PRAISE FOR

"*The Parasol Flower* is an engrossing tale of two impassioned women, separated by a century, both hunting for treasure: one is an artist trekking through a pulsing Malaysian jungle, seeking a singular, exquisite flower; the other, a scholar trekking through the tangles of time-past, seeking a singular, exquisite woman. Beautifully written, utterly engaging and sparkling with wisdom, Karen Quevillon's outstanding debut novel vividly explores the essential urgency of heeding the persevering yearnings of one's creativity and destiny."

– Janet Turpin Myers, author of *Nightswimming* and *The Last Year of Confusion*

"*The Parasol Flower* is a visceral, captivating novel about charisma, commitment, and the need for connection—an elegant and wistful portrayal of two women from different eras searching for each other."

– Monica Carter, *Foreword Reviews*

"[Karen] Quevillon shows an intimate knowledge of the problems women face today as well as those faced a couple of hundred years ago. The juxtaposition of these two timelines is more and more striking as the story progresses and leads the reader's thoughts along the unique paths of everywoman. This is a novel for the thinking person who delights in identifying and solving society's problems. I loved it."

– Elaine Cougler, author of the *Loyalist* trilogy

"With *The Parasol Flower*, Karen Quevillon offers an intricate bud of a story that gradually unfurls to reveal, petal by delicate petal, a rare and brilliant bloom."

– Sherry C. Isaac, author of *Storyteller*

THE PARASOL FLOWER

Judy,
Thank you for your support -
Happy reading! Kar

Karen Quevillon

Regal House Publishing

Published by
Regal House Publishing, LLC
Raleigh, NC 27612
All rights reserved

ISBN -13 (paperback): 9781947548732
ISBN -13 (epub): 9781646030200
Library of Congress Control Number: 2019941545

Interior and cover design by Lafayette & Greene
lafayetteandgreene.com
Cover art from the Biodiversity Heritage Library.
Digitized by Smithsonian Libraries. | www.biodiversitylibrary.org

Regal House Publishing, LLC
https://regalhousepublishing.com

Printed in the United States of America

To my parents,

with gratitude for your unfailing love and support

ONE

Let me be as plain as possible. I don't know with any certainty how it ended for Hannah Inglis. What became of her? The ending here is particularly speculative. So if you're the sort of no-nonsense person—as is my own mother, I am familiar with the type—who won't waste time on anything but the facts, it's best you move on.

Not that I'm not working from evidence. I have done the research. I have documents, scholarship, findings. I have made my own travels. Seen, touched, taken notes, read, re-read her letters. Her art! When I close my eyes, I see the pieces arranged on walls, in galleries, in homes and office buildings. These "botanical portraits" are exquisite, vibrant expressions of lives that may have gone unnoticed. But I must admit that Hannah's *achievement* is as I imagine it. As I have had to imagine it.

"Because it's subjective," Professor Munk said to me the first time we met, shrugging his narrow, cardiganned shoulders. "Art is a subjective matter."

Shrugging off Hannah's work, I thought, and mine.

I'll admit I'm not in the fine art business. That's a point in my favor, isn't it, that I'd make no money from Hannah's success? I'd been funded—shabbily, but funded—to pursue a PhD. My dissertation concerned the social construction of gender. Simone de Beauvoir had written, "a woman is made, not born." Okay, but how does that making happen? Does it happen *to* a woman, or does she do it to herself? These were the sorts of questions I wanted to answer. Because my gurus were French and I looked good on a fellowship application, I was living in Paris while I wrote up, as we put it.

Except that I wasn't writing. I read feminists, gender theorists, postmodernists, postcolonialists, and other sorts of "ists" with a kind of exhaustive fervour that made me feel thoroughly knowledgeable, though it was absolutely useless for my own progress. I couldn't write anything I didn't want to drag to the trash afterward. I couldn't write anything good enough to send to Kenneth Cavanaugh, my dissertation advisor. So I kept on reading, further and further afield, in the hopes I'd find a way to say something.

Ah, Paris! Where I ate pot noodles most nights of the week and washed my clothes in my tiny kitchen's tiny sink. My only friends were a couple of Welsh expats—madly in love with each other—who were studying the history of phrenology. ("Not that there's any future in it!" was their standing joke.) Other moments of human contact involved verbally abusive Parisian clerks and cashiers and the occasional email from my ex-boyfriend. I savoured Paris for what it meant to others who didn't live there (romance) and what I imagined it would mean to me after I had left (romance), then carried on as best I could, tempering my loneliness and desperation with jasmine tea and English detective novels.

I first encountered a reference to *The Descent of Woman* in a contemporary analysis of colonial desire. Published in 1908 in London, *The Descent* was old and foreign (to France) and therefore housed in the Richelieu Library Reserve collection. This was reason enough for me to seek it out. I loved Richelieu. The Reserve Reading Room is an enormous oval, five or six stories high and ringed with bountiful mahogany bookshelves and arched porticos. In the center, under a dome punctured by iron-laced windows, readers sit in quiet solidarity at the long tables, exercising their minds.

The librarian with the flame-red hair fetched me the leather-bound volume, penned the hour of day in her logbook, and I took my kill to the table. *The Descent of Woman: On the Role of Sexual Selection in the Origination and Continued Creation of Femininity*, by Dr. Charles Peterborough and Eva Peterborough. My own line of enquiry had nothing to do with evolutionary biology or indeed any scientific approach to sex identity. In fact, the Peterboroughs' presumably naturalistic theory was what I and my interlocutors wanted to leave behind: the move to root femininity in a "natural" given. I treated *The Descent* as an exotic specimen—quaint, worthy as a spectacle or an artifact. I flipped pages.

What caught my eye, consequently, were the illustrations—etchings of jungle botanicals, ferns, insects, moths, birds and so forth. Page 173 had an unusual flower. THE PARASOL FLOWER, PERAK, MALAYA, read the caption. Resembling a morning glory in shape, this blossom was obviously much larger, ensconced in a jungle scenario of corkscrewing ferns and lianas, moss-covered boulders and towering trees. The life and world of this flower appeared at once substantial and ethereal. Tangible yet fantastical. I peered at the engraving, running a fingertip gently over the page.

The longer I considered the illustration, the more masterful and unique it seemed. I would not have been surprised to discover that Whistler or Degas had drawn it. At the corner of the etching, the initials E.W. meant nothing to me. I stared, wavering between laughter and a conviction I'd struck gold. While around me the other library patrons, with heads bowed, carried on as usual.

In the nearby pages of text there was no reference made at all to the majestic "parasol flower." Odd! But there was nothing to be done about it. I skimmed the section of the book about sexual selection and took a few notes before winding my way home for pot noodles.

There was an email waiting for me from Jason, my ex and a student in a neighboring program of the university. Rumor was, Cavanaugh was leaving for Loyola—did I know anything about this? No, I did not. I'd heard nothing from Kenneth since I'd left the States, thankfully not even a reply to the lengthy, sappy email I'd sent him in winter. If Kenneth left the department, would I have to find another advisor? The thought of this, and the low level of heating in my apartment, sent me to bed early where I tossed and turned, mapping out different futures and different pasts for myself that all involved backing up against a cold wall in Kenneth Cavanaugh's wine cellar, his hot mouth on mine.

At last, I got up for a glass of water. I gulped it down, redirecting my thoughts to the parasol flower, blooming so vividly in its forgotten tome at Richelieu. Surely if such an incredible species existed I would have heard of it. *The Descent of Woman* belonged to a time when science was not afraid of speculation, faith, art, adventure trekking, or storytelling—but it was still science. From the shadowy corners of my apartment, Charles and Eva Peterborough murmured to me in distressed tones; no, they were definitely not engaging in make-believe.

Had they, or had E.W., the artist, named the plant? Such a whimsical, *pretty* name for a jungle survivor. I slipped back into bed, balled up the covers, and shut my eyes. I could see E.W. in one of those white three-piece Victorian suits, pushing his way through the sweating, squawking rainforest and happening upon an almost unbelievable sight.

A few days later I called home. This was rare for me. My mother kept in touch by mailing me homemade cards with her handwritten notes folded inside, plus clippings from our small-town newspaper. Neighbors and former classmates were making good with their lives in various ways. Getting married and having babies, though not always in that order.

"Hi, dear!" Mom said. "How are you?"

"Pretty good, the weather's been good. I've been researching Victorian etching technology."

"Oh!"

"It's interesting. Much more complicated than I thought."

"Oh, I'm sure it is interesting, yes. And complicated." There was a noise as she put her hand over the phone and shouted to my father. "It's Nancy! No, I haven't mentioned it yet. We've only just started talking."

"Mentioned what?"

"Oh, your father! It's just about Christmas. We're thinking of going to Florida. Disneyworld."

It was September and I hadn't given Christmas much thought. The year before I'd flown home to Michigan for a couple weeks. My parents never went anywhere over the Christmas holidays except to visit family, which was no vacation. In fact, I thought they considered that sort of thing ridiculous—jetting off to a beach, leaving commitments behind. Sulkily I said, "And what about Sam and Mikey?"

"Sam and Michael are able to come with us. And their girlfriends! It really worked out just perfectly." She went on breathlessly, telling me the story of the booking of the airline tickets as if it were high drama. My father interjected comments from beyond. There were beaches involved and various options for rental cars and villa types and parking arrangements at the airport. Disneyworld was only an hour on the freeway from the closest beach. To hear her talk, Disney had improved the beach by its proximity.

As she spoke I rolled my eyes and bit at my nails. I stood up from my chair, trying to see out the room's high window past a dying potted plant. Stepping up onto to the seat of the chair, a sea of Parisian rooftops swayed in my watery vision. When my mother stopped talking, I said, "That's so good. Good for you guys!"

There was a longish silence.

"Nancy?"

"So I've heard back about the travel grant."

"Oh!"

"The one from the graduate school?"

"Uh-huh," she said.

"They're giving me the full amount."

"Oh! Will you have to pay it back?"

"A grant, Mom. That's why it's called a travel grant."

"Well, that's wonderful. Nancy's won a grant!" I heard her shout to my father. "You're doing wonderful work, I'm sure. And that's what they saw, and what they're rewarding you for."

I felt myself about to cry and I turned my face away from the receiver, inhaling as deeply and silently as possible. "I don't know," I mumbled at last.

"Nance, come to Florida with us."

I was still standing on the chair. I sank slowly into a squat.

"Now I know you've never liked Disney, but you could just stay at the resort on those days. We've only planned on spending three or four of the days at Disney. And, you know, MGM and the other ones."

"How long are you going to be there? I thought you said a week?"

"Yes."

"How are they even open at Christmas? Of *course* they're open at Christmas. It makes perfect sense, doesn't it? Capitalism run amok." An image visited me: Nancy the freak, reading *The London Review of Books*, walking the beach to collect stones, nipping out for a cup of fair-trade coffee while the rest of her gregarious sneaker-wearing clan piled into a van to go ride roller coasters and hug giant plush mascots. I'd never met Mike's girlfriend but Sam's partner, Summer, was Cinderella incarnate, all curves and kindness. She wouldn't stand for leaving me on my own.

"I…I can't."

"Well," said my mother. "I know you're always so busy."

"I have so much to do."

"I understand, dear. Everybody understands. You're devoted to your paper."

"It's not a paper, Mom." For some reason, my mother had always referred to my dissertation as a "paper," and I always felt bound to correct her. "It" wasn't anything, I thought to myself. It was four hundred pages of notes on other peoples' books and articles and dissertations. It was a draft prospectus I'd really liked and that Cavanaugh had rejected. It was a second prospectus I liked much less but that Cavanaugh accepted, pending further changes. All of this mass of nothingness was so far from understandable, so far from devotion, that it clotted in my throat like a plug of phlegm. I swallowed hard.

"I received an email this morning from Daphne Plewett," my mother resumed after our substantial silence. Daphne was some relation or other, or maybe just a friend of a relation, some woman who lived in England. She and my mother had always swapped Christmas cards. Mom kept up with a raft of old people this way.

"A Christmas card already?" I exclaimed.

"Are you all right, Nance? What was that noise?"

"Nothing. Dropped the phone. Sorry, what did you say?"

"I said it's *not* a Christmas card, it's an *email*. Daphne's even on Facebook now! She wondered how you and the boys were doing. She was asking me all sorts of questions."

"Right. And what did you tell her?" I wiped my cuff under my leaking nose.

There was another long pause. Such a long one I thought my mother was retrieving the email to quote from it. "I've just had a thought," she said, taking another moment. "Nancy, I know you're very busy; but I was wondering if you would do something for me?"

I waited for her to go on.

"Daphne and Bob have been so good to us over the years." She cited a few incidences stretching back to before my birth. None of it sounded familiar to me. "Nancy, would you look in on them over Christmas?"

"Look in on them?"

"Visit them. Stay with them for a week or two. I think it would mean a lot to them. Daphne was more or less begging me, begging us, to come over."

And you chose Mickey Mouse. I didn't actually say this, mostly because it didn't occur to me until much later.

My mother went on in some detail about the Plewetts' apparently miserable existence (kidney dialysis, no adult children, broken appliances, drunkard cousin) and their unflaggingly bright attitudes (charity shop, gardening, knitting caps for preemie babies). Their lives sounded quite full to me. What could I possibly add? The answer was that I would be the Roach family standard-bearer. Show up and please Daphne and Bob. Redeem myself a little for rejecting the Magic Kingdom. Avoid eating pot noodles for Christmas dinner.

"And everything's so close in Europe," Mom concluded. "You're only an hour away by train, aren't you? Think about it, Nancy. I'm just asking you to think about it."

I didn't know it at the time, but Daphne and Robert Plewett happened to live near a stately home called Fulgham House, and Fulgham House would lead me to Hannah. Destiny never looks like destiny except in retrospect.

Two

By the light of a kerosene lamp, on an early morning in March of 1896, Hannah Inglis dabs shades of olive on a busy canvas, covering the kapok's trunk with crisscrossing roots. Stepping back to regard the effect, she chews at the nail of her index finger, too absorbed to respond to the voice.

"Memsahib? Mem?"

The color work, she likes. Also the brushwork. The way she has created a spiralling movement for the eye. Yet there is something unbalanced…which perhaps *should* be unbalanced, given the strangulation occurring…but which she finds herself fighting. She considers this fighting feeling. Is conflict an acceptable effect for a painting? A desirable one? *Strangler Fig Upon Kapok*, although she has not quite decided at this moment in time, will be her submission to the Kew Gardens Amateur Botanicals Art Competition.

Knocking on the door. Bare feet shuffling. "Please, mem!"

She wipes her brush and stabs it into her French knot. As she opens the door he says, "Come please, mem. Come." Anjuh, their *syce* and groundskeeper, is a particularly dark-skinned Malay. The whites of his eyes are shining in his troubled face.

"Good morning, Anjuh."

He motions with his hands and scurries away.

Hannah blinks for a moment at the empty door, considering the kapok and its cage of fig branches, like an exoskeleton. "Oh, all right. I'm coming," she mumbles, undoing her smock. The colonel is a heavy sleeper. No chance he would have heard anyone calling for *him*. Underneath the smock she is wearing her favorite silk day gown. Drawing its creamy lapels to her chest, she tightens the sash and glances one last time at the painting.

Anjuh is waiting by the back door. To her surprise, he opens it and steps outside.

"Oh! Wait." She veers into the foyer to fetch her rain cloak and garden shoes.

The Inglis' little barn, for this is where Anjuh appears to be heading, sits at the end of a long lawn that dips then rises steadily over its length. Her servant hurries on, stiff-kneed. Hannah follows at a slower pace, taking in the once familiar surroundings. Where the forest halts at the edge of the property, a milky mist is lingering, giving the areca palms and the ferns an enchanting prehistoric aura. Why has she never thought of painting the dawn?

Inside the barn, an odious smell assaults her. She sputters, "Anjuh! What on—!" All he does is beckon yet again, leading her to the roomy stall where Cleopatra the cow is tethered, a rope looped firmly around one of the Jersey's hind legs. The rope holds a stump. The leg has been severed at its hock and lies like a tossed dog's bone.

Gorge rises in her throat. A mess of entrails and lumps of flesh are strewn across the sticky floorboards.

"The barn wasn't locked? The pen wasn't locked?" she demands.

"Yes, mem. Everything locked."

The door, she then sees, has simply been pushed off its hinges.

Anjuh wrings his small hands. "Tiger, see."

Hannah pinches her nostrils and bends over the severed leg, her pulse thrumming in her ears.

Back in the kitchen she lights the stove and puts the kettle on it. How long to leave the crime scene intact? Typically, the colonel wakes late. Would he want to see any of the mess? He ought to see it, his beloved cow.

Anjuh's wife Suria, their housemaid, ambles into the kitchen as the water is coming to the boil. She takes the teapot from the cupboard, checks inside it for spiders, and reaches past Hannah for the fluting kettle. "Poor thing, mem."

"Oh, I'm fine, Suria, thank you."

"The cow, mem."

"Yes, yes! Poor Cleopatra. Although I think she must have had rather a lonely life here, don't you?"

Suria shrugs. Eyes Hannah's hair.

Hannah puts a hand to her head and feels for paintbrushes, sliding three free and lining them up on the counter. She watches the old Malay complete the preparations for tea. "There's not much in the way of clean-up," she tells her. "So, I think you and Anjuh can manage it. You two together. That is to say, alone." She'd really rather not ask anyone at the Residency for help.

Suria grunts.

"Find yourself a bucket. Two buckets. And a scrub brush and some hot water. I suppose use the washing crystals, though I'm not really sure what's called for…and take a few rags from the cupboard. We'll have to pitch them afterward but that can't be helped. You may take your time with it, of course. There's no rush."

Hannah cracks her knuckles, thinking. "In fact…*don't* begin the cleaning until I ask you to. Suria? Leave it all be for now. Yes?" She waits for Suria to make eye contact.

"Mm. Sahib woan like."

Won't like his cow dead, she means. No, he won't, Hannah silently agrees.

"Good you doan hear her. Last night." Suria shakes her head slowly from side to side. "Screamin'."

Hannah had heard nothing. Had she heard nothing at all? For a minute or two, the women cultivate their own thoughts, Hannah's straying to strangler figs, Sergeant Singh, and cobalt blue before returning to the tethered stump of leg.

The ayah pours them tea.

"And. I'll tell sahib," Hannah says on the third sip.

She walks back out to the barn on her own, carrying the three-legged stool she uses on her forest treks. First, though, she stands, stooping over the severed leg. Carefully she pivots and crouches, examining it from several angles. She makes little forays like this, into the foul haze of the scene, holding her handkerchief over her nose and mouth, then sits just outside the pool of blood to sketch. The hoof is terribly poignant. Why is that? Why does she have more compassion for the bothersome creature now that it's been reduced to a single body part?

She swabs different blue-reds and black-reds and pink-reds onto a palette, searching for something dark enough to serve as a background. The background will be blood. The foreground, a foreshortened stump of leg culminating in a dirty hoof. The blood must serve the hoof in its complexity, not flatten it out. She will return to the work in the studio, paint it up properly. There will be no second chances there, only memory to rely on. The time to play is now. Quite enough time. George won't wake for a time yet; he came home late, reeking of tobacco and opium smoke.

Early on, the colonel made his expectations plain when it came to whores; they were and they will be part of his life. Hannah's life—somehow, incredibly, now contained in his—involves these women. For the better, she's come to believe. George wants children, though neither of them would cope well with a child's mess or a child's noise, if you ask her, not to mention the extra expense. Besides which the children of Ridge Road are sent home to boarding school by age five or six, before they have a chance to grow too Malayan. It's cruel, she tells the colonel when he tries to bed her. Cruel to be parted from such dears when they are so young and so tender. She couldn't possibly.

Hence his reliance on whores. Their reliance. On nights like last night, when he comes from one, he snores like a warthog and sleeps even longer than usual. Hannah checks her pocket watch. Bright light is leaking into the little stable.

With a number two brush she adds a few veinous lines for the ruptured sinews. Then, separately, a dry brush to try pushing back the hide. Compares how it folds, naturally, where it meets the hoof. Even in familiarity, there is mystery. Such as how the colonel will react to losing Cleopatra, something she cannot completely foresee even after four years of marriage. The back of a vase, the interior of a mountain. What remains unseen generates the effect of depth. The bone of the cow's leg taking shape by her brush, shrouded in stiffened muscle and skin. Or rather, the effect of bone.

She throws everything into her paint box, replacing the handkerchief to her face as quickly as possible, and heads back to the house.

THREE

In their bedroom, the colonel stands before her dressing table mirror, massaging his swollen stomach. He has always complained of stomachaches and indigestion, along with a constellation of symptoms the military doctor calls climate fatigue.

"How are you feeling, George?"

He turns and grunts.

"Sit down perhaps. Have a sip of water," she advises. A full glass is sitting on the table by the bed. "Is it very painful this morning?"

He pinches his eyebrows together. "As a matter of fact it *is* very painful this morning." He shuffles toward the glass she holds out to him. "You've not been in that thing all day, have you?"

The colonel dislikes the shapelessness of her dressing gown. The gown is marvelous—oyster-coloured, smooth as a dream, and meticulously embroidered with designs of pine trees and snow-capped mountains. James, the Resident, bought it for her while on a trade mission in Singapore. It served as a sort of welcome present, or perhaps a wedding gift, for she and George had arrived in Kuala Kangsa during the Resident's absence.

"It's early yet," she protests lightly. "Besides, women should be exempted from corsets in this climate. Do you know they're protesting them in London, Edith tells me? They're quite unhealthy."

"I'm quite unhealthy." He eases himself back onto the bed with a moan. "Far too fat."

"No, you're not," she replies dutifully. "Perhaps you should wear a corset."

The colonel laughs. "And smart as a whip she is, too, ladies and gentlemen." He looks up at her fondly, expectantly.

With a pang, she realizes she doesn't bother much with humour any more. "I'm afraid I have some bad news, George."

He sits forward at this.

"Cleopatra has been killed."

"But. She was...I thought she was perfectly healthy."

Hannah bows her head. Such a waste. "She was healthy, yes. But she was *killed*, George. A tiger, it seems. Anjuh and Suria are cleaning the…remains from the pen."

Hannah studies him a moment as this news settles in. The colonel is not one to think on his feet. Nor is she, and she respects his need for time and deliberation. When he doesn't respond, she turns to her wardrobe and the day ahead, her hands moving shakily over her clothes. The smell, that horrid smell, has attached itself to her insides. Look at her arms; they are no more than bone twigs, waving about uselessly in front of her. And her legs, hiding under the gown—such flimsy, pluckable things, really. Pluckable petals.

She presses her feet into the floorboards. *Shush. You need those legs to stand.*

Behind her he is stirring, she notices vaguely, creaking the bed. Will the colonel even think to thank her? *Thank you, Hannah, for gently bearing and bringing me the news of my beloved cow. For dealing with the foetid mess she became. For tramping out to the barn at five o'clock in the morning, interrupting your—*

"This is outrageous!" The colonel has pushed himself off the bed. "Outrageous!" he repeats, mustache squirming.

"George?"

He shuffles and turns and shuffles and turns, kneading his bearded chin in his hand, a smile slowly transforming his face.

"What is outrageous?"

"The poor thing," he says with fervor.

"Well. Yes." She closes her paint-stained fingers into fists. "George, I'm not sure it's worth trying to keep a cow, do you? I don't mind the tinned milk. Everybody settles for the tinned milk here, don't they?"

"I despise tinned milk." His smile broadens. "And I like cows. I *like* them, Hannah."

It is an unkind thought, but it occurs to her that he might go mad in his old age. She says, "Yes, I know. You find them soothing." If he'd been in the barn and smelled her rotting innards… She shivers.

"Tigers are fifty dollars a head now," he says.

"What? Do you mean the bounty?" Even then she doesn't see where he is heading. She is caught in her own chain of thoughts— one that usually leads to her ceasing, for an unspecified period, her jungle outings. And then the anxious, regretful feeling follows. Not that she and the sergeant ever went west of Ridge Road. But a tiger's territorial range is known to be expansive, is it not?

"I'm going to shoot our way to a new cow," the colonel says.

"What do you mean shoot? *You* are—"

"Oh, not *I*, Hannah. I'll pay some coolies to do it for me." He glances at the shuttered window. "I've told you, it's suicidal to wander around in that diseased wilderness. For any reason."

"You've not said that before," she mumbles. "Suicidal? You've not said that, have you?" She's aware of course that he is not in favor of her jungle trekking. Lately, admittedly, she's not cared to be too aware.

"Well, I'm sure you have already considered it. With a man-eater like this around, it's simply not prudent. It's not reasonable." He clasps his hands together. "No, it's simply not reasonable, Hannah, for you to continue to do what you are doing."

She is taken aback for a moment. Recovering, she says, "Anjuh fetched me this morning and took me to the barn to see for myself. So, as it happens, I've been forced to consider this tiger. Intimately." No response. "As for the treks, I do have Sergeant Singh," she ventures to explain, "although—"

The colonel explodes. "Oh, you have Sergeant Singh! You have Sergeant Singh! Excellent. And Sergeant Singh follows you about, gun cocked." He sets himself laughing.

"You make him sound like a *lunatic.*"

"Look. I'll save your sergeant the trouble. Here you are, putting him to trouble. And I'll save him the trouble. Do you see? I'll save you both. I'll keep you both safe."

"What are you saying, George? What do you mean you'll keep us safe?"

The colonel taps his front teeth. "You'd better stay clear of the tiger hunt. That's what I mean."

"Oh, indeed!" She swats away a fly that is encircling them. It could take the colonel weeks, months, to catch a tiger. If he ever does. She has an overwhelming urge to reach out and tear the gauzy netting from their bed. "What good is a tiger hunt?" she demands. "How can you be sure to kill the same animal that killed Cleopatra?"

The colonel's eyes run over her as he considers her question. Or else considers her. He replies, "I can't be sure."

"Well then!"

"*Tida apa*, as the natives say."

Tida apa. So what.

Yes, Colonel, she has long been thinking about it, the question of What Is Out There. That has always been the question, all these months since she started trekking. Ironically, the only *reasonable* conclusion is that she should keep visiting the jungle. Especially as she continues to make strides in her art. The cats have been out there all along. And she, after all, is not a tethered cow. Sergeant Singh is armed and ready to protect her; that is his very purpose.

And yet. Hannah sighs as she bends to tie the laces on her boots. She will ease off trekking for a while.

"Suria, I'm leaving!" she calls from the front door.

Ridge Road, what the natives call the Street of Big Bosses, is the highest in Kuala Kangsa and has marvellous vistas of the Perak river valley. As Hannah walks she delights in the river snaking into the distance, the abundance of steep, forested hills, and the village sprinkled below her.

At the Cinnamon Hill switchback the road plunges toward the town's high street, and where Roderick, she sees, is perched in his acacia. He swings down and runs toward Hannah, chittering and squealing, then assumes his beggar's pose on the dusty road, eyes upturned, mouth drooping. The red-banded gibbon is sandy-coloured, with a ring of white hair around his tar-black pensive face.

"Good morning, Roddy darling! I did bring one. Hold on." Digging a biscuit from her pocket, Hannah tosses it toward the little monkey.

He catches it without effort and sits for a moment to nibble.

"Tell me," she says, once she's sure he's following her. "The colonel is overreacting, isn't he? I think that's pretty plain."

The gibbon darts forward, performing a forward roll. Where he's learned this, she's never known, but Hannah claps and coos on cue.

"He doesn't consider what anything means to me," she complains. "No, honestly, it was just the one biscuit."

Roderick looks at her as they walk, waiting for her to elaborate.

"Oh, listen to me, I sound like a child! Somehow I'm in this position, Roddy, and I'm not sure if *he's* put me here or I've done it myself.

Or someone else again has set this up for the both of us. And I'm playing the part of the wayward child. I'm not a wayward child."

Roddy stops and scratches his head, which makes her chuckle.

"And you're playing the part of the comical little monkey!"

Though it is mid-morning, the high street is all but empty. They pause for a moment to take it all in: the shuttered state buildings, the little local shops, the slender sycamores in their iron cages, delicately shading the dirt sidewalks. Kuala Kangsa the outpost, holding itself open to a civilized future, but in no great rush for it to arrive.

They make it a block further before the gibbon squeals and shoots in through the open doorway of the barbershop.

"Good morning, Mr. Lim!"

Inside the shop, Mr. Lim raises a hand in greeting.

Roddy, she sees, has already stolen a handful of shaving lather and is applying it to his head and chin.

This, the first Friday of each month, is payday. Today the colonel is sitting with his pen down when she arrives, as if waiting for her to walk into the room. No shuffling of paperwork. No Miss Wing to be found. As usual, Hannah carries a few letters with her to post, including her most recent order of art supplies. That envelope remains unsealed.

"Good morning, George. Miss Wing is not in today?"

He stands. Begins flapping a wallet against his forearm. "In light of recent events, I have decided to reduce your stipend."

"Recent events?" she repeats. He must be referring to the tiger attack. Surely *that* isn't her doing?

"I take it you won't be entering the forest," he says.

"I—no—I think not, actually," she stumbles. "Not for the time being."

"And you'll appreciate that I need extra funds."

Before she can speak, he adds, "For the hunting party."

"Oh! I thought…"

He thrusts the linen wallet toward her.

"Thank you," she says automatically.

The colonel glances skeptically at her parcel of letters. "The new amount will be plenty for the household necessities. Food, cleaning supplies…" He returns behind his desk, his hands sliding toward each other over the back of the chair, coming closer and closer together. Throttling the tepid air. "…a lady's necessities. Buy yourself a new pair of gloves, why don't you."

Hannah tucks the wallet and the stack of letters under her arm, resisting the temptation to look down at her outfit.

In the street, she discreetly unbuttons the wallet and counts the Straits dollars as the colonel's voice drones on in her head, listing necessities. "A new pair of gloves, why don't you," she mimics. Gloves! She's given up gloves. It was only out here, thirty thousand miles from civilization, that she'd worn them in the first place.

The amount he's given her is less than half of what she normally receives.

She walks to the postal office, doing sums in her head. Making plans. And walks home, still dueling with the idiocies of life. Until that day it had not seemed to her that the colonel was on her side. But he had been. She'd taken for granted his generosity and his lenience.

FOUR

I made arrangements with Daphne and Bob Plewett over email. Their messages always included a signature line with both names:

Cheerio,
Daphne and Bob

Take care of yourself!
Daphne and Bob

Love,
Daphne and Bob

So I was never quite sure which one of them wrote any given email. I liked to imagine it was both of them, sitting side by side at their computer keyboard as if they were playing a piano duet.

The Plewetts lived in a place called Frimley, a former village cum suburb of London. It was suggested I take the train from Waterloo Station on the South Western rail line to Farnborough. There was a station at Frimley itself, but making it there required changing lines and it was no trouble, they assured me, to pick me up from the Farnborough main platform.

We have white hair and a red Fiat.
See you shortly,
Daphne and Bob

In mid-December I traveled to London by Eurostar, racing along under the ocean, periodically reminding myself that the odds of the structure collapsing and all of us drowning in the rough waters of the English Channel were probably astronomical. In the three months or so since I'd opened *The Descent*, my research into E.W. and the parasol flower had essentially petered out, and, as far as I knew, I was leaving it behind for good. Nothing was coming up on Google. I'd returned twice more to Richelieu to look at *The Descent*, scouring the front matter and the index and examining the other illustrations.

From my research into book illustration I'd learned that etchings and engravings were completed by a handful of specialists hired to work from original pieces of art, copying the artist's style and subject as best as possible, and transferring it into the print context. That meant E.W. was likely not the creator of *The Parasol Flower*, but rather more like a translator. Indeed, I noted many of the other botanicals for the book had been engraved by E.W. None of those seemed quite as excellent to me.

Nor were they fantastical. E.W.'s other drawings had matching text; they did their job as illustrations. For instance, the chapter in which *The Parasol Flower* was embedded, "Wildflowers," had a section on another huge specimen, the Rafflesia plant (*Rafflesia arnoldii*), whose meaty blossoms could span a yard in diameter. But these petals were spiny, oozed fluids, and stank like decaying offal.

It must be a joke, I thought. The parasol flower! Yet who would insert a joke in their magnum opus?

It occurred to me that something like three-quarters of the planet's species remained undiscovered. That was the tragedy of habitat destruction, wasn't it, that life like this could vanish without anyone ever realizing it existed? Maybe these Peterborough scientists simply hadn't known how to categorize this particular plant, or what to make of it in an evolutionary sense. Or perhaps the illustration had been added at the last minute, after the text had been finalized.

When I looked up "Victorian botanical art," I had been surprised to discover many of the artists were women. The idea that the parasol flower had been painted by a woman piqued my interest. Flowers were deemed a suitably feminine subject matter, of course. And one that you named after a parasol, that quintessentially feminine accessory, that veil of modesty…yet you painted it so big and so bold, dripping with sweaty jungle vapours…? Well, it was a slap in the face, wasn't it? An enchanting, well-placed slap in the face.

Having completed my dissertation research and writing for the day, I often laced up my running shoes and jogged a loop along the canal, over the Seine, and now—since the parasol flower—through the Jardin des Plantes, with its bulging stands of perennials and verdant patches of lawn between trails of crushed stone. I half-expected to turn down a little-known path, tucked away somewhere on the rambling grounds of the old gardens, and find a parasol flower blooming. I could almost smell it, like lemon gelato.

On some days I didn't work at all. I don't mean the days I spent hiding in bed. Other days, when I took a little sketchpad and went to art museums and art galleries—Pompidou, d'Orsay, Montmartre, the Louvre, MAMVP, the Rodin museum—admittedly unlikely to have any nineteenth-century botanical paintings, but still a joy. At first I looked for *The Parasol Flower*, the painting that I guessed was hiding behind the etching in *The Descent*. I looked for Victorian botanical art, art of Malaysia, art by women. After a while, I simply looked. I could sit for fifteen, twenty, thirty minutes before a painting, as eddies of spectators came and went. I loved people's inane conversations, their impatience, their petty bickering over hotel tax and souvenirs and cuts of steak, and how all of this fell away as they moved into a painting's orbit and lapsed into silent communion.

Of course, inevitably, I would arrive home to my studio apartment, with its sprawling piles of paperwork, flowcharts mounted on each wall, and chastise myself for caring about anything but the dissertation. The rumor that Cavanaugh was heading to Loyola had turned out to be true. It seemed that he wasn't even waiting until the end of the academic year, which immediately made me wonder if his reasons were more personal than professional. My ass, with Kenneth's hands all over it. I thought, though it hadn't been stroked or slapped in years, that my ass was quite as good as it had ever had been, quite as good as anybody else's. I ought, perhaps, to have contacted our department Chair to let him know I was still alive and working. But this seemed a facile message to send. I wasn't sure the man particularly cared. And once I told him Kenneth Cavanaugh was my advisor, the Chair would quite reasonably tell me to contact Kenneth Cavanaugh directly. Wouldn't he? I was unsure how close the two colleagues were, or who might have said what to whom. In any case, what did *I* really *want* at this point? A new advisor to approve my distinctly Cavanaugh-esque prospectus? A way to follow Cavanaugh to Loyola and finish my degree there? Virtually, that was to say. I would no more have to go to Chicago than I had to go anywhere.

As the train hurtled toward London, I was working my way through an anthology on "reconceptualizing power." A foreboding feeling had lodged in me that Daphne and Bob were the sort of people who couldn't abide excessive education. Still, I reasoned, I was unobjectionable in person. My mother's Christmas cards over the years would dispose them to like me. I only hoped that at Christmas the Plewetts went for roast turkey with the trimmings rather than blood sausage or pies filled with kidneys.

At Waterloo station, I made my way through the terminal and onto the correct commuter train dragging my cheap, wheel-less luggage. Block after block of brick buildings slid past me and I fell into the comatose state you arrive at when traveling, sometimes before you've reached the destination. I must have looked like a zombie to my hosts. When they spotted me rounding the small fence at the end of the Farnborough platform, their expressions registered something between disappointment and alarm. For my part, I had recognized the Plewetts immediately. They were the only ones standing in place rather than hustling to get somewhere; they were dressed for an outing.

"Aren't you good, dear, coming all this way," Daphne said as I approached.

She was a slightly stooped, slightly larger woman with loose salt-and-pepper curls and orthopedic shoes. I imagined she would have been straight and slender in her youth, dark-haired and sharp-eyed. Her complexion remained lovely, though there seemed to be no appropriate way to compliment her on her skin. Bob was hunched in a similar curve to his wife's. He had a slicked nest of white hair and a sallow complexion. I recalled his kidney disease.

Bob extended a freckled hand and I shook it before realizing he'd been offering to take my case. "Oh, I'm totally fine with it," I said.

His eyes flicked to his wife's. "Well then, I'll open the boot."

Daphne held her hand out, and we shook awkwardly. She looked at me and said, not unkindly, "You're exhausted."

"A bit," I said.

"First things first. You're not to do any work while you're with us."

We turned and started walking slowly toward Bob and the open trunk. I said, "I'm not sure if my mother told you...I'm...uh... writing my dissertation."

"Yes, of course she's told me. *That's* the work you're not to do."

The spare bedroom they'd allotted for me had a little desk in one corner, billowy pink drapes, and textured wallpaper. Like the rest of their home, it smelled of apricot hand cream. The window looked out over a narrow backyard, closed for the season, beyond which I could see a wedge of frosted pasture. Frimley, from what I'd seen of it, was the sort of place where time stood still. Boutiques, charity shops, a brook, a park, peaky churches, and a nearby castle. If time had stopped, property values were in unceasing motion. Bob told me proudly their house had quintupled its value in the thirty years they'd lived there.

I fell back onto the checkered pink bedspread and into a deep sleep.

"It was your mother's idea," Daphne informed me later. They'd given me a grace period of a couple of days. She and Bob were spooning cherry yogurt into their mouths. Dessert.

I rested my spoon. "What was my mother's idea?"

"Daphne," Bob growled. He shook his head.

"Well, she has no intention of listening to *us*," Daphne said to him. "She's up all hours *zoned in* on that laptop. She doesn't do anything else. I think Lauren is right."

"She goes running," Bob offered. "I think she's taken a few photographs. She's taken a liking to that coffee shop too, the one on Magnolia Street."

"*What* was my mother's idea?" I demanded as politely as possible. "What is she right about?"

Daphne said, "Let me put the kettle on first."

My mother had asked me to visit Daphne and Bob, not for their sakes, but for my own. This much I'd already figured out—perhaps even during that first deep sleep—though I wasn't sure what to make of it. I felt guilty for worrying Mom. I felt angry, too, that she'd come to this conclusion. I was so unable to look after myself that an elderly pair of strangers had to be brought in as reinforcements. Or were the Plewetts her meager solution to my supposed loneliness? Well, I *was* lonely, okay, but not desperately lonely. And I failed to see how eating yogurt with pensioners was going to solve anything for me, even at Christmas. I sat in grim silence with Bob, waiting to hear the kettle whistle. I managed not to smack my forehead against the tabletop.

Daphne returned carrying her tea tray. She set it down, poured us our milk, adjusted the tea cozy, and took her place at the head of the table.

"My mother thinks I should give up on my PhD, doesn't she?" I said.

"Oh no. No, I don't think she dares think that," said Daphne, reaching over to shake the teapot. "It's your *dream*, dear. Mothers these days seem to think it's their duty to promote their children's dreams. Promote, promote, promote. Like cheerleaders."

"She's as subtle as an elephant in drag," Bob murmured to me.

Daphne gave him a stern look. "She's worried about your mental health, Nancy. For lack of a better word. Something's happened to you, dear. Something's going wrong."

"Well…" I didn't know what to say. My mental life had been entirely overtaken by scholarly arguments. Truthfully, I was superior at decoding them, at critiquing them, unraveling what led to which and why. How could this excellence possibly be a problem? And yet there were those days spent sniffling in bed, days when the knots seemed too tight for me to ever untie them.

"Your mother wants us to make sure that you take a break." Daphne poured three mugs of orange pekoe then splashed milk in all three. "*I'm* the one who thinks you should quit entirely."

I slumped behind my mug, glaring at the toast rack that was still sitting at the center of the table. When I sipped, I might as well have been sipping pure adrenaline.

"I'm afraid you're just going to have to hear her out," Bob said to me. "Just…just try to remember that she's generally well-meaning."

"You don't even know me!" I exploded at Daphne. "How on earth would *you* know what's right for me? You use a toast rack, for god's sake!"

"Don't know you? I've known your mother for fifty-odd years, dear. I knew her parents. I know what's she's been through and what she's like; what kind of a house you and your brothers have grown up in; that she's thrown you at me like some sort consolation prize instead of visiting us herself; that she thinks I'm going to just do her bidding, like everybody else does; that you're neck-deep in something you can't get out of, Nancy, and all she seems to care about is when you're going to do her and your father proud. But you're absolutely right, my dear, I don't know *everything*. I don't know why or how you've managed to spend five years in graduate school and have nothing to show for it."

"I don't have nothing to show for it!"

"My hunch is that they're not doing you right, those people. Those professors. They should be helping you. They need to be guiding you. They need to be telling you, if it's the case, that you're not cut out for it." Bob made a noise. "Well, they shouldn't be leading her up the garden path, pretending she's brilliant if she's got nothing to—to contribute!"

"Daph, I'm sure she's got something to contribute," he said softly.

"Well, not everybody does, Bob. Despite what the papers will have you believe." Daphne reached for my hand but fell short. "Nobody's saying you have to be *normal*, dear. Sorry. Oh, that didn't come out right."

"What she means," Bob tried, "is that none of us care if you don't want a nine-to-five job with a mortgage and two-point-five children. That's not normal, anyhow." He shot a look at his wife. "Not in this day and age."

I imagined the impression my mother's letters and emails had given them. Single, having fled another boyfriend. (Mom not being aware that I had been cheating on said boyfriend with my married dissertation advisor.) Single, with no known friends, certainly not any good ones, so far from home/family. (Read: reality.) Single, with no church, no hobbies, no sense of style. Single, with ties only to virtual colleagues or strands of thought. Serious addiction to books.

"You need a little *fun*, dear."

"Some balance," added Bob.

"Go to a party here and there," Daphne said, flinging her arms open. "Meet a nice man. Have some—"

"I have…balance," I shot back. "I have friends, real ones. From Wales. Who are studying phrenology. And…I've been going to art galleries lately."

"Well, that's good," said Bob Plewett, nodding, avoiding his wife's eyes.

"And you know what? I'm fine with taking a break from my research." A break, I thought to myself, would probably do my productivity good.

"Yes, that's all we're saying," Daphne said without irony. "Take a little break."

After that, we sat and drank tea and made small talk to prove that everything was still okay. A recent Sainsbury commercial had gone viral. It was a three-minute drama featuring soldiers in the trenches who'd enacted a ceasefire to trade stories, Sainsbury chocolates, and play a game of soccer.

"Imagine that," Daphne commented. "Those men had no idea it'd go viral, all these years later."

FIVE

The rest of my December was cobbled together with crossword puzzles, television programming à la Bob and Daphne, and jogs through the nearby countryside. Sometimes I drove Bob to his dialysis appointments and sat with him while his blood was being scrubbed. Other days I walked to the little library branch in the village. There, I sat in the lounge to read detective novels from the "Page-Turners!" shelf. Although it might sound mundane, life outside and inside the Plewetts' apricot-scented home felt inordinately special to me. Was it Frimley's status in my life as an oasis? The fact I was no longer consuming scholarly arguments all day? The most ordinary of moments seemed richly textured with significance. I remember choking up over the last nub of soap as I showered; the bar had been shaped like a squirrel holding a nut.

Daphne and Bob recommended Fulgham House. In an effort, perhaps, to introduce me to some national culture.

"We've seen it many times," Bob repeated as he wheeled into the car park.

"It's lovely done up at Christmastime," said Daphne.

"Lovely," said Bob.

"And you're sure, now, about walking home?" Daphne asked.

"She's a young lass, Daph."

I laughed. "I'm twenty-eight."

"Precisely."

"So we'll go for our shop, then," said Daphne.

"Yes, we'll go for our shop."

Every Thursday they shopped for groceries together. As it turned out, I spent all afternoon at the Fulgham House estate that day, well past the grocery shopping, and barely made it back in time for dinner. I have no memory at all of walking home to the Plewetts' stuccoed townhouse.

Like many stately homes, Fulgham House is managed by the British National Trust. It's the sort of place you tour via cordoned-off runways, all of you *oohing* and *aahing* over the ceiling fresco in the massive ballroom, pointing at the delicate tea service sent from the emperor of Siam. And somebody will remark on how short they made the beds in the eighteenth century.

I was enjoying myself by venturing off the beaten paths to examine details such as the mother-of-pearl spittoon in the men's drawing room. Through this tapestry of Victorian elegance and oddity, my mind was threading memories of my ex-boyfriend Jason, who had emailed me a cursory Christmas greeting the night before. I debated with myself as to whether I'd been unkind and shortsighted, or rather ethical and courageous, to have broken up with him. He would have wanted me to break up with him, was a recurring thought. Point being, my mood was reflective and somewhat inward-facing, and I was taken entirely by surprise when I encountered it. There, inside a plastic display case, lying open almost casually—was a first edition copy of *The Descent of Woman*. Open to page 173.

There it was, *The Parasol Flower*.

I studied the familiar forest scene again, with its moss-covered boulders, its towering trees and lianas. At the center, that immense pale blossom had unwound itself, ribbed like the delicate underside of a parasol, its petals slightly curling along the edges. The same E.W. in the corner. The familiar opposing page of text, whose first whole paragraph began, "Mr. Darwin has described the sudden emergence of the flowering plants as an abominable mystery." I looked around me. No one else was in the room. No one to tell me that I was on candid camera and that coincidences like this did not happen. The very same *page*!

A printed label affixed to the exhibit stated the book was written and published "by Eva Peterborough and her husband Charles"—a semantically loaded formulation, I thought—"following an extended stay in Kuala Kangsa, British Malaya." The Peterborough family members, I had just learned, were the last inhabitants of Fulgham House.

I stood so long peering into the plastic case that a security guard ambled over. We chatted. Against my wishes, he fetched the head museum tour guide—an enthusiastic woman with a crew cut. Miranda, her name was, told me about the avant-garde atheist Peterboroughs and their time abroad. Fulgham House had been owned historically by the Pellinghams, the family of the wife, Eva, who had left to travel the world.

"Malaysia," I said. "That's where they discovered this parasol flower."

"Interesting name, isn't it?"

"You don't happen to know who the artist is? I imagine that E.W.," I tried unsuccessfully to point through the plastic case at the initials on the illustration, "are the initials of the engraver. Rather than the artist?"

"Yes, quite right." She looked impressed. "That's Edward White. Well-known engraver of the period." Motioning me into an adjoining sitting room, Miranda pointed at two paintings hanging side by side, each one depicting a caged bird. "*That*," she said, "is the artist."

The delicately feathered birds stared at each other, forever separated, toeing their bamboo coops. Exotic, lonely, attractively yet bizarrely ornamented. What a marvelous pair: two lonely little freak shows. I located a white wiggle at the corner of each painting that read H. or perhaps A. Ingles, or Inglis. By then my mind was racing. Compared to *The Parasol Flower* the style here was somewhat more abstract, or perhaps it was simply that the media differed from painting to engraving. The colors were wild yet perfectly pitched; the mood was somehow warm and sorrowful. Beautiful was an insufficient word. The bird portraits were stunning. *Murdo*, read the plate on one frame; *Jane*, on the other.

"Were these birds…the Peterboroughs' pets?" I stammered. But I had a hundred questions—

Miranda laughed. "We think so, yes. They're birds of paradise. There's a whole section about these birds in *The Descent*. Unusual creatures."

I didn't recall the section. "And so, is it H. Inglis? Is this the same artist who…"

She nodded. "Hannah Inglis."

"*Hannah* Inglis," I said, my scalp tingling. "Really! Who is—what was her connection to the family?"

A guarded look entered Miranda's eyes. Or was that my imagination? Had I offended her with my enthusiasm that Hannah was a woman?

"Besides selling them art?" Miranda replied. "None, as far as I'm aware."

Silently I was putting pieces together. If this Hannah Inglis was living in Malaysia at the same time as the Peterboroughs, who had bought her paintings, then in all likelihood they'd known one another socially. The British community there must have been a small one. "Are there any other Hannah Inglis works in the estate's collection?"

No, unfortunately not. *Blah-blah-blah.*

"And so you don't have the original of *The Parasol Flower*?" I didn't hide my surprise and disappointment.

No, unfortunately not. *Blah-blah-blah.*

"What year were these ones painted?"

Miranda looked regretful. "We're not sure. Some time before *The Descent* was published."

"It's interesting," I remarked, "that she painted the birds *in* their cages."

She checked her watch. "You might want to see if Kew Gardens has any of her paintings. They have quite a collection of nineteenth-century botanicals. Do feel free to be in touch with us if we can assist in any way with your research."

I'd told Miranda I was writing a dissertation on pioneering English artists. A lie, of course. As I strolled through the remaining rooms at Fulgham House, my suspicion solidified that Miranda had not been entirely truthful with me either. If Hannah Inglis meant so little to her, why had she remembered, straight away, that *The Parasol Flower* was her creation?

A visit to Kew Gardens was considered touristy fun by Daphne and Bob, so I had no need to explain Hannah Inglis. At the Frimley library, I'd performed preliminary searches on the Kew archives, the world's largest flowers, and variations of "artist Hannah Inglis." Nothing was coming up. But my Kew Garden Info Desk query had been forwarded to Alvin, one of their archivists. He'd confirmed that Kew had one of Hannah's paintings in their holdings. Immediately, I drafted an email to the staff at Fulgham House.

To: info@fulghamhouseestate.co.uk
From: nancyroach21@gmail.com
Subject: many thanks

Dear Fulgham House,

Earlier this month I enjoyed an amazing visit to your property. What a beautiful place! During my visit, I spoke for some time with your museum manager, Miranda (sorry I do not recall her surname), regarding the Peterborough art collection. More particularly, the work of artist Hannah Inglis. I am following up, first and foremost, to thank Miranda for her time.

I also wanted to let her know that I took her suggestion to contact Kew Gardens London. Kew does indeed have one work by Hannah Inglis in their collection: *Strangler Fig Upon Kapok*. It was submitted to the 1896 Amateur Botanical Art Competition and the archivist's records show it was sent from Kuala Kangsa, Malaya.

Regarding a parasol flower, incidentally, the Kew botanist who spoke with me dismissed the idea that such a flower exists or ever existed. Apparently, it defies some sort of biological logic?! Did the Peterboroughs leave any notebooks about their scientific discoveries? I'm also wondering if other works of art by H. Inglis may have gone to relations or descendants of the Peterborough family. Wherever it may be now, there must have been an original of *The Parasol Flower* from which the engraving for the book was made. Thank you in advance for any assistance you are able to offer me.

Kind regards,
Nancy Roach, PhD (ABD)

Had the Gardens acquired *Strangler Fig Upon Kapok* as they did many other works at that time, through donation, Alvin would have had a devil of a time locating it. "They didn't bother to catalogue the donations," he confessed. "S'pose they had a hard enough time cataloguing the plants themselves."

"I'm surprised the Gardens has kept the paintings all of these years," I interjected.

"Kept all the entries," said Alvin. "Property of the Gardens, once you submit work to a competition." He pecked at the keyboard. "Now. 1896. The category was 'women: *other*,'" said Alvin, scanning the monitor, "which seems to have referred to anything that was not a watercolour illustration. In the traditional botanical training." He squinted at the handwritten script in the logbook the Gardens had used to record the entries. "C17," he said, moving out from behind his desk. "I'll fetch it."

"Thank you," I said softly, watching as he whipped a pair of surgical gloves from a nearby cabinet.

He returned quite some time later bearing a squarish painting on a wooden stretcher. It looked to be about a little over a yard in length and a little less than that in width. With his blue-gloved hands Alvin propped it on a low filing cabinet and began gently dusting it with a feather duster. We sneezed simultaneously.

"I'm sorry to put you to all of this trouble…"

Alvin grunted as he torqued himself upright. "No trouble 'tall if it'll help your research. That's why we're here."

He backed away and we stood side by side in his office, staring at the painting. The finished work, as I would later come to describe it, was a calculated assault on the senses.

"Amazing," I breathed.

"Isn't it just," he said.

We took the painting to a conference room down the hall, where there would be more scope for viewing.

"Who's the artist?" Alvin asked me, as we stood again, further back, in contemplation. "Is she well-known?"

"I don't know, actually…I'm trying to find out who she is. What I mean is, I have her name, as you know, but unfortunately that's about all I've been able to find so far." I told him a bit about *The Descent* engraving and the birds of paradise paintings at Fulgham House.

"Lovely spot, the Fulgham estate."

"Yes."

"Nasty family, though."

I asked him for permission to take some photographs. To oblige me, Alvin moved the painting once again, into the reception area of the archives, where it was brighter for shooting without a flash, and went off to answer his buzzing mobile phone. I took a few photographs, front and back, as if I were some sort of art specialist. Then I scribbled a few notes about my time at the archives and what Alvin had found in the logbook. I have to tell you, I was tempted to snatch the painting. Had I not already left an accurate contact address and telephone number for the Plewetts, I might well have. Clearly Kew didn't deserve it. Hannah's painting was going to be submerged again in a stack of amateur botanicals and packed away out of sight.

Alvin eventually loped back in, wiping his hands on the back of his pants. Perhaps after the phone call he'd dashed out back to plant saplings.

"All set?" he asked, and I nodded. He snapped on his disposable gloves.

"It's just so…well done," I said of the painting.

He cocked his head for a last look before gently seizing *Strangler Fig Upon Kapok* by its edges.

On the train back to Frimley I replayed my time at Kew in my head. Stupidly, I'd asked Alvin nothing at all about the Amateur Botanical Competitions or the other works submitted. Which piece had won that year? What exactly were the works competing to show? Would it have been unusual to send in a painting from abroad? Perhaps Alvin assumed that I knew the answers to such questions, being (as I was pretending to be) a specialist in pioneering women's art.

Then there was my grand summing up of the artwork: *it's just so well done.* A particularly inept finale for a supposedly educated specialist. Dwelling on this punishing moment, it dawned on me that H. Inglis must have been an educated specialist. Surely it was unlikely that she painted with such technical skill absent any formal training. As I was soon to confirm, there were very few art schools that admitted women in the 1880s or '90s. I was no longer looking for a needle in a haystack.

Meanwhile, back at the Plewetts', I'd received a promising email from Miranda. Things were hotting up, as Daphne would have put it.

To: nancyroach21@gmail.com
From: info@fulghamhouseestate.co.uk
Subject: Re: many thanks

Dear Nancy,

I remember that afternoon very well. Thank you for your kind words.

I have wondered how you got on at Kew if you ever went there. I have taken the liberty of contacting one of the Pellingham descendents, Dr. Barnaby Munk. He is amenable to being reached at barnabymothballs37@livewire.uk

Best wishes in your quest!

Kind regards,
Miranda

Six

Art is a leap of faith, Monsieur Godot used to say. Faith is necessary but faith doesn't make it any easier. He walks the room as he lectures. After, he visits them singly at their desks while they paint. Other days he paints for them, with wet brushes stashed like weapons in his pockets and belt. One above his left ear. "The picture that looks as if it were done without any effort can be a perfect battlefield in its making."

"Not this kind of a battle," Hannah tells her teacher. "This isn't what you had in mind." She rubs her knuckles against her temples. She is sitting in the public gardens, on a stone bench beside a camellia bush. Not far from where she and the sergeant usually meet.

Sergeant Singh soon arrives through the main entrance, loping in his characteristic way, a slight slouch in his shoulders. He is in uniform: the stark white woollen trousers, red jacket and sash, a sky blue turban wound high and tight. From his belt sways a sheathed machete.

When she first considered painting in the jungle, Hannah sought help. Somebody with know-how and the kind of courage—stupidity, might be just as apt—that it took to fend off the wild animals they all heard at nightfall, screeching, thumping, and barking in the wilds beyond the village. It made sense to her that a policeman came forward; members of the squad had been some of the first inhabitants of the area, she was told, tasked with mapping and clearing "the brush" before civil order could enter the picture. For the past year, or just about, she and Sergeant Singh had met on Mondays.

In the deep jungle, ironically, most animals fled. The fiercest creature they'd encountered was a stubborn tapir.

She can't afford him anymore. That is more to the point.

"Greetings, madam. How are you feeling today?"

She has canceled on the last two Mondays, saying she was ill. "Oh. Yes, I'm fine. Fine now," she fibs. The truth is she is worse than ever; she can't see past her predicament.

He hoists her stool under one arm and takes her paint box by the handle. Naturally, he doesn't realize she's no intention of entering the forest.

"Have you never worn a gun?"

"Gun?" He looks down at himself. "No."

"How odd. I thought…"

"Never, madam. Military are issued guns."

He sets off down the crushed gravel pathway, forcing her to follow. It is not yet midday and already the heat is pressing at her lungs, tightening her sleeves against her damp skin. It would be hot, indeed, to work in the village. The forest is shaded. And private.

"Before you go any further, Sergeant—"

He slows and turns. Seeing her face, he stops.

"I cannot…" Hannah clears her throat. "Cleopatra was killed by a tiger. The colonel, in his wisdom, is seeking revenge on this tiger. On all tigers, by the sounds of it."

"I see."

"Cleopatra is—was—our dairy cow."

"I see."

How much does he see, truly? Drawing a long breath, she continues: "We had rather a discussion, he and I…that's not important. The colonel believes it is not *reasonable* for me to continue to paint outdoors. *It's not reasonable to continue to do what you do*, was the way he put it." The anger is just as close as if he'd told her yesterday. "This, from the man who is funding an indiscriminate war on tigers!"

Sergeant Singh looks away.

"Moreover. This is to the point, now, Sergeant." She loosens the strap of her sunbonnet and fans her neck with her hand. "It seems I cannot afford to pay you any longer for your assistance."

His expression has not changed. He is still holding the stool and paint box.

"Sergeant?" Hannah looks around her, shielding her eyes. "I shall have to start carrying a parasol, along with everything else."

"Pardon me, madam, but you'll not be heading into the jungle on your own, will you?"

"No," she admits, with some vexation. In the past few days she has gone back and forth on this question. She is simply not courageous enough for it. "I thought…I might paint from what I can observe here in the gardens. Or perhaps in the village. It's high time I seriously attempted more work with the figure. I should make the most of our wonderful villagers."

He smiles grimly at her false cheer and her apologies, still clutching the stool and paints, while she expresses her genuine gratitude for his service and the time spent helping her. It is true that he has been so much more thoughtful and useful than she could have ever anticipated.

"Goodness, do you remember that tree snake?" she says, laughing. "And my series of elephant dung paintings? You've put up with a great deal." As she travels through a few other reminiscences, he remains silent. At last, Hannah prompts him to tell her what he is thinking. What will be his contribution to the town gossip?

"I suppose I can only be agreeing with this decision, madam. It isn't reasonable behavior. Not for a lady."

"So, you agree with the colonel?" It feels like a betrayal. Hannah's mind whirs. "I'll tell you why this is unreasonable. Because I am not a tethered cow. And because *you* are here to protect to me from tigers and other wild creatures. That is your express purpose. You and your expertise. And your gun."

"I do not carry a gun, madam."

"Evidently not. Oh, do please stop calling me madam. I dislike being called madam almost as much as being called unreasonable!"

"Sorry, madam. For failing in my express purpose!" Abruptly, Sergeant Singh puts down the stool and paint box and strides away.

Hannah watches him hastening across the lawn only to trip over a bank of miniature roses, his long legs splaying. Better not to go into the forest with the likes of him. It's almost comical, the way men stick together. Almost. She'll just have to finish the strangler fig painting from memory. And create something absolutely moving for the Kew Gardens jury.

Collecting her supplies, Hannah moves to one of the benches and for a long time simply sits, staring up at the changeable sky. Despite their many other disagreements, the male students at the academy agreed the female students were trivial. They did not use this word. Likely, they never spoke their agreement. But it held, just the same. If girls were there at the school, it was as an experiment, one that some people looked on charitably and others with spite. It didn't help that most of the female students were from wealthy families who treated the academy as an exotic finishing school or an excuse to ship their daughter abroad, even when these daughters themselves had grander ambitions. For her, art school was a beginning. An opening. If it weren't for Monsieur Godot...*stop thinking*. Too much thinking leads to no good.

Fishing out a pencil and paper, she lets her hand draw curls over the page. Clouds change so effortlessly. She is a vessel for clouds. A vessel for change. Soon, there is only the task of balancing void and shape, creating forms that generate points of interest, and she goes on until a painting reveals itself—that possible experience, that possible world, that possible way of feeling. The painting is what has asked to be seen.

At home, with the sketch book on her easel, Hannah's eyes leap from purples to greys to airy blues; against these, deep whites are emerging. Quickly she unbuckles her paint box.

SEVEN

As Deputy Resident, George is consigned to the third-floor office, by far the muggiest. Resident Finch is installed on the cooler second floor, and in any case has a boy to fan him and to make ice runs. Miss Wing and Miss Pevens share the space on the ground floor where, ostensibly, a member of the public might enter and require assistance, but where in reality the two Eurasian women play cards and read each other's fortunes. Miss Wing is his, Miss Pevens, Finch's. Though he knows his supervisor makes special requests of the younger, more vital woman, owing to her stronger skills in alphabetization.

Finch has told George to stay put for the meeting that day. They will come up to him. Signifying this meeting is off the record? No. Why meet at the office at all, in that case. He straightens the framed portrait of Sir James W.W. Birch, first British Resident of Perak. Rather heavy-handed in his approach, Birch had been assassinated in his bath-house. The killing had been contracted by the local sultans he was supposed to be advising, thus prompting the Perak War.

"What do you think—why here?" George asks the unswerving Oxbridge gentleman, and Birch looks back at him, askance.

Before long footsteps are echoing on the stairs, at the very moment George notices how grimy the window ledge and slatted blinds have become. With his handkerchief, he dusts crudely and furiously, then shoves the filthy cloth into a desk drawer.

"Ah!" he exclaims. "Come in, of course. Come in, come in, gentlemen."

"You remember…Dr. Charles…Peterborough," says James Finch, still puffing from the climb.

"Yes, of course." George moves to shake the man's clammy hand.

"Deputy Resident…our revenues collector," Finch elaborates for the doctor's benefit. "Good man is George. Discreet. Reliable."

Dr. Peterborough smiles modestly. He looks around the room, his eyes falling to one of the rattan armchairs.

"Government-issued furniture," George says. "But as it manages to support James's, ahem, *ambitions*…I'm sure you've nothing to worry about."

Finch, already easing himself into one of the chairs, guffaws and pats his moist face with his handkerchief. Dr. Peterborough brushes his hands over his trousers, front and back before lowering himself into the second rattan and the three of them talk about nothing of consequence for a while. Finch's mood is characteristically agreeable; the doctor fusses with his spectacles.

At a lull, Peterborough scratches his forehead and says to George, "*You* are on good terms with the sultan? Do I hear correctly?"

George thinks of the raja, the slight old man in his bright yellow *kefti*, invariably topped with the military jacket he was so fond of. The raja was a shrewd man and a kind one, who'd lived too long in a compromised position. Yes, I am quite fond of Izrin, he wants to say, I'd rather be chatting with him. Instead he tells Peterborough, "I've known Sultan Izrin for twelve years now, thereabouts."

"And he has his people's interest at heart?" Expressed in the same skeptical tone.

"To a point," Finch interjects. "We've always been able to pursue our own best interests, where money is involved."

At this, Dr. Peterborough looks a little skittish.

"Haven't we, George?"

"Yes," he admits. "The raja has usually considered it prudent to negotiate where it concerns money. Or for certain commodities with which we can supply him. Pocket watches. Dickens," George adds. "Izrin is a fan of Charles Dickens' writing."

"True!" James bellows. "Funny little man!"

Dr. Peterborough smiles at them both, a dead smile.

Before long the doctor is on his feet and, wiping his hands again on his trousers, makes an excuse to leave. He stops at the image of Birch.

"Ah, Sir James," chuckles James. "A pity, isn't it."

"That is what you get," Peterborough responds drily, "for depriving a people of their slaves." With that, the man rises on his toes then strides from the room.

George and James go to the window to watch Peterborough's suited figure exit the building and cross the high street toward his waiting blacktop.

"Uses a blacktop," George remarks. The rest of them, even Finch, make do with bullock carts and oxen. "Long drive, I suppose."

Finch resumes his seat. "He's rich as a horse with papers. And damn well-connected."

"Connected? Do you mean, Swettenham?"

This *is* impressive. Swettenham is the governor of Malaya and founder of the colony. He served as the Resident of Perak for its first fifteen years.

"A whiskey wouldn't go amiss, George."

On Finch's request, Miss Wing was dismissed early that day. George makes for the liquor cabinet himself and sorts out the tumblers and the whiskey, considering whether James is going to let him in on this great stress of his, this cloud of anguish and bother associated with the evolutionary scientist he's brought to see him. "I'm not going downstairs for ice," George mutters. Miss Wing would have been there and back already.

"Why do you think he came here in the first place?" Finch says.

"What, the Peterborough fellow? You brought him."

"Not here *today*. Here to Malaya."

"To conduct his research, was it? What did he say he was studying? Something about the Indo-Malaysian line."

"Pinky, think of all the places in the world you can find savages and dark races. And the Peterboroughs happen to headquarter themselves in Perak, the very province where…"

George considers this coincidence. Families as ancient and wealthy as the Pellingham-Peterboroughs may well have decent connections in any of the colonies. In fact, didn't Charles mention they had lived for a time in New South Wales? The Peterboroughs must have come to Perak around the time he had brought Hannah back with him. Magical, that journey feels in retrospect. As if he'd gotten away with an impressive trick. Her new skin against his mouth, under his nose, on his tongue; the constant, faint nausea induced by the roll and pitch of the seas.

"Hallo in there!" booms Finch. "You've not heard a word I'm saying, I'll venture. What's the matter with you? Gut troubles again?"

George is about to reply that nothing is the matter when he hears his own voice, plaintive, saying, "A tiger killed my cow."

"Christ. Lucy mentioned something." Sternly, Finch growls at him. "If we have a man-eater on Ridge Road…"

The Residency, where Finch and Lucy live, is the nearest neighboring home on Ridge Road. The insinuation is that George has been putting them all at risk.

Finch says, "Why do you need a cow, eh? Use the tinned milk, like everybody else."

"Tinned milk is a…a capitulation." George hands Finch his drink. "Besides, I like cows. They… I have a *right* to pasture a cow. Surely you're not blaming this unfortunate event on me!"

"Easy does it," Finch drawls.

"I'm arranging for a hunting party, you know."

"Good then," says Finch. "Good." He surveys the near-empty bookshelf beside them. "And is Hannah, is she all right?"

"Yes, of course. Why do you…We were in *bed* when it happened, James. She was nowhere near the creature." They hold each other's gaze for a moment. George has confided in Finch in the past about his younger wife—her coldness, her painting, her unsociability, her jungle treks. He adds, "As a matter of fact, Hannah has given up the forest trekking."

"Has she?"

"And I've reduced her stipend. Why should I pay for any of it anymore?"

Finch raises his remarkable eyebrows. Two lengths of frayed rope.

"What?" George demands.

"I'm only…a little surprised at that, my dear fellow."

"Well, don't be."

"From our previous conversations…"

The man is insufferable! "What? From our previous conversations, what?"

"We both know Hannah's not like my Lucy."

"Oh, is she not?" George snaps. One evening, when newly married, George and Hannah had hosted supper for their Ridge Road neighbors. Hannah brought out her book of copies, something she'd made in art school. A painted record of all the "famous" works that inspire her. The Rembrandt had impressed Finch, in particular. In what he'd said, and more so how enthralled he'd looked as Hannah answered his questions, it was clear to George that his new wife could only make things worse between the two men.

"She's complicated," Finch says vaguely. "Creative types, you know."

George lets the matter drop; he's in no mood for indulging the old man. There is this new mysterious task for Peterborough, this providing of Malayan women. For it will be *his* task, no doubt. On top of that, the need to scrounge up a hunting party. He gulps back his whiskey. God, he'll be spending all week groveling with the natives.

On cue, Finch announces, "So. I've told Peterborough we can support him."

The royal *we*. The reason for Peterborough's visit, then, must have been to acquaint himself firsthand with his agent.

"You're sure he approves of me, then?" George quips.

"Of course. You're my man. And Izrin trusts you. You'll be able to get his cooperation."

"And what exactly...I mean, what should I tell Izrin that he wants them for, these women?"

Finch swabs his forehead. "Interviews. We've told you."

Whether Izrin finds this idea as preposterous as George does remains to be seen. He doesn't press the question. Were it unproblematic, Finch would have already related the truth. The fact is George is pleased to be relied upon for such an apparently inconvenient matter. It bodes well.

"Izrin trusts you," Finch repeats.

"Yes, well, I've spent a good deal of time with him."

The Resident rests his empty glass on his belly. "And it's a considerable sum of money. Considerable."

It strikes George as a pity he's to leverage his hard work with Izrin for this doctor's queer research. Evolutionary science, hadn't that fallen out of fashion?

EIGHT

Fruits, fish, vegetables, spices, candles and kerosene, cut flowers, fabric, chamber pots, bamboo chairs, pickles, parakeets, holy water: at the market, you can get most everything. Malu watches from across the stalls as the English colonel limps into the hut of the opium dealer, Ah Sip. Malu takes good notice of the *longos*. Her father, whoever he is, is one of them.

Before she can spy the colonel leaving, Omar, the jeweller, calls her over. "Hey, girl, what you looking so mean for?"

"Born with this face!" Malu retorts, furrowing her brow even harder. She should not speak this way to an elder. But Auntie Nattie dislikes Omar, and besides, Nattie is busy with Bird Mem. As with every customer this month, her aunt is singing the praises of their new monkey.

"Fifteen," she hears her quote the woman. "He can play domino!"

Bird Mem bends to watch the creature scratching vigorously at his toenail. Her face, Malu thinks, is almost as ugly as the monkey's. The same close-together eyes and puffy upper lip. Her bright eyes shift and flicker, coming to light on Malu's. "No, I don't need a macaque," she tells Nattie.

Bird Mem has been coming to them for years now. To buy birds, mostly, but she sometimes asks them to catch her other animals— fish, reptiles, even insects. So the fact that she is bothering to look in the cages is curious.

"Bird today," prompts Nattie. "Bird you like? What bird?"

"Give me a twirl," Omar says behind Malu. "Old times, girl. Come on."

When she was a kid she twirled for him, this was true, and some-times received a coin to buy paan. Malu twirls theatrically, coquettishly, then holds out her palm. This, Nattie certainly wouldn't allow. Omar laughs and tosses her a five-cent piece. Malu is saving money for En-glish medicine. Her mother has stayed faithful to the fortune teller's cures all these years, and now she deserves some English medicine, whatever Nattie thinks of it. Malu turns the coin between her thumb and finger, wondering, as she does these days, about how to get more.

Bird Mem and her aunt have moved close enough that Malu must appear attentive.

"A bird of paradise. *Paradisaea apoda*, preferably. You don't have any." Bird Mem measures the air with her gloved hands.

"We'll catch one for you. Or two," says Malu, entering the conversation. "We always do."

Auntie Nattie's mouth opens. This is too confident to the Malay ear. Nattie still hasn't learned that the English like confidence.

"Yes," Bird Mem smiles, "you *are* reliable. I…I wonder…"

"Describe which bird you are looking for, please?" Malu says to the strange woman. It comes back to her that she needs to be patient when dealing with this woman. Bird Mem's words are sometimes uncommon, and she has trouble—or else refuses—to use simpler ones. Nattie, impatient and poor with English, has steered Bird Mem to Malu. Catching Malu's eye, her aunt fades into the background.

"The males are dark blue or grey in color and they have a…sort of ornament hanging from their facial plumage. Like a worm from a fishing line." Bird Mem demonstrates by holding her arm out in front of her forehead, her gloved hand dangling like bait in front of her face. "And they *dance*." She totters back and forth on the straw-strewn floor, kicking her legs out and waving her arms in circles.

Malu feels Nattie watching them through the cages. "Yes. I can catch one for you. One? Pair?"

"A pair? A pair would be… Yes, thank you. But these birds are notoriously reclusive. Shy."

Malu nods. "We know these birds, memsahib. These are called God's birds, the *manuk dewata*." She is already familiar with one place where the birds come together. The usual way of hunting them is to hide under leaves until daybreak. An arrow, fitted with a plug of rubber, can knock them dead without tearing the brilliant feathers. As for taking one alive… "Yes, they are very shy. Special price for shy birds."

One of her straggly eyebrows arches. Bird Mem is plainer even than most Englishwomen, with big teeth and gaping nostrils. Wearing that crumpled hat, you'd think she never bothered to look in a mirror.

"All right," she says, "I will pay your 'special price.' But only once I return and find that everything is in order."

"Of course."

They trade numbers briefly, ending on something that makes the job well worth the effort. Malu offers a shallow bow to conclude the transaction.

But Bird Mem does not back away. "Is she your mother?" she asks Malu in a low voice.

"Mother's brother's wife."

Bird Mem waves Nattie closer. "Speak? Can we…? I wonder if I might hire your girl. Not for catching birds. For something else."

Nattie is struggling, her face contorted. "Higher her?"

"Employ her. Pay her to work for me."

"Oh!"

"I need a helper for my daughter."

Nattie smiles broadly. Her aunt would be happy to get her out of the way. Wasn't it always Umi's good-for-nothing child who ate the last cup of rice? At market, Nattie complained that Malu tripped her up and put off the customers. *Too dark-skinned for your big ideas, too light-skinned for hard work.*

"Charlotte doesn't need an ayah. She's too old for that now. But… this girl," she points at Malu, "has always seemed to me to be…tenacious and reasonably articulate. I think she might prove a suitable playmate."

"Genduk," Nattie names the Malay work for such care. "Aw, she is so good, my Malu. Sensible. Very valuable for me, see?" Nattie puts her hands on Malu's shoulders.

Bird Mem's eyes narrow slightly. "I will pay the *ordinary* wage for a genduk, whatever that wage happens to be. No more special prices." She adjusts her crumpled hat. "If it suits you, I can take her back with me when I come for the birds. My name is Mrs. Peterborough. We live out of town, on the former Boonstra plantation."

"Ah. Yes, memsahib," agrees Nattie. "Excellent girl. Clean, very friendly." She continues to haggle as if Malu were one of her caged pets. "Half-breed bastard," her aunt says brightly, tapping the side of her forehead. "Good thinking."

"Excuse me?" says the lady.

"Two dollars a week," Malu interrupts them. "That is the ordinary wage." In fact, she has no idea about genduk pay, but this number is at least more than Malu and her mother's portion of the menagerie profits.

"Well, I will make inquiries as to the ordinary wage."

"I don't leave for less," says Malu quietly.

Nattie growls at Malu and shoves her out of the way. Pivoting toward Bird Mem, she says, "We will settle price. We all happy together. So we settle price, eh? Price can be settled. You come back, mem."

Malu is red-faced—hopefully Omar has not seen any of this—as she watches the crumpled hat bob away with the dark heads of the native shoppers. She doesn't like Auntie Nattie, but to work out there, so far out of town on that abandoned plantation? To have to make play with an English girl she's never met? It's all as strange as the lady herself, with her tangly words and her special requests.

Her pay could go for her mother's medicine. English medicine. Somehow, *inshallah*, with this new work, she will make sure of it. Incredible, Malu says to herself. Three-fifty per bird. Then two dollars a week! Was it the manuk dewata who'd brought her some courage? She is still lost in thinking this through when the white-suited officer limps past their stall.

NINE

The parcel postage for the art competition, not to mention the entry fee, must be deducted from Hannah's diminished stipend. She decides therefore against placing a March order to Schlauerbach's. "It is really no way to work," she writes to Godot, "when the practical part of your brain measures each blob that hits the palette and demands to know that it is going to be put to good use." Confining herself to the most developed version of *Strangler Fig* seems to bring her further and further from its completion, maddeningly. Whereas *Tethered* she finished in a day!

Even if she manages to purchase supplies next month, what will she paint? Rehash old studies? Or else "the figure," as she put it to the sergeant so pompously. Well, it is one thing to draw a paid model indoors. Quite another to approach Malay villagers on the street.

In the end, bulging vines fill the plane of the canvas until it looks as if the canvas might torque and rupture. Contrary to her expectations, the excess of vines makes the mostly hidden kapok appear even sturdier and stronger.

"Yes," she says at last. "Yes, I think so."

The timing is tight. If the painting had been able to dry before she needed to ship it, she could have rolled it into a cylinder. As it is, Hannah nails lined crate boards over the stretched canvas and binds the entire thing in strips of old linens, all of which she encases in brown parcel paper and twine. Her entry form is sealed in an envelope, stuffed within. Checking at the window, she sees their bullock cart is gone. A walk, then, to the post office.

But the sandwiched crate boards are awkward, the parcel too deep for her to hook under one arm and too heavy to hold out in front of her. After some fumbling on the front lawn, Hannah decides to balance it on her bare head. By keeping her posture erect she can at least move steadily.

Out on the road, the air is warm and fragrant with the scent of *kemuning.* As she nears the acacia, Roderick comes running, chittering and squealing.

"Hello, Roddy darling! Yes, I did bring one," she says. "Hold on."

Hannah concentrates for a moment before carefully removing her left hand from the parcel and even more carefully inserting it in her pocket while keeping her upper body, neck, and head perfectly still. Withdrawing the biscuit, she flings it, not daring to look down.

The sound of the little creature's crunching makes her smile. Hannah proceeds, both hands once again gripping the painting. Roddy, she knows, is scampering along beside her. By the time they turn onto the avenue of the high street, her neck and arms are aching. She halts, releases first one arm and then the other to let each fall loose and rest for a minute. The post office is another three or four blocks away, nearer the other end of the downtown.

"Best get on then, hadn't we?" she says.

Roddy chitters and dashes ahead, nearly tripping her. The barber-shop, no doubt.

As she passes, Hannah calls out, "Good morning, Mr. Lim."

In the final block, her forearms begin to burn and her scalp goes prickly. Meantime, the sounds of hooves and rolling wheels grow louder behind her.

"Hannah?"

"What on earth does she have on her head?"

"Driver, slow down."

"Goodness, is that monkey…wearing shaving lather?"

The cart slows to a stop just in front of her. Hannah tilts the crate board carefully to confirm the speaker is Lucy Finch, the Resident's wife. She and Hazel Swinburne, another Ridge Road neighbor, stare down at her from their bullock cart, eyes goggling. Roderick scampers over and begins flicking shaving lather at them from his fingers.

"Shoo, you little beast!"

"Roddy," Hannah commands. "Stop that! Go home now!"

"Good morning, ladies," she adds before she sets off again, moving past their cart as fast as she is able. The postal office is only twenty yards away.

"Hannah, let us help you!" the women cry after her. "Driver, go! Go!"

"Ask one of the police officers to help you," Lucy calls out loudly.

The Sikh police officers have a habit of gathering on the shallow steps of the postal office. Ahead, she hears them arguing with each other in vociferous Punjabi. She'd forgotten about the Sikhs, with whom she ordinarily exchanges a few friendly words. No doubt *they* will be laughing at her now as well. At least that mischievous gibbon is no longer in sight.

Deputy Onkarjeet rushes over. "Madam, madam," he says. "I will carry this for you."

"Thank you, Deputy, but I'm delicately balanced," she replies, continuing to mount the stone steps. Sergeant Singh, amongst the officers she passes, is smiling broadly.

The deputy bounds ahead to hold open the door.

"Wonderful, thank you kindly." Hannah slips in sideways as elegantly as she can manage.

Vast and dimly lit, the foyer of the postal office has always put her in mind of a harem courtyard. Its grandiose, three-story ceiling is held up by numerous embossed pillars. Two shriveled *punkah wallahs* pull the ropes for the two enormous ceiling fans. The tidy Eurasian clerk, behind his far-off counter, is serving three or four customers who twist to look behind them.

"Morning," Hannah says under her breath. She raises the parcel in her tired arms and with a groan ducks out from under it, levering it against her hip to bring one end down carefully against the polished floor. Moments later, Lucy and Hazel burst through the door. The three women stand catching their breath and letting their eyes adjust.

Hazel loosens the chin strap of her sun hat. "Hannah, I can't believe you walked all the way here with this monster."

"More difficult than I expected," she admits. She is still breathing hard. "Although, I do love the walk."

"At least it was downhill," Lucy says. "It's a painting, I take it?"

"Yes." Hannah discreetly attempts to fix her hair, after the look Lucy has given her. "For the Kew Gardens competition, actually." Her bun is squashed and multiple pins have been pushed out of place. Lank strands of dark hair droop over her ears.

Hazel tugs up one end of the painting, prompting Hannah to take hold of the other. "Best get out of the doorway."

As Lucy shepherds them toward the queue she says, "You've been a stranger lately, Hannah."

"Have I?" Having been greeted with fervour by the small community of expatriates and drawn firmly to their perspiring bosoms, she had wanted to please. She'd fooled them all for far too long by acting sociably. Which is to say, normally. There's nothing more suspicious than an unsociable woman. At the end of the queue, they set down the painting. "I've been rather occupied lately."

With a start, she feels fingers moving over her head. Lucy is unpinning and re-pinning her braids. The other customers, mercifully, have turned back to their business.

"Painting can be such a struggle, I must admit," says Hannah. "There is something about completion that is ever so difficult to gauge, I find. With this one, I was desperate to be *done with it*, ten times over." She half-swats at Lucy's hands. "But I couldn't finish with it. Well. Until it was finished with me!" She laughs heartily at her own joke. "And how are you both?"

"Never mind about *us*," says Hazel.

"I've nearly fixed it," says Lucy. "There. Passable."

"Of course she doesn't have a hat for the return trip," Hazel remarks. "In this sun…"

Lucy takes back her packet of letters from Hazel. They stand together for a minute or two, watching the clerk process and release his customer, punching his stamp loudly.

"I hear the colonel has hired a hunting party."

"I suppose so."

"A hunting party? Whatever for?" Hazel asks disingenuously. There is no news Lucy wouldn't have told her already. The two of them are thick as thieves.

Lucy answers on Hannah's behalf. "There's been a tiger attack. A man-eater."

"A man-eater!" Hazel repeats, loud enough for the word to echo.

"Really, it's more of a cow-eater," Hannah says. She addresses the women in the queue who have turned in alarm, adding, "Our Jersey was taken recently."

"In her pen. At night," says Lucy. "Hello, Beatrice. Jane."

Beatrice Watts is the minister's wife and Jane, her eldest daughter.

Hannah does not recognize the other person whose back remains to them as she deals with the clerk. A tall, angular woman, wearing a crumpled felt hat.

"And now," Lucy tells them all, "the colonel is going to hunt the beast down."

"He's hired a hunting party," Hazel marvels.

"Can one hire a hunting party in Kuala Kangsa?" asks Beatrice.

"Apparently."

Fifteen-year-old Jane squirms at the prospect. "How exciting!"

"They're natives," Lucy informs them. "Off shift from the mines."

"Malays?" asks Beatrice.

"Apparently a certain strain of them are quite expert hunters."

There is a lull as they separately consider what off-shift Malay miners know or do not know about the sport of hunting.

"Well, I don't like the thought of a man-eater on the Ridge Road," Beatrice tells them. The Watts live on the other, poorer, side of town, though her sympathy is obviously heartfelt.

"At least your husband is doing something about it," Lucy says to Hannah.

"One dreads to think," says Beatrice, "if the children are out playing…"

The Watts have seven children ranging in age from fifteen to infancy. One or two to spare, is what Hannah thinks.

"This tiger is not a man-eater."

The contribution, the pronouncement, is made by the woman in the crumpled hat. She has turned toward them to reveal a bare, freckled face of perhaps forty-five. Pulling on her gloves she says, "A man-eater is an animal who has incorporated human flesh into its diet. Human flesh is a distinctive taste. A tiger who is bold enough to poach a cow from a stable, or a chicken from its coop, is not the same animal as a man-eater."

The women grimace and freeze, unsure how to respond. Hannah realizes this is the biologist, Mrs. Eva Peterborough, the woman who refuses to have anything to do with the Ladies Association of Perak. Lucy, chairwoman of the LAP, has been pursuing Mrs. Peterborough's membership for years, and it occurs to Hannah that, however awkward, Lucy might take this opportunity as well.

It is Hazel who speaks, belatedly. "So you don't think we should be worried?"

Eva Peterborough moves past them with her collection of letters. "If you keep a cow, yes."

They all watch her exit the building, silent until the heavy door thuds shut.

"'Human flesh is a distinctive taste!'" Jane bursts into giggles.

"Next, please," the clerk announces.

"That is the most I have ever heard that woman say." Hazel tugs Lucy's arm.

"So pretentious," Lucy murmurs approvingly.

"Next, please."

"Oh, I suppose it's our turn," Beatrice says, awakening and nodding vigorously at the clerk. She pushes her daughter toward the counter.

As they are waiting, Lucy inquires about Hannah's painting. "Come now," she insists, when Hannah politely demurs. "If you're submitting it for a competition, you must take some pride in it."

"Pride? Why, yes, of course!"

"Well?"

She meets Lucy's eyes—eyes that, unless she is mistaken, seem to be smiling. "It's called *Strangler Fig Attacking Kapok*. Depicting a strangler fig. Obviously. They can grow to enormous size in the forest, these vines. And this one, when we encountered it, was breathtaking. The tree itself was enormous. A mighty old kapok. It was covered in a webbing of vines, for you see the vines can become quite solid, I suppose you'd say. They meld together to become like branches, or rather a trunk, for the vine is literally eating its host and sending the nutrients up and down its length, as required. It's a parasitical relationship."

"Wherever did you learn all this?" Hazel asks. "Not at your art academy."

"No. Sergeant Singh explained it to me." Hannah hurries on. "I was, of course, interested in depicting something of this *smothering* action, this elegant depravity of one life feeding from another."

"Of course," says Lucy.

"In portraiture, you see, the artist reveals something of interest about the sitter. There is a definite thing to be said. But in the best portraits, a great deal more can be apprehended by the viewer. It is the triadic relationship of the artist, through the sitter, communicating with the viewer, that allows for such wonderful complexity. In the best portraits."

"Portraits? But this is a *tree*, is it not?"

"And a vine," says Hazel.

The clerk is finally free. A small, pale man with a mustache like a caterpillar, he calls them forward. As Hannah hoists the crate board onto the counter he lunges to receive it, then peers at the address label. "Oh! Good luck, mem." He winks as if the contents are their little secret. Hannah sighs inwardly.

Working his measuring tape and scale, the clerk soon tabulates an outrageous postage.

"Are you sure?" she says to him as discreetly as possible.

"Sorry, mem. Big size plus big weight equals big price, heh?"

Hannah pays, fishing out the last of her coins, and he lugs the parcel to a back room. All the while she can hear Hazel and Lucy discussing her jungle treks in low tones. They agree she will have to stop, with a tiger prowling around. It's the lighthearted way they reach their conclusion that makes Hannah want to wail.

"Sorry, there are no incoming letters for you today, Mrs. Inglis," the clerk reports.

"Come home with us in the cart," suggests Lucy, as Hannah turns to go. "We'll drop you off."

"No, thank you. I enjoy the walk."

Hazel and Lucy exchange a look.

"But it's all uphill in this direction," Hazel says. "Just the thought of it makes my lungs ache." She fans her hands over the prow of her breast. "Mind you, I suppose you're not carrying…anything… anymore."

"Leave her be," sings Lucy. "She's obviously a lost cause."

"Excuse me? What…did you say?"

"I said that you obviously love to walk."

Hazel waves. "Toodle-oo!"

The ladies step toward the clerk. Hannah pushes open the heavy door and walks into the blinding sun.

TEN

Daphne and Bob recognized that they were making great strides with me. By mid-January I'd stayed in Frimley two weeks longer than planned, and I was no longer "hiding," as they put it, for hours on end behind a screen or a book. I made jokes. I'd learned how to properly watch *football*—i.e. in the pub, with a beer and a bunch of Bob's friends. Daphne told me stories about her younger life, when she'd worked as a trauma nurse. No one, she said, had ever asked her the kinds of questions I did, and she meant that as a compliment.

What the dear Plewetts didn't know was that as much as I genuinely liked Frimley and their apricot-scented company, I was lingering because of barnabymothballs37. I'd written to Barnaby Munk the very day Miranda sent me his address. I was still waiting for a reply. I'd discovered he was a professor emeritus at Oxford so I assumed, maybe incorrectly, that he was living somewhere nearby and also assumed—in the unfair, exuberant way people do when they are engrossed in their own projects—that the old man would have nothing better to do than to facilitate my quest to find Hannah Inglis' art. Yet with each day that passed, I was coming to accept that this "line of inquiry"—as the police always said on Daphne's programs—might well be a dead end. In the meantime, I began familiarizing myself with British Malaysia, Victorian customs, tropical trees, and art movements of the nineteenth century. I'd even tried to trace the Pellingham-Peterborough lineage on a genealogy site.

Most importantly, I'd discovered the only art school admitting women in the year that *Strangler Fig* was painted was the Academie Julian, a college in Paris. This was a remarkable breakthrough. The art school was still in existence, incredibly, and, as Parisian institutions tended to, Julian had its own archives. When I mapped the Julian address, I saw that the art school was a stone's throw from Richelieu library. I must have walked by the place dozens of times before. Now, I would go inside.

It was time for me to return to Paris, I told Daphne and Bob when I came down one morning.

"My…uh…phrenologist friends have invited me to a party," I said. This was perfectly true.

"What kind of a party?" Daphne asked. "Hopefully some other singles are there, Nancy, and some dancing."

"I have no idea," I said, picturing a sixteen-year-old Daphne doing a foxtrot in her nursing uniform. "I think it's just dinner." I flicked on the electric kettle and prepared the French press. It was another grey day—rain pelted the patio door that opened to their yard—and I came to the glass to look out at Bob's garden sanctuary, no more at that time of year than humps of burlap-wrapped shrubs and ice-covered garden beds.

"And I really shouldn't impose on you any longer."

Bob had the newspapers out in front of him on the table and Daphne was standing at the stove, boiling eggs. They both looked up and insisted that I hadn't been imposing.

"Bob," I said, turning back to the window, "have you ever heard of a plant called a parasol flower?"

That was how the whole story came spilling out—about *The Parasol Flower*, *The Descent*, Alvin and the *Strangler Fig* painting, my visit to Fulgham House, the rise of Impressionism in the art salons of Paris, where the saying *running amok* originated. (Answer: British Malaysia, of course.) Everything. In the middle of this, the egg timer buzzed. Daphne transferred the soft-boiled eggs one by one into our waiting cups (mine was a bunny) and brought them over to the table. I contributed a steaming French press. Bob plunged, then poured.

"I really can't wait on this Dr. Munk guy any longer," I told them. "Miranda said he was amenable to being contacted, but clearly he isn't amenable."

Neither of them had said anything so far. Daphne's mouth was open and she looked confused.

I said, "Miranda emailed me… She's the one at… Never mind. The point is the lepidopterist ancestor is not replying and I really need to move forward."

Bob rubbed under his scruffy chin, pondering this a moment before cracking into his egg.

"And since there are only so many files that the academy has converted to digital holdings, I can't do it from here."

"I thought you'd stopped," Daphne said quietly.

I spouted something about conducting real research, the kind that people had forgotten how to accomplish, what with everybody Googling and Googling! "Stopped what?" I replied.

"Well, obsessively researching!" Daphne's head shook rapidly, like she was short-circuiting.

I'd sat down across from Bob, who was spooning out his egg with deliberation. I said, "Ooooh. Actually, this has nothing to do with my dissertation."

"Pardon me, sweetheart?"

Bob said, "If this has nothing to do with your dissertation, then why are you so keen on finding this parasol flower woman?"

"Parasol flower?" said Daphne.

"Daph, you weren't listening to her!" he growled.

I had their full attention now. The Plewetts drew themselves up as straight as their backs would allow and waited for me with wide eyes.

"Why? I don't know why!" I laughed outright at myself.

They looked at me warily as I cracked into my egg.

I had no reason to care about Hannah Inglis and her parasol flower. Not this much. And when had I ever done something for no good reason? When had I ever acted on instinct? Never. Well, at no time that I could remember. Probably not since I was a small child. I told my eighty-something-year-old friends all of this in my rambling way, spearing toast crumbs with the tips of my fingers. No, there was no good reason for me to care, but I did.

Whatever I said seemed to brighten their mood considerably. Two days later, they dropped me off at the station with a toot from their little red car. I promised to email them regularly.

On my visit to Julian, a new world opened for me. I leafed through the notebooks of former students, some of them women, some written in French, some written in English, even some in Japanese. The academy had been a cosmopolitan crossroads. An experiment ahead of its time, whose young women were "educated as human beings, first and foremost," wrote Amelie Beaury-Saurel. A former student, Amelie had married the founder, Rodolphe Julian, and went on to manage the women's atelier that opened in 1880. Like her classmates, Hannah must have been intimidated by the feisty "Madame Espagne." (Amelie had been born in Spain.) If Hannah, my Hannah, had indeed attended. There was no "Inglis" on the rosters or any of the documents I scanned, where everyone was recorded by surname.

It was a conversation with my Welsh phrenologist friends that renewed my hope. I'd never seen so much of Chris and Zoe. They were leaving Paris soon, to be married in Zoe's home town in Wales, and I suppose they were trying to cram in as much casual socializing as possible. The three of us had always bonded over bookstores and cheese markets, so we alternated visits to their favorite venues. Our conversations were wide-ranging, as usual, but now suddenly our *lives* struck me as wide-ranging in random ways; it wasn't just that we jumped topics readily, but people like us jumped the globe and jumped into different lifestyles, jobs, habits, relationships. We were making changes, huge, irreparable changes to our futures, based on precarious circumstances. We joked about it, but opening a bookshop or becoming cheese experts seemed just as likely as anything else we might do. I asked Zoe and Chris about where they were going to live and work after they graduated in spring. They were both gunning for history and philosophy of science instructor positions.

"The rule is whoever gets hired first," said Zoe, "the other person has to follow."

"Whoever gets hired first," Chris repeated, "the other person has to follow."

They locked eyes, smiling goofily, then pulled each other close, mashing their faces together.

"Good rule," I remarked.

When they didn't let up, I turned away to sample some Brie-like cheese and experienced an epiphany. Hannah had gone to Malaysia. Why? Why all the way to Malaysia? Not to paint it. No, she'd gotten married! Inglis was her married name, and she'd had a different one at the academy.

God only knew what that name was.

Still, I kept snooping around the archives. As it turned out, I wasn't in need of Hannah's maiden name. During my second week, I was working my way through the books on hand and encountered *The*

Late Godot: Conversations with Young Artists, written by one Edward Coles. Henri Godot had attended Julian himself. A portraitist by specialty, he graduated and went on to be a charismatic young teacher for the academy. Later, he emigrated to America and became a founding member of the Ashcan School.

Skimming the book's index, I froze at "Inglis, Hannah." Twenty-two of her letters to Henri Godot were included in the volume. I still get chills, recalling that moment. Godot had kept in touch with many young artists, apparently, and communicated fervently and publicly about art-making as the right of every human being. I reckoned that his correspondence with Hannah was not unusual. Though it felt like a private banquet all my own.

Edward Coles made several claims about Hannah, some of which were borne out by the published letters. (Had there been more letters from which to choose, I wondered? What other sources did he have at his disposal? The citation was spotty, quite frankly.) Born Hannah Bliss, she was the illegitimate child of a prominent English politician and an innkeeper. She'd grown up in a London neighborhood, presumably in her mother's care. There were no details on her parents' liaison or whether her father remained part of Hannah's life. Had art school been his idea? Almost undoubtedly his money had funded her to attend; he must have at least consented. Coles stated that Hannah had married one Colonel George Inglis, a distant relation, and relocated to Kuala Kangsa where Inglis was stationed as a customs officer.

By then of course I could already picture the village, having read a variety of memoirs, government reports, and historical documents associated with the young colony. Small though it was, Kuala Kangsa was the de facto cultural capital of Malaysia by the time Hannah arrived. It had acquired a cricket league, a barbershop, and even a traffic warden.

In Malaysia, Hannah evidently went on drawing and painting. It was plain from the letters to Godot that she fell in love with the tropics, that "bright, excessive, exotic, HOT, fly-infested clime." In her first months away, she mailed him sketches of mammoth insects. Of various neighbors' pets and garden plants. Of the views from her veranda and dragon fruit in a bowl. Then came more polished works of undulating blue-green hills and panoramas of a stunning river valley.

After a hiatus, Hannah's trajectory swerved. That is to say, from what I could tell by her replies to Godot's responses to the studies she was sending him. She let go somewhat of perspective and dimension. The color work became wilder and bolder. She was sending her mentor dozens of botanicals. Odd botanicals. Trees with roots shooting from their branches. Rotting logs hosting alien mushrooms and vibrantly colored slime molds. Miniature violets growing from a smear of bat dung.

This shift, this tectonic shift, coincided with a major change in her process: namely, Hannah began painting *en plein air*. In June of 1895 she wrote:

> Today I will be taking my paints into the forest. I am warned (in gentler terms) that this practice is unsafe and inexplicable. I feel rather that I am being called unsafe and inexplicable. I would throw names back in their faces—de Valenciennes, of course, and Mr. Constable, also Rousseau, Millet, and the entire Barbizon Group. Then there are your Impressionists, especially M. Monet. It is nothing new at all to be out of doors! And quite necessary if I am to produce anything of interest! I thought it prudent, though, to hire a man to assist me in bushwhacking and staving off any troublesome animals. He is one of the Sikh police guard here, a great mountain of a fellow topped with a sky-blue turban. That said, I can admit to you, monsieur, I am very nervous—!
>   (Coles, p.337)

The strangler fig and kapok duo I had seen at Kew must have been one of the subjects Hannah encountered on a forest trek. I wondered where the other paintings she mentioned had ended up.

Armed with Hannah's surname, I reviewed the academy's archive of images. There was one class photograph taken during her time at Julian, circa 1890, that included an H. Bliss. The ladies in this anatomy class looked young and determined. One or two had bangs cut into their hair, the new fashion. H—the one I felt to be Hannah, although it was not entirely clear from the legend—was seated on a high stool toward the back of the group, leaning forward a little, as if she were trying to see the photographer behind the apparatus. As if she might break from the formation. Her dark hair was swept up like a storm cloud, her regard quizzical.

Now that I'd found Hannah, how to find her art? The Coles book was of no use here. The Ashcan School inheritors, when they returned my messages, let me know that nothing by Hannah Inglis or Hannah Bliss could be found in *their* archives either. I debated with myself about bothering barnabymothballs37 with a third follow-up message. Professor emeritus he might be, but he had zilch in the way of netiquette.

The time came for my friends' departure for the unpronounceable town in Wales. To celebrate, we went out for *moules frites* with some of their other friends at the local brasserie. I brought Zoe and Chris a wedding gift: a pair of Bauhaus-looking stainless steel salad servers, which seemed a suitably adult present. I also brought my tiny dilemma with me—to email Dr. Munk, or not to email Dr. Munk—and criticized myself for even thinking of broaching the subject. Here were these two people planning on growing old together, washing each other's laundry, having children that would need constant supervision. *That* was serious stuff, and Zoe was already drowning, in my humble opinion, in a sea of rules and expectations that the two sets of parents—opposites, in every way—had applied to the wedding preparations. By dessert, though, I was tipsy enough to ask the people around the table for their opinions on my humble conundrum: how could I find out more about a little-known artist.

This was an educated, equally tipsy bunch and they pounced on my offering like street dogs on a carcass.

"Hannah Inglis…is she a performance artist?" Zoe asked. "The one who dresses in drag and scales buildings?"

"No, no. She was a painter in the late nineteenth, early twentieth century." I described *Strangler Fig* and *Murdo* and *Jane* to everyone, and they made shiny little offerings: "search eBay," said one person; "I've got a friend who works at Sotheby's," said another; "I'm assuming you've checked the library"; "Is she in any of the galleries?", etcetera. The answers to which prompted me to lay out the research I've performed to date.

"This isn't for your dissertation," Zoe surmised. Keeping her eyes on me, she slurped a mussel from its casing.

"It's not?" said someone.

"Can you do that?" asked another.

"Maybe she's given up on her dissertation. Not everybody makes it." This, from the American graduate student.

"Why, then, are you looking for old paintings?" The only French native at the table was a slender, impeccably dressed woman who worked as a labor relations lawyer.

"To see them," I said, sensing immediately that this was too simple an answer. I added sheepishly, "For my own personal development?"

A debate ensued at the far end of the table as to whether my current pursuits should be considered brave or escapist, an anti-capitalist statement or a form of free-riding. A more meandering discussion opened up around me. Was I right to expect to find anything more at all? Was I perhaps tricking myself into thinking there was more to the story, a habit acquired from years of watching films and reading novels?

"Humans are innate storytellers," the documentary filmmaker informed us, as if we'd never heard this said before. He was from Colombia, or maybe it was Brazil, and we forgave him a great deal because of his accent. "It is only natural that Nancy is pursuing for something more. Some grand finale."

The English redhead, a friend of Zoe's from some other era, had been agreeing with Mr. Colombia all night. She told me now that I was pinning my hopes on Barnaby Munk because he was all that I had left.

"Yeah, maybe," I said, hating her. "I see you what you mean."

"Just because he's all you have left," she elaborated, "doesn't mean *he* has anything good for *you*. Anything that will help you find this woman's art."

"People disappear into nothingness all the time," the filmmaker said mysteriously. I wasn't sure if he was referring to Hannah Inglis or to Barnaby Munk, or possibly someone he'd filmed. The statement carried an air of finality.

"Yeah, I get it," I said. "I should just leave the man alone."

"No! We're not saying that," Zoe told me. She cocked her head at the others. "Have low expectations, that's all. Don't make this a 'big deal.'" She used her faux American accent.

"Are those two dating?" I whispered in Zoe's ear, referring to the redhead and the filmmaker.

"Yes," she whispered back.

Down the table, I heard Chris and the labor lawyer sparring about neo-liberalism and the impoverishment of ideals of meaningful work.

"So, what you are saying is that she is fucked, regardless." The French woman's manicured fingertips stirred the salty air. "Whether she finishes or not."

"Yes!" said the American student. "Unless she sells the movie rights!"

A lull in both conversations having coincided, the seven of us looked around at each other, moorless for a minute or two.

"Let's order a round of shots," Zoe suggested.

March 11, 1896
Dear Monsieur Godot,

We have been struck by that most clichéd of colonial events: a TIGER attack! I am hiding in my writing garret—less from the tiger, mind you, and more from the colonel.

And I have been re-reading your letters.

I cannot express to you the reassurance your words have given me over the past years (and continue to give me!). Particularly what you say about *seeing*, as to how this is the most important aspect, and a more difficult accomplishment for any artist than technique or its mastery. Although I am no longer in a position to study formally, I do try to have my eye on reality—the inner reality—of what I want to convey.

It is easy here, so far from the hustle of modern city life, to recognize the beauty in ordinary things. I take consolation in that.

Now if my way of *seizing* what I see of this inner reality, this inner grace, should be rude and imperfect, as it no doubt is, I must still seize it and drag it onto the canvas. I am compelled to do so, though I fall short of my own standards again and again. (Is there ever any other way? Should I be reassured by my frustration?)

On a practical level, I do not paint as much as I would like. (How much is enough? Will it ever feel enough?!) I spend most of my days trying to maintain a style of life that neither suits myself nor my situation. And I am expected to take pride in this struggle. I know it's no more than any woman bears. But I cannot pretend to do it in earnest. I am surrounded by friends who do not see the absurdity—who do not *see* at all, at least not beyond their own petty noses. The village administration is no different, which I fear has created significant grievances with the natives.

And then there is the colonel. How can one man be so intelligent and yet utterly dense at the same time? Monsieur, it so hard for him. *Everything* in his life is so difficult, and I am sure he would say I am one of the chief troubles.

I am no Master. I intend that my paintings ask forgiveness of their audience, forgiveness for their roughness, while still offering something. Some small thing that deserves and requires to exist— and exist NOW!— and the matter cannot wait until one woman's arsenal is complete or her conceits are clear and thorough. As you said in one of your lectures, even the Masters were not masters in a strict sense. I would say that Art, the exquisiteness of it, lies in how it records the attempt to take stock of a moment.

I am enclosing a revised version of the lotus flower to show you how I have taken to heart your comments on colour—viz. for colour to be used for its building power, as a tool. So, I have remade the water in hues of grey and green, mostly, and now I think the petals simply glow, do they not? They now have an aura, in the water. How is it I had not appreciated colour as a technical element in quite that way?

As always, I await any comments you may have with keen interest. Do please write. The academic session will soon be done… and then what are your plans for summer? Will you be traveling?

As ever,
your student, H.I.

ELEVEN

In Malu's judgement, Miss Charlotte does not need a playmate. She needs a pet ape. Memsahib could have bought Bad Boy at the menagerie and taken him home instead. The best games are simple ones like hide-and-seek and kite flying. Anything that involves making up rules, or speaking, is a chance for the Miss to order Malu around using fancy words.

Except the doll house. This is Miss Charlotte's special toy, and the girl is barely willing to have Malu involved at all. She is supposed to look on without saying or doing anything, often for an hour at a time. "Good evening, Mr. Jeremiah," says the Miss, steering the dolls in and out of their rooms. "Good evening, Mrs. Cornelia. Would you like to take supper with, or without, the children? The children are outside having their…"

Malu turns and glances out the window. Manang, the gardener, is pulling up tiles from the earth, just as he has been doing every day since she arrived at the estate. His chest is bare and glistening with sweat. His face turns like a dial as he heaves a block upward onto its side and struggles to turn it end over end until he can lever it into a wheelbarrow. He is strong and young, only a little older than she, but why don't they have some help for him? The job would be faster and easier for two or three people.

"Not another vocabulary lesson, Mr. Jeremiah! Next you'll be telling me they…"

"What is in that cabin in the orchard, Miss?" Malu asks. Charlotte seems to know everything, so why not ask her. Malu has seen house girls coming and going, though mem was very strict about keeping Charlotte away.

"Papa's studio." The girl rises from her knees and joins Malu at the window. "Where he does his experiments and writing and thinking."

Out there? Malu wonders.

"I'm going to start collecting butterflies this summer. Papa promised."

It's silly to collect butterflies, she wants to tell the girl. Catch a bird that sings, maybe. Catch a monkey you can train to fetch coconuts. From what she can tell, the girl has been promised many silly things.

"What does it mean, 'vo-cabulary?'" Malu looks at the doll in Charlotte's hand.

"Why, words." Miss Charlotte springs to the bookshelf and returns with a thick book whose pages are edged with gold. "Every day my tutor tests me on the words in the dictionary." She sighs. "Their spelling *and* their sense, including the provenance. I wouldn't mind if it were just the meanings. But I have no time for spelling. Spelling is such a formality." She flips open the book and searches its pages. "There it is, you see: vocabulary. 'From the medieval Latin *vocabularis*, from Latin *vocabulum*. One. The body of words used in a particular language. Two. Words used on a particular occasion or in a particular sphere. Example: The term became part of the medical vocabulary. Three. The body of words known to an individual person. Example: He had a wide vocabulary. Four. A range of artistic or stylistic forms, techniques, or movements. Example: Folk dances have their own vocabularies of movement.'"

Every English word is in that book? It seems too good to be true. Malu says, "Will you teach me, Miss? English vocabulary?"

"Me?" Miss Charlotte starts. A grin fills her face. "I would be pleased to teach you, Malu." She heads straight for the table in the center of the room, sweeping aside its contents, abandoning her dolls to their imaginary lessons. "I'll teach you all the idioms, too. Those are the sayings that don't make sense if one simply adds up the words."

"Oh. Thank you," Malu says. She attempts to pronounce the word "idiom."

"It's like when I'm tired because I've stayed up past my bedtime. Mummy asks me if I'm a fried egg yet."

Malu frowns. "A fried egg?" This was going to be trickier than she thought.

"I say, 'I'm a fried egg.' It means, 'I'm tired out.'"

"Ohhh."

"But I don't know if everybody says this." Charlotte taps her chin to think. "Maybe that one is just for me and Mummy."

This idea Malu likes: she will keep aside some words to share only with Amah.

The Idlewyld servants are allowed to return home on Sundays until suppertime. It seems like the whole neighborhood comes out to greet them as the carts roll to a stop. In the midst of many welcomes and questions, Malu bows her head and starts walking, desperate to see Umi. Auntie Nattie and Nattie's sister Roula hurry to catch up.

"How is tuan with you?" Nattie asks.

Malu doesn't bother to answer. Silence shows how little this question matters.

"Well?" Nattie puffs. "Speed walker!"

"Tuan? I barely see him. Fine. They're all fine."

Roula adjusts her blouse and looks knowingly at Nattie.

"Truly, aunties, I have nothing to complain about." Malu has always found something stifling about the aunties in the neighborhood. They squint at her when she speaks, as if no good could ever come from her mouth. Here are Roula and Nattie now, expecting bad news when Malu has discovered good. Sahib is a doctor. An English doctor, of course. Of all the people she could have gone to work for, this man is the one who will cure her mother. It is up to her to convince him to do it.

"How is my mother?" she asks them, slowing as their stilted hut comes into view.

"Same."

"Still with the demon in her."

Although Malu managed to catch the manuk dewata birds and pocketed three dollars for each one, she hasn't had a chance to visit the chemist on the high street. It's bad that Umi has to wait. But if Nattie looked after the extra money she'd only spend it on fortune tellers and betel paste. Malu concentrates on looking responsible and grown-up as she enters the house. When Umi calls out a greeting from her bed, she runs over and starts blabbing about everything. They ask her about being a genduk. What is the Miss like? What sorts of things do they do together? Malu lists the games they play. Yes, while the Miss is at her tutor, Malu must also do some cleaning.

"Ah," each of the women say in turn.

"Dusting, tidying," says Malu. "There are so many decorations."

They look at her with wary eyes.

"And I am learning English vocabulary," she adds, pleased to have this as a topper. She is already known as a good English speaker. "It means I am learning three new words every day! I am learning many more from listening to the Miss. But there are three new words each day from something called a 'dictionary.'"

"Dix... That is a new word! Are you counting that word?" Nattie bursts out laughing.

"I am learning how to print the letters too."

"Amazing," Umi says in her soft voice. "Tell us your study words this day."

Malu thinks for a moment. "I have none for today, being Sunday. But yesterday's were... *anodyne*, *bassinet*, and *cardiac*." Then she tells them what each one means.

TWELVE

One of the places Hannah goes to paint is the harbor quay. She enjoys the atmosphere here, amplified by the light on the water. There are shrimping boats, long lopsided crescents that cut through the river. There are the shrimpers themselves, with their grasping fingers and lean brown bodies. On the wharf she paints hawkers, a customs official, children fishing, but mostly she paints the prostitutes who have made the wharf their unofficial headquarters. They wait near one of the paths to the lower town, talking together and spitting blood red betel paste over their shoulders; they take catnaps curled upon the huge coils of dirty white rope that is used to hold the steamships that come into port. The prostitutes make good subjects because they spend so much time waiting around. Plus, they are used to being looked over.

One of them, a girl with high cheekbones and an asymmetrical mouth and eyes, Hannah finds particularly striking. The girl poses without being asked. Motions with her arm, then stands against the side of a shed and lowers her chin demurely.

"How old are you?" Hannah asks her, but gets no reply.

She makes several studies. Her favorites are the paintings with two or three of the girls standing together against a wall of a boathouse, whispering and smiling. Do they know who she is? To whom she is married?

Generally, her new experiments with the figure have been more rewarding than she expected. On the first day out she was mortally afraid. Of what, exactly, she couldn't say. She uses a restricted palette, partly because she's run out of colors and hasn't the money for more. Fewer colors, though, means she can work faster and more freely, without dithering about "getting it right." Fewer colors also make for brighter, bolder combinations. Like this white sarong she's turned a tomato red. Hannah concentrates on the folds—what they conceal, what they reveal—and where they move the eye. Taking her number five brush, she continues strokes of red across the girl's forehead and, more heavily, on her bottom lip. The Malay's feet are characteristically wide and bare, scuffed, with the toenails caked in dirt. In the portrait, Hannah accentuates the feet, lifting the sarong over them like a rising theatre curtain.

Lost in her labor, she doesn't notice Sergeant Singh watching her from one of the stairways to the pier. Until he clears his throat.

"Sergeant! Hallo!" she calls and waves, then lays down her brush.

"Good evening, Mrs. Inglis."

"How are you?"

He seems to be stuck on the final stair. "Thank you, I am well. Uh, they...they have your parasol." He indicates the other girls who are playing at the mouth of the shed, around the corner. Teasing each other, poking and preening, and gossiping (she supposes) in their language. Hannah leans over and spies one of the Malays twirling her parasol and strutting coquettishly. Another holds her hands out to receive a turn.

"I let them borrow it. Can't balance a parasol while I am painting."

He says, "I suppose not." Sergeant Singh, she notices, is not in uniform. The turban he wears is smaller and mocha in color.

"What time has it gotten to, Sergeant?"

"Half past five." He checks his pocket watch. "Five thirty-one."

Her girl in the sarong is picking at her fingernails now and bumping her rear gently against the shed. Business must pick up in the evenings, thinks Hannah. How else could they possibly feed themselves, poor things. Sergeant Singh has not moved. Is he waiting for her to come over, perhaps? Something in the way he is looking at her makes her put her brush down. The four natives turn at once to see Hannah rising from her stool. The smallest rushes over with the parasol.

"Thank you." She receives the lace-trimmed umbrella, folds it, and sets it down next to her paint box, intending to join the sergeant. When she looks up, however, he is gone.

It's not for several days, on a morning when she happens to be in the public gardens, that she has an opportunity to speak with the sergeant. Hannah is working at a wilted *Camellia japonica* that has somehow escaped deadheading, playing with her brush to recreate the damage and the fraying of the blossom, when she happens to look across the center oval. On a bench facing the stone birdbath, Sergeant Singh is referring to a small notebook. As she watches, he slips the notebook into a breast pocket, checks his watch, and starts off across the lawn.

"Like Alice's White Rabbit!" Hannah giggles to herself. She gets to her feet. By the looks of it he is heading for the south gate. *Their* gate, as it used to be. Moving quietly and swiftly along the pathway that encircles the outer ring of flowerbeds, she emerges at the stone archway just prior to his arrival.

"Madam! Mrs. Inglis!"

"I'm sorry to startle you, Sergeant Singh. I was painting over there…and I noticed you on your way." Again he is sashless, without his machete, and wearing the smaller brown turban. "On your way where? If you don't my…?"

He leaves the question unanswered long enough for her to recant and confess that it is none of her business. It's obvious enough *where* he is going. They both know the south exit leads into the forest via a brief expanse of scrubby meadow. There is nowhere else he could be going but the forest. She gazes through the stone archway. "I thought perhaps you had wanted to speak with me, the other day at the dock."

"I recall that I did speak with you."

"I meant at greater length." A disagreeable lump of emotion slides down her spine. What is the matter with her? *Let him be. Save your twiddle twaddle for Hazel and Lucy.* Only, they had rather gotten along, she and the sergeant. Probably because there'd been no need for twiddle twaddle. Absurdly, she feels her eyes tearing. Hannah backs away. "I'm sorry to have disturbed your, uh—"

"No, no—"

"Please! You, you be on your way!"

"I'm going into the forest."

"Yes, of course. I mean, why shouldn't you be? As a matter of fact, I've been told it is not a man-eater, the tiger that killed Cleopatra."

He nods. "I would agree with this. I have seen the results of a man-eater before. Back home."

She clears her throat. "You don't have your machete."

"Oh. I use that to clear a path for you, Mrs. Inglis. I myself have always managed with an unclear path."

Hannah smiles. Thinking of his notebook, she says, "And do you… are you documenting something? Is that what you are doing?"

"I record specimens of interest. This I have always done, ever since coming to this country."

"Oh, really! Have you?"

"It is one of the reasons I wished to assist you with your own excursions. Another opportunity to explore." He takes his notebook, turns to a dog-eared page, but thinks better of opening it. "For example, I am keeping a record of undocumented botanical specimens. Those which are not listed in *The Almanac*."

"May I?" she asks. "Please?"

She looks at the page he holds open for her, skimming over his neat handwriting. Each entry appears to have a brief description, a basic sketch, and measurements. There are symbols as well: blacked-in triangles and Latin alphabeticals.

"Are there many specimens, then, not listed in *The Almanac*?" she asks. "Whatever *The Almanac* is, it must be the authority on jungle botanicals. "How do you know what to call them if they haven't been documented?"

"Good question, madam! You will see that I have suggested some Latin names."

She takes a second look. "*Carnivorus empiriosa*," she reads out. "My goodness!"

"That one you decided not to paint." He points to a black triangle in the margin.

"I had no idea you were cataloguing wildlife, Sergeant Singh."

He leafs through the book. "You had your own aims. Rightly so."

"I'm most impressed," she says. Evidently *he* is not about to stop because of a rogue tiger. "Are you planning to write to the editors of *The Almanac*, then? And tell them about these new specimens?"

He shakes his head.

"Or you could prepare your own book, Sergeant. *A Guide to Malayan Forest Botanicals*. And here I thought you were a police officer."

"I am still a police officer."

"I'm quite serious. Did you think I was poking fun? No, I think it's admirable, and fascinating, and I... Well, I suppose you know already how I feel about the jungle. I'm the last person in the world to question the time you spend there. If none of these species has ever been discovered, then you ought to be given due credit."

"Mrs. Inglis, you are the friendliest Englishwoman I have ever met."

Hannah laughs. "'Friendly' is not the received opinion, I'm afraid." She holds up her hands. "Do you see these stains? The colonel thinks there is something wrong with me, and I pretend not to notice him. And Lucy and Hazel and the others… Well, I pretend not to mind what they say about me. Sometimes I think they are genuinely concerned.

"Then I consider: they don't have a creative bone in their bodies, do they? Absolutely no scope for the imagination. No *openness*! Monsieur Godot used to say that artists are people who open the book and show that more pages are possible. Others try to close the book. They are closed people. But anyone who has an artist's spirit…" She falters. It's obvious that he's listening intently, but of course how can he possibly comment? "I must admit, though, I sit on my hands during dinner parties. Actually sit on my hands. Unless I'm eating."

She starts to laugh. Sergeant Singh follows suit, letting out the little booms she remembers. He has a sense of humour underneath all his seriousness.

"I wish to tell you something foolish about myself," he says, looking around them as if there might be bystanders in this remote corner of the garden.

"If this is in service of making me feel less foolish, Sergeant, believe me there's no need."

"I've been meaning to tell you this before. I only hope you won't be angry with me, madam."

"Angry?" She is intrigued. Touchingly, he appears to be working his way up to an opener.

He says, "I am looking for a special flower. I was looking for it on our treks, too."

She considers this strange confession. "So you're saying you were secretly leading me to places where you thought it might be, this special flower?"

"It is called the parasol flower. That is, I call it that, because it blooms as big as a lady's parasol. Sometimes even as big as a carriage wheel, the locals say. It is something of a legend here."

"Goodness, that large? It's a wonder we *hadn't* come across it in three months walking."

"It is notoriously rare. Yes. And it blooms only once in every seven years. Blooms for a fortnight."

"Once in seven years! Incredible." She admits that she has never heard of such a thing.

"The foliage is totally unremarkable—resembling a young nipa palm, merely an unassuming clump of fronds. So, one must, practically speaking, catch it in bloom."

"Really!"

"You must know that I followed your explicit wishes, Mrs. Inglis, whenever you made them known to me. And *never* did I compromise your safety. Never! If I had ever found any evidence of a predator, I would have alerted you."

When they first began on the outings, Sergeant Singh trained her as to what to do if they came across a tiger, or it came across them. Tigers are shy creatures who will not want to see you. Freeze, then back away slowly and wait for the animal to leave. If for some reason it is curious and comes closer, remain very still unless and until it bats you with a paw. In this eventuality, smash its face with whatever you have at hand. Then stand your ground; never run from a tiger.

"I don't think it's foolish to search for a parasol flower," she tells him. In fact, it would be a coup to paint such a spectacular bloom. A life-sized portrait! She should be painting on a larger scale. She should be in the wilds, not in this pruned and preened facsimile of nature. It's simply wrong, sitting in this soupy air, being so prudent.

"No, no, I don't think it's foolish in the slightest," she avows. "What's foolish is to keep out of the woods on account of a tiger who has been there all along!"

"Well. There are probably several."

"Precisely." She bites her lip. "But why ever didn't you tell me about this flower before, Sergeant? I would have loved to have joined you in the quest." He bobs his head apologetically. "And you don't mean the carrion flower? I've heard of that one. The huge one that smells of rotting flesh."

"The *Rafflesia*." He pulls a face. "No, no."

Before long they say goodbye, offering each other good wishes for their pursuits, as there seems nothing else left to say.

"Do let me know if you find one!" she calls after him.

THIRTEEN

By late February in Paris, the newlyweds were honeymooning in Majorca, and I was more alone than ever. I had been quite unable to turn up any more of Hannah's artwork. Nothing at Julian. Nothing in any of the local galleries. Nothing in the Sotheby's database or on eBay. From the Ashcan people in New York and Philadelphia, I'd learned a little more about Edward Coles. Of course, there was also a lot out there about Henri Godot, and I'd been occupying myself learning about his life and his work after Julian. He'd lectured extensively and his lecture notes had been compiled into a lovely little work called *The Spirit of the Artist*. I bought a copy for myself at Shakespeare & Co. and marked it up with my musings as I went along. I could see why Hannah had liked him so much, and why she'd cherished their relationship. Once in a while, I took out my phone and flipped past the images of Zoe and Chris, kissing and holding their new salad tongs, to the pictures I'd taken at Kew of *Strangler Fig Attacking Mighty Kapok*. Shrunken and digitized, there was nothing much mighty about the kapok and barely any strangulation effected.

Whether it was Godot's enthusiasm or my own anxious aimlessness, I decided to try some oil painting myself. In high school I'd taken a few art electives that involved mostly sketching and design, and I'd earned A's. My oil painting, however, was an expensive disaster. I was left with three little canvases, an indelible stain on a place mat, and a box full of chemicals and gear. My scenes were interlocking fragments of color, muddled in perspective and without depth. They managed to convey less feeling than the photographs on which I'd based them. A bridge over the Seine looked like a playground slide. An iconic Metropolitan sign resembled a giant bullfrog-green lollipop. My paintings were not so much communicating my spirit, I told Henri Godot, as insulting artists. And other people with eyes.

A postcard arrived from Zoe and Chris of a turquoise strip of ocean, white sands, resort towers. Funny, I'd never considered them beach people. On the back, Chris had drawn a picture of his hand giving me the finger (an inside joke of ours), and Zoe had added an earnest little message: *Thank you so much for the new kitchen weapons! Everyone at the farewell party thought you were lovely. xo Zoe*

Everyone at the party thought I was *lovely*? Lovely! Everyone at the party. She made it sound as if their friends had gone with them to… Cala Millor, the caption said, and the group of them were sipping margaritas and swapping impressions of me. It was only slightly less unnerving to imagine that the four of them had been separately in touch with Zoe to share their feedback. Zoe, I reckoned, must be inventing the group's impression. After all, which one of those people would have seriously called me lovely? Yet it wasn't a word in Zoe's usual repertoire either.

I'd reflected on that evening a fair bit, and I'd thought about, mostly, what I hadn't said: what hadn't felt sayable. I'd not even mentioned the engraving of *The Parasol Flower* or *The Descent*, for instance. Had that been some unconscious attempt to protect it and preserve it for myself? Most of all, I was uncomfortable about the way the conversation had pivoted at a certain point. It had become about me and not Hannah. Had I caused that? The French lawyer had wanted to know why I was bothering with old paintings. My response, looking back on it, was a cheap and convenient one, like I'd reached for a premade shrink-wrapped sandwich. Yet it was inauthentic. I wanted to find Hannah's art because of the *art*. Because of Hannah. I was doing this for her, not for me, and certainly not for "self-development" or whatever I'd said that sounded like an explanation. I was doing this because I loved the paintings I'd seen and I loved the promise of the paintings I hadn't yet seen. And the voice I heard in her letters—it felt as if we could be good friends, she and I, as if I should have been her best friend and ally. I reread the postcard. *Everyone at the farewell party thought you were lovely.* Maybe this had come across somehow, in spite of my own ignorance to it; people could sense that I was full of love. What a terrifying prospect.

I pinned the postcard on the corkboard in my kitchen and hurried to change into my sports gear and running shoes. "Don't make a *big deal* of it," said the Zoe in my head. "Congratulations on your *lovely* wedding," I replied, giving both of them the finger in jest.

To: nancyroach21@gmail.com
From: barnabymothballs37@livewire.uk

Subject: Re: Fwd: hoping to reach you

Dear Nancy,

Forgive me for my delay in replying to you. I have been away on a walking holiday in Morocco. Invigorating!

For various reasons, I had not thought about the family art collection for quite some time before reading your requests. I happen to be making a trip to London this coming week and there I will consult with my sister-in-law as to the works in storage. Stay tuned, as the young people say. Regarding the parasol flower, I looked into this many years ago and concluded that its existence is highly doubtful. From a scientific perspective, it makes very little sense. Yet, as you imply, the inclusion of a fantastical flower in *The Descent* is itself curious. Have you read *The Descent*, by the way? One must get beyond considering it all a nasty business, in my humble and outdated opinion.

More anon, Barnaby

Keenly aware of his use of the plural "requests," I sent Barnaby the briefest of replies. I would wait to kindly hear from him again, after his trip to London. I would stay tuned, indeed. Dancing around the living room, I busted into a *Saturday Night Fever* freestyle.

Coming back to his email, which I tended to do first thing in the morning and again while I ate dinner, I was careful to contain my expectations. At the very least, it would be interesting to compare notes. "Have you read *The Descent*?" Barnaby's email kept asking me. "One must get beyond considering it a nasty business, in my humble and outdated opinion." I growled these words at my reflection in the bathroom mirror, trying on different fuddy-duddy accents. Clearly Barnaby was the sort of man who felt his opinions would never grow outdated.

What nasty business? I wondered. He'd dropped the reference so casually, as if I should know what he meant. I returned to Richelieu and sat down to properly read *The Descent* in four-hour increments— the reserve library lending period. Perhaps there would be some clue within the book about Hannah or the parasol flower. If not, at least I'd be able to go toe to toe with the globetrotting Barnaby when he resurfaced.

FOURTEEN

There is nothing in Kuala Kangsa's year quite like the queen's gymkhana festival. In addition to the horse-racing, the cricket match, and the brass band, there is bobbing for apples, a kite-flying competition, boat races, shaved ice, a tent-pegging competition, stilt-walkers, a clown who juggles knives, donkey rides, an egg toss, three-legged races, and the large baked goods table hosted by the Ladies Association of Perak. Festival day is excess and exception. Even the vigilant members of the Ladies Association encourage their customers to eat too many sweets.

Like the rest of the village, Hannah is in a bright mood as she weaves her way up the sloping parade ground to the LAP baked goods table. Chastened by her encounter with Lucy and Hazel at the post office, she has volunteered for two shifts this year. Around her, Malays are strolling in sisterly chains, their colorful headscarves floating on the breeze behind them. A family of Dutch homesteaders are laughing at each other as they attempt the apple bobbing. She makes a large detour around a queue of Chinese women and children waiting for the egg toss. Two English officers—she remembers their faces but not their names—strut through this same commotion in uniform, looking like smug peacocks. They are heading for the racetrack, she supposes, where the colonel will be found.

She herself will not spend a penny that day. Not even on a kebab, she tells herself. Their spicy meaty scent seems to be following her, making her mouth water. Her measures of austerity brought her through to the next installment of her stipend, from which she promptly removed payment for an order from Schlauerbach's. A reduced order, but an order nonetheless. Knowing that seven tubes of paint and twenty metres of canvas were making their way from France is as gratifying as anything she could enjoy at the festival.

"Is it going well, then?" Hannah says as she reaches the LAP table. "The location is good this year."

"No, it's not. We're well out of the way up here," grumbles the lady manning the table, Myrtle Something-or-Other. A flushed, porcine woman, she is married to the bank manager.

"The view is inspiring!"

"But *they're* not going to trudge all the way up here for the view, are they?"

"I suppose that's why we have the baked goods." Hannah moves in around the tables, assuming her place in the second empty chair. "Such a lovely breeze, too."

Myrtle is so overheated that droplets are forming on her temples. "Did you not bring any baking?"

"No," Hannah admits. She'd not wanted to squander pantry ingredients, but this decision seems churlish and wrong now that she sees how generously the others have donated. "I'm afraid my upside-down cake fell flat," she fibs.

Myrtle peers at her skeptically.

Hannah turns to check the roster, hoping Myrtle is about to head off shift. No such luck. When she looks up again, she sees the crumpled hat coming nearer through the crowd. Soon the Peterborough woman is standing across from them at the baked goods table, hand in hand with a girl of about ten. Behind them, a light-skinned Malay servant waits.

Hannah greets the mother and daughter warmly, giving a brief tour of the goods on offer.

"I'm Eva Peterborough," the woman interrupts her.

"Oh yes, I know." Hannah laughs nervously. "Though I didn't know you had a daughter."

"The gossip mill failed to report that I have a daughter?"

Myrtle snorts.

"Well it...probably not," allows Hannah. "I just don't take much notice of gossip."

Eva's mouth crooks into something resembling a smile. "You're telling the truth, aren't you? This is my daughter, Charlotte. Charlotte, this is Mrs. Inglis. The artist."

Charlotte looks much like her mother, though shorter and somewhat fairer. She nods politely and they exchange greetings.

"She's lovely," Hannah says to Eva. Exactly how the lady knows who *she* is, "the artist," is that owing to the same gossip mill?

The Peterboroughs order two plates of various squares and biscuits and two slabs of fruitcake. Myrtle, recording the tally on a clipboard, brightens considerably.

"I think you should know," Eva says, as she and Hannah come together over the fruitcake, "that Lucy Finch has just cautioned me against you."

"Why? What do you mean, cautioned you?"

"Just what I said." They confirm that Myrtle is busy dispensing cups of lemonade to Charlotte and her girl. "I'm not sure of her *purpose*." Eva squints. "I believe the charge was fraternizing in the public gardens with an undesirable."

"What? Good grief!" Hannah exclaims. Lucy, or one of her spies, must have seen her with Sergeant Singh. "We were discussing… It doesn't matter. Sergeant Singh works for me. Or rather, he used to. When I painted in the jungle." It's a false characterization in more ways than one. That anybody should be "cautioned against" her! And that Mrs. Peterborough should confide in her about it!

"Don't worry, darling," says Eva. "I understand completely." She stands, chewing a macaroon, for a few moments longer before bidding Hannah goodbye.

"Well, that was very odd," Hannah says to herself.

"She's an odd duck, if nothing else." Myrtle mops her brow as the Peterboroughs disappear into the shifting crowds below. "I'm surprised they came into town today to fraternize with the hoi paloi. Hannah, do make sure to replace the doily over the lemonade jug if you're serving from it. The wasps are voracious."

"What is that?" Hannah points. At the corner of the parade ground, a party of servants is struggling over something massive. *What on earth are they hauling between them?* She strains to see as onlookers crowd in; the little mob moves slowly across the field. Others rush across the grounds toward the men. Hannah comes around the table. "That's not a game. I don't think that's part of the festival."

"Mrs. Inglis?" calls Myrtle. "Where are you going? You're on shift!"

She wanders down the lawn, side-stepping darting children and their ayahs, pursuing in fluttering sarongs. The newcomers at the center of the melee are natives. Their miners' jumpsuits are rolled down their waists and bamboo poles are yoked to their bare shoulders. Hannah stumbles and falls into a horseshoe pit. "It's George's tiger," she says, righting herself. Back on her feet, she continues down the slope.

The majestic cat is upside-down, bound by its legs to the crossed poles. It is large enough, and the men short enough, that the back of the body is dragging against the scrubby grass as they travel. As Hannah nears, she sees that one of the arm bones protrudes near the shoulder. The surrounding flesh looks to have been hacked at. Even in this state the fur—a warm apricot brown with strokes of jet black—appears exquisitely sumptuous. Instinctively, she puts out her hand.

"Is this for sahib colonel?" she calls to them.

Some in the crowd move aside as she nears. The hunters do not turn or break stride. The weight must be staggering. She runs to the head of the party and catches a glimpse of the beast's sympathetic countenance. Dead. Riddled with bullets.

The crowd forming around the tiger and its hunters causes them to slow and finally stop. Malays and Chinese and Europeans alike are poking and pinching and jeering at the carcass. Two men lift the great muzzle by the lips, exposing the fangs. They drop the head back down with a crack. Hannah becomes aware of the flies buzzing over the body, especially at the anus and along a gaping wound on one flank. When the breeze shifts direction, forcing a metallic wet-fur stench upon her, she claps a hand over her nose and mouth. Eva Peterborough, she notices, is watching, farther up the slope.

"Please," Hannah says to the men, raising her voice even louder. "Are you bringing this animal to Sahib Colonel Inglis?"

One of the miners, struggling to keep his footing near the beast's head, looks up at her.

"Then I'll fetch him! I'll fetch you the colonel. Just…stop trying to move the poor thing." Then she shouts, "And the rest of you: go away! Leave it alone. This animal is not your property."

Swallowing her disgust, Hannah turns and runs.

For George, gymkhana festivals give diminishing returns. The best bit is early on, when he directs the opening military maneuvers. It is a duty he enjoys immensely, leading the cadets in formation, putting them through the drills. Not a hair out of place. The crowd cries out in appreciation as the trumpets crescendo and, at the finale, cannons boom. *Thwock. Thwock.* The sound that all will be right in the world.

He turns to the crowd, hoping he will see Hannah in the audience. And fearing that, seeing her, he'll lose his resolve. Arrangements have been made; he is hard-pressed to recall just how it unfolded. But concern is widespread. That is what he knows, and how he thinks he will start. *Concern for you, Hannah, is widespread.* Though this sounds too impersonal? *All of us here are worried about you.*

George is sitting trackside now with some of the other officers. Each of his damned horses has turned out to be slower than the last. He drinks and curses their lungs, ill-suited for tropical heat, and mulls over his wife's disregard for propriety. Was it her unconventional upbringing? That ridiculous academy? His gut feels like someone is trying to cut through it with a butter knife. Foolish woman. Too young, perhaps, to realize what an opportunity she has on a frontier like this one, to perform above her class. To relocate herself socially. Leaning back in his chair, George closes his eyes and concentrates on breathing.

"Pinky, how long have you been out here?" It is Dennison's voice, to his right.

"Three or four hours I should think."

Oakeshott answers to George's left. "Ten years, isn't it?"

"Christ, that's a lifetime in ordinary years, old boy!"

"We should be celebrating *you*, never mind Her Majesty."

The officers laugh. George puts on a smirk he hopes will pass for good sportsmanship. Tallying the years in his head, it is in fact closer to thirteen since he set out for Malaya. It is surely some sort of paradox that the past three years—years in which he's had the greatest means, the greatest respect of the Resident, the company of a beautiful young wife—have been outstandingly the worst. He opens his eyes and announces he needs a walk.

Past the north side of the racetrack, he makes out teams of Sikhs, their towelled heads in two rows, standing at the ready. A whistle shrills and sends them scurrying.

"Rather pointless skill, isn't it," mutters George. "Not as if one often needs to raise a tent at breakneck speed."

Dennison and Oakeshott appear to be suddenly on either side of him. As they stroll, Dennison leans in toward him. "Let's put in for the hill cottage, Pinky. We'll bring our wives up, escape this dreadful heat for a week or two. What do you say?"

Oakeshott says, "Finch could supervise your hunt for you. He's plenty of safari experience."

George doesn't respond to any of this. Is it Dennison who came to him last year? Oakeshott, or Dennison? Dennison, he thinks, who had been unfortunate enough to witness Hannah and her sergeant walking up the high street together, sopping wet, laughing, their clothes stuck to their bodies. Oakeshott must have a story, too; they all have stories. Who is the one who saw her at the docks, paying prostitutes to pose?

"So, will you have the head stuffed?" Oakeshott is saying. "Finch's trophies have taken over the entire lounge of the Residency."

"To Lucy's chagrin," sniggers Dennison.

Their chatter irks George. Their need to point out the obvious. They're too young to have any tolerance for suffering. "I haven't caught a tiger yet, gentlemen. I have *matters pending*."

Waving them off, he shuffles away. Ahead, the sultan's family is billowing in the breeze like a parachute. Standing next to Izrin is Resident-General Swettenham himself. Yes, those are unmistakably his pin-thin, navy limbs. A yellow cravat blooms at his throat. Has Swettenham come to pressure Izrin personally, about Dr. Peterborough's request? More likely he's come for the pomp, like everybody else.

The colonel steers away, too, from the sultan, the resident-general, all of them, veering back toward the tent-pegging competition. Dozens of color-coordinated Sikhs are still running about like trained monkeys. Where is *he*? Where is *her* trained monkey?

The team in white has nearly unfolded their canvas and is already fixing the poles together into a brace. George eliminates one sweaty face after the other until he's located Sergeant Singh.

Singh is bending to hook down the skirting that edges the canvas; his team is behind their rivals, with the hardest part still to come. They must position the canvas precisely over the main pole so its perimeter reaches the ground evenly, with enough slack on each side to fit over the brace, yet not so much slack that the peg wires become useless. With a deep-throated "three, two, one!" from Singh his team hurls the canvas over the central pole. So, he fancies himself a leader.

"Go, Perak!" shouts a filthy boy in a topknot. "Kick their Hindu-loving arses!"

A crowd of natives surrounds him: Indian mothers and sons, gangs of Malay children, a few Eurasian railroaders sprinkled throughout.

"George! There you are! I've been looking all over for you."

"You have?"

Hannah is standing before him, a hand pressed to her side. "The men at the track told me you'd wandered off." Panting, she glances at the Sikhs in the clearing, hammering their pegs and hollering directions.

They watch the final seconds of the competition together. Sergeant Singh's team wins. Hannah claps and cries, "Bravo!" as if she were at the theatre. For a moment, it looks as if she catches Singh's attention.

"They've killed your tiger, George." She turns him by the shoulders and points. "Look."

He does see the commotion. It went unheard, drowned out by the cheering at the tent contest. "Sphectacular!" he slurs.

She purses her lips. "Come with me. They're destroying the poor thing."

Indeed, a throng of darkies seems to be pecking at it, the thing he still can't quite see. The procession is carnivalesque. He feels Hannah's fingers hook into his own as she pulls him along. It's a good start, he tells himself. This is a good start. "I'm ill, Hannah. I don't feel right."

"You're drunk."

"No. Not so much. What I need..." *I need your help. I need you to care for me.*

"Sahib Colonel, tuan Colonel," he hears the natives addressing him as they approach.

Soon after, he is face to face with the red-foamed mouth of the great carnivore.

FIFTEEN

In the cool of the evening, most of Finch's guests are slumped in chairs on the patio or on the large deck, exhausted by the heat and the day's activities. On the upper balcony of the Residency, George sips water, with a good view of it all. Though his eyes are mostly on Hannah as she picks her way through the flowerbeds, examining every frond and petal. He is utterly sober.

Doling out the wages, he discovered two of the Malays had died in the bush, fighting the tiger. Why should he feel bothered? They'd each of them agreed to the danger. They'd each of them taken half their wage at the outset. George had split the remainder of their pay amongst the survivors; he wasn't about to give money to corpses.

"Those hunters must have left their dead friends in the bush."

Beside him, Finch leans forward, elbows on knees. "Happen they couldn't carry out the tiger and the men."

"Happen they weren't friends." George chuckles, but not for long. Finch is known to be a Malay man.

"How's your stomach?" Finch strokes his own rotund belly as if it were a pet. "Feeling any better?"

"I don't know if I can go through with this, James."

"What?" He looks alarmed.

"Tonight, with Hannah. She's going to be…"

"Oh, with Hannah! Well. Lucy's been like a dog on a bone with this, I have to say. And she's probably right. Best to talk to Hannah before things get out of hand." The Resident waves a houseboy over for a flute of champagne, then watches him saunter back to the door. "Everything is in place for Peterborough, isn't it?"

"I told you yesterday. The girls have already begun heading out there."

"How?"

"I don't know. On foot, I suppose."

"Long goddamned walk, isn't it?"

"She'll be humiliated, James. Maybe I should just have another word with her at home. A stern word."

"Look. If she were the sort to feel shame, my dear fellow, she wouldn't be up to all sorts in the first place."

"If she isn't the sort to feel shame, then how is this going to help?" he asks lamely.

Finch drains his glass. "Check in with Izrin, will you? See if they're managing all right. Because they're not going to come to us, these girls, if they have a problem."

In the garden, Hannah picks something and winds it into her hair. Like a child, George thinks, always playing. She is nearly out past the last torches. "Yes, all right, see if they're managing," George echoes. "And if they're not?"

Finch sighs and puts a hand on George's knee. He's often more touchy-feely than makes George comfortable. "I'm sure you can figure something out."

"Why does Hannah feel the need to traipse into the darkest corners of your garden? What's so bloody exciting about the unknown?"

The Resident bellows with laughter. As he gets to his feet, he says, "Ready, then?"

George shoots air from his nostrils. "Ready."

Hannah picks a flower from the royal jasmine. Ordinarily she avoids cuttings, but the plant is flowering in abundance out where no one is there to appreciate it, past the torches and the congratulatory chitchat. She is well aware she should be socializing, but if the colonel is going to hole up somewhere, she's not to going make excuses for him, or accept compliments. On the contrary, it's with growing disgust and anger that she thinks of that poor, ruined creature, its mashed and maimed body.

And she feels a fair degree of responsibility, she must admit. It was their cow. He is her husband. Whatever his warped views of revenge and protection, she did not try to stop him from pursuing and killing an innocent animal. A majestic animal. She inhales the delicious scent of the jasmine before fitting the stem into her hair. The tiger was probably baited. By now she has heard enough speculation about this to believe it to be true. The wounds to its shoulder and flank were consistent with its falling into a staked pit. Plus, the timing was too perfect; a spectacle for the village's largest celebration.

Making her way back towards the rambling mansion, Hannah scans the thinning population of guests. No sign of the colonel. Oh, why are they are even here if neither of them is feeling festive? She spies Lucy, fluttering about inside, passing out plates of cake. Hannah approaches and begins to make her excuses and bid their host good-night.

Lucy feigns great distress. "Hannah, don't go yet! Have some cake! At least have some cake," she begs. Thrusting a plate into her hands, Lucy dashes off.

It is a lovely cake, in fact. Layers of pastry and custard and a sort of pinkish jelly. In the sweetness of the jelly is a hint of lychee.

"Good, isn't it?" Hazel Swinburne is standing near enough to comment. "Too good for some people to appreciate." She and Myrtle Something-or-Other are side by side, clutching empty plates and looking ill at ease. Edgar Swinburne sits behind the two women, his eyes drifting shut. "I've told you, he's a district officer," Edgar murmurs, "what else can the man afford?"

Hannah turns to see a young interracial couple standing awkwardly by the punch bowl.

"It's just so very unlike Lucy," Hazel comments. "Her hand must have been forced."

"Hannah, dear." Now James Finch is coming toward her. Hiding behind him is the colonel, his round eyes fixed on her last bites of cake, with Lucy bringing up the rear. George looks guilty. About the tiger? About his earlier drunkenness? "Step into the drawing room, will you?"

"Of course," she replies to James, and follows them all through. To her surprise, Hazel, Myrtle, and Edgar pile in after her. The group of officers talking together in one corner of the room politely vacate.

"What's going on?" Hannah sets down the plate of half-eaten cake. *Lucy Finch has cautioned me against you*, Eva's words come back to her.

Before anyone answers her there is a knock on the door. Beatrice Watts, the minister's wife, is ushered in by a housemaid. Beatrice is red-faced and wearing a simple sundress which is too plain and cheerful for evening wear. The colonel clears his throat as he steps toward Beatrice. He fails to speak.

"Mrs. Watts," says Lucy, taking up the charge, "indeed, all of us have…"

"Concern for you, Hannah, is widespread," the colonel says.

Does she detect a wry note in his voice? "What do you mean?" she says. "Concern for me is widespread? Why?"

"Now, now," the Resident drawls. He is a big man, standing at six-and-a-half feet, and his voice seems to issue from his whole body. She's always liked James Finch, always felt herself to be somehow under his wing, knowing that he could appreciate the challenge of being married to George. He bends and looks her in the eye, his bushy eyebrows pinching together. "Several residents have noticed you painting out of doors, in the village."

She tries to recall having seen any British residents while she was out. "That may be," she says. "I have been painting in the village."

"Mrs. Watts, can you please relay for us what you saw the other day?" asks Lucy.

Beatrice clamps her arms to her sides and nods. "Yes, Lucy. I was passing through the lower quarter. As you know, the missionary church is situated near the wharf in the lower town and I was walking there to deliver Mr. Watts a tin of noodles which he forgot to bring with him for his duties that day at the missionary church. I happened to be looking over the carapace, toward the water, as I passed the area overlooking, indeed, the harbor front. For I do sometimes enjoy the glassy look of the river water."

Hazel releases a sigh, prompting Lucy to ask, "What, Mrs. Watts, did you see at the base of the pier?"

Hannah is so angry she could swing for them all. They all know what the good lady has seen; they are waiting, rapt, to witness the shame and humiliation Beatrice's disclosure is supposed to bring her. She draws herself up in anticipation.

"I saw Mrs. Inglis seated on the pier. In front of an easel. Painting." Beatrice fumbles with her hands. "She was painting a…a lady of ill repute. A Malay, the girl looked to be, wearing a bright pink sarong. You know how they fold them for—"

"Thank you, Mrs. Watts," Lucy interrupts.

Beatrice scans the little crowd apologetically. "Should I…?"

"Go," the colonel says stiffly.

Beatrice glances warily at Hannah before exiting the room.

As the door shuts, James Finch starts chuckling.

"Dollymops, Hannah? I didn't think you had an interest."

"James!" Lucy objects. "There's no need for vulgarity."

"My dear, if I wished to be vulgar, I'd call the miserable wenches 'harlots' or 'three penny uprights.'"

At this, Edgar starts laughing.

"This is not humorous in the slightest," Lucy hisses. Hazel growls her husband's name.

"I think we are missing the point here," the colonel ventures, sounding uncertain.

From their mounts on the high, wood-paneled walls of the drawing room, Finch's stuffed heads witness everything through their glass eyeballs. "Yes," says Hannah. "*I'm* missing it. What exactly is the point?"

"I saw you as well, Mrs. Inglis," pipes up Myrtle. "I saw her. Doing... something concerning in the public gardens."

Hannah cries at Myrtle, "You didn't think to mention anything to me this morning, about this great concern of yours. We spent two hours together!"

Myrtle bows her head.

"Go on, Myrtle," says Lucy. "We cannot help the Inglises until all the facts are made plain."

"Well...er...first Mrs. Inglis was painting out there, in the gardens. But she sprang up. Left her belongings strewn across the walkway."

"Odd. Where did she go, do you know?" asks Lucy.

"She ran over to a policeman. The big tall one, who always seems amused by something?"

"Sergeant Singh."

"But he wasn't in uniform," Myrtle adds.

"So there was no emergency."

"Heavens, no! They stood talking for quite some time near the south gate. Deep in conversation." Myrtle bites her lip, glancing at the colonel. "They..."

"Go on," says the colonel, looking bullish.

"They were sharing a book. Passing it back and forth."

Lucy says, "It was Myrtle's impression that the book belonged to Sergeant Singh. And they were laughing together. At a certain moment, Hannah became quite emotional—"

"Goodness, how long were you spying?" Hannah snaps at Myrtle.

"Lucy, do we really need this level of…?" James mumbles.

His wife holds up a delicate hand. "Myrtle has also shared with me that she had the impression that you, Hannah, were *pursuing* Sergeant Singh."

Hannah shakes her head. Dashing to the south gate, intercepting his exit. Of course she pursued him, though not in the way they are insinuating. "That is false, Lucy. And this is all nonsense. I would like to leave. I wish to go home to bed, as it's been a very long day."

They look at the each other, unsure what to do next.

"So are you going to indict me for something? Some crime? James? Is that how your regime works?" This is going rather too far, Hannah knows; anger has gotten the best of her. "Or are you all spewing these impressions at me simply to try to humiliate me and my husband?"

George's face is pained—a raw, murky blend of crimson and burnt umber. "Hannah, *you* are the one who is humiliating me. Don't you see? You are humiliating all of us with this mad behaviour."

"Mad behaviour?" She wipes her hands over her face. "I'm an artist. And I am painting."

"Painting whores," says Hazel.

"Yes!" *At least I'm not screwing them*, she wants to say, *like our husbands do.*

"Why can't you just stop?" demands the colonel. "I've asked you to stop. And yet you go further."

"No, George, you've never asked me to stop. You've never *asked* me about art, about painting, about anything that matters to me. In fact, you've never asked me anything! Not even to marry you—it was my father who obliged me to do that."

Myrtle gasps.

"What you do, George, is make threats and arrange ambushes."

"Let's go," he replies, rubbing at his sternum.

But James is closest in the room to Hannah, and he draws even closer to her until his presence eclipses the others, until she registers the longing in his eyes. "This," he gestures, "may have been a little much, Hannah, bringing everyone together here. But…do you see why we are concerned, my dear? Why your husband is concerned?"

"Of course," she replies, letting her chin fall toward her chest.

"Well?"

"Well, he shouldn't *be* concerned."

James recoils as if she'd slapped him.

"Good Lord!" Lucy exclaims. "We're your friends."

"Do you not care about your reputation?" warbles Myrtle.

Hannah grits her teeth. "I do *care*. Somewhat. But it's not—I—look, I don't expect you to understand this, any of you. But painting is like breathing to me. Like being able to breathe."

Edgar is wrinkling his nose at her like she's a hunk of stale cheese.

"Of course, none of *us* would understand," Lucy says softly.

"Enough of this theatre," barks the colonel, on his feet. "Let's go."

Hannah is out of the room before him and doesn't wait for him to catch up. Outside, the air has cooled to a chill. Carts wheel and turn in all directions over the expansive front lawn and guests wave at each other as they totter away from the party. Hannah dodges them, cutting across the adjoining lawn toward their home. Pain clots her throat and she concentrates on trying to dissolve it.

Mounting the veranda steps and daring at last to look behind her, she sees the colonel chugging nearer with a sour look on his face.

He looks down as he moves past her into the house. And upstairs, he turns away as she undresses. Maneuvering out of her gown, petticoat, corset, stockings, she tosses each layer aside until all there is left is silence.

"Hannah?"

"Yes."

"I didn't know what else to do."

She pulls her nightgown over her head. In bed, the colonel is snoring, as if to prove his carelessness, even before Hannah has finished brushing her hair. Drained as she feels, her mind is active and works its way backwards to visit the people they have left behind at the Residency. The women, she imagines, have moved to different seats in the drawing room, conferring with each other. Eating second helpings of cake. *She's so unreceptive! What can be done, James?* James Finch, fatigued with the topic, makes a remark to that effect before retiring to bed. *She's more trouble than she's worth,* somebody else says.

Hannah wipes her face. What if she had calmly explained to them all why she was painting the locals? It was not just the dock girls but the coconut man and flower seller at the market, the customs official at the pier. Children playing in mud puddles. Would it have made any difference? And if she could have calmly described the jungle painting, how marvelous it is to discover and amplify the hidden vibrating love that is all around them. What if she had shared Sergeant Singh's exciting and unusual news: there is something called a parasol flower, a most astonishing wild creation. Would it be deemed an appropriate object of emotion?

In her mind, she takes Lucy and Hazel (with Myrtle struggling along behind them) on an imaginary walk through the public gardens. Shows them the camellia she is painting. *The petals look burnt, she tells them; here, where the edges are decaying and dried, isn't that endearing? It's remarkable how life, even scorched or clipped or damaged life, struggles on in whatever manner it is able.* She points out Sergeant Singh in the distance, consulting his little notebook. *Wouldn't you have been curious enough to want to intercept him?* Now Beatrice Watts is looking at her over the carapace and Hannah waves her down to the shore. *I want this embarrassed girl to look up at all of us from my canvas,* she tells Beatrice. *I want her to catch us staring at her swollen feet.*

Other thoughts and memories come as she lies in bed. Lucy and Hazel, pouring her tea. As Hannah sips, she compliments them on their homes. This is genuine; they are impressive women. Pioneers, friends who tell her stories of their children and sisters and mothers, their plans to build a hospital in Kuala Kangsa. In the first and earliest meetings, they shared important information about flying ants and scorpions and the greenfly season, how to withstand homesickness. In turn, they asked her questions and listened as she described the academy and the Paris cafes, the Salon exhibitions, the Louvre, Monsieur Godot's little gallery and the "Impressionists" who came and went. They appeared impressed, though perhaps in the way that people are interested by frivolous oddities. "You don't say!" They asked about her teachers and about the other female students. "And your family? Were they happy for you?" Suddenly the whole room is shaking with her silent sobbing. Hannah slips out of bed and, through the blurry darkness, finds her way downstairs.

SIXTEEN

She wakes on the chaise longue in the conservatory. The colonel is standing over her with a steaming mug in each fist. His brow is split, his face puffy and pale.

"George. Are you all right?" she asks, sitting up.

He sets one mug down on the floor beside her, casting a glance at the nearby work-in-progress on the easel. "Brought you coffee."

"Thank you." She groans. "What a horrible night."

He looks away. "What is this?" He nods at the painting on the easel.

"A papaya."

The colonel drags a wooden chair over to the chaise longue, first removing a pile of rags from the seat. Looking through his eyes, she sees the chaos. The room is a mess. And for what? Once seated, he sips before saying, "I didn't sleep well. It was—it was perhaps a mistake to confront you in such a way."

She lets these words swell in the air between them.

"However, I…uh…" he shakes his head. "I felt I had no alternative."

"George, is it really so terrible to want to paint? People have been doing it for centuries. Women, for decades. Longer. I'm not claiming I'm a great artist like Rembrandt or Delacroix, but…"

"It's not the painting, per se," he grumbles. "No, it's these, these situations that you…"

"Goodness, do you honestly think I am romantically 'pursuing' Sergeant Singh?"

He examines the rim of his mug before replacing it in his lap. "That's how it looks, Hannah."

"Well, that is *not* how it *is*. Myrtle's stupidity," she mutters, "elevated to testimony by Lucy Meddlesome Finch."

The colonel chews his upper lip. How vulnerable he is when it comes to her. It has been so from the beginning, she realizes, whether on account of her younger age or for some other reason. Despite the fact she's traveled halfway around the globe for him!

"I feel, George, I mean I wonder, whether the others haven't rather a prejudiced notion of the life of an artist?" she ventures, careful to diffuse any blame. "I was up most of the night as well. Ruminating. I didn't conduct myself very well with…with everybody at the party. I think perhaps if I have a chance to properly explain what I am trying to do with my artwork… If I were to, for instance, show them my portfolio. Or this studio!" She throws open her arms. "Tidied up a little, of course. Perhaps it's a case of the unknown being off-putting, you see? Do you think so? I…I confess I don't fully understand why they would be objecting. I don't go around objecting to the way *they* deal with the natives."

He looks around him uncertainly. "Studio?"

"George, I don't think I've ever properly shown you my botanical studies. From my jungle treks."

He looks puzzled, as if she were speaking Dutch.

After a pause, she tries again. "Or I could perhaps do a portrait of James. Esteemed Resident of Perak. Or, for instance, one of the Swinburne's dog. Or of you, George, if you like. Make myself useful, as it were."

His eyes narrow. "So you're not stopping."

"Stopping?"

"What you're suggesting is that you make *more* art, and talk *more* about painting. You'll try to bring me and the others onside so that you can keep doing what you are doing in the village and in the forest."

She is sitting on her hands. Her left index finger smarts at the tip where she's bitten it too deeply. "I'm trying to help people see."

"Rubbish. Who are you to help them see?" His neck flushes its characteristic puce, rose madder deepened with ochre. "What about our home? This room is a conservatory."

She gets to her feet just as he does. "What about our home?"

"I don't think you were hearing us yesterday. There's something *wrong* with you, Hannah, that this…mess should matter so much to you." He gestures at the cluttered table, the easel, the stacks of stretchers upon which her various canvases lay drying. "Good God, you *slept* in here last night."

"You humiliated me, George! You arranged for my friends to humiliate me! Do you blame me that I couldn't bear to be near you?"

He strides to the doorway, head bowed. "Clean it up, please. All of it." Turning, his eyes scan the room. "I want this room returned to a proper conservatory."

After he's gone, she picks up her full mug and pitches the coffee onto the potted lemon tree. "God damn this!"

In the kitchen, she is pleased to find there is a mugful of brew left in the biggin. Hannah pours herself a fresh cup and stands drinking it, recalling the early morning of the tiger attack. The dewy hem of her daygown against her ankles. The tiger prowling through her mind. Suria, tottering into the kitchen, as she may do even now. *She was screamin', mem. Poor thing.* The smell of rotting flesh, so strong she thought it might corrode the canvas or curdle the paint as she worked.

There is something wrong with her. Look at the trouble they have all gone to, in their sincere conviction to help. And they know nothing about the morning she spent hunkered over a fragment of bloodied bone.

It isn't until she's penned not one but two letters to Monsieur Godot—and walked to town and back to post them—that Hannah can bear to return to her studio. She enters only briefly to fetch *Songs of Innocence and Experience.* On the veranda, the hibiscus bushes have grown high enough to conceal her with their branches and leaves and no one comes to find her except Roddy. The little gibbon sleeps next to her chair as she reads, balancing his lithe body along the railing.

> *Oh rose thou art sick.*
> *The invisible worm,*
> *That flies in the night*
> *In the howling storm:*
>
> *Has found out thy bed*
> *Of crimson joy:*
> *And his dark secret love*
> *Does thy life destroy.*

Hannah begins by boxing up her old palette knives. Cuvier, the first shop where she purchased art supplies on her own. It was last on the list provided by the academy—the cheapest option, and the furthest from Monmartre. The shopkeeper looks through his *pince nez* at her, wondering why she's bothering to remember him. Then, in a blink, she is standing at Monsieur Bougereau's desk with several other girls, listening to Bougie's opinions on the use of palette knives "beyond mixing," as he puts it.

There is a curled photograph in the box. The image was taken just before an anatomy class, she remembers, by a young woman from America who was on holiday and persuaded her family to let her stay on in Paris and attend the school. Diana. What ever became of Diana? They all so look young and determined. She smiles at the one or two women who have had a fringe cut into their hair, the new fashion. Hannah herself is seated on a high stool toward the back of the group, tipping forward a little; she'd had trouble getting in place, it was so crowded. The cautious look on her face to mask the exuberance she always felt in the studio. It was a space of absolutes… Absolute freedom? Devotion? Yes, they were all such slaves, such sponges, so utterly willing to prostrate themselves to the making of art.

There were openly exuberant girls at the academy, and she envied the ease with which they spoke. And there were others, not necessarily so loud, who could hold their own with anyone, female or male; these, Hannah admired and loved on principle, even if they were sometimes disagreeable people. She'd felt rebellious, but the truth was she was quiet and ever-acquiescent. For her, to rebel was to vow. To grow quieter still and take firm hold of her convictions. And then, of course, to paint.

In those days she was closest with Jane Hemming, for no particular reason except that Jane had sat down next to her on the first day. And there is Jane, standing next to her in the image, a slight smirk on her squarish face. Jane proved to have a delicious, dark sense of humour, which she applied in good measure. At Julian, teachers encouraged the pupils to speak, especially about art, but just as often about any topic of the day. It was a point of pride for them all to exist in friendly conflict. They were meant to be as far as possible from the stuffy, disciplined corridors of the Academie des Beaux-Arts.

Tucked into an anatomy textbook she finds a lavender-scented note from the directress congratulating her on her marriage and wishing her well in Malaya. Madame l'Espagne! "Ah, you have a *wonderful* model today, ladies!" Madame would announce, strolling into the room as she always did during the life drawing portion of the afternoon. They were all *wonderful* models to Madame Julian, whether old or young, fat or thin, female or male. *"Formidable!"* she would say in her accented French, rolling the *r*. And just as predictably, the three Japanese ladies would titter.

She folds the note and replaces it, boxes up the textbooks and manuals, collapses her two easels and her drying racks. The round hatbox is filled with letters from her mother that she cannot open. Her mother must have already been dying that year. Hannah's first at Julian.

Her satchel, however, she empties onto the floor. Nothing in this collection is superfluous. Each pencil she has need of, and each curled tube of pigment. No, she doesn't need any of it, she reminds herself. That is the point. She tucks it all back inside the bag and draws the strings tight.

Her notebooks are treasures. Godot's portraiture class in the first semester! In the margins she has sketched his face. She has no memory of drawing this, and yet there he is, winking and pointing comically to his nest of hair.

"Do you understand him?" Jane asked her on the day Monsieur Godot first spoke to them at any length.

"My French," Hannah replied, wincing, "is not *so* bad as it was."

"No, I mean, do you feel you *understand* him?"

That their learning was a spiritual matter. That making art was a way of living. Not something extra, a hobby, that one tacked on. Yes, she felt she understood him deeply.

She and Jane smiling smugly at each other across a café table. Little fools! Probably they'd had too much sugar in their hot cocoa. A new way of being in the world had taken root that year inside her and inside Jane, and they were vain enough to think they had a measure on it.

Flipping pages, Hannah's eye falls on:

> *The Great Difficulty: to decide between own natural impressions*
> *vs // beliefs about what should be perceived*
> *how do you know diff??→instincts, heart, experiences… cultivate these for*
> *genuine art*

In retrospect, how easy it had all been. The triangulation assignment. On backgrounds. Choosing a palette that suits your subject.

Depth perspective. Was she in love with Monsieur Godot? Does she still believe what he told them?

> *What is art? trace*
> *footprints that show I have walked bravely and in great happiness*

The word *happiness* makes her break down. She clutches the notebook to her chest. If only he would write back to her! Why doesn't he write anymore?

Hannah makes several trips to the third story, hauling her boxed supplies and books to her writing garret, where she piles them against the wall and, sitting down at last, slumps over her desk.

Later, in the new conservatory, she and Suria pull the furniture back into the center of the room. Hannah had cleared a space to spread her studies over the floor. A space where, at other times, she would pace or pirouette, shaking inspiration into her arms and hands.

"More help, mem?" asks Suria, when they are done with the furniture. The old woman looks puzzled at the changes but, uncharacteristically, has not shot off any questions.

"No, thank you, Suria, I'll do the rest."

With a duster, broom and mop, Hannah works at cleaning away her traces.

SEVENTEEN

Another supper to arrange; it's practically obscene how they keep coming. Hannah stands in the pantry, examining the mostly bare shelves. Rice. Reliable rice. Half a dozen boxes of stale biscuits.

Three weeks ago she took fifty Straits dollars, over half of the amount he'd given her and, exchanging them for English pounds, completed her Schlauerbach's order. Hoping for what, exactly? That the colonel would change his mind?

She shifts tins, inspecting labels. Has he always eaten in needy forkfuls, plowing into second and third helpings as she sits in agonized silence? No wonder his stomach ails him. Could he be overeating deliberately, so that she's forced to spend every penny on household staples? No. Why bother to go to such lengths when he could just reduce her stipend further if he wished.

Hannah finds the syce in the back room he and Suria use as a lounge. "Has the colonel mentioned anything to you about his tiger hunt?" she asks.

Anjuh pops to his feet. "No, mem. Mention, mem?"

"Does he mean to go on with it. That's what I want to know. If I had some sense of how long we… What do you think, Anjuh? He's killed one tiger."

The servant doesn't raise his eyes.

"I'm sorry. Why am I asking you such things?" Looking at the old man's lined forehead, she decides it doesn't matter when or whether the colonel stops the hunt. She must do things differently. Making art is a way of living. "Prepare the cart, please," she instructs.

In the side garden, Suria is throwing clothes over the line and swatting greenflies. They have just come into season.

"Oh dear," Hannah says. The midge-like flies have settled over the wet laundry. It will be a devil of a job removing their tiny carcasses from the fabric. "Suria, I'd like to come to market with you."

"Huh?"

Hannah smiles. "Or you can come with me, whichever way you'd prefer to think of it."

The housemaid spits a fly from her lips. "Why?"

Cheeky thing. Hannah sighs. "To purchase food for meals. Well?"

"Oh, uh-huh," says Suria, nodding. She goes back to wrestling with the laundry.

"Right now," Hannah adds. "So, you finish up here, and I'll meet you at the cart."

This isn't how it's done, of course. Servants are sent to market for the fresh items; wives order supplies from the dried goods catalogue. At a financial loss in both cases, Hannah surmises. And for what? So that people have Atmore's and Brown's in the pantry. So ladies may be spared the hustle of the natives and the "overwhelming" scents and sights at market. She and the ayah sit in the cart together, a stack of woven baskets sliding back and forth between them as they descend to the village.

"I'll follow your lead," Hannah says to Suria as market stalls come into view up the road. "Just do what you normally do."

Suria holds out a small, cupped hand and Hannah fishes coins and a couple of folded bills from her purse before thinking better of it. "No. I will keep hold of the money."

"How I know what to spend?"

"Ah! Spend what is a fair price for the item."

Suria looks blankly back at her.

"Imagine." Hannah taps her forehead. "Imagine you are buying for *only* you and Anjuh."

The old woman squeals. "House for me on Street of Big Bosses!"

"No, no, that's not what I mean." They have come to a stop outside the marketplace. A gang of bare-legged children emerge from nowhere to surround the bullock cart. "Run along," Hannah urges them, waving them away. But they smile so deliciously she laughs and tosses a few pennies in the air. Cheering, the children scrabble for the coins before sprinting off.

"Imagine you are purchasing for your own selves," she tells Suria. "For a house on the river."

Suria wrinkles her nose. "A stilt house, mem? Or can we get a bungalow?"

"A stilt house."

Suria shrugs and climbs out of the cart. Slinging the empty baskets over one shoulder, she plods across the dirt road. Hannah tucks her purse away and follows, scolding herself for feeling nervous. It is only a market. One she has passed by many times.

From the wide central aisle—where Hannah is already drawing furtive glances—they enter a much narrower one flanked with pails of shrimp and squid and river fish. Overhead, ducks dangle by their webbed feet. Hannah is tall enough to risk striking them with her forehead so she veers to her left and right, at one point struggling not to topple onto a pile of leathery kelp. The housemaid pokes at various watery wares, stealing backward looks at Hannah, before coming to a stop beside a huge bass. They do sometimes eat bass. The fishmonger, catching sight of Hannah, hurries over. He exchanges several words with Suria in Malay, and the two seem to come to quick agreement.

Suria turns to her expectantly.

"What about prawns?" asks Hannah, pointing along the bench of wares.

The seller is visibly deflated.

"Yes. Let's buy some prawns instead."

After assisting in the purchases of a half-pound of shrimp and two bunches of onions, Hannah asks Suria, "Why aren't you haggling? You've not been haggling, have you?"

Her eyes pop open. "English not like haggle."

"You're not English."

Suria smiles coyly. "No, mem."

"Listen to me, please. I am giving you permission to haggle. Don't be afraid. I want you to do so." Hannah repeats what she's said, insisting that Suria be her teacher, and eventually the other woman nods.

Apart from the aisle dedicated to fish and meats, there appears to be no order to the vendors. The two of them walk from bunches of herbs and vegetables to mounds of sandals, from stands of colored, swaying fabric to a table lined with pineapples and pocket watches. Suria purchases various leafy bundles, Asian pears, a packet of pigeon peas. The bartering is straightforward, from what Hannah can tell, but seems to involve patience and an uncomfortable measure of stubborn silence. One time, Suria points to a defect in a fruit and purchases it and three others at a discount. Another time, they move on without a tub of coconut oil, only to circle back later. Hannah plucks up the courage to ask about some of the unfamiliar wares on display. Brown candle-like cakes turn out to be sugar made from coconut palm.

There is a flower vendor whose stall is stacked with orchids, heliconia, torch ginger, and other exotic blooms. Hannah drifts there automatically and is greeted by a plain but sweetly smiling Malayan girl. "Buy flower, memsahib?"

"They're gorgeous. Actually, I'm just wondering, have you heard of…or rather, have you ever sold any parasol flowers?"

She shakes her head slowly.

"Par-a-sol," Hannah draws the shape of the umbrella in mid-air, then grasps an invisible handle. "Oh! But aren't you one of the girls who… We've met at the docks, haven't we?"

A hostile expression contorts the girl's face.

"Perhaps not. My apologies. Well. I don't suppose you'd be selling something so large. And so rare." Hannah turns her attention to the flowers. All of them will wither and die before long, and she can't help but see the shimmering blooms as death masks. To be polite, though, she treads the length of the display table, feigning interest, then nods at the salesgirl. "Thank you for your time."

Suria is waving at her from behind a barrel. "Mem? The poison?"

Rather than trying to eliminate all pests, Hannah has taken to regulating them by leaving out strategically placed substances—a crust of bread, fruit peelings. Although a steady thread of ants travels through the pantry, they have at least stopped invading and spoiling the supplies. She has been keeping up a pretense of hostility, in case the colonel ever wanders into the pantry, by storing empty boxes of poison. "Oh, let's not bother."

Reaching Suria, she says, "Do you ever disobey Anjuh?"

"Ha!"

"What does that mean?"

"Ya, mem."

"When?"

"Nnnh." The ayah tugs her sarong against her hips. "Whenever he is wrong and I am right."

Hannah smiles. "That makes perfect sense."

With the woman selling chickens, Suria appears to embark on an extended discussion. Hannah drifts to the menagerie next door, peering in the cages at the tiny twittering birds and fending off the blunt saleswoman. An awkward coincidence that the live birds are exhibited next door to the dead ones. The little finches, in particular, are darling. They meet her regard with curiosity, cocking their tiny feathered heads. Looking back to Suria, Hannah sees her and the vendor bowing to each other. "What do you think?" she asks the songbirds. "Better to be bright and caged than a fat dead chicken?"

"I should have said, I might not have enough money left for a whole chicken," she tells Suria, coming over. She stirs the coins in her purse. "How much?"

"Choose," says Suria.

Hannah sighs. "Meaning?"

"Pay her what you want to pay. She is sister to my mother."

"She's *your* aunt?"

"Much younger sister to my mother."

"Well, that's very kind of her. And of you."

Suria holds her head up proudly.

"Now, I think we'd better stop," Hannah says. She reserves a few coins and, bowing to the chicken woman, hands the rest over to her.

They lug their baskets to the main road. This could well be her saving grace, the discovery of the market. For the savings have been significant. To cut down even more, perhaps she could learn a few local recipes… And with the money she will save she can still afford small orders through Schlauerbach's. Then, too, might there be local materials? Local paint suppliers? She has heard of Oriental artists painting on bamboo boards, on burlap sacking, even on banana leaves… She twists to look behind her as they exit, wondering if she has seen the market after all.

Anjuh appears mildly impressed as he helps them into the bullock cart. "It went very well," Hannah reports, setting down her baskets. "Next time, I will try the haggling."

They enter into a stretch of scorching hot days where the shutters must remain drawn and the house never seems to cool. Outside, only the faintest breeze blows along the ridge. It is ill-advised, as Lucy would have put it, for any fair-skinned folk to expose themselves during the daytime. Anjuh and Suria, meanwhile, walk up and back from the lower village on a daily basis.

The colonel has been at home on account of the weather. While he could be, Hannah suspects, squaring the accounts from his home study, instead he spends his days playing dominoes, smoking, and sipping gin—venturing through the house on the occasional rampage to chase away a lizard. Is it her imagination, or is he tacitly keeping track of how she is spending her time? Housework, is Hannah's emphatic answer. Tidying, dusting, sweeping, mopping, scrubbing, laundering, mending, replacing, unplugging, watering, waxing, fluffing, turning out, turning over, tightening, loosening, darning, ironing, wiping, and polishing. Hannah's exertions have failed to siphon away the full extent of her frustration. It is nine days since the gymkhana festival, eleven since she's held a paintbrush. Instead, she's attempted to create *nasi lemak* for their supper.

"So?" she asks the colonel. "What do you think? This one is my *sambal.*"

He stirs his rice. "I think it's bloody hot. What do you mean it's *your* sambal?"

"I prepared it. It's my proprietary mixture. I may have to reduce the chilies."

"You may have to cook proper food!"

She pours herself another glass of wine. The first one she drank while cooking. "They eat this dish for breakfast, the natives. I thought that might be pushing it a bit." He grunts. "It's an interesting…it catches you right at the back of the throat, doesn't it? Salty."

The colonel gives her a strange look. "You are…insufferable. There is always something new for you to learn, isn't there? Something of new and dramatic interest. Some further boundary to cross."

Hannah frowns. She plans to speak to him after a dinner someday soon, after a "proper" meal without spicy sambal, when he is full and relaxed and perhaps smoking his pipe and looking over the *Illustrated London News*. She is beginning to recognize that she does not manage him, or her situation, well. It takes patience and foresight, and she is short on both. If not management, there is fortitude. How good her mother had been at accepting uncertainty and strife! Even when she was very ill, and Hannah was still protesting, Mum took what she'd been given and made her peace with it. *God gave me you, a beautiful girl with a great talent. What right do I have to question Fate?* The true talent was in extracting happiness from misfortune.

In this future discussion she will ask the colonel what she is supposed to do about God and the way He made her. Her nature. Does George truly expect her to close her eyes to what she sees, even now as she moves around the house and the light sways in heavenly parabolas upon the drapes and the puddles on the road turn to blood in the setting sun, and her eyes in the mirror beg so exquisitely. How can these things not be painted? How can all those moments simply be lost? What, she will ask him, is *his* solution?

The colonel refills his water goblet and wipes his mouth with his napkin. He is looking at her placidly. Suffering through his time with his insufferable wife.

"George, I know I am capable of…I am capable of…" She brings her hands to her face. Her fingers smell sharply of bleach. *I am capable of greatness.*

What if she were to use the garret? This she could propose. In this heat, three in the morning would be the only feasible time to paint. Not that she would mind three in the morning, nor the heat, particularly, if she were painting. She needn't wear much of anything, holed up in the garret. When she is painting, anything is possible.

"Hannah? What were you saying?"

"Sorry, George. This heat is…" She takes a short swallow of wine.

The colonel sets down his fork and goblet and appears to be concentrating keenly. A great effort is being made on his part.

Suddenly, she is angrier than she has ever felt in her life. It startles her how quickly the fury invades her senses and propels her from her chair. Hannah strides out of the room, not bothering with the plates. Seething and striding, that is all there is.

She ignores him calling out to her and sits down by the door to lace up her boots. Then bangs past the colonel and his silly expression, out of the house and into the tepid black evening.

The surprise is that it's not George she hates, it is the academy. With its silly debates and "open days" and its high-minded instructors with their pet projects. And every one of her over-confident classmates, including Jane. Especially the ones who are painting and holding shows and arguing with each other about palette knives and Degas and the "new futurism." How viciously she hates them and their false lives!

Hannah stomps down the middle of Ridge Road, barely present to her twilit surroundings, not registering the howler monkeys' chorus across the river, nor the pothole. Her foot lands heavily and awkwardly in it. Over-extending her knee, she topples to the ground in what feels like a circus stunt, pain lacing her shin and ankle. Inadvertently she cries out—a single gasp of protest. On the dusty road she writhes for a time in silence, clutching herself.

The moon is already high overhead. A pearly eye on her indignity.

"And what do you know about it?" she scoffs.

Hannah squeezes the bright orb between her thumb and forefinger as she lies back, letting her breath loosen, feeling the earth where it cradles her body.

EIGHTEEN

Barnaby Munk and I arranged to meet in a pub called The White Dog. I'd never been to Oxford and was surprised to find it entirely under construction, my preconception being that it was an unchanging and ancient place. The roads, the bridges, the old stone buildings of the university—everything, it seemed, was framed with scaffolding and hazard tape. I walked in circles under a cool March sun, enjoying the icy boughs of the weeping willows and the yellowed church spires, priming myself for the relief of a cozy pub. (I'd located said pub upon arrival. Out front, the sidewalk was being re-leveled and two enormous pylons marked a potentially hazardous bump.) I entered at one p.m. sharp, and as I stood looking around me, rubbing my cold hands together, an elderly gentleman rose in one corner, his eyes locking on mine.

"Nancy?"

When I nodded, he beamed like the Cheshire cat. The professor emeritus wore a pink cardigan over his rounded shoulders and sported a frizzle of grey hair. He extended a hand to shake mine, but in the process of moving out from behind his little table knocked against it. Over went his pint. The glass crashed to the floor, ale sloshing dramatically. Barnaby apologized to the servers who came running, to me, to the other nearby customers.

"I drop things," he told me, when we had settled down together at another table. (The staff needed to mop the floor.) He looked over his shoulder at them. "Oh dear, I do drop things."

"I do, too," I confessed. "Sometimes I drop myself. I sit down and find there is no chair under me." I told him about the most recent occasion, at Richelieu. And the librarian who'd walked the length of the open floor to shush me like a five-year-old.

Barnaby laughed. "Ah, les francophones. So," he said, looking conspiratorial, "have you read *The Descent of Woman*?"

"Yes."

"Good."

I held his gaze for a moment. I'd contacted him about Hannah

Inglis and her art, and he kept rerouting me to the Peterboroughs' book. It was true that Hannah's art appeared there. Did he feel the book provided us with some sort of common ground?

"It's an interesting book," I prevaricated.

"In what way?"

"I suppose it's a sort of systematic hodgepodge, isn't it? As if they felt they had to include everything they'd ever studied. One of those Theories of Everything books."

He nodded cautiously.

"Or," and this had just occurred to me, "perhaps the two Peterboroughs couldn't agree on what to include? There's something of a mixture of styles, maybe? Something odd. I can't put my finger on it. Something patchwork about it."

Of course, I remembered the comment in Barnaby's email concerning the "nasty business." I'd learned that Charles Peterborough had performed studies of the natives in the Malay and Indonesian archipelagos as well as Australia. Physiological tests, the "evidence" of which informed the most contentious section of *The Descent*, two chapters concerning the sexual traits of human beings. Whereas Alfred Wallace had collected everything from crayfish to orangutans, which he'd brought back to England pickled in barrels, apparently Charles and Eva Peterborough felt that to fully understand humans they had to study humans. Whether that study represented Barnaby's "nasty business," I wasn't so sure. In any case, I wasn't prepared to do what he wanted: namely to prove, by mentioning the "nasty business" reference, how closely and keenly I'd been hanging on his every emailed word.

I said, "Is *The Descent* considered to be their magnum opus, so to speak?"

"It's the only book-length volume she wrote. He wrote several others."

"*She* wrote? I thought it was a—"

"Oh, it was published under both of their names."

We broke off to receive menus and order drinks. Were we eating? the server wondered. Yes, we were eating a proper lunch, he informed her. I wanted to ask Barnaby if he'd found out; did his family have any more of Hannah's paintings? This seemed so direct as to be impolite, however. I inhaled and smiled as my companion addressed his menu with as much gusto as he'd welcomed me.

"The operative question," he said, folding his menu at last, "is what to consider that document. Do we address it as a contribution to truth? As a historic artifact? Literary work? Triptych to a global adventure tour? Is it a book of theory, a sort of philosophy of sexuality, or is it a scientific treatise?"

"Uh. What do you consider *The Descent of Man?*" I countered. "Isn't the Peterboroughs' book some kind of response to Darwin?"

"*If* we treat it as a contribution in the service of scientific truth," said Barnaby, "if we do so...then we can discount *The Descent of Woman* thoroughly."

"Can we?"

He shrugged, making an it's-always-debatable expression. "Well, I can tell you the dominant view is decidedly *not* that sexual differences arose from sexual selection mechanisms. Nobody followed Darwin in that direction."

"And is the dominant view correct?" This was as an innocent question on my part. It set Barnaby off, and he seemed pleased for the opportunity to put me straight. In the process, he told me about his own research in the field of lepidoptery, which centered on moth migration and various accomplishments associated with moth migration. In the midst of his monologue we ordered our food. By the time it arrived, Barnaby had exhausted himself.

"Now tell me about your own research." He unrolled his knife and fork from their napkin. "You're looking for this Inglis woman."

"I am, yes. Her artwork."

"Quite. She herself would long be mouldering, wouldn't she?"

Irrationally, I felt a pang of sadness. Surely I hadn't been expecting to meet the woman? I reviewed for Barnaby what I'd seen at Fulgham House, as well as Alvin's unveiling of *Strangler Fig* for me at Kew Gardens. I worked in how difficult it was proving to be to find any more of Hannah's art, and I expressed hope that his family might have some pieces in their collection.

Soberly, Barnaby said, "I did speak to Celia." He wiped his hands, fished in his shirt pocket, and produced a heavily creased piece of paper. Squinting for a moment at it, he turned it over to me.

It was a typewritten list. A very long one. Some line items had been crossed out with a blue fountain pen; others involved additional penciled-in information. I scanned the numbered entries until I found what I was looking for.

16. H. Inglis, *Murdo* and *Jane* (2 pieces, companion; oil)
17. H. Inglis, *Still Life of Cut Flowers* (oil)
18. H. Inglis, *The Cabin* (sketch, charc. on paper)
19. H. Inglis, untitled of Sikh servant and fruiting tree (oil)
20. H. Inglis, *Nude House Girl* (oil)
21. H. Inglis, *The Parasol Flower* (oil)

My hands shook a little as I moved my beer aside and my bowl of curry. Beside the entries for 20 and 21, someone had written: *give to Tommy.*

"Do you, do you have these works?" I asked.

"No, unfortunately not," he said, forking off a chunk of battered cod. "Well, as you know, *Murdo* and *Jane* are at Fulgham House." He took the sheet back and, pulling a pair of reading glasses from the pocket of his cardigan, reviewed the list with great care. "I believe the Trust also took the still life, and this one called *The Cabin.*"

An annoying confusion. Miranda had told me the Fulgham House collection had no other Inglis works at all. "And the others?" I pressed on. "Does 'Tommy' have those?"

He laughed. "Presumably. Celia and I do not."

"Does Celia perhaps know where I can find Tommy? Or how to contact him?"

Barnaby sucked his bottom lip for a moment before shaking his head. "We're not sure who he is. The list was probably drawn up by Charlotte. She was my grandmother, Charlotte Peterborough Munk. Or, you know, somebody working for her. But the list itself is sixty years old or more."

I hid my frustration with showier mock-frustration. "Oh, no! And so *no* idea who this 'Tommy' is? Do you think it was Charlotte who wrote that in?"

"Well, it could be Thomas Ealing—he was a second cousin of Charlotte's, apparently. Celia went through all this with me. You see, I'm afraid I've never taken much interest in these old dead buggers. Tory toffs, the lot of them." He cleared his throat and gave me a rueful look. "Or it's possible 'Tommy' was no relation at all. One of the estate staff, perhaps. An art dealer. A friend of Charlotte's?"

"Quite a close friend, to give him two oil paintings," I observed.

He looked frankly miserable. For a moment, I thought he was going to reach for my hand to squeeze it. "Charlotte may not have valued the pieces as much as you do, my dear."

How delicately put, I thought. I must look a fool to him. People like Charlotte Peterborough, people who lived in places like Fulgham House, had so much art they had to list it to remember it. They treated it like a commodity—bought, sold, dispensed with. I had no inkling of this kind of life. Barnaby was at least familiar with it.

"Forgive me for being blunt, Ms. Roach, but I must ask you: why is this woman's art noteworthy? *Is* it indeed noteworthy?"

"I believe so," I managed to say.

"But art is subjective, isn't it?" He shrugged. "Art is a subjective matter."

"Not *merely* subjective," I protested softly. "There are elements— line, balance, composition, color—elements that can be judged on the basis of known standards and known strategies. Anyway, you can't go discounting everything with a subjective element to it. *Intersubjective*," I drawled the word. "How else could there be art criticism. Art appreciation. Art history."

"And yet Hannah Inglis has *not* been part of that history or that criticism, has she?"

My fingers began tapping the table of their own accord. "I don't know that that matters for considering the quality of the art itself."

"But you've just said it does."

"The question is *why*, then? Why has she been excluded?"

I took a swift pull of my pint, a beer that he'd recommended, which smelled and tasted to me of meadows. Excusing myself for the toilet, I locked myself in a dimly lit stall to try to get some purchase on my motives.

Hannah's paintings had moved me. Because they were a contribution, I vowed, a true contribution. Not because they hadn't been appreciated, *she* hadn't been appreciated. I couldn't deny that her gender and the lack of reception were factors of interest for me. Of course they were. I, more than Barnaby, surely, knew how very *alone* she must have felt as she was making these works…. But how exactly did Hannah's story matter to an appreciation of her art?

Perhaps her art had been forgotten for good reason, and I had simply become obsessed with it in the way people became obsessed with stock car racing or comic book heroes or their local football team. I stared at my face in the tiny mirror over the sink, habitually going over as I did now, the pouches under my eyes and the blurring line of my jaw.

Did I have a right to be angry with Barnaby? Yes, I decided. Not because he was clueless about his family history. He could have saved me a trip to Oxford. He could have just written back to me and said he'd checked into it, sorry, there was no art, he had no clue where else to look. Instead, I'd come all the way here and walked in circles for two hours; it had all been one great big tease. "He'd better be paying for this meal," I told my reflection.

When I returned to the table I found that he'd done just that and was chatting with the server. The two of them were discussing the sidewalk construction—some ins and outs with the city council. I thought I might ask Barnaby to introduce me to Celia. I considered how to accomplish this request without making it seem that I distrusted him, while also subtly pointing out that he'd wasted my time.

"Did you like the unfiltered beer?" he asked when the server bowed out of the picture.

"Yes," I said decidedly. "Very much." There was an inch left in my glass, and I set about finishing it.

He played with his paper coaster and smoothed his dress shirt with a knobbled hand, shooting me furtive looks. A crusty old codger, that was the bottom line. Which is not to say I didn't like him. On the contrary.

He leaned toward me. "I have letters in my possession."

"Oh. Uh. Letters? You mean…"

"Letters written by your Hannah Inglis." He paused to enjoy the moment, a sly look on his face.

"More letters?" I said, deliberately deadpan.

He looked a little deflated, which pleased me. "More? I—well, I don't know about that," he said stiffly. "At any rate. You're welcome to have a look at them."

I told him I'd love to have a look at the letters in his possession. I told him about what I'd found at the Academie Julian: namely, the Coles book. That Hannah had attended the academy in one of the first classes of female students and she'd left for Malaysia, possibly even before she'd graduated, but that she'd kept in touch with one of her instructors. Presumably the letters in Barnaby's possession were more mundane, though perhaps more personal, if she'd been writing to one of the Peterboroughs.

"She kept up quite a correspondence with this famous artist." I smiled at him. "Mind you, I've only seen a few of her letters as they have been reprinted. Appendix A. Not the originals. A Frenchman named—"

"Henri Godot."

We frowned at one another.

NINETEEN

The Peterboroughs' large and cluttered sitting room is stocked with objets d'art. Dreading and longing for the moment that Eva is finally finished flipping through her portfolio, Hannah flits from one exotic item of décor to another. Hannah's plan is to let her art speak first and as much as possible. Far better that Eva Peterborough is moved to help her because she's seen some promise in her work. Pity, in any case, seems out of the question. It's not in this woman's character.

"Idlewyld," Hannah says, unable to stand the silence any longer. "Was that the name of your English home as well?"

"No."

The Peterboroughs' estate is vast. It's nestled in the lush, hilly countryside, about a twenty-minute cart ride upstream from Kuala Kangsa. Judging by the state of the coffee orchards, the plantation was abandoned long ago. Perhaps the family got a good price. Though they'd hardly needed one, by the looks of the opulent furnishings.

"You've obviously traveled...extensively..." Hannah picks up a carved elephant tusk to examine the workmanship. "Is this from India?" she guesses. She's seen nothing like it locally.

"That's a *shiva lingam*," says Eva, glancing up.

"Oh?"

"In honor of the penis. A sort of penis idol, if you will. From the tantric religion of Goa."

"Oh!" Hannah puts the tusk down and bends to look at it. "Oh, I see what you mean."

"I think these are wonderful," Eva says levelly. "Very bold. Expressive. There is something wavering about them, about these spaces, that...draws me in."

Hannah receives these compliments gratefully and, as the tea service arrives, answers the lady's many questions about craft and subject matter. They even discuss her training and her life in Paris. Eva Peterborough may not be an artist but she's obviously an educated and accomplished woman. It's a pleasure just to talk with her.

When their conversation finally slows, Hannah attempts to explain.

"I'm sure you're wondering why I'm here in the first place, Mrs. Peterborough."

"Please, call me Eva."

"Eva. The thing is, and this is why I thought of you, here, at
Idlewyld... The colonel has forbidden me to paint."

"Forbidden you!" She laughs outright. "You're serious."

"Perhaps not in so many words. But I—I have been warned."

"Hmmm," Eva muses. "This has something to do with the Ridge
Road ladies, I'll wager. Mrs. Finch and her cautionary tales. They're a
fearsome bunch, aren't they?"

Hannah sighs audibly, which feels luxurious, but holds back her
scorn. "I suppose they think they are helping me."

"People like that always do." Eva adjusts her collar. "What do you
mean you thought of me? To be frank, we hardly know each other."

It's true. And the reasons for Hannah being there, making her ap-
peal, are all patently self-serving. Swallowing, she vows to become
a better human being. "Mrs. Peterborough. Eva. At the moment I
have very few means, practically speaking, to keep painting. George
has reduced my stipend and diverted the money to his tiger hunt.
Which...I cannot see an end to."

"No end to it? Wasn't that bloodied spectacle at the festival a tiger?"

"Yes, it was. The colonel says he cannot be sure that one was the
man-eater."

"There is no man-eater."

"Quite!" Hannah looks at her stained fingers with their bitten nails
before thrusting them behind her back. "I may be able to manage as
far as paints are concerned. However, I have no place to work. For a
while, I was painting in the village."

"But?"

She can't bear to mention the confrontation at the Residency. "But
that was not practical."

"Oh, my dear, surely none of it is *practical.*"

"No, I suppose not." Hannah rubs her eyes. "It was objectionable,
then." She shifts herself on the chesterfield. "They say I should stop."

"They?"

"Everyone! All of the other residents!"

Eva rests her chin on her fist for a moment or two. "Why do they say you should stop, Mrs. Inglis? It is matter of your reputation?"

She nods. "It's not that I don't care about reputation or, what is the right word, 'social graces'? I simply care more about art."

Eva smiles shrewdly. Could it be that Hannah's misjudged the strange woman? Will Eva report to George or Lucy the latest install-ment of her foolish obsession to paint? There is nothing for it now but to press her case further. So she says, "I don't exactly know why, but you've always seemed to hold an appreciation for the fact that I paint, Mrs. Peterborough. It's obvious that you have an independent mind. I respect that very much. And I don't believe the colonel would suspect anything if I were to…come here occasionally. He'd think I'm visiting you to socialize. That we are becoming closer friends."

Eva blinks slowly.

"Which of course I would like to do as well, to become closer friends. I really would."

She's skipped over the major consideration: the Peterboroughs are recluses who live well outside of town. No one would find her here.

"Let me be clear, Mrs. Inglis. You are requesting that I—that we—permit you to paint on our premises? And that we lie to your husband about it."

"No, no, I would lie to him. You need not have anything to do with him. Just as it is now."

"So: condone your deceit and the very practice you say your hus-band has already 'forbidden.'" Eva's expression is neutral.

"I promise I wouldn't be in your way," Hannah hastens to add. "I had in mind to paint out of doors, you see. In the forest, with your permission. I needn't come in the house at all." She looks around her. The main house must be thirty rooms or more for the three of them. It's hard to imagine how anyone could be in the way in a place like this.

Eva refreshes her cup of tea. "You say you have no means to con-tinue painting." Hannah shakes her head warily. "And that you face opposition from your friends and your husband."

"Yes."

"Then why don't you stop?"

"I—uh. I don't know."

"I think you do. You've gone to a good deal of trouble to pursue something that, to put it mildly, continues to cause you suffering. Why?"

What happened to the praise and memories of Paris? The woman is formidable when she wants to be.

"Surely, given the circumstances, this is a reasonable question for me to ask."

"Yes, yes, of course." Hannah says. "Of course it is. I suppose I don't stop because I cannot stop. I need to paint."

"Explain."

"Only that I cannot stop, Mrs. Peterborough! I'm not sure if I ever could. Certainly not since the academy. I find that I need to make art. And I would like to try—" She draws a deep breath. "I wish to *contribute*. I feel that I have something to contribute to whatever it is that we're all…trying to fathom. This life. Mostly, I admit, it's personal need. Whether that's selfish, I'm not sure. But whatever else is expected of me here, on earth, I need to paint. I'm sorry, but I don't know how else to put it."

Eva Peterborough watches her in stillness for what feels like an age. Then says, "Bravo, darling. Of course you may paint here."

"Really?" With shaking hands, Hannah replaces her cup and saucer to the table. "Thank you, Mrs. Peterborough. Thank you very much."

"I believe in a woman's right to meaningful work. I'm better known around here for what I *don't* believe in. They can't seem to get past that."

"Oh yes, right." The Peterboroughs are atheists. That is their scandal. At the moment, Hannah couldn't care less whether the lady stuffed cloven hooves into her shoes and hid a tail under her frumpy dress.

They sip tea and trade happy glances for a minute or two before Eva says, "Really what you need, Hannah, is a patron. Like Michelangelo had Pope Julius." Her laugh is an awkward wheeze.

That the woman knows about the ancient master's patronage makes Hannah want to squeal with joy. "Well, I thought I might do some paintings for you and Dr. Peterborough in return for your hospitality. I could paint your estate, or the mansion, if you like. Or your portraits? Or if you'd prefer, you could choose something from my existing collection."

"How kind of you." Eva opens the portfolio and begins flipping pages, but soon shuts it. "Is it truly a question of having the colonel's permission?"

"Goodness, I didn't think. Am I putting you in an awkward position with *your* husband?"

"Not at all." She looks out the open casement window. Past an enormous weedy planter, a scrubby meadow slopes away from the house. "Charles will take no notice of us, I'm sure. He's very busy these days with his research." Eva gets to her feet and Hannah rises, on cue. "In fact, he and I hardly take any notice of each other. It suits us that way."

"Sounds heavenly!" she blurts out, feeling her face redden. "But then, I'm frightfully anti-social."

TWENTY

The entrance to Idlewyld is two stories in height, incorporating the main spiral staircase to the upper floor. Several enormous gilt-framed mirrors decorate the walls, refracting the light into multiple channels and creating, in certain angles, reflections of reflections of reflections. Descending the winding staircase from the upper floor, Hannah feels a small shock—part delight, part discomfort—seeing fragments of Sergeant Singh copied in the mirrors. The original Sergeant Singh is standing a few paces from the double doors of the entry, inhabiting a fiercely professional attitude that is only briefly disturbed when he notices Hannah on the landing.

Eva, it seems, has already welcomed him in and now dismisses the servants.

"I believe you've met Mrs. Inglis," Eva says to the sergeant.

Hannah flashes her a look. Already she regrets the way they've summoned him: on false pretenses.

The three of them move to a nearby room. Not the Souvenir Shop, as Eva has dubbed the formal sitting room, but a much smaller, barer space with yellow-papered walls and wooden chairs set round a wooden table. On the table, a surveyor's map has been unfolded.

"I have title on two hundred and fifty acres to the southeast of the formal grounds," Eva tells him. "As I'm sure you've noticed on your ride here, Sergeant, the terrain is hilly. Outside of the orchards, and the main road of course, it remains completely untouched. Please, do sit down."

Hannah clutches her elbows, avoiding both of their glances. What on earth is Eva doing? They summoned him to report a theft, yet she isn't reporting it.

"I would ask that the two of you stay out of the orchards and off the formal grounds," Eva continues, "but you are welcome to any part of my jungle acreage. Now, the easiest and most convenient point of entry would be behind the stables. The woods come in closest there and you will have some privacy whilst—"

"Madam, forgive me, but—"

"Yes, perhaps we should *explain*?" Hannah interjects.

Eva clears her throat. "I was mistaken about the ring, Sergeant. I've just now found it in the pocket of an apron I rarely use."

The sergeant draws himself up even taller on his chair. He has the decency to look perplexed.

"Heaven knows how it ended up there!" Eva throws up her hands. It is a terrible piece of acting. "Seeing as you've come *all this way*, Sergeant… Well, as I say, the two of you are welcome to any of our jungle for your trekking."

Sergeant Singh looks from Eva to Hannah and back again, his eyes darkening and his frown deepening. She's never seen him like this. Hopping mad, she thinks.

At last he replies, barely able to unclench his jaw. "The first thing I would suggest, madam, is that before you summon the police in a criminal matter, verify the missing item is indeed missing."

"I am truly sorry for the inconvenience, Sergeant. However, I'm not sure how I could have verified that status without actually finding the ring. Which I've only just done."

After a stretch of silence, he rises.

"And the second thing you wish to suggest?" Eva asks. "You said, 'the *first* thing I would suggest'…implying…there were others? Other suggestions?"

"No. There are not, madam. Good day to you both."

In Hannah's ear, Eva says, "I've had them pack you a pannier for the first outing."

"If I am not needed here," Sergeant Singh announces, "I will return to work."

"You *are* needed!" Hannah exclaims, desperate at how things are unraveling. "Please, Sergeant, give me a chance to explain."

The white picnic basket bobbing along in front of her is shrinking again as Sergeant Singh lengthens the gap between them.

"Do hang on a minute," Hannah says, but not loudly. She's in no position to make demands.

Her ankle, healing well these past weeks, is sorer than she expected. There is nothing quite like forest walking. Each step a little different from the last, with roots and rocks and saplings to dodge. The flora at Idlewyld is lighter and more delicate than the forested sites in the river valley she and the sergeant have explored. Over each new rise and around every corner is a miniature clime with its own unique inhabitants. It seems incongruous for such a subtle, charmed world to take her breath away and make her thighs burn and her back ache.

"Clearing," the sergeant announces.

They struggle through a thicket of thatch palms, tumbling into a wide ditch that has been recently scythed. The open air strikes her like a furnace blast. Even the sergeant staggers.

"Oh, it's the road!" she says.

He sets down her easel and stool and wipes his face with his sleeve. "The road to Ipoh."

Hannah, likewise, drops her satchel. "This isn't the road to town?"

"It goes in both directions, madam."

Fixing him with a mock glare, she rolls her eyes. Then climbs up onto the empty carriageway and looks backwards and forwards, shielding her face with her hands. Cicadas whine loudly. "We haven't had much luck today, have we?"

"Depends on how you measure it, madam. There is nothing that pleases you to paint."

"I've been holding out for a parasol flower, I must admit."

At this he brings his chin to his chest, pulling a sour face. She made it clear, at the house, that she couldn't pay him; the opportunity to trek would be strictly voluntary. In fact, she repeated that he mustn't feel obligated, that he could simply decline and she would heartily wish him well. Hannah sighs, trooping back down from the roadway. Probably she'd sounded like one of the cleaning supply salesmen who used to call at her mother's inn. No wonder Sergeant Singh is rankling. In a single afternoon he is lied to, inconvenienced, and prevailed upon. And now he is carrying a pannier the size of a tortoise.

"I hope you aren't missing anything important at the station," she frets, squinting up at him. "We could decide on a schedule, couldn't we? Choose some mutually convenient days and times."

He makes no reply, but stands looking through her, rubbing at his chin. White is creeping into the stubble on his neck and runs in thin rivulets through the longer hair of his beard.

"Shall we find some shade?" she suggests.

They retrieve their supplies and head for a lemon tree that escaped scything some years ago and is casting an oval pool of shade up the bank of the ditch. Hannah plonks herself down, not bothering to spread the blanket they've brought, and takes a swig from her wine-skin. "Oh, how marvelous water can taste!"

The sergeant is occupied with the straps on the picnic basket. "What is in this thing, the crown jewels?" he mutters. "No, something heavier."

"Sergeant?"

"Madam, I feel I must make clear… This is the strangest turn of events. To be summoned out here on false portenses."

"Yes," she agrees heartily, smiling a little at his bastardization of the word. Hannah reiterates the apology she offered him at the house and admits, "We simply got carried away, I'm afraid. It was like something out of a childhood novel; the mistress of the great house summons the fretful butler and the local constabulary in order to put a secret plan into action. Though, there was no butler in our case."

He puts his hands to his waist. "This is the problem, madam. I am but a pawn for your secret game."

"No! No, that was bad comparison."

"*I* am not a game, madam."

"Of course not. I-I felt I made the situation very clear in the end. Unfortunately I'm not able to pay you—"

"I am not caring about money!" he thunders. He makes several adjustments to his turban, his long nose twitching. "So what has happened, eh? Has the colonel changed his mind about tigers?"

"Oh, I see what you mean. As a matter of fact, no." She debates for a moment or two and says, "I don't have the colonel's permission to paint. In fact, everybody we know in town is quite against it. So I asked Mrs. Peterborough if I might paint here at Idlewyld."

He looks up at the gathering clouds for a long moment. "You came here without your husband knowing. You don't wish your husband's permission?"

"Of course I do. I would. But he's not going to give it." Suddenly she feels as winded as if she's just climbed Cinnamon Hill. "Well, it's a solution, isn't it? If we came here."

"We *are* here. We have come already!"

"Sergeant, Eva seems discreet and quite willing to help, believe me.

She's given me a room in the house for my studio that will serve perfectly. And the trekking, well, I'm sure you can tell already how promising it is. I really believe there may be a parasol flower in bloom here. Or even a whole slope of them. Can you imagine? Waiting to be discovered. Ever since you mentioned that incredible flower…" She closes her eyes. "It's almost as if I have seen it already."

The sergeant has closed his eyes too. When they flick open, he shakes his head, brushing invisible dust from his jacket. "No. No. I cannot do this, madam. Not any further." His dark eyes flash. "Do you think I have nothing to lose from this…arrangement?"

She opens her mouth and cannot speak for a few beats. "Oh," she says lamely.

"My character. My job. My sanity!" He shakes his fist in the air. "I will not be accused of ruining you."

"That's absurd."

"I know. *You*, who are the one so willing to deceive your husband."

"What I mean is that it's absurd to think of either of us…or both of us… Ruination is an absurd prospect." Yet he's right. This is exactly how Lucy and the other ladies, not to mention the men, would frame her disloyalty.

"If you are not paying me," he grumbles, "then I must ask myself: what am I doing this for? Who am I?"

She jumps up, for he is striding away. "Sergeant? You're not going to leave me here? What about the pannier? Sergeant!"

He halts with his back to her, bunching his fingers to his temples. Then stalks back to heave the pannier over his shoulders and stuff her folding stool under one arm. "There is a roadway, madam. And… we can both use this roadway to return to the estate."

Hobbling along behind Sergeant Singh, Hannah occasionally urges her body into a shuffling sort of jog to try to decrease the gap. Her feet throb, along with her entire left ankle. The road enters the woods after a time, mercifully, so that the worst of the sun is blocked by the treetops, and the voice inside her settles into a kind of numbed babbling, her mind touring, as it were, the same subjects—ruination, her Idlewyld studio, tiger hunting, Eva's friendship—until they are nearly entirely drained of excitement and prospect. Has the sergeant increased his pace, or she is she growing slower? Her legs are sluggish and stumbling, her sight spins dizzily. Too proud and too ashamed to show she is suffering, Hannah remains quiet as long as she can.

"We must have…set out in the wrong direction…don't you think?" she calls to him at last.

Sergeant Singh turns toward her. "Sun is here." He points. "Village, here. If we are not getting anywhere it is only that we are moving *very slowly.*"

"Village!" she gasps. "But we're returning to Idlewyld, aren't we?"

With a grunt, Hannah thrusts herself forward and stumbles over the toe of her boot. She's forced to put a hand down to the dusty road to break her fall.

"Damn these boots! They're impossibly confining."

He dashes to her side. "They are not the proper size?"

"Yes, of course they're the proper size!"

"Can you rise, madam?"

She cannot, is her estimate. Why not sit? "What are we going to do if nobody ever finds us?" Hannah laughs at him, spinning from all fours onto to her bottom. "Then again, what would we do if somebody *were* to find us? It would be ruination. Oh dear, Sergeant, I'm feeling a little light-headed. So terribly hot. And life is…life is such a puzzle."

His eyes well with feeling. "Water, Mrs. Inglis!" He hoists her to her feet and walks her from the road to a shady glade along the shoulder. Locating her empty wineskin, he then fishes an extra one from his pack and thrusts it into her hands, gently commanding her to drink. He watches closely as she sucks at the lukewarm water.

"Sometimes I act against my better nature," he tells her. "Please, accept my apology."

"We all do, Sergeant. It's civilization that corrupts us, don't you think?"

He looks thoughtful. "I'm quite fond of civilization, madam. I've seen how badly men act without it. Come," he says, smacking the picnic basket. "Let us eat something."

As she sips water, he unpacks the basket. Eva's kitchen staff has made a five-course meal, it appears. There is a full silver table setting for each of them, salt and pepper, serving utensils….

"No wonder it was so heavy," he comments.

"Roast turkey! She's incredible. Naturally, they've included the carving knife."

"What is this?" he asks.

"It was a jelly."

They discover, too, a bowl of potatoes marie and a tiffin filled with tapioca pudding.

"I would sooner have my nuts and cucumbers." The sergeant's trekking staples. Durable and convenient for packing, refreshing and sustaining by nature, as she often heard him say. He pulls out a bottle with a Harrod's label. "Cranberry pickle," he reads.

After the water and a few bites of food, Hannah is already feeling relief. The pain in her feet and ankles has subsided.

"Good," he says, when she reports this. "Very good." He is studying the land survey, moving his compass this way and that against the map.

"Eva's writing a book. *Sexual Selection*, it's called. In many species, apparently, there are striking differences between the males and the females. In peacocks, for instance, only the males develop the colorful tail feathers. And in butterflies—males are brilliant and shiny while the females are mostly drab and brown. It's fascinating. If you want to explain why they are so different, Eva says you have to use this idea of sexual selection."

Partly to see if she is able, Hannah goes on to describe the difference between natural selection and sexual selection. It takes some time for it all to come out as it should. Natural selection refers to adaptations that are preferential for fitness, she tells him. Adaptations created by the struggle to survive. Whereas sexual selection refers to the business of mating, which may or may not be a struggle, may or may not be a choice. She says, "Some animals seem to choose partners based on preferences about certain traits. *Even* if the traits aren't helpful for survival. Like the cumbersome tail of the peacock."

"You are indeed feeling better." It is a warm appraisal, colored by relief.

"So why do they have these preferences?" she asks.

He admits he does not know.

"They are *aesthetic* preferences. That is Mr. Darwin's theory." She is pleased by this punch line, the central role of art in this story of what is. It is surprising, though only in the way of something that one has long been looking for, when it turns out to be right under one's nose.

"I think," he consults his compass, "if you are able, we ought to head northeast from here. It will be a quicker return than the roadway."

"It's such an odd branch of study, biology. Listen to this, Sergeant. A female spoon worm is two hundred times larger than her mate. But this is so that Mrs. Worm may inhale Mr. Worm and he will live inside her body! This is the best vantage point, apparently, for fertilizing her eggs. Eva said to me, 'If Charles and I were spoons worms, he'd be the size of a pea.'" Hannah hiccups loudly. "That man might well be living in her gullet, for all I've seen of him."

The sergeant snaps the last breadstick in two. "Actually, that is all rather frightening."

"I suppose the spoon worms present a case of *natural* selection at work. See, I'm getting the hang of it!" Hannah says.

"Here is an idea, Mrs. Inglis. I will run down the roadway to the estate—it cannot be too far to the laneway—and come back with the horse to collect you. Or of course the Peterboroughs may wish to send their carriage for you."

She imagines him bringing word to Eva. *Mrs. Inglis has overheated and is stranded at the side of the road with the roast turkey.* "Carriage! Pssht." Hannah gets her feet under her, trying to ignore the ache that radiates as soon as she puts weight down. "I don't want them thinking I'm a liability on the first day they let me loose." Nor, come to think of it, is she keen to be left at the roadside. "Please, don't leave me here alone."

He studies her face.

"I'm serious, Sergeant. I can manage."

"You are certain?"

"*I'm* no delicate flower, am I?"

He begins packing away the picnic basket, a strangely determined look on his face. "May I, madam, may I, uh, let you know that my name is Darshan Singh. I would be pleased for you to address me by name rather than my title."

After all, he's not on duty, is he? Nor is he in her employ; they've made that very clear.

"Dar-shan," she tries. "Right, then. I shall call you 'Darshan.' Darshan Singh. And you may call me—"

"Mrs. Inglis," he interrupts her. "I could only ever call you Mrs. Inglis. Or madam."

"God, not madam! I've told you how I feel about that. Haven't I?"

Gently, he helps her on with her satchel, then takes up the rest of her gear himself, as well as the picnic basket. "Well then, Mrs. Inglis. If you are fit to walk, overland is a more direct route."

She follows his sightline into the dense, sun-dappled jungle. Mossy boulders dot a crowded forest floor that rises and falls unevenly.

"And a more scenic route," she says gamely.

TWENTY-ONE

Miss Charlotte is not allowed to touch the brown bottle of chloroform. Charlotte nets the butterflies, all the colors of the rainbow, and it is Malu who kills them.

The insect in this bottle has pale, veiny wings that remind her of the petals of lilies. With tweezers, Malu draws the body from the jar and rests it lightly on a square of towel. Taking up a straight pin, she works it through the brittle abdomen.

"Good butterfly. Good girl." At the nearby corkboard, she presses the pin carefully until it catches in the cork.

In the beginning Malu tended to grip the tweezers too tightly and sliced some of the butterflies in half. More commonly, a wing is ripped. She rubs her bleary eyes with her knuckles before closing the clasp on the case. The quiet of the nursery is pleasing, so she takes her time corking the bottle of poison and boxing the equipment, all the while practicing her request inside her head.

Malu takes the request to Slow Roki, who is loading up sahib's tray for delivery.

Roki listens and says, "Where's the kid?"

With her broken mouth, it sometimes hard to hear the words Roki speaks. Malu concentrates, then answers, "With tutor."

"And you want extra work? You're coconuts." Roki honks like a goose and swings her arm toward the tray on the counter, her bangles chiming theatrically. "Sure, half-breed. Be my guest."

"What are *you* doing?" asks Manang, when Malu walks past him at the rosebushes.

"Taking sahib his tray."

The tray holds a squat jug of water and two empty goblets. She brings it all with care to the door of the little cabin, knocks, and waits. Looking back across the grounds of the estate, she makes out Roki lounging on the balcony, her feet up on the rug she is supposed to be beating out. The sun shines hot into Malu's hair and upon her shoulders. She is doing her best for her mother. Dr. Peterborough will know what to do. He probably has expert medicine right in there, on the other side of this door.

Just as her arms begin to burn from the weight of their load the cabin door swings open. Sahib doctor leans toward her, studying her face through slitted eyes. "Ah," he says. "Wait here." He takes the tray by opposite sides. "Wait here."

A minute later he reappears in the doorway of the cabin. "Fetch my extra pair of spectacles. I'm missing my spectacles."

"Yes, sahib." She darts off toward the great house. Not knowing where he keeps his extra pair of spectacles, and being too proud to ask Roki, it is some time before she locates them and returns to the cabin. He opens the door at once and extends his arm.

But Malu keeps the spectacles to her chest. Her heart pounds. "Tuan sir, I need to ask you a question."

His mouth drops open. "To ask *me* a question?"

"My mother is very ill, tuan. She cannot walk and she…shakes. She is sometimes, um, mad," Malu says, following the English words she has practiced. "Like a demon is waking inside her."

He stares.

"Please can you help her, tuan sir?" Malu pushes on. There is nothing to lose now. "You are a doctor, sir. Can you please check her for what is wrong?"

"Ah, well, I am not practicing here as a medical doctor. I am occupied with my research."

Malu pleads, "But it will not take long for you. And there is so much *benefit* for her. I am sure you do not forget your powers of medicine."

"Benefit?" he says, tilting his head.

Malu is almost certain the word is correct. She has been studying it, and others, from Miss Charlotte's books.

"No. Decidedly not," he says, though something crosses his face that gives Malu hope. He does look interested. "Spectacles," he says, pointing.

Unsure what else to say, Malu hands them over and trudges up the hill to the scullery.

That night, she sits with Manang under a full moon for their evening meal.

"What did you want from tuan?" he asks. He hands her a banana leaf.

"Help for my mother." Like everyone else, Manang knows of Umi's sickness. In the lower town, Manang's family has a stilt house not far from her own.

He scoops a handful of rice onto each of their leaf plates.

"Tuan didn't want to help," she admits. Saying it out loud makes her feel sick. She pokes finger holes into her sticky rice, ignoring Manang's frowny face.

"May be for the best," he says.

"How can that be for the best?" she cries. "Yes, better to waste my time playing hide-and-seek and killing butterflies than to help *amah*. You're so stupid, Manang!"

She chews a mouthful of rice ferociously, watching his face grew stony and his shoulders slump. Other people call Manang unintelligent, witless; he is slow to learn and slow to say his thoughts. So she is only saying the same. But he is also kind, and he works hard. She remembers the way his muscles strain along his backbone as he digs his spade into the earth and each time he lifts the handles of the wheelbarrow. There's no reason it should be easy to get sahib's help.

"Sorry," she mumbles.

Now it seems she will have another chance. After Miss Charlotte went to her tutor, Malu was summoned to the kitchen.

"Mem's orders: starting now, *you* deliver sahib's trays!" Roki honks.

"*Mem's* orders?" Malu is amazed.

"You heard me, half-breed. Not *my* idea!"

Why is Slow Roki is so angry? What's so special about delivering trays?

"Who will kill the butterflies?" Malu wonders.

Cook, puttering nearby, snorts. This time, Malu doesn't wait long before sahib opens the studio door.

"I'm expecting someone shortly," he says. "Bring that inside, please."

"Yes, tuan."

He disappears through the doorway and she follows with the tray. Instinctively she heads for the curtained window, trying to make the most of the weak light.

"Sahib, it is me you were expecting? I was told to—"

"Set it down. There."

A strange smell in the cabin. Like a barbershop and a butcher shop mixed together.

"I understand you are good at keeping secrets," he says. "You mustn't talk to anybody about anything you see or hear in this cabin. Do you understand me?"

"Yes, tuan."

"Here." He hands her a small bottle of what looks like cooking oil. "It's castor oil. Tell your mother to take three teaspoons each morning until the vial is finished."

"Oh, thank you, tuan sir. Thank you!" Malu holds the oil to her chest a moment before twisting it into an inner fold of her sarong.

"I don't have great hopes for it, child. But it can't hurt to try that first."

"Thank you, tuan sir."

"What are your mother's symptoms? What precisely happens to her?"

Breathless, she lists all of Umi's struggles, careful not to forget any details, even though her mother's health has been poor, she explained, for several years. Malu tries to quiet the hum in her mind that threatens to jumble up her spoken English. Dr. Peterborough has selected her to wait on him, and now he is going to help Umi!

As she is speaking, he walks to one of the counters. For there is a high counter, she observes, running all the way around the cabin, like a shelf. Underneath it in some places are cabinets. In the center of the room stands a dining table, at least in shape and size, laid over on one side with soft blankets. She comes to the end of her rambling description of Umi and sees that tuan is nodding.

As he looks over what lies on the counter in front of him, he selects things. Tools? Metal tools that clang when he sets them on a metal tray. Tools whose names she will come to learn and never to forget.

"You speak very good English indeed."

Malu curtsies. Realizing his back is turned she adds, "Thank you, tuan."

"And I'm sure you understand even more. You see, I find that I have need of an assistant." He takes the metal tray to the center table.

"An extra pair of hands. Truthfully, I am told they are not permitted to be alone with me."

"They, sahib?"

"And if it turns out that you could translate, that would be even better."

There is a soft knock at the cabin door.

"For today," he says, "I want you simply to watch what I do."

He opens the door to let in a small very dark woman Malu recognizes from mosque. Seeing Malu, she lowers her chin even more. Dr. Peterborough greets her politely and offers her a glass of water from the tray. He invites her to sit on a stool in the corner that Malu has not noticed. Behind it, a white bed sheet is tacked to the wall.

Afterward, Malu runs up the hill to the house. She darts past Manang, busy laying new tiles.

"You okay?" she hears him call out behind her.

Inside, Cook and Roki fall upon her instantly.

"Where you been?" Roki demands.

Cook snatches the tray. "We didn't see you out there."

Malu secretly runs her fingers over the vial of castor oil, as she has been doing all afternoon. *God is good, God is merciful.*

"The tutor left an hour ago," says Roki.

Malu feels no concern for this. Only tiredness. *God is good, God is merciful.* She is almost out of the kitchen before she thinks to ask, "Where is Miss Charlotte?"

"How should *we* know?"

"*You're* her genduk!"

Chasing butterflies, expects Malu. Outside chasing butterflies.

TWENTY-TWO

Barnaby invited me home with him to read his letters. It was no more than a ten-minute walk from the pub, and he passed that time bad-mouthing his sister-in-law, Celia, whom he believed to have driven his brother to an early grave. The best I could make out was that Barnaby's elder brother, and thereby Celia, had inherited Hannah's letters with the rest of their mother's estate when she passed away in the late 1980s. Surely Barnaby had gotten *some* of what must have been a huge inheritance? I didn't ask how these decisions came to be made.

Arriving, Barnaby fetched the letters directly. They were on loan from Celia; he'd borrowed them, I gathered, in anticipation of showing me. Inside a plastic Marks & Spencer's bag, the letters were tied together with a strip of brown velour. (Celia had recalled they were re-upholstering a couch in that velour at the time Alice Munk's "worldly possessions were dumped upon them.")

"And this is my mother she's talking to me about," Barnaby marveled.

I stood with the bundle in my hands, somehow hesitant to pluck at the soft knot with Barnaby watching. I imagined both he and Celia had read the letters, on separate occasions, and returned them to their original wrapping.

"I'll put the kettle on." He nodded at a sofa behind me. Dutifully, I sank onto it.

There were perhaps two dozen letters, all addressed to Henri Godot ("Dear Monsieur Godot"), written in a sloping script of middling size. Occasionally, generous loops and capitals obscured letters on the lines above and below. But it was all legible, and wonderful, so much more than reading the typeset, justified passages prepared by Coles and his publisher. A distinctness, uniqueness, in the bunching and leaning and inky pools. What minute control of her pen! There were a few mistakes that went unnoticed, and some that she'd noticed and corrected. Other crossings-out and slithery additions were not corrections but rather adaptations after the fact. I could almost feel Hannah's hand moving across the page, her eyes skimming along behind it. She had a tendency to resort to dashes and the word "meanwhile," and she had so much to say—there were so many layers to her ideas about art—that she circled back to a subject again and again, making something fresh from it. All the while, it seemed to me, revealing more about herself than the coconut palm or the horizon line or the need to use tones of red in certain shadows. Did she know how revealing it all was? I grew very conscious—especially in the places where Hannah faltered and flailed around and threw darts at herself and others, or when she wrote from one of those black smothering holes we dig ourselves into—that she never meant for me to see her like this and would not have allowed this intimacy, most likely.

When at last I awoke to my surroundings I noticed a cold cup of liquid on the low table near me and the soft clickety-clacking of fingers on a computer keyboard.

"Professor?"

"Barnaby," he grumbled in response. The clacking ceased after another moment and I heard a chair leg squeak against wood flooring. He entered the lounge, eyebrows raised. "Will they be useful for you, then?"

Useful for what, I thought? What was I going to do with the traces of this woman's life? All I could sense, in that moment, was something like the opposite, a countermotion, was occurring. That Hannah was going to do something with me. That maybe she'd already started.

"They're lovely to read," I said. "She writes such a lot about the art she is creating. It's quite exciting, isn't it, how conscious she is of her process. The experimentation. The struggle."

"Mm."

"And I find her…" I searched for a useful word. "She's more, like, *open* in these letters. They read differently."

Barnaby scratched his chest. "You mean…these are not the same letters? As were published?"

"Oh, no!" I lunged for my briefcase and pulled out the photocopied packet I'd made of Appendix A from *The Late Godot*. "No, they're not."

"Well. I suppose that makes sense, does it?"

I flipped to Coles' last published letter of Hannah's, dated March 11, 1896. Then spot-checked the letters on my lap. "These are slightly later. They're all written later, I believe, but…why are they here?" I asked him, struck with the thought. "How did her letters to Henri Godot end up with your family?"

"Jolly right," he said. "For God's sake, I'd hadn't thought of that."

We looked through each other for a moment or two.

"Shall I order some takeaway?" he said. "There's a nice Thai place I get sometimes."

Barnaby allowed me to lay out the letters on his dining room table, having cleared and stacked the bills, cat treats, newspaper clippings, travel magazines and *The Lepidopturus* article reviews on a nearby credenza. The room smelled of cat, and I soon spotted the culprit perched on a spare dining chair in the corner, squinting at me skeptically. Never the mind the cat's odor; I was conscious of my own. An aggravating fuzz covered my teeth and my armpits stank, quite frankly, ruined from a long day of nervous excitement. I promised myself that as soon as I'd eaten supper I'd leave the poor man alone and head for my hostel.

I skimmed back over the letters with my pen and notebook handy, interested in documenting the enclosures that were mentioned. For in almost all of the letters Hannah referred to "a sketch" or sometimes "a study." I showed Barnaby my list.

"No *Parasol Flower*," he said.

"No *Murdo* or *Jane*, either. But this could be the same still life, potentially. And there are two or three letters in which she mentions working on either a *Naked House Girl* or *Nude House Girl.*"

His eyes flicked away from mine. Good grief, I thought, surprised at what I took to be Barnaby's prudishness. Wait until he heard my idea that the parasol flower was an enormous Georgia O'Keefe-style vagina.

"What size do you think these paintings would have been?" I wondered.

"I suppose they could have been any size," he muttered, poking apart the blinds to peek out at the road. "She could have mailed them in tubes or between boards or some such. They sent all sorts in the post, in those days, it was really quite extraordinary."

"And then the letters could have been attached, physically attached. Rather than the other way around. 'Enclosure' is a misleading word,"

I said. "It could be that the art was the main thing she wanted to ship to Godot, and she was adding notes to personalize the shipments." I had been asking myself this question already, of the letters Coles had reprinted: had Hannah written the letters as a point of context, or explanation, for the art she was sending Godot? Or was their written communication the primary purpose, and the art a happy addendum?

The letters reprinted in *The Late Godot* were quite short and straight-forward, and now I wondered if Coles or somebody before him had excised portions. These later letters were generally longer, a good deal more rambling, and more intensely personal. I pointed out some of the differences to Barnaby; he seemed intrigued by my observations. He sat down to read the letters in my photocopy of Appendix A.

"My impression," I told him, "is of a lonely, embattled person who is…well, joyful. Intensely joyful. Is that a contradiction?"

He looked up, pulling his reading glasses aside. "Possibly. But aren't we all?" I could tell by the guarded look on his face that he was coming to care for Hannah, too.

As we ate, he asked me about patterns in the letters. Had I noticed any? Timing, themes, events? I don't think my responses satisfied him, because after we'd boxed up the leftovers he hunted down a magnifying glass—a great round one, like something Sherlock Holmes would have used—and began inspecting the pages. We spent another hour or so, he and I, simply reading and rereading, studying the documents from opposite sides of his table, swapping out letters and putting them back in place, maintaining their chronological order.

"Things get worse for her," I said, struck by a line I'd just read. "They just grow worse and worse, somehow, no matter what she tries. Is that a pattern?"

"And yet…as you say, *she* grows somehow fuller," he replied. "More human, for lack of a better way to put it. However, *I* am still struck by your original question."

"What was my original question?"

"How on earth these letters to Godot the artist ended up in my family's possession."

My eye fell on the magnifying glass, resting on a corner of the table. "You don't think they're reproductions?"

"And the originals went to Godot," he said. "It was a thought. But, no, I don't think so. Why would anyone transcribe someone else's letters?"

"Well, to keep a copy."

"But doesn't that seem odd? And then of course to transcribe them, this individual would have had to have them in his or her possession for a time, at least. Which sends us back to the original question: why was someone who was not the addressee in possession of so many of her letters?"

"Someone who was not the addressee," I repeated. "Wasn't that someone likely to have been Eva Peterborough? The Peterboroughs are the only connection between Hannah and your family. And, of course, Hannah mentions Idlewyld and Eva throughout these letters."

"Yes," Barnaby said absently. He was mulling something over himself. "So the letters never reached Godot."

I thought of what I'd read, considering this hypothesis. "I suppose not," I agreed. "I mean, that has to be the case if these are the originals. They never reached Godot. It's true, Barnaby, it's absolutely true that she doesn't make reference to receiving anything from him. She keeps asking him to write."

He was skimming letters furiously. "She makes reference to his *lectures*, to things he has told her before she left—"

"To old letters, too," I interjected. "Maybe that explains the change in tone, from the Coles' letters to this group? She's on her own. It's not a true correspondence."

"And, as you say, in increasingly difficult circumstances. Difficult circumstances change people."

We each picked up a letter to peruse.

"But there are, what, twenty-five or twenty-six letters," I said.

"Mmm. Over a roughly nine-month period."

"Why did she keep writing? If Godot wasn't replying, why did Hannah keep writing to him? Barnaby?"

He was rubbing his eyes. "I haven't the foggiest. Hope? I suppose if we had the envelopes we could see whether they were posted or had a 'Return to Sender' or whatnot."

"Good point!"

He stifled a yawn.

"I'm so sorry." I saw that it was nearing ten o'clock. "I shouldn't have taken up so much of your time with this!" The moment I had been mentally preparing for had arrived. I took a breath in preparation. "Look, I can take the letters with me...if you don't mind. I'll photocopy them in the morning and bring the originals back to you."

He made another yawn-filled noise that seemed to signify consent, and he didn't object as I began to stack them carefully. As I gathered up my own items I made sure to mention the second cousin Tommy and ask for his contact details. This may or may not have been *the* Tommy to receive the paintings, but there was no harm in asking the fellow. I added, a little glumly, "I'd be happy to be in touch with Celia directly. Then I wouldn't have to bother you any further."

"No, no," he said quickly. "I—I quite like the bother."

That night I lay in my narrow bed at the hostel pretending to sleep—most of my roommates arrived in the wee hours, loudly and staggeringly drunk—while contemplating the many oddities surrounding Hannah, the Peterboroughs, her letters to Godot, my lunch with Barnaby at the White Horse. Why had he not mentioned the letters in the first place? Was it something to do with this Celia woman? Was there something Barnaby wasn't telling me? Yet he'd been a great help, after all.

I fell asleep with Hannah's letters tucked under my pillow, one forearm raised to protect them. They were so close I could smell the musty-sour scent of the paper.

TWENTY-THREE

Some days, she and Eva play chess. This is Eva's idea. Hannah herself has played only three or four times in her life, and she's uncertain of the rules. She'd rather just talk. Eva has plenty of stories and ideas for the both of them. But that's just it, thinks Hannah. The woman is so intelligent, so knowledgeable, her companion does not offer enough in return. The chess set is magical, though. Quirky little pieces carved clumsily from ebony and ivory. She strokes a rook, whose turret has somehow grown out of the head of an elephant.

"Yes, don't forget that you can castle," says Eva. And after another moment, "Tell me, darling, why did you marry the colonel?"

"Oh my. Do you want the long answer or the short one?"

Eva parts her lips into something resembling a smile. "Both."

Hannah castles, then says, "The short answer is that my father obliged me to do so."

"Really? How terribly old-fashioned."

"Actually, it wasn't about fashion, so much. My mother and father were estranged when I was born. The truth is he never married her. He was already married. And highborn, as Mum would have put it. He had a family. My mother was an innkeeper." Eva's eyes widened, as people's usually did. Hannah added, "Maybe you'll think this odd, but I believe they were deeply suited, my parents, in their own way."

"I don't think it odd at all."

"He doted on her when they were together."

"And how often was that?"

"Several months of the year, I suppose. Off and on, a week here, a week there. A whole month, sometimes. It changed over the years. He stayed at the inn, you see, whenever he was traveling through his constituency. And I suppose his family was in London, though they owned a great home in the area. I-I won't tell you which one. You know I'm not sure how he managed to avoid them so much."

"Men like that are practiced at it," Eva says drily.

"Sometimes he would enthusiastically renounce his situation, de-clare to hell with 'society,' that he'd disappear with us and they'd buy a farm on the Isle of Man, or an olive grove in Spain, or some such fantasy."

"And so she, or rather the two of you, waited for him to make good on his promise?"

"Not really. My mother had no illusions; she was a very practical person. I think she must have considered her situation mostly a beneficial one. She advocated for us, for me in particular, and she knew how to get what she wanted. He provided everything she asked for and more, as far as I knew. And I do think he believed in his love for her, at least when he was with us. He was genuinely caught."

"And he wanted you to attend Julian? He must have seen something special in you." There is an edge to Eva's voice that Hannah remarks upon only later. What rankles her in the moment is the presumption it was Father who wanted her educated, who saw what the academy might open up for her.

"I'm not sure how I learned of the academy," she demurs, "whether he planted the idea with Mum, or whether this was from her own 'research.' She was always talking to somebody, a guest at the inn, someone in the village. She was always scheming." Hannah laughs nervously. "I applied, and I was accepted." As if it were as simple as all that. It was a mountain, she thought to herself; it felt like she had climbed a mountain, one that put her childhood irretrievably out of view. "I remember that afternoon as if it were last week."

They have stopped tending to the chess pieces. Eva looks entranced. So much so, Hannah worries the other woman is somehow inhabiting her own favorite memory: of Father arriving and ducking straight into the kitchen at the inn, where she is kneading dough, and silently and inexplicably shaking her floury hand very formally before embracing her. The smell of his skin and the roughness of the stubble on his neck against her forehead; her mother looking on at them with watery, smiling eyes. Hannah could not recall another time when he had held her like this. Mum must have already known the good news and agreed to let him tell her. For the two of them had been in the process of making the very *tarte tatin* they would eat that night in celebration.

"It probably never occurred to my father that Mum would die before him. He was a fair bit older than her, you see."

"I'm sorry," Eva says with feeling. "I didn't realize. And you, so young."

"Yes, well. I suppose I took it rather hard. Such a stupid phrase, that. How else are you supposed to—?" She blinks to clear her eyes. "But when you are young and away from home already…you don't have the capacity to…weather things."

Eva looks thoughtful. "Ah, so you were in Paris when she passed?"

Hannah nods. Practically the only time in her life she'd not been at her mother's side.

"Did you tell the school what had happened?"

"Oh, yes, of course. Madame Julian was wonderful. The girls—the ones who were not too scared themselves by the news—they were kind to me as well. And I pretended to manage for a time."

"For a time?"

"There was a boy, a student at the college, with whom I became involved."

"Oh, darling."

"I think now that perhaps loving him felt like a way to counteract her death. To counter death itself. Silly, of course." Turning to the chess board, she plunges her knight forward then surveys the result. "You know, I've never talked about any of this. Not even with George."

Eva's eyes seem to glow a tiny bit brighter. "And so what of George? In all of this…?"

"Oh, I suppose George was generous to agree to me. Father could dispense with me before I had a chance to sully his name or show up on his family's doorstep demanding attention. He'd only really wanted my mother, I suddenly saw quite clearly. Not me." She laughs shortly again, feeling uncomfortable with this old line of thinking. "I'm not sure that's a fair assessment. I imagine he wanted me to have some status, some kind of life, but whether that was for my own sake, or his, or hers for that matter, I don't know. And relocating to the end of the earth, well that was a fresh start for all of us, wasn't it?"

"And was it?"

"No."

"No," Eva agrees. "I don't believe in fresh starts." Sliding her bishop down the board, she scoops up Hannah's knight. "The past remains part of us."

"The evolutionary past, you mean?"

"Even more broadly, our choices, our situations. The situations and choices of others. They are sedimentary. Like rock."

"I'm not following, sorry," Hannah says, feeling fatigued.

"Consider it in the restricted case of your art, darling. Or my scientific work. I could not do what I do if Mr. Darwin had not studied and contributed as he did. And he could not have done what he did had he not relied on von Humboldt, who in turn relied on Wildenow. Now, I happened to have studied very little Wildenow, but when I address Mr. Darwin's premises, I am also in a way addressing Mr. Wildenow. His work is a part, a hidden part, if you like, of my own body of work."

"A hidden part. I think I see what you mean. Although nobody has written a book before about the genealogical descent of woman."

Eva bows her head, almost shyly. "No, this is true."

More and more lately, Hannah feels an enthusiasm about Eva's ideas. How cleverly, how solidly they have been built. Eva often spoke quite humbly, but she and Charles had met Mr. Disraeli and so many other famous and learned people, it turned out. In the company of these influential men she had spoken her ideas, had stood behind them as their champion even with so many dissenters, as Eva called the horrible ones—the ones who banged on their desks and pulled on their collars and told her she was a menace, a distraction, a perversion, a "female Napoleon." Eva and Charles had responded to these dissenters in writing, patiently, thoroughly, in such painstaking detail, over and over again. There could be no doubt Eva Peterborough was making a true contribution.

"I do so admire you!"

Eva has devoted herself to the board again. "The middle game is always the trickiest. Too many options."

"Oh. Is it my turn?" Hannah says miserably. She nudges a pawn ahead, then pulls it back. "I feel rather badly, Eva. I'm not a good enough opponent for you." And she has no patience for it today, she should add.

"Charlotte is getting rather good."

"I'm sure."

"Concentrate on moving your queen into play, I would say."

Hannah concentrates for a minute. "And you? Why did you marry Charles? Was that a case of sexual selection?"

They laugh a little too hard at this joke.

"Charles expressed an interest in me as opposed to my family's wealth. In the end, I got quite good at it, you see. I could spot a pretender during the introductions."

"My. That sounds...efficient." Hannah thinks of the carriages rolling in at Fulgham House, the suited men dropping like swatted flies as they climbed the front steps.

"The fact is I'm ugly. And beauty is what all men seek, even if they claim otherwise."

"No!" Hannah objects. "But Charles doesn't..." She stops herself, realizing she may be inadvertently affirming Eva's self-directed insult. She knows nothing about how Charles views his wife.

"Charles is half-blind." Eva moves her bishop close to Hannah's king, clinging to it a final instant. "Checkmate in three moves, darling."

On other days, they talk about Charlotte and the difficulties of mothering, about Kew Gardens, corsets, the morally insane, the Boer conflict. Together they solve the political problems of Kuala Kangsa, honing in on improvements to the Ladies Association of Perak, which they delight in poking fun at. Hannah also tells Eva about the jungle acreage surrounding Idlewyld, its limestone outcroppings and delicate waterfalls. It's an enchanted world, from the tallest towering tree to the tiniest phosphorescent toad.

TWENTY-FOUR

It is toward the end of a long and typically hot afternoon in an area of the forest they call the Giant's Playground when Hannah and Darshan first see them. Here, an enormous yellow *meranti* has fallen, tearing an opening in the forest canopy, and the relatively brighter light in the vicinity causes a jungle riot of corkscrewing vines and a crop of saplings. Several durian trees are making good use of the sun, too, thickening with their spiny fruits. When the "men of the forest" arrive that day, Hannah is painting alongside the fallen trunk: a foreshortened view down its length that geometrizes the grey blades of shelf fungus.

Darshan moves in behind her, touching her lightly on the shoulder even before she sees or hears anything. It is an extended family—he points out three matriarchs, with several young between them. The orangutans swing down from the tops of the surrounding trees, crashing spindly branches and trunks against each other, until they are well-positioned on two of the durians. She and Darshan are perhaps twenty feet from the closest animals. Close enough that when the smallest one peers directly at her, Hannah can make out the curiosity in its brown eyes.

The adults are already busy whacking at the heavy fruits and tugging them from branches. Some of the riper fruits crash to the ground with this movement, thudding like great stones into the peaty floor of the forest. The spiky rind of a durian fruit is practically bulletproof; in Kuala Kangsa, the locals axe them open with machetes or beat on them with mallets and chisels. Will these hairy clowns succeed at splitting them open with their bare hands? Stealthily, Hannah slips out her sketchbook.

To her surprise, the orangutans organize themselves in a production line, the adults calling out with hoots and groans. She and Darshan watch as one of the matriarchs swings into position at the far end of the line, which descends from the trees toward a lichen-dappled boulder. The children dangle in positions along a route that begins at the durian trees, where the remaining adults continue to strip branches.

One by one, they toss the balls from ape to ape along the line. It is a delight to see the children hanging on so effortlessly with their long fingers and toes, catching and hurling the big treasures as if the whole thing were play—and it *is* play to them, no doubt! Hannah strains to see what is happening at the end of the line, where the adult female is receiving the durians. She squares up, aims, and throws each one at the face of the boulder.

"She's trying to break them open." Hannah turns and mouths this news to Darshan. Behind her, he too is frozen, eyes riveted on the furthest orangutan.

Before long, the two adults abandon the closest durian trees, swinging up the line and scooping up children as they go. At first Hannah fears that her comment has caused the animals to move, but they appear to be focused on the durians. Hooting to each other, or perhaps more so to their children, two of the mothers descend fully to the forest floor. It is here that she and Darshan creep around the fallen tree for a better view. The apes are taking up each fruit and smashing it against the edge of the rock with casual emphasis. The impact is enough to crack the woody rinds open—she can hear the durians splintering. Once split, the females toss the orbs above them, where the younger crew are waiting.

Soon, all of the furry redheads are smacking their lips, settled in the branches of the trees. They pry open the durians and scoop out their pulpy flesh with long dark fingers and wildly roaming tongues. Hannah's mouth waters as she eases a little closer to observe the feasting. The adult orangutans now finally appear to take notice of her and Darshan, apparently without concern. *Have they never known humans? Or are the durians too good for them to care?*

The orangutans have certainly known durians. There is slurping, chomping, sucking, licking. Full bellies that are smacked and rubbed. Feet flex. Noses are picked. In the pauses, when their mouths are not busy, the family members hoot at one other and blow sounds with their lips. Hannah is mesmerized, and a little embarrassed, to be spying on these naked persons so intently. One of the youngsters distinguishes himself by stretching out on his belly along a limb of the tree and letting out a loud belch. By the time the last of the rinds has been picked clean and tossed to the ground, the sky is greying. The orangutans seem to awaken suddenly to the fact that night is falling. Giving Hannah and Darshan a last glance, they leave as quickly and noisily as they came, swinging off into the forest.

She and Darshan move immediately toward the aftermath, examining the area below the feast. Rinds and trampled vegetation are evidence of the party. The boulder retains a few smears.

Hannah touches one. "If you hadn't seen it, you wouldn't have believed it, would you?"

"We have seen it, Mrs. Inglis." There is reverence in his voice. "Now we'd best get back to the estate. It's late."

They arrive as the Peterboroughs are sitting down to their evening meal, though it is Hannah alone, of course, who enters the mansion and weaves her way toward the sounds of cutlery chiming on crockery.

"Thank God you're not lost," says Eva in her unflappable manner.

"Oh, no! The sergeant is an excellent navigator." She can't contain her excitement and offers a rushed account of their orangutan encounter.

"Stay for supper," Eva interrupts, "tell us all about it."

Famished, Hannah hesitates. Charlotte is picking at her plate, head down. Next to her, Charles has half-turned toward her, perhaps to appear hospitable, but he looks lost in his own thoughts, or perhaps simply tired. She says, "I'd best get home. George will be waiting for me."

By the time Hannah arrives home, the colonel has made his way upstairs.

"He eat, he eat, not worry," Suria informs her as they make for the dining room. The dark little chamber, lit with a single candelabra, is like a surgeon's waiting room in comparison to the Peterborough's spacious, elegant surroundings. A portion of roasted chicken and vegetables sits at Hannah's spot. The colonel must have had Suria serve him in her absence. To prove a point?

She's not surprised to find the colonel awake. He pats the bed.

On the ride in she contrived an excuse for her lateness. God forgive her, she is good now with excuses.

"Come to bed," he says, voicing the directive this time.

She is about to tell him how hungry she is and remind him of the food waiting for her downstairs. The orangutans. How incredible, when they came swooping through the trees! And the little one who had looked at her, how indescribably…

"Hannah."

She climbs onto the bed. "It's durian season," she remarks. The orangutans hadn't *looked* particularly powerful but they were incredibly strong. To toss durians as if they were oranges. To smash them open, too.

"What of it?" He pulls a face. "You like the taste of durian?"

It's an acquired taste, admittedly. One most Europeans didn't try to acquire. As Hazel once put it, "They smell like the insides of house slippers!"

The colonel runs his hand down her side. "You're losing weight."

"I don't think so."

"Too much walking."

She must be cautious. As far as George is concerned, she is no longer walking. Not in the forest. Why would he say this?

"Skipping meals doesn't help," he adds. "You missed supper."

"Yes, I'm sorry about that. Eva and I—the time escaped us."

"Did you eat supper there?"

"No. I came home."

He is touching her breasts. "And the time just 'escaped' you, did it? What were you two doing? Something so compelling you lost track of hours."

Her plan is to transpose something she did in fact do on another occasion, so as to sound convincing in the details and to be able to answer questions confidently.

"Did you know Mrs. Peterborough is a scientist?" she says, prefacing her story. Stalling.

"*Mrs.* Peterborough?"

"Yes. Thus far, Eva has published her research under a male pseudonym. I won't get into the irony of *that* being a necessity within a community of truth-seekers."

The colonel looks at her strangely. "What are you trying to say?"

She wishes now she'd invented something mundane.

"The point is that Eva is studying birds, for the book she is writing."

Hannah doesn't bother to mention evolutionary theory, natural selection or sexual selection. These things would be of no interest to the colonel. "And she bought two birds from the menagerie in the town market. Birds of paradise, they're called. She's been studying their behaviour. This sounds odd, I know, but Eva wanted to show me their mating dance. It's, well it's a bizarre sort of performance. And it's somewhat unpredictable."

Hostility, it seems to her, is lurking under the colonel's skin as he listens. The recognition of this startles her into silence for a moment.

"We waited ever so long to catch a glimpse of the male dancing. How comical the bird is!" She forces a laugh. "I've never seen the likes of it, George, the way this poor bird darts from side to side. He has a bit of plumage, like bait on a fishing line, dangling in front of his own head." She forces another laugh, then yawns loudly.

"You're saying that Mrs. Peterborough had them hold off on supper for the entire household until this bird did his mating dance for you?"

"Why, yes, I suppose she did."

"And she had you waiting…outside I take it? Absurd." He mutters something about the priorities of the upper classes.

Hannah pushes the heel of one hand into her empty stomach when it growls audibly. "I didn't want to be impolite," she says, for he's about to protest. *Surely you could have told her you have a husband waiting, a household to attend to.* "Let's not argue," she whispers.

Without waiting for the colonel to reply, she leans over and kisses him softly on the cheek. Something occurs to her and she kisses him on the lips, deeply, hungrily. As if she has been waiting all month to be alone with him.

TWENTY-FIVE

The colonel brings his morning coffee into the conservatory. It consoles him that the room is unchanged and unchanging these past months; the same catalogues and newspapers arrayed in their holding pattern, the same half-dead plants in their pots. Not one scrap of sketching paper. Not one whiff of paint, nor stick of charcoal. He chooses one of the lesser-used armchairs, allowing his gaze to wander in case his eyes happen to pick out a hidden detail. It is useful to review matters from different vantage points.

This morning he feels balanced in his limbs—a pleasant, almost drowsy heaviness that radiates from his center to all corners of his world. He is not so stupid as to believe his wife cares for him any differently. Though he recognizes her as being obedient, and this pleases him nearly as much. Perhaps more. If he loves Hannah more deeply than she will ever appreciate, then that is her failing, not his. There is even something noble in this inequity.

A strange shape under the chaise longue. George gets down on his hands and knees. It turns out to be a curled leaf, fallen from a nearby potted tree.

What to make of all this time spent with Eva Peterborough, and Hannah's new friendship with the strange woman? Of all the diversions she could have turned to, she decides to find company out there, where that doctor has the Malay women coming and going. Mind you, he can understand Hannah holding a bit of a grudge against her old circle of friends. He tried to explain this tactfully to Lucy when she appeared at the door the other day.

"How is Hannah?" Lucy asked with some gravity, after they'd exchanged pleasantries.

"Very well," he answered, hinting that she was causing no further concern.

At this, Lucy looked disbelieving. She fluttered her eyelashes. "She's very well? I have to tell you something, George. Something odd has happened, and it's why I've come over, to be honest."

"Oh?" He exhales slowly. Once Lucy got hold of you, it was difficult to extricate yourself.

"Hannah still won't return my calls."

"I reckon she's been, well, licking her wounds, as it were."

"Wounds?"

He feels his colour slowly rising. God give him the patience for Lucy flaming Finch after a hot day's work. She must have seen him arriving home and beetled over. He says, "It was something for her to live through, wasn't it? That night of the festival. Us ganging up on her."

"Goodness. George, it was all for *her* benefit." Lucy looks past him into the house. In the kitchen, Suria is singing, if you can call it that. "Is Hannah in now?"

If Hannah were in, would *he* have come to the door? "She's out."

"At this time of day?"

It's just gone half past four, hardly the witching hour, though the sky has blackened like night in preparation for its daily thunderstorm. George steps through the mesh outer door, closing it behind him and causing Lucy to back up further on the veranda. "What is this *odd* event you mentioned?"

"Ah. Last week I bumped into Hannah in the village. Fortunately, for as I say, she's not returning my calls. I invited her to join us for a game of bridge this Friday past."

"Did you? Nice of you." He doesn't recall anything special about the Friday past.

"She agreed to come. Hazel is my witness. I thought at first I must have been losing my mind! But Hazel is my witness: Hannah quite clearly agreed to come at half past two. 'I'd love to, Lucy,' she said to me. Now, I don't know if she was in a hurry—she seemed to be heading to the east side, perhaps to the market? That was all she said, really, was 'I'd love to, Lucy,' and she was off again."

George frowns at the mention of the market. "She sometimes shops at the market rather than sending our girl."

"Oh, I've gathered that. The *odd* thing is that she never showed up on Friday to play bridge. Which, as you can imagine, when one is arranging numbers it's quite inconvenient to have players go missing. We had to fetch Anicka Gnudsen as a stand-in, and nobody wants that, George."

He tries again to remember anything at all about the Friday past. There is a crack of thunder, an opening gambit. Shaking his head, he says, "I...I'm sorry, Lucy."

"Oh, you don't be sorry!" she flutes. "It's not your fault, George. I just thought you might have had a bad turn with your stomach. Or, I thought, maybe she became ill. She's so slim, it's a wonder—"

"No, not that I recall, no." Though his gut was feeling worse by the minute. He looked out at the road—that cheeky little gibbon was strolling by, chittering to himself—and told Lucy that he'd speak with Hannah.

George redirects his thoughts to the moment when he's first pushing himself inside her. It gives a precise sensation, and an echo of the pleasure that shouted from him. He tours the conservatory one last time and sets his empty mug down on a hall table, smirking to himself. Hannah could sleep for hours yet. He might as well go in to the office.

"What is he up to, this doctor?" George will simply ask point blank. As it concerns his wife, he will simply ask Finch for the truth.

At the office, George bides his time, smoking. It's better if Finch comes to him, as he will, the gregarious creature. Finch soon appears in the doorway. "Hallo, Pinky. *You're* here early today!"

"Am I? Not really."

The Resident enters the room and takes a seat. "And you look... chipper."

"I slept well," George mumbles.

"Yes, you do look chipper." Finch twirls a moustache, regarding him. "Ah! Another tiger in the bag, is it? I saw them hauling it up your lane. Well done, I say! Looked like a cracking specimen."

"Yes," he agrees. A smaller cat, with a lighter hide. A female. This time the head was better preserved. The two talk about work matters for some time before Finch gets to his feet. "Uh, before you go?" George comes around the desk to shut his office door. It's still early enough they won't swelter without the air flow. "I...don't know whether to be concerned about this..."

"Spit it out, Pinky. Not worth bottling anything up."

"It has to do with the Peterboroughs."

Finch's face falls. "Does it now?"

"It seems Hannah has been seeing rather a lot of Mrs. Peterborough. Out at their estate."

"And?"

"Well, I don't know." He lowers his voice even more. "We've arranged for those women to go there. The Malays. For...for whatever purpose..."

"Hannah is not party to that," Finch says. It sounds like a warning.

"Of course not. That's why I'm asking. I don't want her to be inadvertently involved in...whatever it is that...look, do I have cause for concern here, James?"

Finch has turned to the wall, arms crossed over his belly. His chin triples as his head falls forward. "God, I hope not. What is she doing out there?"

"She seems to have become fast friends with Mrs. Peterborough. Says she's a 'fascinating woman.'" They exchange glances. "I stopped Hannah from painting, James. We all did."

He points a finger. "No, we didn't all do that."

"I'm saying, well, she's been left with a good deal of time on her hands. And no desire to be friendly to the women who've...intervened."

"Hmm." Finch rubs his chin. "What a cock-up. Wouldn't Hannah be nice all plumped up with a babe, eh, Pinky? She would make a wonderful mother."

George doubts this is true. But it's no reason not to want her pregnant. A family may not be far off now, he tells Finch with conviction. The feeling memory comes again—of his cock pushing, pushing, prying. Into Finch's silly grin, he says, "*Until then*, Hannah won't appreciate any further restrictions. But there's no need for that, yes? There's nothing to worry about with her visiting this Idlewyld place?"

Finch frowns. "Can she not socialize with this 'fascinating woman' at your house?"

"I rather think they're avoiding the rest of the civilization." George sighs. "But, yes, point taken."

"That would be my advice, then, Pinky. Keep her away from the estate as much as possible."

"Right."

"And get her pregnant."

Twenty-Six

Sergeant Singh rides out to Idlewyld on the lone horse owned by the Kuala Kangsa police squad.

"What if there's an emergency?" she teases him one afternoon as they head out from the stables. "What if Merrylegs is needed to chase down a criminal?"

He waggles a finger. "Not so very funny. I have been lying awake concerning this eventuality."

"Oh." She bites her lip. "And?"

"I am taking my chances." He looks so disturbed that Hannah offers an apology. She wonders whether any of the other policemen know where the russet mare disappears to on a regular basis.

Hannah is lying awake nights, too, thoughts hopping around her head like rabbits. Though she now lets the colonel win her over in bed on most occasions, she avoids conversation with him. Suppers, practically speaking the only occasions they are forced together, feel long and dismal. Too much time spent feigning interest in his affairs whilst trying to avoid accidentally exposing her own. And all of it seems to point at how poor a wife she is. How poor a person. And yet they are all unreal, the events of Ridge Road, as if they are happening outside of life, outside of the time she is truly alive, painting and moving through the wilds.

"Are you worried your colleagues will discover where you're going?" she asks him as they enter the forest.

"They know I am trekking with you."

"They do?"

"Certainly. What they don't know is that your husband has now forbidden it."

She laughs. George's decree is exactly the sort of open secret that travels like wildfire through one community and not a hair beyond.

"Besides, I am an odd duck to them, Mrs. Inglis. I am already teased mercilessly."

"What for? Not for spending time with me, I hope."

He adjusts his turban, smiling mysteriously, and they travel in silence

152

for some time. *I must ask myself, what am I doing this for? Who am I?* What answers did he supply to the questions he'd posed to himself, that first day in the mountains?

In the forest behind the estate they have worn a rough path that extends perhaps a hundred feet before it dissipates. Darshan stops where the brush thickens, pulling his compass from his pocket.

"Would you sit for me today?" she asks.

"Me?"

"Yes, you."

"I don't…really sit. Though I am honored."

"You don't sit?" She plants her fists on her hips. "You could stand, then. I'm asking, would you let me paint your portrait?"

Darshan's eyes flit in their sockets. "Potentially, Mrs. Inglis. Potentially."

"Let's look first for a parasol flower. A good hike first, and instead of a botanical specimen…"

"A human specimen."

"Please? You are willing?"

"Am I able to read while you…?"

"Oh yes. You needn't be perfectly still. Not the whole time."

As they wind their way between the mossy outcroppings of limestone and sun-dappled ferns, Hannah's cares slip from her mind, as they always do. It's as if the ferns reach out and take them from her, holding them aloft to be dissolved in the fragrant air of the forest. There is no other time or place on earth she'd rather be.

Ah, but let them find a parasol flower.

Eventually they make camp near a cannonball tree at the edge of a whispery grove of bamboo. Darshan keeps his word. She positions him, standing, in front of the cannonball tree.

"Am I not rather upstaged here?" he says, twisting around to look.

True to their name, the fruits are as large and hard as ammunition. They dangle from a series of liana-like branches.

"You, Sergeant? Not at all," she assures him. "Besides, my intention is to keep all of that firmly in the background."

"They are very good for healing burns, by the way. The juice of the cannonball fruits."

He stands patiently for some time, occasionally breaking the posture to swat at an insect or stretch. Then he fetches his notebook from the inside of his jacket and begins leafing through the pages.

"What are you reading?"

"Ah." He shuffles his feet and says, "I can attempt a translation."

"It's not your own notes, then?"

"Guru Nanek Dev," he replies. "I intersperse."

Hannah paints through the long silence that follows, blocking out the background of the work, and is almost surprised when he begins speaking again.

> This Earth is flower-dyed
> With diverse species of life,
> This Earth teems with their
> Infinitude;
> As we do here so shall we be judged,
> The court of God separates
> Chaff from wheat, there
> Shall be measured unto us
> Our raw and ripe;
> Each man shall stand alone;
> His own deeds shall hold on
> After the life of this Earth.

"Well. That's beautiful," she says. And a little intimidating, she thinks to herself, just like the sergeant. "'His own deeds shall hold on after the life of this Earth.' I do like that. Very much."

"'Hold on.' 'Persist.' 'Bloom.' I am not sure of the best word, Mrs. Inglis. It carries all of these meanings."

"Not much longer now," she tells him. "I can work up the rest of it indoors."

He nods, replacing his notebook with his pipe, which he lights and puffs on for a time. "People may see this painting, Mrs. Inglis?"

"Yes, they may."

"What about Madam Peterborough?" he asks shortly after.

"What about her?"

"You are not concerned that she will say something about us to... somebody?"

"Of course not." She concentrates for a moment on bronzing the shade of orange she is using. "Besides, what is there to say?"

"You have good reasons to trust her, I imagine." Unsheathing his machete, he begins swinging it lightly beside him.

"Eva *wants* me to keep painting. You don't hear our conversations. She's what people might call a progressive woman. Which is quite difficult to describe. She believes in the equality of the sexes. That women should be allowed to freely pursue their own goals."

"She appears to believe in marriage."

"As an adaptationary device. She's developed a theory about the evolutionary benefit of longstanding bonds."

He swings the blade, a light sidearm motion, in the way boys skip stones. "Well, then. That is reassuring."

"I think you'd like her, Darshan. She's a brilliant woman. And she would be astounded by your knowledge of the natural world."

"Mrs. Inglis, it is entirely inappropriate for her to be astounded by me. Not to mention the three of us to be chitchatting."

"Well." Hannah wipes her brush. "She might be astounded just the same."

They pack up and she follows him back through the grove and across the stream they have forded, going down on hands and knees over the fallen java olive that serves as their bridge. By the time she touches solid ground again, her blood is pumping and an idea has worked its way into her mouth. "Let's take Eva to the waterfall. The one with the seven stages. We could make it a nice outing for the day."

He stops and turns to face her as she is brushing the worst of the grime from the front of her. "Why?"

"This is her property, after all. Let's show her how beautiful it is!" Darshan looks uneasy at the prospect. "What?" she demands. "Why not?"

As they hike back toward the estate, she considers the sergeant's discomfort. Maybe he has put his finger on something, in all these queries about madam. There is a distance, an awkwardness, that exists between her and Eva that isn't dissipating, no matter how many games of chess or pots of tea. Once she sees this fact, there is no way to squelch it out of her consciousness. What if she got the lady out of her stuffy mansion? Would that change things?

"I *do* trust Eva," she tells him as the coffee orchards come into sight. "But you're right, there *is* something. Something not quite...right."

TWENTY-SEVEN

Malays and Chinese and mixed blood natives, all of them women, come and go on the slender pathway worn into the meadow. They say nothing to Malu as she greets them, serves them water, holds open their sarongs, translates their questions. It seems, very nearly, that they don't see her. By now, the whole of the lower town must know she is helping the doctor sahib. And the whole of the lower town will call her a traitor?

Manang knows, too, of course, but how much? As he weeds and plants and prunes, he watches for her coming and going from the cabin. One afternoon, he drives his pitchfork into a flowerbed and beckons to her. Malu nods toward the studio door and lifts her tray, to explain she cannot stop to speak. But he waves again. So she walks over, balancing a large bowl of figs and a jar of antiseptic.

"New job," he says, jerking his head toward the cabin.

"Yes."

"I hear things," he says.

She shrugs, looking away from him.

"What does he do in there? Sahib?"

Malu purses her lips and shakes her head. Even if she wanted to, there is no way she can talk out loud to Manang, of all people, about the tools sahib uses and the ways his hands push and poke at the women's bodies. The questions he asks. The drawings he makes while they wait with their arms and legs stretched apart.

He says, "The women are paid, yes?"

Though she did not know this, it's not surprising. Nobody would come to that cabin otherwise.

"My sister Marayam," he continues. "We owe money to the sultan."

Malu shakes her head. "Tell her no."

"She wants—"

"Tell her no," Malu repeats. "It's not enough money."

A day comes that is different than all the others, a day with the power to change other days. For the better or for the worse, she is afterward unsure.

156

"Malu, we'll spend the whole day in the jungle! Trekking and picnicking and swimming!" Miss Charlotte has run into the servant's quarters with her news.

"Who?" asks Malu, leading her back down the corridor.

"Me and you, silly! And Mama and...uh..."

Malu sucks in her breath.

"...Mrs. Inglis and her sergeant."

"Not your papa?" Malu says quietly.

Charlotte's smile falls. "No. But it'll still be smashing. I'm *sure* they'll pack us cakes. And we're going to go swimming! And I can bring my butterfly net."

She smiles at the girl. It does sound good. And she likes Mrs. Inglis, who always speaks to her in a kind way. As for the police officer, she's not sure what to think. All morning he's chopped out the rough patches for them, helped them over fallen trees, told explorer stories. For fun, he shows her and the Miss into a little cave that feels as cold as an icebox when you shimmy into it. Auntie Nattie taught Malu never to trust police officers. Well, it wouldn't be the first thing Nattie was wrong about.

After hours of clambering uphill—with mem complaining every step of the way—they arrive at the waterfall. Malu is familiar with the falls closer to town, which are full and broad and foamy. This one is different. It is so high. Higher than any building she's ever seen. Up at the top the water splits itself over a jagged rock and hangs in sheets that float like silks and sound like thunder. A plume of mist rises toward the treetops. For a while, all she can do is stare.

"It's the limestone." Mrs. Inglis' voice reaches her. "What an incredible color."

Following Charlotte, Malu jumps from rock to rock below the falls where the river pools in ledges. Directly under the falls is the deepest and widest pool, its milky surface rolling and shivering like a drum. Malu and Charlotte stand at the lip of the main pool to watch the water plunging. Endlessly.

"Mrs. Inglis!" shouts Miss in surprise. "Are you going to *dive?*"

The lady is standing on the opposite bank. She is wearing a bathing costume that leaves her arms and legs bare but falls in lumpy folds over her middle.

"I don't know how to dive," she calls back to them. She grins and leaps, swinging her arms high. Her legs cycle the air for a moment before she crashes.

Charlotte is squealing with delight. The police sergeant, grinning. They all watch her surface, sputtering and laughing.

"It's magnificent," says Mrs. Inglis. She stands up, then lies back, kicking, then stops kicking. With a twist, she is on her stomach, pushing the water apart with her arms. Her wilted hair and her droopy grey costume make her look like a muskrat.

Miss Charlotte jerks at Malu's hand, tugging her away from the falling water to one of the calmer eddies farther from the falls. She wants help searching for caddis flies under the river rocks. The move brings them closer to the adults. Mrs. Inglis soon comes out of the water.

"You're not coming in at all?" she asks.

"Thank you, but I shall stretch out here," mem answers.

A large tartan blanket has been spread over the ground for the women. Malu steals glances as Mrs. Inglis towels off and the memsahib digs in the picnic basket. Sergeant Singh is nowhere to be seen.

"How is Charles managing with his research?" Mrs. Inglis asks. "Has he been able to get on in this heat?"

"I've hardly seen him he's so productive."

"Really?"

The women lower their voices. With Charlotte singing nearby, Malu strains to hear what they are saying.

"...worked out perfectly."

"Oh? I'm surprised she's able to help him."

"...extra pair of hands. And her English is quite good so she can translate."

"Translate?" Mrs. Inglis leans toward the basket and pulls out a mango. "I thought you said Charles was studying insects."

The memsahib looks over and her eyes strike Malu's. Turning away, Malu plunges her hand into the water and pulls a stone free from the creek bed. Clinging on the underside are three caddis flies inside their bubble homes.

The sergeant pushes his way through the milky water of the lagoon, bypassing Malu. His thick arms and shoulders are bare. His hair falls long behind his head because he has removed his turban.

"Where's he going?" asks Charlotte.

They watch him hoist himself up out of the pool, climb the ledge to the next.

"He's going toward the falls," the girl says, answering her own question.

The sound of crashing water, which had faded in Malu's ears, is thunderous.

Suddenly Malu's feet are hopping along the shoreline, rock to rock to rock, winding her toward the sergeant. Behind her she can hear Miss set out, calling as she slips and sloshes her way upstream. Ahead, Sergeant Singh is swimming and wading through the rushing water. He seems to know exactly where he is going. Malu wills him to look back. The water is roaring now, the shoreline narrow.

When Miss Charlotte slips and comes up coughing, Malu backtracks and hauls her upright out of the water. "Okay, Miss?"

"I'm coming, too!"

Below, both ladies are standing on the blanket; the mem is scowling and talking in an excited way to Mrs. Inglis, who touches her shoulder and points at Malu.

"Wait!" Malu shouts at Sergeant Singh. She and Charlotte struggle to close the distance between them until he slows, looking around him. "Wait! Please!"

"We want to go too!" Miss shouts.

Sergeant Singh watches them approach, then reaches to haul Malu up onto the ledge where he is standing. The three of them talk at once, uselessly, until he shouts, "Stop! If you are coming with me, then *I* am in charge of this…expedition." He cracks a smile.

Far off through the trees, on their blanket by the lagoon, the memsahibs look like miniature, perturbed versions of themselves.

"First rule," the sergeant says, gathering them closer, "do not look backward."

"Malu, are you frightened?" Miss Charlotte squeals.

"Second rule: do what I do, and *only* what I do."

Why didn't they think to ask him what that was going to be? All at once they are clambering after the sergeant, using the great tumble of rocks near the cliff as a ladder. The air spits at them, and Malu's ears, her whole body, fill with the thunderous movement of the crashing river. When they stop climbing, she struggles to see past the sergeant's wide back. Where exactly are they going? When Miss Charlotte's cold hand slips into hers, Malu squeezes back. Surely they're not going under the falls!

"Here, ya?" the sergeant shouts, barely audible. He points where they must go. "Take a big step—through there. Watch."

There is an outcropping he steps onto, then steps again beyond, disappearing around a curtain of water. Malu's breath catches until Sergeant Singh reappears, grinning at them. He extends his hand, beckoning them onward.

Miss Charlotte picks her feet up and down and asks a hundred useless questions. *Go, just go!* Malu wants to shout. Now that they are here, she feels nothing more than the need to reach the rushing water and have it pour over her. If she slips and falls, praise Allah, the water will still pour over her. At last Miss moves shakily forward, reaching for the sergeant's outstretched arm. When it is her turn, Malu steps to the outcropping without any help and joins them in the moving tunnel. Spray floats over them; the sound of the water drowns everything in one mammoth hush. They stand side by side like this for the length of a morning prayer.

Then Malu holds out her hand, palm up, and the river crashes it down. Laughing, she wipes water from her eyes. It was "irresistible," she tells Miss later. A new word this week.

Sergeant Singh leads them carefully along the ledge, testing the footholds. As the ledge widens, Malu is able to come around Charlotte and drop herself down onto a jutting stone to offer the girl help. For the Miss can barely put one foot after the other, now, on her own. She seems tamed, as if the falls have washed away her boldness. Slowly, slowly, the three of them descend until they reach the foot of the falls on its opposite side and the roaring is replaced by ordinary jungle sounds. Further below, mem is still glued to their progress, having crept closer along the shore. She beckons vigorously.

"I will take her back," Sergeant Singh says to Malu over Miss's head. He points to an offshoot of the falls, where water splashes from a low overhang into a shallow pool. "This is a nice place to visit. But go slowly, it can be slippery."

Malu follows the sergeant's suggestion, glancing back to see him hoist Miss like a sack of flour over his strong shoulders to carry her down the last stage to the bottom. At the little pool she shimmies toward the falling water. A cool jet strikes her in the back and makes her gasp. Her feet push against the rock, with its skim of slime, until she finds her balance, and all the while the water keeps coming, stroking her hair from the back of her neck and tugging at her sarong. Enfolded by the contours of the rock and the fragrant branches of an agarwood tree, she has moved out of everyone's sight. For a moment the fact panics her; her legs twitch. But she keeps her feet planted, holds herself until the stillness supports her. Slowly, the inside parts of her give way and her thoughts ooze out of her skin and float away downstream, one by one, until there are none left at all.

TWENTY-EIGHT

As the little party winds its way down the mountain slope and back to the estate, rumbles of thunder chase it. As before, Sergeant Singh is clearing and leading, followed closely by Charlotte and the genduk, while she and Eva bring up the rear.

Eva is much quieter on the way home. No complaints about blisters, disease-carrying insects or the uneven terrain. The river—which, for Hannah, was a heavenly escape and refreshment—could have done nothing for Eva, who put no more than a toe in the lagoon. And then there was Charlotte's adventure. The girl emerged from the falls no worse for wear, really. After she'd eaten and regained some of her strength, they couldn't shut her up about it. Though Eva certainly tried. She seemed somehow embarrassed by her daughter; the poor genduk serenely bore the brunt of her mistress's disapproval.

"Does it have a string, your hat?" says Hannah.

Eva stops and turns, breathing hard. "What?"

"I only thought…if your hat had a string, you might take it off and let it fall behind you on your back. Easier to see."

Eva feels for the string that is coming up under the flesh on her chin, making it bulge unattractively. She looks around her, then at Hannah, who is hatless. "You're not worried that insects will fly into your hair?"

"Not really."

"Or that something might drop onto you?" Eva looks up.

Hannah looks up too. "Drop onto me? No, I can't say I am."

"Bird feces. A worm. A snake."

"You must do what's most comfortable for you, Eva."

"You're rather more courageous than I gave you credit for, darling. And I am entirely unfit for this sort of thing. To my great annoyance." Eva heaves an exasperated breath.

"Hardly! We've made wonderful progress today. I've simply had more practice than you stomping around the wilderness, haven't I?"

Looking deflated, Eva turns back to the makeshift path, her hat still in place. "We've fallen so far behind them!"

"Don't worry, he'll stop and wait for us." They strike out again and accomplish another few yards before Hannah says, "You know, I'm very grateful you've come at all." Eva grunts in a congenial way. "I thought you might like to experience what I've been working from."

I thought you might love the forest as I do. I wanted you to feel how inspiring it all is. It's become obvious that love and inspiration are not part of Eva's experience that day.

"Of course," adds Hannah, "I'd also like to show you the paintings themselves."

"Yes." Eva turns. The red of her face makes her green eyes glow even cooler. "Excellent idea. And that would have been easier, wouldn't it?"

"Well, yes," is all she can think to reply.

"I must admit I've been curious."

"Have you?"

"About your art."

"Oh, yes. I haven't forgotten that I will be doing something special for you and Charles."

Another boom of thunder, almost directly above this time. Ahead in the shivering green, Darshan halts with the two girls. He is looking at her expectantly while the children fidget in place. Hannah raises her hands as if to say, *What else can I do? She doesn't move any faster.*

"What does he want?" snaps Eva.

Darshan bends toward Charlotte, telling her something. A rainstorm doesn't pose them any real threat, here where they are well protected by the canopy of trees. It's just not good for the nerves.

"He's telling them not to worry, they can't be harmed by a sound." Hannah circles back, saying, "I'm not sure if you've seen anything out here that you *particularly* like, Eva. Any subjects, I mean, which would make a desirable painting for you and Charles. The orchids we saw on the way out? Orchids can be quite amazing. Even the ubiquitous ferns are such expressive creatures."

Eva coughs and waves her arms, dismissing the idea that she would care about ferns over orchids or orchids over ferns. Is it all the same to her? Wild. Reproducing. Adapting. Does she imagine that the only refinements, the only points of interest, come from the ideas that are applied to life? If Hannah's time out of doors has taught her anything, it's that nature is full of peculiarities and personalities and singular stories. A moth-covered rock, a phrase of birdsong, a flying frog—at any moment, life forces you to change what you think is possible.

"I haven't painted it yet," Hannah ventures, "but…there is one flower in particular…"

She looks ahead to the sergeant's bobbing turban. Surely Darshan won't mind if Eva knows about their quest. After all, Eva is making the whole thing possible. "I believe this one would be interesting for you as a piece of art but also as a, well, a marvel of nature. This flower has never been recorded in *The Almanac*. Actually, that is the case for several of the botanical specimens we've encountered. But *this* one…. It's called a parasol flower. Local legend says that parasol flowers grow in this area. Unfortunately, it's proving quite difficult to find one in bloom."

Eva looks intrigued. "Local legend? My goodness, Hannah."

"The sergeant has told me all about it."

"So you haven't actually seen one?"

"They bloom only every seven years, for a fortnight or so. The blossom is meant to be extraordinary." Hannah holds her hands out wide in front of her. "The size of a lady's parasol, you see—a wonderful whorl of petals the color of…of daybreak. And the flower smells of vanilla and fresh cream, with a hint of citrus. Wouldn't that be glorious if we could find one? It would make an absolutely unique painting."

"The size of a parasol?" Eva stops and arches her back, letting her head loll and her eyes close for a moment or two. "Why, I've never heard of such a thing. Not even in Wallace's jungle memoirs, and he traveled extensively on the peninsula."

Hannah's tongue prickles. "I suppose I can't promise we'll find one. It's just that I did want you have to something absolutely special."

"Oh, darling. I'm moved. Truly." Eva looks exhausted. Her face is flushed, her skirts dirty. And yet she somehow maintains her preferred expression—something between neutral and mildly pleased, that tells you that you are *under consideration*. She says, "You are so entirely and beautifully sincere."

TWENTY-NINE

Even before I knocked, I knew Barnaby had been stewing about something. I saw him in an upstairs window, pacing. His hair was in a state, whipped, as if he'd been tossing and turning all night. I myself had had a restless few hours at the hostel. I realized I'd been overlooking an important factor when it came to the letters Barnaby had procured. Namely: where were the enclosures? Whether or not the paintings matched up with any on the family's "official" list, they had to have gone somewhere, and it wasn't to Godot. Who had taken them?

"Good morning, Professor Munk." I greeted him with some caution. He was still in his pajamas. Nice ones, mind you. A silver chain with a blue evil eye charm lay around his tanned neck.

"You've gone formal on me again," he grumbled as he propped open the door.

Nervously, I regaled him with my adventures with the photocopier at the Boots store near the hostel, though I could see he was too preoccupied to enter into my technological frustrations. I set down the bundle of letters, in its original plastic bag, on the kitchen table.

"I've had a terrible night, Nancy. Terrible night."

I waited for him to elaborate. Instead, he offered to make us coffee. I confessed I was desperate for one. I'd had no chance to seek out a coffee shop that morning. To my surprise and delight, there was a European espresso machine in his kitchen. "Celia and I spoke," Barnaby told me as he went about the preparations for our drinks. "Please, have a seat."

I sat. "And...Is that why you had a bad sleep?"

"No. Celia and I spoke this morning. About an hour ago." He knocked used grinds from the portafilter and turned toward me, his chest sagging visibly. "I've been keeping things from you, Nancy. Immorally. Absurdly. I detest deceit of any kind and what I told Celia is that I won't be engaging in it any longer." He turned back to his machine to fiddle with it some more.

I chewed on this for a minute then said, "Was it Celia, then, who asked you not to tell me…whatever it is you're not telling me?"

"Cappuccino okay?"

A cappuccino, I told him, would be amazing. When at last he'd finished, he came to the table with two frothy cups and a plate of cherry and custard pastries. I reckoned he didn't eat like this every morning. Perhaps he'd nipped out to a bakery after he'd told off Celia.

"Professor Munk," I said, "I want you know that I don't feel *entitled* to know what happened to Hannah Inglis' paintings. If there's some sort of private family matter that you or your sister-in-law don't want me to know about, that's fine. Totally okay."

"Really?" he replied, looking me over. He could sense that I'd overreached myself with my little speech. It was true, I was dying to hear what he'd been hiding.

"Celia was concerned you were some sort of American journalist. 'Citizen journalist.'"

"What?"

He bit into a pastry, chewed, and swallowed. "Hear me out for a minute. She was concerned you were rooting around at Fulgham House, investigating the scandal of the Peterboroughs, and were going to publish some sort of something that would discredit our family. It's not even her family, technically. She married into it. But," Barnaby sighed, "she's a strong defender of family heritage, Celia is. Family values. And she's an even bigger believer in prestige."

Bizarre, I thought. "I'm not a journalist," I told him. "I'm doing my PhD."

"Ah. But not on Hannah Inglis and pioneering women artists." Barnaby arched his eyebrows. "Just because I'm seventy-six doesn't mean I don't Google. You can find out anything online these days."

"Not anything," I snapped. "Believe me, I'm not interested in Eva or Charles Peterborough, however much you and your sister may think otherwise."

He hung his head. "Yes, I know this now."

"I really couldn't care less about anything your ancestors did or didn't do!"

"Which is why I told Celia that I'd met you and I believed you were genuinely interested in Hannah Inglis' art."

"Yes!"

He looked at me over his raised cup. "You really don't have a clue, do you?"

"About what?"

"Some years ago there was a fellow who approached Celia and Teddy. Well, through Fulgham House. This was before Miranda's time. Somebody, some tabloid press, had given the young man a mandate to come up with dirt on any of the old families in the county. He'd got hold of the notebooks and the writing of Charles Peterborough and various materials that were part of the Fulgham archives at the time. Who knows, he might even have spotted them on a visit to the estate. As far as the racial science part of it, that was published scholarship of the day. Public knowledge. But, as you know, nobody reads journal articles from 1880. Anyway, there were also family photographs, letters, notes, that this fellow dug up. Charlotte was rather a messed-up woman, and she'd kept diaries full of bizarre stories.

"Ultimately, this hack journalist published a series of articles. David Maikin, his name was. He insinuated that Charles was a pedophile and a sex offender. That Eva was a frustrated lesbian. She had 'covered' for him." Barnaby laughed shortly. "As if they were some sort of dynamic evil duo."

"You're kidding," I said. This was all getting to be a bit much to take.

"I don't think pedophilia even existed in 1900," said Barnaby.

"Well, I mean…the ancient Greeks, weren't they known for…" I fumbled, irritated. I was trying to work out how any of this concerned Hannah, if it did at all. I asked, "Did this guy's story involve Hannah Inglis?"

Barnaby gave me a meaningful look. "Obliquely."

"Oh. Eva's lover?" I guessed.

He exhaled heavily. "Something like that. I can't remember if he claimed it was requited."

"But there is no existing correspondence between the women. Is there, Barnaby?" I leaned forward.

"No! No. Just Hannah's letters to Godot. Eva wrote letters home to her brother, her publisher, colleagues. Ordinary letters, all of them, and none of them mentioning Hannah. Of course, Eva kept notes for research and chapters drafts and such. There was Charlotte's diary at the time, full of childish speculations. I suppose Maikin waded through all of this. Probably felt that he'd earned himself a bit of intrigue. You see, *he'd* argue," went on Barnaby, "Hannah and Eva had no need to send each other letters if they were in each other's pockets. If they saw each other every second day."

I scoured my memory bank to think of anything in Hannah's letters that suggested a romantic or sexual relationship with Eva, or then again some sort of child sex ring in operation in Kuala Kangsa. I would just have to read these Maikin articles. As soon as possible.

As if hearing my thoughts, Barnaby said, "It was interesting, reading over Hannah's letters again. I can see some of the elements Maikin was drawing from. None of his conclusions, mind."

"So you think he's just wrong?"

He dipped a finger in the froth remaining at the bottom of his cup. "The whole thing was something of a witch hunt. It was a strange time, Nancy." He paused to reflect. "Six years ago now or so. The Peterboroughs were not the only old guard to be hacked to pieces. Left, right, and center there were upstanding people—telly presenters, politicians, children's authors, venerable cultural icons—all of these men quickly became monsters, accused of various forms of depravity. The Peterborough scandal was minor by comparison, and it came at the tail end of this public shaming. The mob, squeezing the pus from one last blemish. The family had already fallen so much financially, and the crimes, if they were even committed, happened so long ago and so far away."

He'd spoken of the Peterboroughs as "the" family rather than "our" family, I noted. "Is this what you meant in your email? The 'nasty business'?"

He nodded.

"Honestly, I had no idea."

"Yes, well, I realized this in retrospect. As I told Celia this morning, I said, 'You have to remember, the Americans have no idea what's happening in the rest of the world.'"

"I'm not—"

"'They have a different kind of royalty,' I said. 'Hollywood. It's not as if they have venerable old dynasties or intelligentsia to topple.'

The Peterboroughs were not as influential as Darwin or Wallace, but the name is not insignificant here in the relevant circles. They were a powerful family who had made a large contribution to scholarship, all of which was called into question by what was unearthed. A century later, mind you. And it's not even clear what was unearthed."

I'd taken out my pen and notebook. "David Maikin?"

"M-a-i-k-i-n. The articles came out in the *Daily Mail*, I believe. Could have been *The Sun*. Celia feels responsible for Maikin's articles. She gave him two interviews before she realized quite how he was going to twist her words. And then Celia, being of Asian descent—the whole thing didn't play out well for her and Teddy. I was spared most of the kerfuffle; I was in South America at the time, doing fieldwork."

Ironic, I thought, for this Celia to worry I was an American journalist, come to stir up trouble. I couldn't get a scholarly article published if I tried. As Barnaby reminisced about his South American research, I doodled cubes with holes in them.

"Wait a minute," I said, interrupting him. "If all this scandal was already brought to light by this Maikin guy, I mean I can understand why you'd be cautious about speaking to me. But the two of you thought I *knew* about it. So, like, what are you actually keeping from me? You said you had a terrible night. Because you were *keeping* something from me."

"Mmm," said Barnaby, looking pained. "I was getting to that."

He squirmed in his chair before he came out with it: "We have her paintings."

I may have actually snorted. I peppered him with questions. Which paintings exactly? Who does he mean by "we"? Where are the paintings located? Might I be able to see them? *When* might I be able to see them? You'll appreciate I was much too excited by this news to make any issue of the fact Barnaby had lied to me.

Celia was in possession of the enclosed studies and sketches mentioned in the twenty-five letters he'd shown me. Which made sense. Would she be inclined to let me see them? I tried to put Celia's prickliness to the back of my mind for the time being. Of the works on the official catalogue, Barnaby insisted four of them were housed at Fulgham House: *Murdo* and *Jane*, of course, as well as *The Cabin* and *Tropical Still Life*. The two works called *Nude House Girl* and *The Parasol*

Flower—the two I was most interested in—were indeed with Tommy.

"Thomas Munk," said Barnaby. "Celia's son."

"Celia's son!" I exclaimed, remembering how the professor had shamelessly proffered guesses about second cousins and art dealers. "And do you think Thomas would let me look at them?"

"Yes, of course. If Celia or I vouched for you."

My appreciation was gushing. "And your nephew lives in…?"

"Brighton."

"Brighton! Excellent." Mentally, I scanned the list of known works.

Barnaby beat me to it. "The other one, of the Sikh servant, I have that. When Mummy's estate was being divvied up no one else wanted the thing. I don't know, I have always thought it a striking portrait, myself. Unusual."

"It's here?" I looked around me. Had I understood him correctly?

Indeed, the painting was upstairs, hanging on a wall of the guest bedroom. To think that I had spent so much time at the professor's home and might never have seen it! Barnaby led me to it, puttering nervously around the room as I took it in.

He was right, it was a striking portrait. Warm greens and amber-browns with highlights of yellow and orange on a 24 x 30-inch canvas, I reckoned. Someone had had it framed in brushed gold. The Sikh's stance was open, angled toward the corner of the canvas, though he was looking at the viewer with an expression I would characterize as loving concern. The stance, the way the man's head was turned, gave the portrait a casual feel. As did the fact that he wasn't in uniform. He wore dark shorts and a light, almost filmy shirt, a tight topknot of mocha brown crowning his head. There he was, in his element, idly swinging a machete. Perhaps he was clearing away the nearby vines? Harvesting one of the fruits? He looked thoughtful, comfortable, happy. It was amazing, I marveled, what could be conveyed by a few strokes of paint. The tree in the background was garlanded with what looked like glowing orbs of light and looping lianas. It made for a festive mood and gave lovely movement to the work. While *Strangler Fig Upon Kapok* had made me feel almost claustrophobic, this painting opened me—to a world, a moment—and offered…was it hope? Renewal? I looked for long minutes, entranced.

"It's called a cannonball tree," said Barnaby. "*Couroupita guianensis.*

They're quite remarkable. The flowers smell incredible—the flowers are not depicted here, mind you—and then it grows these very big fruits, that hang so heavily before they drop."

I told him I'd mistaken the branches for lianas.

"Yes, well, people consider it a rather a messy-looking plant, on the whole. In actuality, the fruit is a dingy grey-brown color rather than this orange."

"Aha. Whereas everything here seems to be glowing," I mused. "This man must be the Sikh policeman she hired to help her trek." I told Barnaby that several of Hannah's letters reprinted in Coles concerned her decision to paint *en plein air* and that this trekking, in my opinion, had really been the start of her own voice, her own style. And Hannah's long love affair with the jungle wilds.

With Barnaby's permission, I took several photos of his painting. I made plans with him to visit Celia in the near future, though he promised to email her first to "soften her up," as he put it. He also promised to connect me with Tommy. As I set out for the Oxford train station, I was feeling on top of the world.

THIRTY

Idlewyld is not as George remembers it in the days of the Boonstras. Ten years, God, how they pass in the blink of an eye. The orchards are a mess now. The plum trees flanking the long laneway have suffered, too. As they come into the almost blinding sun at the front, west-facing entrance, he tells the driver to stop.

"I won't be long," he tells the man. He's had to borrow Finch's cart and syce. "Just wait here."

But the Malay is looking anxiously about him and talking gibberish to the oxen.

"Well, take them to the stables, then," he says loudly. "Let them have a drink."

Alone, and looking up at his task, George reconsiders his initial impression. The mansion is just as imposing as ever.

A house girl answers his knock. She is confused by his request to see Hannah.

"What about Mrs. Peterborough?" he tries. "Memsahib? Is *she* here?"

"No. She no here."

The girl has a cleft palate and he can hardly understand her speech. He wants to shake her by the neck. "Well then, where on earth are they?"

"Forest," she says.

"The forest? Is that what you said? Look, can I speak with somebody who knows what's what?"

Abandoning the useless house girl, he heads around the side of the house, where the syce is still in the process of unhitching the bullock. George walks past him into the cart house. Inside the shelter sits the Peterborough's ostentatious blacktop carriage as well as his own family bullock cart. So she *is* here somewhere. Crossing back through the stable his curiosity is further aroused. In one of the stalls a police mount sways its collared head.

George strides back across the lawn, already drenched in sweat. He will not sit and wait for his wife—*his* goddamned wife!—to emerge

172

from the jungle. "Where is sahib?" he demands of the idiot house girl, having rapped on the front door again. "Tuan? Where is *he*?"

"*Caarrin*?" she says.

"Is that an answer, or a question? Do you not know anything? Can you not find out? No! Wait!" he corrects himself, as she starts to shuffle away. If she goes searching he'll be stuck waiting, and he's not interested in waiting. He is interested, come to think of it, in seeing firsthand what the precious doctor has in his laboratory. "Take me. Take me to him."

The house girl looks even more uncertain than before.

"Listen to me." He grabs her flimsy forearm. "I am Colonel George Inglis, Deputy Resident of the Province of Perak. Take me at once to Dr. Peterborough."

She leads him through the house—an incredible house—to the back of the property and walks him to the edge of an expansive patio lined with palms. A wooden cabin is just visible where the lawn ends and the orchards begin. Perhaps, in plantation days, it was an overseer's hut.

"*Caarrin*," she says.

"*That*—? He's in there?"

"Nnnh," the girls says emphatically, almost viciously, before turning back to the house.

George puts a hand to the now pulsing pain in his gut and resumes walking. At the cabin he knocks loudly, reminding himself that he has good reason to interrupt the doctor's work. His administration has made that work possible; he, personally, continues to make it possible. A little due diligence is to be expected given Izrin's recent protestations.

"Dr. Peterborough?"

There is no answer. George squeezes the catch and pulls. "Hello? Doctor?"

His first impression is of an old wardrobe. The room is heavy with private, worn-in smells, the overlapping odors of bodies and their habits. Shaving ointment, tobacco, and lemongrass mingle with the nutty smells of palm and coconut creams. Underneath these, like a chord being constantly played, is the sour scent of female sweat.

What windows the little building possesses are rectangular gaps left under the eaves. As his eyes adjust, George sees that counters line the room on two sides. Directly opposite him, on the wall facing the door, a bed sheet has been tacked up by its edges and pulled taut, like a blank canvas. A three-legged stool sits in front.

He drifts to a table that holds a tall bottle of green liquid. Two scalpels and a long-handled pair of scissors stand inside the bottle. Next to the antiseptic, laid out meticulously on a checkered cloth, is an arrangement of steel tools. Measuring tape, calipers, a doctor's hammer, a tongue depressor, various thermometers. Then a series of things he cannot identify: thin metal sticks like cake testers, probes that thicken into paddles, and a double-paddled device that hinges in the middle. He picks up one of the tools—two pointed legs joined by a screw—and twists the pea-sized knob at its middle. The legs spread slightly wider.

"Certainly well-outfitted," he remarks.

Looking up, George notices two anatomical maps tacked to the wall in front of him. The first is a hand-drawn profile of a headless, naked woman. He shivers. In firm, looping penmanship, someone has written all over her body. *Elongated dorsal muscle slender calves narrow hips…* Dozens of phrases tattoo the skin; others are attached to the body's contours with ruler-straight threads. Good grief. This business is uglier than he imagined.

The next map is titled "External Genitalia." And there it is, fully and completely exposed, split open and pricked with dozens of needle-fine lines affixed to labels. Words frame the margins of the chart paper: *outer labia aubergine pigment anus downy hairs Mons Veneris hair thick straight Clitoris swollen overdeveloped Vagina often freckled.*

George checks behind him. If Charles Peterborough were to return? The thought makes his knees buckle and he steadies himself against the counter. He should not be here. He should never have entered. What was that house girl thinking of, leading him here?

Map of the Secondary Characteristics: (i) the Breasts small. Aureola light burgundy to burnished black, of varying size (largest at 3 and 1/4 inches d.). Secondary Characteristics: (ii) the Face. Eyebrows fine to none. Lips: protruding…

An uncomfortable stiffness is slowly spreading inside his chest. He turns away, kneading his forehead with his hand. This is the man's science?

Scanning the outer walls more carefully, he finds a second door he had not noticed, on the other side of the tall cabinet. This door, he realizes, faces away from the main house. Could it be that the doctor exited as George knocked? Is Charles Peterborough hiding in the fucking forest too? George remembers their formal introduction in his office, how the man had looked askance at the furniture before he'd deigned to sit in it. How he'd pressed George about Izrin's reliability. Yet the man isn't ashamed of this, this wreckage. Blue-blooded scum.

A logbook is open on the desk, a pen resting next to its inkpot. George bends over the page *…remarkably similar sexual characteristics. Her musculature is slender and she presents with sleek dark hair, which though nearly absent on the body is yet abundant on the Mons Veneris. Together with her flattened pelvic contour, this elegant structure suggests a racial typography well-suited to sexual pursuit. Observations of the permanently engorged state of the clitoris confirm…* On the page facing, the even, looping penmanship comes to an end. *Stratz has characterized the Javanese type as indolent, fearful, and without initiative. I have as yet been unable to corroborate his findings in the case of the Malay female.*

So Charles is making the maps, not just consulting them. Probing these girls' bodies with those steel tools. Testing their flesh. As the scents of skin and anxiety intensify around him, he feels his bile rising and some shame over his squeamishness. For others might call him that, squeamish. No better than a woman.

Yet he has objections, hasn't he? Logical, grounded objections, and it seemed he'd always had them. Finch should bloody well materialize this instant. Like a fat genie from a bottle. Let him see if he can stand for it. "I don't want this to become a problem for Peterborough," Finch grumbled, when some of the natives began complaining to Izrin. George looks around. Some problems are not so easily put right. Should he take something with him to show the Resident? Some sort of evidence?

His fumbling fingers locate the catch for the desk drawer and it releases. A jumble of dark-skinned, straight-mouthed women stare back at him, every one of them stark naked. Photographs. He was hoping for a mickey of whiskey. A girl barely older than Peterborough's own daughter, cupping her budding breasts. A grandmother with her wrists crossed behind her head. Another woman stands with her brown back and naked pinkish rear to the camera, peering quizzically over one shoulder. Yet another woman is obviously pregnant. Legs splayed, her hands rest at her side.

George stirs the cards in the drawer. He pauses when he recognizes the house girl who greeted him at the front door, the hare-lipped dolt. In the image, she is sitting on the three-legged stool, her work-worn hands pushing her knees wide apart. Dark eyes glistening with the same dumb certainty. George pockets the photo card and shoves the drawer shut.

Fat drops of rain have begun striking the tin roof. He fights his way free from the cabin and jogs toward the big house as the heavens open.

THIRTY-ONE

In 1896, the northeast monsoon season breaks hard on the Malay peninsula. Whether it has broken early is a matter of debate in the Inglis household.

"You're unprepared," the colonel accuses. "You've never been quite this unprepared."

Hannah and George are standing in the mostly empty pantry. Even without food, it is a squeeze for two people. Around them, the outer layers of the house—shutters and screen doors, roofing and eavestroughs—rattle and thump as the rain and gale winds lash the building.

"The storm's come early," she replies. "Over a week early, I've heard some say. I'm not a fortune-teller, George. I can't predict the onset of a monsoon."

"Ha! You could be prepared *two* weeks in advance. That's what preparation is!"

Catalogue goods are the only kind that keep for any period of time. The local stuff goes off almost the same day she brings it home, even the cooking oil. She and Suria swap out their market visits, now going three and four times a week, because most of what they buy is fresh, not meant to be stored. The ants and rodents would only take what's left over.

Knowing none of this is acceptable, she says simply, "I don't purchase that far ahead."

This sets him off again. For it is precisely her work to manage the pantry and the meals and the general state of preparedness in the household. Lucy Finch and Hazel Swinburne, even Beatrice Watts, would never allow their homes to become such *barren*, haphazard places, he tells her. And she *is* ashamed. And it is shocking—how poorly organized she has become, how little she cares! There is no comfort for either of them to be had from this pantry.

Tender, numbed, she would flee except the colonel is blocking the doorway. He's summoned her in there to trap her and make her steep in her negligence. To rub her nose in it. To hit her? To force her to

177

admit she's spending much of her stipend on pigment and canvas? *He doesn't know I am painting*, she reminds herself. Knitting her fingers together and bowing her head, she waits for him to finish. If he hits her, so be it.

"I was at Idlewyld yesterday," George says grimly. "Make us a pot of tea. If there are any bloody tea leaves left. We'll talk in the parlour."

Hannah's mind fidgets as the water comes to the boil. Suria and Anjuh have been sent out to see if they can scare up supplies. Does the colonel plan to confront her about painting? Yesterday, he'd said. When she arrived home yesterday he was locked in his study. Drinking, she'd assumed. And when she knocked, he told her to leave him be. Nor did he emerge for supper. She should have taken more notice of this; it wasn't normal for him to take a plate of food into his study. Instead, she'd been only too pleased to be left alone with her considerations of the Peterboroughs and whether they'd enjoyed their outing to the waterfall. Had they found it too strenuous? Was Eva angry with her about Charlotte's escapade at the falls? They had created an exceptional day together, the five of them. At the center of it something troubling shimmered, and Hannah could not release herself from searching for it, circling the events in her memory, hearing each crack of thunder and the girls' gleeful panic. Was it something about the genduk that seemed out of place? Of course she was shy, and downcast, as ever, but then again she'd bolted after Darshan! And Eva had been so harsh on the girl, and yet so praising of her. For whatever she was doing for Charles.

The whistling kettle awakens her. She's done it again! Concentrate: what to say to George? As little as possible, surely. He must have come out to the estate while they were journeying to the waterfall. All right and good, then. She has an explanation, at least. She has Eva to back her up. Hannah rubs her eyes, exhaustion surfacing in a yawn.

In the parlour, the colonel has chosen the dark wingback. As the tea tray touches down he startles and pops to his feet, then rather formally waits for her to settle in. The way the chairs are angled, they can sit for a time looking past each other. Then Hannah pours the tea and adds a splash of tinned milk to her own cup. The colonel now drinks his black.

"How many tigers have you caught now?"

"Three."

"And…will you be buying a new cow?"

"Hannah, I'm not sure quite how to begin." But he does begin. "There is something going on at the Peterboroughs' estate. Something that I…that I now know about. And it's causing me some concern to think of you out there."

Hold your tongue. Cradle your tea. Say as little as possible.

"Now, I don't know what you are doing out there." His hands seize his thighs.

"I've told you, Eva and I—"

"I know what you've told me."

"We play chess, cards. We talk to each other. The Peterboroughs have quite a large collection of curios from their travels. Eva has a large collection of stories."

"Except you weren't there when I called in yesterday."

"No, not yesterday." She tarries, steeling herself to wait.

"One of the house girls told me you were out. From what I can tell, she meant out *in the forest.*"

It occurs to her that the house girl—which house girl?—might have led him to her studio room at Idlewyld, and her stomach lurches. Looking at the colonel, she senses this didn't happen. He would be livid. Instead he is nervous and strangely apprehensive about speaking. She tells him she was indeed in the forest, on a walk with Eva and Charlotte Peterborough. They'd trekked to a nearby waterfall for some amusement on a hot day. As simple as that, she says.

This news doesn't seem to bring him much relief. He looks at her blankly.

"What were *you* doing at Idlewyld, George? George?"

Abruptly the colonel leans forward, fishes something out of his breast pocket, and holds it to his chest a moment before handing it over to her. It is a photographic postcard of a naked Malay woman— dull-eyed, posing with her knees so wide apart Hannah can see she has been shaved. She is one of Eva's house girls, unmistakably—the girl with the cleft palate and the bangles. In the photograph, she is still wearing her precious bangles.

"What is this?" she asks. "Where did you get it?"

"I found it in Dr. Peterborough's cabin," he replies at last. "In the field behind the house there is a cabin where he…where I suppose he is doing his research. There were dozens of photographs in his desk drawer. Forty, fifty images."

She cannot take her eyes off it. The light is diffuse, the pale background reinforcing the dark contours of the woman's limbs and the sheen on her skin. She is exquisitely rendered, dimensional yet flat, hiding beneath or within her own body. How has he achieved such an integration of expression? Her open legs, her open wound; her closed face, her closed mouth. This instant—that such a precise instant can be captured with a camera—it is all a marvel. Is it something about time, such violently stopped time, that causes life to spill itself open for the viewer? She feels as if the camera has pulled her own clothes to her ankles; so strong is the sensation that Hannah puts her free hand to her abdomen and pinches the fabric of her blouse.

The colonel clears his throat noisily.

"What…were you doing there?" she mumbles.

"That's what I'm trying to tell you." His hand is out for the photograph. "Hannah." Reluctantly she obeys, giving it back to him. "Dr. Peterborough is conducting scientific research involving women. Women of the dark races, here, in Malaya. He is documenting them scientifically. Some time ago, he sought assistance from the Residency."

"Assistance from you and James."

"I had no choice but to be involved."

All of these weeks at Idlewyld, she's seen Charles in passing and made nice to him. She's fretted to Eva about the long hours her husband keeps. Admired his dedication. Poor man, cooped up in that cabin! "And if you were Resident, George—because you will be Resident one day, so you tell me—you would have chosen to do things differently, I suppose?" She is in no mood for mercy.

The colonel looks like he wants to climb into his cup of tea and dissolve. "Believe me, I was never told any of the details. Finch said Peterborough would be interviewing the women."

She makes a disgusted noise.

"I know, I didn't believe that either. But I didn't know what to think. Certainly not that he'd be measuring them and…and mapping them and…"

"Shaving them!" she exclaims, then feels her cheeks pinkening.

They sit in silence for a time, looking wretchedly at each other.

"Did you say *measuring* and *mapping* them?" Hannah asks in a quiet voice. "What do you mean?"

"The point is, Hannah, now that I've seen it for myself I'm not sure…not sure what to do about it. If anything."

"Was there a picture in the drawer of Suria?" she asks.

"Not that I saw."

She chews at her fingers. "You're right, George, *something* is called for. Isn't it?"

"It's tricky. Finch feels he can't deny the man."

"Money," she says.

"Peterborough has been paying them all handsomely. Especially the sultan."

Them, she thinks. Does he imagine her an idiot? If George has been involved, he's been sharing in that wealth. How much has he been receiving from the Peterboroughs for his "assistance"? But she says only, "Money or no money, decent people wouldn't allow this to happen. Even to their servants."

The colonel looks at her fondly. "I took the photograph so that I could show it to Finch. You know, show him what the bugger is actually up to. Then I thought better of it, considering that we need my salary."

"Oh, but surely James wouldn't…" Surely James wouldn't have colluded in the first place.

"I'm sorry to have exposed you to such depravity, Hannah. I've been up all night trying to think my way around it. Trying to forget what I saw. My digestion is… I feel horrible, absolutely horrible."

"You were right to show me the photograph, George," she tells him firmly.

As the storm continues to batter the house, they discuss the ins and outs of bringing the matter to the Resident: whether it can be done without jeopardizing George's trustworthiness in the Resident's eyes, and the possibility of his inheriting the Residency when Finch retires, which is bound to be soon. Does Dr. Peterborough suspect him of snooping through his studio? No, says George, likely not. But it's impossible to know what Finch is aware of already—perhaps "all aspects," he notes—and if that's the case, he would be doing nothing more than antagonizing his superior by flagging something he's chosen to overlook.

"You'd be reminding him of his moral duties," she counters.

"Precisely."

"Perhaps there's something I can do?" she offers.

"It's help enough, my dear, to talk it through with you."

It's true, this is the best and possibly the only conversation of any depth they've had in months. As it nears its end, they even reach for each other's hands.

"So please, Hannah," he says, "stay away from the place for now."

She nods and excuses herself to make a dash through the pelting rain to the outhouse. Drenched and shivering, she perches over the dank hole, wondering at the photograph and the unexpected turn of their conversation. Poor George. Poor Roki! For the colonel to be distressed enough to come to her for help… She tries to recall another time when he's sought her judgment, and cannot. No, the colonel won't go to the Resident, will he? He's already thought through the permutations. He's thought everything through and decided to bring Slow Roki to her attention rather than James's, so that he can warn her away from Idlewyld.

Back indoors, Hannah towels off in the scullery. The weather will be a struggle for a week or two. After that the storms will subside and the daily rains will become predictable, manageable, and life will revert to a wetter, windier normal. Would the colonel really be quite so conniving? No, perhaps not. But he'd make the most of a bad situation.

"George?"

He's upstairs in bed, groaning and panting.

"Shall I get MacGillivery?" she asks at his bedside. The military doctor.

"No. Had enough of that quack."

Hannah sits on the bed, observing him until the spell passes and he looks up at her. "I have an idea," she tells him. She feels his hand reach for her leg and grab onto it, as if she were a piece of flotsam in his sea. "This is a dreadful situation, George, and I know it's not your doing."

At this, he makes an emphatic noise.

"The next time I go to Idlewyld, I'll broach the subject with Eva somehow. Eva deserves to know what's going on in her own home. In fact, I wouldn't feel right if I didn't speak with her. And, if I'm correct, George, she'll put a stop to it. She has that kind of power over Charles. At least, I'd wager she does." Hannah looks at him, trying to judge if he's thought through this particular permutation.

"I don't want you there," he whines.

"Because of these 'studies,' yes. If they were to stop, the problem would be solved. And this way, you won't have to confront James about anything."

"I don't want you going there," he repeats more forcefully, trying to prop himself up.

"Oh, *I'm* in no danger, George, good heavens. I must go. Once the rains die down a bit."

And she must keep going—to hike, to paint. But she won't think too far ahead. Hannah gets to her feet. "I'll make you some peppermint tea. Without any milk to temper it, I think the black coffee is too acidic for you."

He grunts. The grunt that means he's temporarily defeated.

THIRTY-TWO

Three weeks pass, spent fixing leaks, diverting puddles, and restocking the pantry as best as possible. The colonel, content perhaps with her presence, leaves her and Suria to the many chores. It is the promise of going back to her artwork that sustains Hannah, primarily, as well as a rereading of *The Tenant of Wildfell Hall*. Her dreams and daydreams sprout disturbing images of naked house girls. If the colonel has kept the photo card, and she would bet that he has, it will be in his study. Roki, looking sullen and caught out and calmly inching toward terror; Roki, hiding in a drawer or a file, concealed by paperwork. Hannah plans a visit to Idlewyld that does not involve a trek, so as to make herself completely available for Eva. At last she is able to slip away from Ridge Road, throwing biscuits overboard to Roderick as the cart bounces away.

At Idlewyld, a house girl—thankfully not Roki—helps Hannah off with her slicker and Wellingtons. Eva appears during this process, welcomes her with air kisses and, with a finger to her lips, leads her upstairs.

"What…?" Hannah says as she follows.

In the corridor, Eva pauses at the door to Hannah's studio room. "Oh, don't looked so worried!" she hisses.

They enter. Competing with a stale smell of turpentine is a floral aroma. By the window, arranged in front of an easel that has been dragged rather too close, is an enormous vase of cut flowers. Roses, camellias, orchids, heliconia, daisies, dahlias, with sprigs of fern and spikes of palm. At the center, an oozing bird of paradise flower points its snobbish beak to the ceiling.

Hannah is paralyzed by the phantasmagoric centerpiece. When she finally speaks, it sounds like false cheer. "Good Lord, you must have bought up all the flowers at market! I can't believe they had such a selection, two weeks into the monsoon."

"Three weeks." Eva has found another lamp and lights it. "And I commissioned it."

Hannah touches one or two of the blooms, bending closer to inhale their scent and avoid facing her friend. "It's very kind," she says with emphasis. She dislikes the arrangement, fake and gaudy and overpowering as it is.

"I've bought them for you to paint, of course."

"Oh!" Despite the location and the easel, it comes as a surprise. "But…why?"

"That's what you do isn't it, darling? Paint flowers? You won't want to tramp around outside in a deluge, and now you needn't. I fully appreciate that cut flowers are outside of your budget, but not mine."

Good Lord, if she's to gain any inspiration from these baubles she'll have to pull them apart. Hannah cocks her head. Maybe she *should* do that. *No, don't let's be quite so queer and pitiful.* She sighs inwardly. She thought Eva understood what she was trying to achieve with her art.

Proceeding as tactfully as possible, Hannah says, "In the forest the rain is quite manageable, actually. The tree canopy is thick enough that even a torrential storm only reaches the ground in trickles. Well, you saw for yourself on our trek home from the waterfall. And in the rainy season, the air is somewhat cooler."

This information has no apparent effect on Eva who is circling the flowers, pinching a leaf here, adjusting a stem there.

"Though, I suppose I could paint indoors today," says Hannah. "In light of the fact… In any case, there is something I need to talk to you about, Eva." Her wobbling stomach has not let her forget.

"Sounds ominous." Eva checks her pocket watch. "I'm due for Charlotte's science lesson this morning. There's no point in the tutor struggling through the old science, you see, when I can teach her the new."

"Oh. Yes, of course."

"So I shall return in hour or so for the ominous news, if that suits you."

"Ha! Fine. I'll…I'll be here!"

Unsmiling, Eva glides from the room, clicking the door shut behind her.

"I'm sorry," Hannah says to the bouquet. "I don't imagine this will go very well."

The candy-coloured flower heads witness her thrashing around, trying to settle, throwing the window open, drawing her shoulders back, sighing over her pencil. Trying to paint their group portrait. Like an audience of vain dowagers, they await her failure: curious, self-satisfied, not caring a cent what she's going through.

Later, she and Eva discuss her unfinished painting. It has been a rare opportunity for a still life, Hannah admits. She hasn't painted one in years.

"You don't like still lifes," Eva surmises. "Or does one say, 'still lives'?"

Hannah doesn't mention they were considered a lesser form of subject matter, traditionally. "I used to quite like them. I think I've just fallen out of the habit of them, as it were." She feels a little dizzy and imagines her blood spiralling through her limbs. Soon she'll be pulling a rug out from under her friend and patron. Building her courage, Hannah busies herself with drying her brushes and scraping down her palette. "How did Charlotte's lesson go?"

"Fine, I suppose. It's difficult to tell with Charlotte how much she actually absorbs." Eva, who has been idly pacing the room, turns back toward the painting. "Aren't you going to finish it?"

"Yes, of course," replies Hannah. *To paint right over this mess!* "But I like to clean the brushes as soon as possible. Even for a short spell away. Preserves them longer."

Eva crooks her mouth. "I do admire your dedication. Although, these fumes…how do you do it? They're positively corrupting."

"Yes, horrible, aren't they? Shall we—"

"How about I meet you in the souvenir shop."

She finds Eva in the formal sitting room, nibbling at a sandwich. The servants have brought out tea and elevenses, and two house girls are arranged behind the sofas, waiting to assist further, another one by the entrance. There are house girls everywhere these days it seems, flicking glances to each other. How silently they move, how expertly they shift and glide in their sarongs; they are in all places at all times, helpful in every way expected. Yet how quite different each one is, in look and in voice. In breasts and hips and…

"Your book is going well?" Hannah inquires politely. A familiar, reliable topic.

"Stalled, as a matter of fact."

"Oh no!"

"It happens." Eva pinches a crumb on her plate. "Doesn't it happen to you when you're painting? That something's not working? And for a time, you can't go on."

"Of course."

Eva puts a toothpick to her mouth and digs for a moment. "So. What is this ominous matter?"

"Oh, it's not *ominous*, Eva. You seem to have seized on that word…" Hannah looks over at the house girls, waiting with pleasantly arranged faces, eyes down. "And you've made this all rather fancy, for the two of us. I just—could we ask them to leave?"

The toothpick jutting from Eva's thin lips makes her look for a moment like a farmer's wife. She stands and asks the house girls to leave, following them to the door. "I suppose you want the doors locked as well!" she jokes.

But Hannah only nods, gulping, and Eva takes her time bolting each exit with a flourish.

"Charles' research…I think you told me he specialized in fish?"

"That's simplifying it somewhat. Concerning fossilization and its support for evolutionary theory, fish are his area of specialization."

"But Charles is not studying fish here. *Here*, at Idlewyld."

"No. That would make no sense."

"He's studying something else." Hannah folds her hands and pushes them out of the way. "Eva, I think you ought to be made aware of what's happening in the cabin in the orchard. Charles' cabin. Charles has been photographing native women. Naked…and…and posed, like…prostitutes. Some of them, apparently, are as young as your Charlotte."

"He's been taking photographs of them posed like prostitutes?"

"In the cabin. George—well, apparently, George came out here looking for me on the day we were hiking to the waterfall. There was nobody to be found, and so he asked to speak with Charles. One of the house girls led him to the cabin."

Eva lifts her eyebrows, expectant.

"I suppose Charles didn't answer at the knock. George let himself inside and—"

"'George let himself inside.'" Eva blinks furiously, the rest of her struck perfectly still. "What is this nonsense?"

"I'm sure he was hoping to find Charles."

"And why wasn't the door locked?" Eva demands. "The stupid man!"

"I...uh... It must have been unlocked."

"The stupid, stupid man! Leaving the door unlocked!"

There is something unusual in this reaction, Hannah reckons, but then again everything about the situation feels unusual and she's having trouble keeping fossilized fish from swimming through her head. She persists, "I know this must be a shock. But I have every reason to think George is telling me the truth. He showed me one of the photographs. In fact," and in that instant she decides not to implicate the Perak administration, "it seems that Charles is trying to document these women. Specifically, their..." Hannah gestures down her front.

"Their sexual organs," says Eva. "Primary and secondary sexual characteristics."

"You know that this has been going on in your back garden?"

Eva's green eyes trip around the room. "Of course. I'm developing a key distinction: ornamental as opposed to adaptationary *sexual* traits. I've told you about the distinction more broadly. We've talked many times about it, haven't we? If I can show that the ornamental traits are particular to a population, then I'll have shown...Well. I can see by your face that it doesn't matter what I will have shown."

"It's just. I thought you'd feel *badly* about the women who... Don't you think the way he is forcing them to—"

"Stop being such a prude, Hannah. Women have bodies. They have sexual organs and sexual histories. Charles and I have discovered that there are *no* essential differences in skull shape or pelvic curvature between Europeans and natives. None. Though that's not what some scientists maintain. *They* would have you believe that the dark races of this world are well-adapted to breeding and maladapted to thinking. Such assumptions are scientifically unfounded, and we need to prove they are unfounded. All the compassion in the world means nothing when it doesn't rest on fact. So don't bleat at me with your squeamish concerns. What George saw in that cabin is science in the service of equality. Equality of the sexes and the races."

"But—"

"And nobody is forcing anybody. They come voluntarily. They're paid."

The hare-lipped house girl's chemically fixed expression materializes on the screen of Hannah's memory. "But what about those women?" she repeats. "They're not animals. Surely they must feel ashamed and violated."

"Oh, well then!" Eva balances her empty palms, two trays of an imaginary scale. "Weight of scientific evidence and unpleasant feelings for a few natives. Frankly, darling, science is in the service of something greater than any of those women. Greater than either of us."

"Do they know why he is examining them?" she says quietly.

"Hannah, think. If you can't grasp the utility of these studies, then how can we possibly explain them to illiterate Malays?"

So what have they been told, she wonders? What do their families think about this? She tries a different tack. "George was shocked by what he saw in that cabin. So much so that he doesn't want me coming here anymore."

Eva laughs. "Well, we both know who that would serve. Did your caring husband share with you that *he* persuaded the sultan to procure the women?"

Hannah shakes her head, shamed into silence.

"Granted, I dislike the way we've had to go about this, Hannah. Skulking around as if we were criminals of some sort. But six years! Six years I've been working here without any institutional support, because the institutions don't support equality. Not for those of us living in an inbred Oriental backwater." She nudges her plate, overhanging the ottoman, fully onto its brocaded surface. "So we resorted to doing it the old-fashioned way, by waving a bit of money around. And now here are you, the live-and-let-live artist, the furthest thing from the hand of moral propriety, I would have guessed, bothering herself about—how did you put it?—'what's happening in my back garden.' Why is that?"

It is the most volatile she's ever seen Eva Peterborough. The least collected. Even when Charlotte disappeared behind the flow of the waterfall, even then Eva was less panicked. The woman is afraid. Of what Hannah might do? Or think?

"Why?" Eva snaps, repeating her question.

"I don't know, Eva. I love this country. And its people."

"Tosh. You might love them as subjects for your paintings. But that's not quite the same, is it?"

She takes this in—a foreign body she'll have to probe and salve and possibly winkle free, later. "This is as much your project, then, as it is Charles'?"

"Yes."

Hannah gets to her feet. Whatever has happened here, she's done nothing but make things worse. She presses a hand over her mouth and chin, side-stepping the coffee table, eyeing the bolted door.

"You're a progressive woman," says Eva, following. "You know what it means to carve out a space of freedom and try to live as if that little pocket of air were an atmosphere. We're alike, the two of us."

"I don't know that we are." Her thoughts are dimming and shrinking away. She reaches for the bolt on the door.

"Hannah, wait. I'm glad that you've spoken your mind. I have something I want to tell you, too. So let us both clear our consciences."

"You have no conscience." Afterward, hunched in the bathtub back on Ridge Road, Hannah would wish she'd flung these words and run.

Instead, she takes a step back from the door, to face Eva.

"Your Sergeant Singh. He's lying to you about this parasol flower."

The idea jars Hannah awake. Through everything, until then, she'd been dozing.

"I asked a botanist colleague about your parasol flower. I wrote to him several weeks ago, when you told me about it. You see, I was suspicious from the first. Neither Templeton nor any of his colleagues at Cambridge have ever heard of such a plant."

"It *is* unrecorded. We realize that."

"No, Hannah, it's a fantasy!"

She is supposed to have recognized this Templeton's famous name, is she? And to put some store in the fact that he's a learned specialist at Cambridge? Cambridge is the fantasy, she thinks. "This is just one circle of colleagues, at one university. Why should they have knowledge of every flower on the planet?" Hannah demands. "Why would Darshan lie to me?"

"Why?" Eva moves even closer. "To trick you into spending time with him, of course. If he's lied to you, it's obviously for his own gain."

"His own gain? What gain?" There is a muffled thump in the hallway. Hannah lowers her voice, drawing even further back from the door. "What are you insinuating? He hasn't gained anything from the time he's spent with me."

"Oh, come now. Use your imagination." Eva backs away, coming to prop herself against the back of the closest chesterfield. "Payment. A sympathetic ear. The satisfaction of compromising your position as a British Resident. Compromising your position as a wife! He's had you on a wild goose chase, Hannah."

"He doesn't have to trick me into spending time with him." She throws her shoulders back and faces the poisonous woman. "I am happy to consider Sergeant Singh my friend and colleague."

"Friend and colleague?" snorts Eva. "You're not serious."

"I really don't understand you." Her voice rises. Who really cares who may be listening behind the doors? "You're suddenly concerned for what, my reputation? *Your* reputation? I thought you didn't put any store in reputations and society. I thought you wanted to help me. You facilitated this whole arrangement!"

Later, Hannah will recall her friend, in that moment, so vividly as to be able to paint her portrait. The attitude of her body and limbs, pressed against the furniture, recoiling, wounded, in stark contrast to the expression on her face. The chin jutting, and her cheeks and lips a vivid pink-red. A strand of hair has loosened itself from her normally severe bun to softly frame her face, though her eyes shine hard and bright with discontent.

"You came here, begging to be rescued," Eva says. "*You* came to *me*."

Hannah concentrates on the bolt, the knob, the open doorway, drawing rapid breaths as the hallway's narrow roll of Turkish carpeting flies under her feet.

"More fool me," she hears Eva call out behind her, "for commissioning the painting of an imaginary flower."

THIRTY-THREE

When it is her turn, Malu is required to touch herself as sahib watches. She minds this less than helping to arrange the others. Take Slow Roki, for instance, who has never liked Malu and always calls her a half-breed and sneers when she walks past. In the cabin, Slow Roki only shivered and bit at her broken upper lip, bowing to Malu and lowering her eyes like Malu was her elder. It was nearly impossible to convince her to raise her head and look toward the camera.

There are plenty of other women Malu does not want to meet again in the neighborhood. So she does not go home for many weeks. Until one day, after the worst of the monsoon is over, she does.

To her surprise, nothing has changed in the lower town. The air smells, as ever, of river fish guts. Uncles stretch in the doorways of their stilted huts, groggy from the afternoon sleep or too much nipa toddy. Women are rinsing their hair in rain buckets. They lean over the railings, chatting to each other from one landing to another and the village rings with voices. A few young kids scamper to keep the ball aloft in game of *sepak takraw*. Malu smiles to herself. She's forgotten how good it feels to kick a ball.

She gives the wet grass a couple of practice kicks before climbing the slippery ladder of Nattie's raised hut. Three broken rungs, she counts, and one rung completely missing. Nobody fixes anything around here! Nobody cleans anything, either! Uncle Nito's shrimpers spend all their time squabbling and chewing betel. Their conversation is so loud they don't notice her come in. Or notice the rat scurrying along the rafter above them. Five or six men are seated around a low table which is laden with an ulam spread, heavy on the shrimp, with extra spicy sambal for Nito.

"Take this problem to the raja," says one man. "That's what I say."

"He is part of their shame, I tell you. Who do you think is spreading the monies for their visits, heh?"

"The longo, you fool." Nito pushes a hand through his black hair.

"Yes, and the raja's receiving his monies."

"So what? He will still hear us on it. He may even give us some of those monies."

Auntie Nattie, who is bringing the men a fresh bowl of rice, happens to look over. "Malu child! What are you doing here?"

The shrimpers turn and stare. Nodding to the men, Malu walks to the bundle of blankets in the opposite corner and kneels beside it. Her mother moans.

"Amah? Are you cold? What's wrong?"

Umi's eyes are tired and small. She struggles to sit up, her head bobbing on its slender neck. "Like this with me now. Better not to see."

Nattie is tugging at Malu's sleeve. "No work tomorrow? Want to help me at market?"

"No."

"You know, your longo medicine is no good," Nattie spits. "None of it."

Malu ignores this. She tucks the blankets around Amah's knees.

"There's some trouble for you, my girl," Umi says. "I see it in your face. Something bad going on inside of you."

Could it be that none of the women have said anything yet to Nattie? Or else, more likely, Nattie is sparing her dying sister the shame. Malu leans gingerly toward her mother, closes her eyes, and holds herself there, afraid to rest the full weight of her head against the frail body. Like everything else in Nattie's house, the blankets smell of brine. She fights the tears. She doesn't care what happens to her. But she needs Amah. Without Amah, what is left? "Please," she whispers to her mother, "please don't listen to what they say about me."

"Come and eat something." Nattie is trying to pull her up by the armpits. "God knows you've gone too skinny, whatever else you've done."

"Leave me alone. I want to rest with Amah. I just want to rest."

"I'm sick of her ulam, too," Umi whispers. "Stay here with me. Leave them to their politics."

Malu puts her head on her mother's lap. As she closes her eyes, she sees Auntie Nattie's eyebrows rise in surprise. Dr. Peterborough measured Malu's eyebrows: each one is two inches long, "decidedly European in texture." He measured her pubic hair, too, pulling the strands upright against the cold metal of his scale. He wiped the scale in the vinegar water before he brought his scissors down. "Be still!" he said. "I'm merely cutting a lock. Parasites live in hair. Different parasites for different kinds of people."

Hush, you are home now, in Amah's arms. For the moment, this is enough.

Waking, she hears Nattie circling. Light as a flea, walks like an elephant, Umi always joked about her sister.

"So? What's going on, long face?" Nattie asks, poking Malu's leg. She sets down a bowl of rice topped with curry. "Sahib doctor bothering with you, heh?"

With relief, Malu sees that Amah is asleep beside her.

Nattie looks over at the men.

"They all upset now about sahib doctor. Allah, these white people mixed in the head!" Nattie's eyes grow wet as she strokes her own forearms. "I should never have sent you to work there."

"What?" says Malu. Can she be hearing right?

Her aunt squats down. "Stay. Don't go back there, child."

Malu pulls the bowl of rice and curry closer and eats while Nattie watches. She says, "Dr. Peterborough has promised to come here to see Amah. To help treat her sickness."

"Ha. And you think your uncle will allow that visit, girl? Uh-huh." Nattie blinks fast. "Don't matter how many fancy words you know for asking. You can stay home with us from now on."

"No." Malu is surprised at how hard the word comes out of her, like an arrow to a target.

Nattie stares. "What do you say to me?"

"I'm going back," Malu answers. "And Amah *will* be treated." She raises her head to look in the direction of the men as they pick over the spread of food between them. "Tell me, where is the money going that I am sending home? Huh?"

"In the tin," Nattie says, avoiding her eyes.

THIRTY-FOUR

Rounding the exit platform, I spotted the Fiat with little trouble, and Daphne waving by its side.

"Where's Bob?" I asked, slipping into the passenger seat.

"He's taken a bit of a turn with his health."

"Oh! Is he okay?"

"He'll be just fine, dear. He's in the hospital for the time being, to make sure everything's sorted. How was your trip to Oxford? Did you get what you needed?"

"What happened?"

"Sepsis," Daphne said.

The word sounded familiar, but I had no idea what it meant.

"Infection of the blood." Daphne's fingers gripped the steering wheel loosely. In every way, she looked perfectly normal.

"Oh." I didn't want to let on how horrible that sounded, an infection in the blood. Or to ask any stupid questions about Bob's health that might hurt her feelings and reveal my own ignorance. "I'm glad he's going to be okay."

It wasn't until we went to visit Bob in Frimley Park hospital, the next morning, that I mentioned my adventures with Barnaby Munk. Daphne and I had settled in amongst various machines and were trying to ignore the noises of the ward—sporadic shouts, whimpers of pain, a nurse talking with exaggerated loudness and slowness. My excursion provided a welcome distraction.

I told them in detail about Barnaby and his sister, Celia, Hannah's letters, the progress I'd made, the lovely painting of Sergeant Singh, the many more paintings Celia would be able to show me. I speculated about the two that her son in Brighton owned: *Nude House Girl* and *The Parasol Flower*. Thomas Munk, a solicitor in Brighton. Daphne and Bob offered little coos and murmurs of support as my tale unfolded. They kindly offered for me to stay with them as long as I needed.

"Who is he again, Nancy, this fellow you met?" asked Bob. I wondered how closely he had been listening, after all. Were the two of them simply impersonating themselves, trying to appear engaged? I couldn't blame them for being preoccupied.

"A descendent of the Peterborough family," I said. "You know, Fulgham House?"

I asked if they remembered ever hearing news of the Peterboroughs being involved in a sex scandal. By then I'd read Maikin's piece in its entirety—it had originally been released in three parts, over three Sundays, as part of a series titled "How The Mighty Have Fallen." As Barnaby had hinted, Maikin stripped everything of its context and was over-generous with his inferences. Hannah's name was mentioned only in passing, as "one special friend who, having become embroiled in the goings-on at the Peterborough plantation, was never heard from again."

Plantation? I thought. He made it sound like they'd done her in.

"The sex scandal, of course," said Daphne. "They're all funny, those elites. Some sort of child pornography ring they were running back in the nineteenth century!"

"*The Mail* broke it, if I recall correctly," Bob added. I remembered his avid daily reading of the papers. He had *The Mail* and *The Evening Standard* on subscription.

"I had no idea about any of this," I said. "Barnaby told me about it."

"Why should you?" Daphne exclaimed.

"And you didn't mention anything, when you suggested I visit the estate."

"Should we have?" Daphne asked herself. "Should that have mattered for visiting the estate? It's a beautiful stately home."

"Lovely grounds, too," added Bob. "Gives you some good ideas for the garden, it does."

Daphne reached over and patted his hand. She turned to me. "Oh, I think they were probably both rotten to the core, Nancy. It just goes to show that money and power don't make for happy families."

I returned home with Daphne and went about my day doing much of nothing, my conversations with Barnaby looping through my mind. It would have been right and good if I, like Daphne, quietly missed Bob and was concerned about his recovery. I did, and I was! But it was the Peterborough-Munks who were distressing me.

During a long shower, I came to the nut of it. It bothered me that Hannah's paintings belonged to the Munk family. They were not Hannah's heirs. It was a definite possibility that Eva and Charles Peterborough had themselves never purchased the art, certainly not the works that Hannah had intended to send to her mentor. And who knew what kind of arrangements had been made about the other paintings, or what kind of duress Hannah may have been under. A young penniless artist amongst wealthy, unscrupulous elites. *Forgive me for being blunt, Ms. Roach, but I must ask you: why is this woman's art noteworthy? Is it noteworthy?*

Forgive me for being blunt, Dr. Munk, but who are you to ask?

The Munks had made no attempt to have any of the works appraised, as far as I was aware. Nor to search for any of Hannah's heirs, the people with a legitimate stake in her belongings. Far from championing the large number of works in her possession, Barnaby's sister-in-law had locked them away. Out of indifference. Or worse, some sort of homophobic hostility spurred by baseless accusations that the woman was their great-grandmother's lover. The more I thought about it, the angrier I grew. If Hannah appeared nowhere in Eva's correspondence with the engravers and publishers of *The Descent*, if I could believe Barnaby in this, then it was even possible the Peterboroughs had used her botanical art for their book without her knowledge. Stewing like this for a day or two, it started to seem to me that Barnaby and Celia Munk were actively trying to suppress Hannah's contribution. To silence her voice so that she was forgotten.

When an email came through from Barnaby, I squelched whatever annoyance was lingering. I needed him, and he appeared to be helping me now. The best I could do—and I vowed I would do it—was to honor Hannah's contribution and to advocate for her, if and when it came to that. Barnaby's message cc'd Celia, who replied shortly after. They suggested an upcoming date for us to "raid the lock-up," presumably where the family stored their considerable art collection. Celia, the key-holder, would let all of us in, supervise the extraction of Hannah's studies and sketches, and offer us a room in which to view them.

"That date works for me," I wrote. "Happy to make the trip!" I was almost certain I didn't sound like an American citizen journalist.

Bob returned from hospital before long, his infection having cleared up sufficiently enough to be on oral antibiotics. He looked quite weak to me. Shrunken. Yet his tolerance for Daphne's help had grown. So too had his desire to talk. Hospitals, I imagined, were both very boring and very stimulating. Whatever the reason, Bob was newly and keenly interested in my future.

Daphne chided him one night after *Jeopardy*. He'd been questioning me from his La-Z-Boy about my marital and career prospects; I'd been lobbing noncommittal answers back at him from where I sat working at the table. "Leave the girl alone," she cried, "*I'm* the one what does the meddling, and *you're* the one who stops me!" She was folding a dark load of our laundry and stacking the clothes in piles on the couch beside her.

"I'm not meddling," Bob replied gently. "I'm letting Nancy know I respect her."

"You are?" said Daphne, voicing the same surprise I was feeling.

"Here she is, working away on so many important things, uncovering this famous artist. The discovery of a new flower species. She's taking good time to see it all. Through. Properly." He nodded with satisfaction. "Which is just what the world needs. It's all too slapdash these days. Young people, you'll excuse me, are all so slapdash these days. And here you are, my dear, taking the time to cultivate your knowledge. Working on something until you get it right."

"Sorry, what does the world need?" I asked. "See *what* through properly?"

"Your book," said Daphne. "He's referring to your book."

"What book?"

Bob said, "Your book about this artist woman."

"Hannah Inglis," said Daphne. "Her avante-garde artwork and then the trekking through Malaysia in search of a parasol flower…"

"And these sinister benefactors, the Peterboroughs," Bob chimed in. "Who knows what they'll do to her."

"It's all very romantic!" said Daphne.

I considered whether Bob could be experiencing some sort of delusion or emotional overload as a side effect of his medication. (Daphne needed no explanation.) True, I'd *lied* to a few people that I was writing a dissertation on pioneering women artists. But I'd lied. I had no plans for a book. I was having a hard enough time writing an email. I'd started a draft message that I returned to periodically. It was addressed to Kenneth. In it, I told him Europe was my oyster, that I was making good progress on my dissertation, that I'd learned of his recent move. How I should go forward, I would ask him. (Would I?) I hoped that he could still advise me. (Did I?) And if so, would I need to transfer to Loyola for this to happen?

I told the Plewetts I was not writing a book.

"But you're doing all of this work!" Daphne exclaimed, ever a gauge on efficiency.

"Yes, well, more fool me," I said sulkily, flipping my laptop closed. "I'm…I guess I'm just exploring."

Bob was quiet. He waited until Daphne stood up with an armful of folded laundry and chugged away with it. "Why not?" he asked me.

Why not write a book? I could remember the feeling when the words were flowing, when my dissertation project had made sense and given me purpose, a voice. It was the same feeling when, as a kid, you threw up your kite and the wind finally caught it and swooped it aloft. From a practical perspective, it was true that I now had plenty of notes to work from on a bounded subject. With no particularly challenging conceptual apparatuses to square, confront, or niftily sidestep. No requirement that I make a "unique contribution" to display my prowess.

"I'm not an artist, Bob. I'm not an art critic, or an art historian. I have no special expertise about, like, post-expressionist art and the Ashcan School, or the rise of the avant-garde and how that transformed the critical reception of works by the general public in relation to forms of mass consumption."

"You don't say?"

"It wouldn't have to be a book *for* the art community, I suppose. Or about the art in any technical sense. I could make it explicit I'm not a painter. Sometimes I think the viability of a project is truly all about the delimitations, if you see what I mean? But…I don't know."

Bob pursed his lips in the way he did when he concentrated on a crossword. "Why would a painter be any better at telling the story?" he asked. "Painters are good at painting."

"Plus I'm not English!"

"You speak English."

I rolled my eyes at him. "I'm serious. I wouldn't be able to properly convey her nineteenth-century English sensibilities."

"Neither would I," he said. "Got no imagination, me. Least that's what all my teachers told me, and lo and behold, I ended up as an accountant. Go figure." He winked at me. "Now this David Maikin fellow. He's English and you told us what a dog's breakfast *he'd* made of everything. Didn't you?"

"In my opinion. I suppose—I suppose he was entitled to…no," I rallied, "he wasn't entitled to come up with a bunch of self-serving lies and pretend they were the truth." I picked a shirt off the top of the pile and refolded it less neatly. "But the thing is, I'm better than David Maikin. I know life is more complicated. I know it's—"

"*You'd* be doing it for the right reasons," Bob said.

"—too complicated."

Daphne came back into the room, heading for the other piles of laundry. Her face stretched comically when she noticed the refolded shirt and she looked sideways at the two of us. "Far too quiet in here. What are you two hatching?"

THIRTY-FIVE

Already a poor sleeper, since his visit to Idlewyld George now wakes for two or three hours each night. One thing he arrives at fairly quickly; talking the matter through with Hannah was a poor decision. Now he feels her scrutiny, too, and her disappointment. He should have realized she's too childishly principled to recognize the benefits of lying low. As a mature adult, one is entitled, indeed one is often required, to evade responsibility for the actions of others. At least she appeared to have given up on approaching Eva Peterborough about the matter. When he gently broached the subject again, after sex, Hannah surprised him. "Oh, don't worry," she replied hotly, "I have no intention of returning to Idlewyld."

Hannah is not the only one urging him to take action. An alligator, his mother, and a talking pair of scissors appear in his dreams. His mother, God love the woman, suggests he raise the matter with Lucy Finch. "Clearly she is the moral seat of authority, Georgie, if not also the actual one." The alligator proposes a confrontation with Charles Peterborough. This ends, in several versions of the dream, with the two men tearing strips of flesh from each other's naked bodies and pinning them to a corkboard. As for the long-handled scissors, they warn him to document the matter thoroughly and bring it to the attention of higher authorities in the administration. *The natives won't stand for this*, the scissors intone in their distorted, metallic voice. Speech that is not unlike the hare-lipped house girl's, a hollow sawing of syllables.

On the other hand, George's dream father appears on occasion—dressed as a butler—to remind him there is nothing to be gained by intervening. Andrew Inglis, delivering a tray of drinks, reminds George that he has already consulted with Oakeshott and Dennison. In actuality, he has done no such thing, though George's sleeping mind remembers this as a conversation that took place in front of a primitive-looking mural of trees and animals painted on the side of the government building. (As vivid as this "memory" is, there is no such mural; George takes the time to check.) The lads say: "stay the course," "follow the plan," "keep it to yourself," "nobody wants to listen," "Finch won't bail you out." His father the butler reports these phrases, over and over again, with professional aplomb. As if the man were in a sort of trance, thinks George. But of course he is: a dream trace.

With so many nights of interrupted sleep, George's stomach ailment flares up and his headaches worsen. He is in bed when Suria delivers the message that the Resident-General has entered the village. "Big boss at the Residency," she shouts from behind the door.

"Come in, come in," he directs her.

She shuffles to the bed to hand him a folded card. The message is in Lucy's handwriting. An invitation to attend a "welcoming soirée" for a new British resident, one Brigadier Arthur Effingdon-Watts. Swettenham will apparently be in attendance.

"Swettenham? Tonight?" George groans loudly. "How long have you had this card?"

She looks meekly at the footboard.

"I don't want to attend any fucking welcome party." He scans the paper again. "Effingdon-Watts," he snarls. "Why does that name sound familiar? Where is memsahib? What does *she* say about this?"

"Ill, Colonel Sahib." The housemaid shakes her head, then points through the wall. "Other bedroom."

Arthur Effingdon-Watts went to the same public school as the Resident-General and is in fact a personal friend. A soft-spoken man, he turns out to be bald under his safari hat, but sports a thick and meticulously groomed auburn beard and mustache as compensation. Inside this nest of hair, his rosebud mouth moves now as he relates the plodding tale of the death of his wife. Trapped beside Resident-General Swettenham, George is forced to stand by and wait.

"Are you feeling quite well?" Effingdon-Watts interrupts himself to inquire of George.

Swettenham peers at George, looking displeased.

"Yes, certainly," he assures them. Though he takes the opportunity to excuse himself for a glass of water.

"Pinky, you look as sick as a skunk!" James Finch exclaims when they run into each other in the hallway. He gestures at the staircase. "Have a lie down upstairs."

"I'm not going for a nap *now*, Finch. Good God."

Finch grimaces.

"I'll just...maybe I'll just take a moment alone." George trudges up the stairs. "Colossal bore, anyway," he says under his breath.

The evening has been mainly an elaboration of the many exploits of Resident-General Swettenham—which is to be expected when the Resident-General is in town. The Brigadier, E.W. as they all call him, is effusive in his praise of Kuala Kangsa, Swettenham, and Finch, something about which George can't help feeling suspicious. Most travelers prefer to commiserate with those who live there more permanently.

He stops at a mirror in the upstairs hallway. Eyeing his reflection, he adjusts his new cravat. He does look unusually pale. They must have the same sickness, he and Hannah. Some sort of flu. He'd thought these were the old symptoms flaring up but, no, these are new ones. He pictures her in the guest room, the bed sheets twisted around her ivory ankles and her dark hair, wild and unbrushed, fanning from her troubled face. His heart melts again at that moment, despite himself. When he goes home he will visit her in her bedroom and kiss her brow and wrists.

He could send Hannah back to London, just as soon as he's taken over the Residency. Why hasn't this occurred to him before? Once he is Resident he could afford both homes. She would be safe there. She appears not to be fertile in any case. Then, after he's served the few years remaining on his ticket, he'll join her.

"Good!" he says to his reflection. "That's settled."

The colonel wanders on down the hallway, considering how he might put his own stamp on the place. Yes, if she doesn't care for him, just as well to have her in London. He squeezes the frilly sash of a drape.

In the wood-paneled study, George gravitates to the pedestalled globe in the corner. It was a gift from one of the local rajas, one of Izrin's competitors in the decades before British involvement. The miniature earth is a solid, deftly carved ball of mahogany and the continents are worked in gold and secured with thin screws to the dark wood. When George spins it the shiny formations blur together before regaining their familiar coastlines. The globe, he feels sure, is considered government property. Finch would be leaving it behind. He spins it faster, enjoying the optical illusion.

"Colonel?" Swettenham is standing in the doorway, fists planted on his hips.

George draws himself up. "Resident-General, sir." What on earth is he doing up here? Following him? The globe squeaks to a stop.

"E.W. has just told me something astounding. You've made some sort of deal with the sultan, is that so? You have promised not to tax 'his' opium."

"Er...that is not precisely the case, sir," George stutters, discouraged to be on the defensive. The brigadier must have spoken in confidence with Finch. Or Izrin himself? The man had been in town two days! "What I told the sultan was that the *chandu*, ah, in fact *would* be taxed. He...he was to assume control of the taxation for a period of—"

"Stop waffling," Swettenham declares. "That amounts to the same bloody thing."

"Does it?"

"I spoke with Izrin yesterday when I came in."

"You did. Ah."

"Izrin is under the impression that the *chandu* will be tax-exempt as of the new year." Swettenham's delicate nostrils flare. "I told him that would not be the case. However, until now, I have remained curious as to who had given him this impression."

"I must tell you, sir. This 'research' of Dr. Peterborough's is proving to be a...a *significant* antagonism to the natives. In my opinion, they are likely to revolt if it continues much longer. What I arranged with Izrin, you see, was a stopgap measure, sir, for a difficult situation."

Swettenham gives him a patented withering look. "Believe it or not, Inglis, what worries me more than the loss of revenues is a situation in which a glorified tax collector takes it upon himself to rewrite the laws of this land." The laws of *his* land, Swettenham's tone implies.

"Surely—" begins George and then closes his mouth. In the ordinary course of diplomacy, how many laws has he been ordered to bend thus far? How many favors are routinely required to establish a single policy? Besides, Finch is quite as responsible for the *chandu* strategy, having approved it. "I—I hadn't considered the matter in quite that way," he manages to reply. He wipes one sweaty palm against the other.

The Resident-General fixes his clear blue eyes on George for an uncomfortably long time.

"Oh!" George remembers, laughing loudly. "You *are* aware, sir, that I had not planned on following through on the promise?" He is relieved to have discovered this vital ballast of information. "Raja Izrin, sir, has a certain amount of inertia, as it were. Once the arrangements with Dr. Peterborough were in place and the monies distributed, I felt certain there would be no need for something as significant as, uh, taxation diplomacy."

Swettenham sighs audibly. "You felt certain, did you? Inglis, do you have any idea how annoying it is to have to play politics in the middle of a party?"

George nods. Yes, he has an inkling.

"I know Izrin better than you do," continues Swettenham, "and I am not certain he would be content with a broken promise. Not in this case." He picks a fleck of lint from the hem of his navy blazer. "Damn hell, if this thing was to be done, it had to have been done properly!"

He is seized with spine-racking hatred for Effingdon-Watts. This was absolutely none of his business! If the foul man had only kept his trap shut, Swettenham would have been none the wiser. George clenches his fists, trying to quiet his breathing in case the slight wheeze bothers the Resident-General. But the man appears to have given up on him. Without issuing an order, he strides from the room.

After a minute or two, George ventures out himself. He's not the first man to have been dressed down by Swettenham, he knows. Nothing much usually comes of it other than public humiliation, though this is painful enough. His head is freely pounding now and there is a new throbbing sensation in his abdomen. Has his appendix perhaps burst? Doesn't that occur in times of great strain? He takes the stairs slowly, concentrating on smoothing the crease from his brow without putting a hand to his face. If he were thinking clearer, he could puzzle out how this E.W. became so involved with everything.

"—illness after illness. And then there's the drinking. I'm not one to refuse a tipple, but *this* goes…"

George halts in mid-step. Swettenham's left arm with its familiar tweed elbow patch is poking out at the bottom of the stairwell.

"No, no, no, you've been entirely respectful, James. More than respectful. The man is a loose cannon."

"That's lost its balls!" somebody jeers.

Laughter follows.

"We've made the right decision," comes Swettenham's voice again. Finch's reply is inaudible. The elbow disappears.

As the colonel slowly descends the final flight of stairs, the nearby rooms vacate. It is all something from a very bad dream. Except for a petite girl in a pink sari, who glides up to him. She holds a tray balancing a single flute of champagne. It strikes him as excessive, even for James, to have gone to such lengths to welcome an old friend to town. George takes the flute. As he stands watching the tiny bubbles cast themselves off the side of the long glass and fly upward, he hears a commotion rising in the great room—the chiming of many forks against many glasses. Feeling nauseous, he makes his way toward the others.

"Thank you, thank you, gentlemen," James Finch's voice booms. "At long last, some of you might say, I'm being put out to pasture."

Laughter and some applause.

What? George's stomach heaves. He buckles, staggers sideways, rights himself. Retirement? Retirement! How could he have missed this fact?

"And I'd like, now, to invite Resident-General Swettenham," Finch continues, "to kindly introduce my successor."

Standing next to Swettenham at the front of the room is Arthur Effingdon-Watts, smiling like a Cheshire cat.

George barks, loudly and involuntarily. The guests turn, amazed, in time to see him vomit into his hand and onto his shoes.

August 11, 1896

Dear Monsieur Godot,

In anyone's life there are stretches of bleakness. Of blackness, even. Yet I have lately thought to myself how grateful I am, knowing that I will be all right. Unlike others, I have art to help me through anything.

Enclosed is a letter I received from the jury of the Kew Gardens Amateur Botanical Artwork Competition. I have sent it on to you for your impressions, of course, if you have any to offer, but just as much to get the blasted document out of my house.

Does it sound prideful of me to suggest that the jury members do not understand my aims with this painting? I could easily admit I had not *accomplished* those aims, if only the aims themselves were appreciated. I agree, the composition is wildly imbalanced. I agree, the colour is displeasing and limited. The difference being, I suppose, that I had thought those choices were serving the overall effect, and that overall effect being neither childish nor obscure! And really, how could an effect be both childish and obscure, as the third juror writes?

Possibly these sentiments are nothing more than sour grapes. Would I feel the same if I'd won the competition on the basis of some misapprehension about my work? Oh, how very challenging it is to perceive one's worth objectively.

I realize, now, that in some ways I have always been painting portraits, monsieur, even with these botanical subjects. How I wish I'd sent you one of the *Strangler Fig* studies for your ever-honest impressions.

As ever,
your student,
Hannah

July 5, 1896

Regarding: *Strangler Fig Upon Mighty Kapok*, entry in the juried competition (Category of Women, Other)

Dear Mrs. Inglis,

Thank you for your entry in this year's Kew Gardens Amateur Botanical Artwork Competition.

We regret to inform you that your piece was not selected by our jury as a finalist. There was an unusual abundance of very fine entries in all categories this year. Notes from our three jury members, specialists in art appraisal, are included for your edification and in gratitude for your efforts. We hope you will consider submitting an entry next year.

Sincere regards,

John Simcoe, on behalf of
Artworks Judging Committee, Kew Gardens

- *Composition wildly imbalanced. Work risks self-decomposing.* AK

- *Colour range rather narrow; displeasing palette.* JG

- *What is the interest here? Everything strikes the same childish note.* EEM

Hannah hardly recognizes the marketplace, deserted of vendors and customers. Well past nightfall, the area is layered with shadows, menacing enough that she hurries through them, swinging her umbrella. It's proved useless, in any case, against these gusts of rain-soaked wind.

She is emerging from illness, and the world feels ominous and slightly shimmery. For days, for lifetimes, there had been only the frames of dark and bright to dwell in, a drudgery in which the hours stacked upon themselves and expectations reduced and reduced—a slide toward nullity. All the while, the most meaningful and compelling ideas floated before her as she lay helpless. Now that she is upright, now that she has wormed her spirit back into its flesh, the ideas are congealing into blood and breath. Hadn't she realized something about portraits? Something revolutionary and exciting about how she might paint portraits? There is so much to tell the sergeant.

Hannah pulls her cloak further around her waist, re-cinching the tie, and mops cold drizzle from her face. She could have perhaps sent him a note. That said what, exactly? She needs to see Darshan to discern what there is to say within this abundance of feeling. As soon as she determined the colonel was attending that silly welcoming party, her evening took its shape and purpose. She lay in bed, thinking it through in all dimensions, pulling it toward her like a handle, until the front door closed behind George. Then she dressed herself hastily and clumsily, plumped pillows to lie under the blankets where she was meant to be sleeping, and snuck out of her own house.

As for Darshan's house, she deludes herself into thinking she will recognize it when she nears it. But the neighborhood is a labyrinth of alleys and thatched bungalows. A man pokes his head out of a window and Hannah seizes the opportunity.

"Excuse me! Pardon me! Where does the police sergeant live? *Di manakah*," she practically shouts into the man's stern face. "*Di manakah* Sergeant Singh? Where?"

Luckily, he has only to point. She hobbles away along this invisible trajectory until she is toeing the flooded ditch that encircles a dark bungalow. Could Darshan be asleep? Not a flicker of light from within. Hiking up her skirts she wades through the filthy water, hoping there are no leeches. At the side door, she knocks softly.

The door swings open soon after to reveal Sergeant Singh standing barefoot inside the threshold, blinking and scratching his bare, hairy chest. He is wearing nothing but a pair of cotton pants that fall just above the knee; his long hair is tied behind him.

"Mrs. Inglis!" he exclaims.

"May I come in?"

"Uh, yes. Yes! Come in, please." He ushers her inside, looking her over with growing alarm. "What are you doing here? You are wet. Are you all right?"

She swallows. "I'm ill. Though not very ill, I suppose. But when you're ill, it always feels as if you're very ill."

"Oh, I'm...I'm sorry for you, Mrs. Inglis."

"My apologies for calling on you so unexpectedly."

"No, no, please, come in. Sit down. No, no, wait there a moment. On the mat." He dashes off even as he is speaking, returning in a minute or two with a glowing lantern in one hand and an arm full of towels and blankets. By then, she has shed herself of her sopping boots and raincoat. He hands her a towel to dry her skirts and legs then wraps a woolen blanket around her shoulders and guides her into the lounge. He's put on a patterned *kefti*, the cotton Malay shirt that falls to the knee, but remains barefoot and bareheaded.

"*Malasa chai?*" Darshan says, depositing the lantern on a table. "Indian tea. This is always good for a sickness. Clears the passages. Warms the heart."

She thanks him for the tea and tells him she is not congested. "It feels rather more like my future is unraveling."

"Tea is good for that as well," he says. He heads to the kitchen, where another lamp soon bursts to life.

"You're in bed early," she calls out.

"I am an early riser, Mrs. Inglis. Five in the morning."

Hannah explores the lounge as he clinks and clanks with his pots, and the scents of vanilla, cinnamon, and other warming spices infuse the air. It is a simple home, furnished sparely, and neat as a pin. Along one wall is a low chesterfield draped with a bolt of gold fabric. Next to this sits a well-loved chair, its seams splitting a little along the arms. The sergeant's pipe and tools are arranged on a side table. In another corner, a round prayer cushion. On the walls hang three portraits of the Sikh gurus, she supposes—bearded, beatific-looking grandfathers with cherubic smiles and knowing eyes.

When Darshan finally emerges from the kitchen he is holding two mugs of milky tea. He sets them down on a bamboo mat on the table.

"Sugar!" He points a finger in the air. "One moment."

Hannah sniffs, then tastes the brew. It is less like tea than warm spiced milk, but what does that matter?

"Try with some sugar," he advises as he returns with the sugar pot.

She takes a spoonful and stirs it in, observing the tiny tornado she's set in motion. Before too long she must explain herself. After a few gulps of the fragrant tea she wants nothing more than to curl up under the woolen blanket and close her eyes. "Do you know," she realizes, "I'd forgotten all about George's ridiculous tiger hunt."

"Ah." He regards his cup. "I have not."

"George doesn't know I'm here." Though this hardly deserves

saying. They both know that if the colonel should find out she'd come, on her own, after dark…. "I've come," she continues, "because Eva and I have fallen out, and I don't suppose I will see you any time soon at Idlewyld."

"I'm sorry to hear that." He sips, avoiding her eyes. "I was expecting as much, Mrs. Inglis."

"Were you?"

He shrugs, looking oddly bashful. "Well. It has been some weeks."

Hannah's mind vaults back to her confrontation with Eva, stitching details together: the thump behind the door—*Hannah, it's a fantasy!*—a toothpick poking from Eva's thin lips—*equality of the sexes and the races*—the overbearing, musky scent of the bunched flowers.

"I've been ill," she says, "and the worst of the monsoon…"

"It is no criticism, Mrs. Inglis."

She'd heard nothing from Eva since their quarrel. Even in the unlikely event the Peterboroughs decided to shut down their laboratory, the damage to their friendship felt permanent. And the damage to the Malay women, what should she do about that? Here she sat in front of the chief of police, and still she said nothing! But what *could* be said or done?

Darshan is looking at her warily. "Are you all right, Mrs. Inglis?"

The administration itself had organized everything. The acts were plainly lawful.

"There are…so many thoughts," she murmurs.

Composition is wildly imbalanced. Work risks self-decomposing. If she tells him about the Kew Gardens rejection, how can he possibly respond? With a meaningless platitude about her artwork? He'd never even seen the final *Strangler Fig*.

"Darshan, I have to ask you…" She leans toward him, gripping the sofa. Her long hair, which in her hurry she did not bother to tie up, falls forward. "Oh, I'm such a mess!"

"No," he says softly. "Not at all. Take your time, Mrs. Inglis."

Gratitude ignites within her. Here is her sergeant, welcoming a confused, bedraggled woman into his tidy sitting room when he would normally be asleep. What does he get from associating with her besides a pain in the backside and the risk of public humiliation? Nothing. Except perhaps the same things as she has gained: some company in appreciating nature's wonders. So much in life is better done on one's own, she is coming to believe. However the appreciation part really does require others.

"I am fond of you," she says. "I think—I think you are my best friend."

He smiles and then the smile grows. Running a hand over the top of his bare head, he mumbles, "I'm glad, Mrs. Inglis. Yet, why do you look in pain?"

"Because I have to ask you something rather difficult. And I—I hope you don't think me the worse for asking it." He nods, his eyes widening and his smile fading. "And so I'm just going to ask."

"Okay."

"The other day, Eva and I, we quarreled about you. Actually, never mind about Eva. None of that matters." By now she is up and pacing under the watchful eyes of the gurus. "Darshan, have you invented the parasol flower?"

He strokes his beard. His chest is heaving. "This is why you are here? This is the difficult thing you must say to me?"

"Yes."

"I thought…somebody had died! Or your husband had found out about us!" He looks embarrassed. "Or you came to tell me you were leaving for England. Something serious, madam."

"Well, I would consider it serious," she says with feeling, "if it turns out that you have invented this parasol flower. And have been deceiving me all this time for…for degenerate purposes. That would be very serious to me, Sergeant Singh."

Color has crept into his cheeks. "And if I have been lying to you all this time, Mrs. Inglis, you would trust me now to tell you the truth?"

"Well?" she demands.

He sinks back in his armchair. Looking beaten, she thinks.

"I do not have any 'degenerate' intentions toward you, Mrs. Inglis, and I never did."

"Then answer my question, please! Is the flower a fiction?"

"I wish it were not." He bites at a thumbnail.

"You wish it were not. So you are saying the parasol flower is your invention?"

"I told you: it is a local legend I'd heard of. I've never met anybody who has seen or smelled or touched one." He looks up at her. "I made up the name, as you know. I made up some details. Who knows what color it is, or what it smells like."

"But there *is* none!" she exclaims.

"No, probably not."

She watches him closely. "Why? Why would you lie to me?" Was Eva right about him? Her instincts tell her there is more to the story.

He shakes his head, unable to speak.

Guilty! Guilty as charged. She makes her way to the door of his bungalow and, with the room spinning, begins wedging her feet into her wet boots.

"Mrs. Inglis. Please wait." Soon he stands looming over her, hands on hips. "You are feverish. I am really worried about you like this."

"Are you? So you're going to walk me home, then?"

He draws a great breath and releases it. "You know I cannot do that." If she's not mistaken, he is almost teary. "The flower," he says softly. "It was a beautiful idea. I thought simply, I want to share a beautiful idea with Mrs. Inglis."

"But I *believed* you! I believed it was real. I told Eva I was going to paint her a prized picture of it. And all this time, whenever I mentioned the thing, you must have been having a grand old laugh at me." She could cry over it on the walk home. Please God, preserve her from falling to pieces until she'd left his house.

"I'm sorry." He catches her arm. "Truly. I never was laughing at you, Mrs. Inglis. It may exist, you know. We may find this flower."

"No. We won't." Marshaling the last ounces of her strength, Hannah shakes her arm free and glares at the doorknob until he twists it, releasing her.

THIRTY-SIX

The kerosene is kept in the second shed, nearest the men's quarters. Malu notices when she goes to fetch more butterfly poison. Kerosene is *reliable* and kerosene is *expected*: such useful words. In the cabin, Dr. Peterborough uses a kerosene lamp. The kerosene becomes her first discovery.

He watched her strip off her clothes and climb onto the counter. For the first while, until her mind learned a trick of crawling out of her skin and going to sit on the roof, she had to concentrate all her energy on keeping still.

"Don't move," he told her more than once, his face disappearing from view. "Just jotting something down."

Once, he left something inside her that felt like the blade of a knife. She dared to whisper, "It's cold."

After, he helped her down to the bare floor, where a beetle scuttled quickly away. Under the counter, closest to the examination table, a plank of the cabin's siding is cracked and broken away. Her eyes happened to follow the insect as it ran for the broken board.

It is only later, when Malu is lying in her hammock thinking of the running beetle, that she realizes the loose board is a door. Sahib locks the proper doors and pockets the key. Yet with the beetle, she was lucky. The broken plank becomes her second discovery.

The night after the photographs, Malu couldn't concentrate on her letters. She dug her pencil into the paper and made a hole. Outside the women's quarters, the others were teasing and quarreling and she got it in her head that she wanted some rice toddy, too. By then, none of the other servants except Manang would go near her, let alone share their toddy. When she approached, they turned away with their cups. On a whim she went to find sahib, wherever he was relaxing in the great house. If not toddy, the truth.

She spoke up once she had his attention. "Please, sahib, when will you visit my mother? For treatment?"

Only then did she notice memsahib was in the room as well, sitting in the other corner, reading a book. Malu curtseyed. "Good evening, mem. Sorry to disturb."

Memsahib smiled. "It's fine, girl. You're quite right, you deserve an answer."

"How about next week?" The doctor touched the rims of his spectacles. "Sunday? I assume you would like to be present?"

"Charles," the mem said, before Malu could answer. "Just tell her the truth."

"I *can* visit the girl's mother," he said in a quiet voice.

"Charles, what is the point of all this, if not for the truth?" said the mem. She set her book down with a plonk. "Tell her the truth! Or *I* shall."

Sahib folded his newspaper and, glancing at his wife, made a very heavy sigh. "I'm afraid your mother's condition is incurable." He attached a long English name. "It's not your fault, child. And I do regret...I regret not telling you sooner." He glanced again at the mem. "But the fact is you oughtn't to waste your money on 'English medicine.' You're an enterprising girl. Use it to better yourself."

Malu kept looking down at her toes. She knew what "incurable" meant. What did it mean "to better herself?" How could she make herself better, without medicine, without Allah, without the comfort and the knowing of a mother? Some people were changeable, maybe, like light on water. Maybe those people could become someone better.

"You're an intelligent girl," said the mem. "You deserved to know."

It is Malu's third discovery, of the incurable, that fuses the other two discoveries together. The third discovery makes them all into discoveries. It is a miracle that each night, as she lies in her hammock, no one can tell she is divining her own fate.

By chance, the next moonless night is a cloudless one. No rain to douse a fire. Although the September air is still lukewarm, Malu shivers in her hammock, listening to the servant women breathing and snoring. She keeps one hand pressed to the sleeve of matches she's wrapped inside her sarong. If she is caught sneaking out, she'll say she's going to the privy. If she is caught past the privy, she'll say she's on an errand for tuan.

As it turns out, nobody is there to question anything.

Once she locates the loose plank, she pushes it in with little trouble.

Water has rotted out the board. Malu squeezes inside, right under the examination table, and lights the lamp to work by. She hurries from the one corner of the room to the next, dribbling kerosene along the floor. Around the camera on its stand. *Look up! Don't move!* she told them all. Malu tears down the sheet, strikes the jar of green liquid, tipping it off the counter where it smashes it to pieces. Spilling more petrol, she rushes over the places sahib lingered. Near the entrance that she's torn open, Malu lies on her belly for a while, breathing the heady fumes.

Her plan is to stay. But she isn't brave enough. Choking, she turns and wriggles backwards out of the hole. Then she lights three matches, one after the other, and tosses them in.

Malu hears the shouting and twists in her hammock, thudding onto the floor. Pain flashes up her back. Other women are rousing. Soon they crowd up through the doorway and spill out into the yard. One of the water boys sprints past, nearly knocking Malu over as he dashes up the pathway toward the main house.

His arms flail. "Fire! Fire!"

Malu stares. Has it all been a dream? Where the cabin had been, bright yellow flames are leaping into the sky, billowing streams of black smoke. The little box is so consumed it looks like a funeral pyre. Nothing will be left of it. Nothing. Around her, women begin muttering prayers and bending to touch their foreheads to the dewy ground. *Allah save us, Allah in your mercy.*

"No rains tonight!"

"A miracle."

At least that is the word that Malu thinks she hears. She hasn't noticed Roki come up, hasn't prepared her ears for Roki's broken speech. Roki's red-rimmed eyes are leaking.

One of the stable boys arrives and begins herding the women away from the servant's quarters toward the front of the house. "Come this way! Police will come soon," he tells them.

"Police will ask questions," Cook says. A murmur of concern goes through the group.

Manang runs by in the opposite direction, Hakim, the syce, on his heels.

"Manang!" Malu calls out. Where is he going?

He slows, locating her in the crowd. Then he gives a little bow before the two men break hard toward the flaming studio.

"No!" she shouts.

Roki frowns hard at Malu, then at the backs of the men.

"Why are they going *there*?" says Malu. "No one is in there."

"Come," urges the stable boy.

"We're staying here, you old fool!" snaps Cook. "We're in no danger."

As a compromise, they shuffle toward the scullery entrance, never letting the blazing building out of their sight. What of sahib and the mem, two stories up? Are they pulling off their crisp bed sheets, coming to watch from a window? An empty pail of kerosene lies under a bush, as far into the black jungle as she dared to stumble. The rest, God willing, will be burnt and gone. Their shame will be burnt to white feathers.

Malu holds her shaking hands behind her back, straining to find Manang's form. The smoke stings her eyes, cleansing them.

"Allah protect him," she whispers.

She prays so hard for Manang that she doesn't notice the police carts bouncing up the long driveway, or the light rain that has begun to fall.

THIRTY-SEVEN

Hannah's art was being kept in a self-serve lock-up in the Hampstead Village area of London. Celia Munk paused, key in the lock of Unit 33, to look back at me. "I'm afraid they're not as impressive as you've been imagining, my dear."

Celia had turned out to be a petite, upright septuagenarian with a meticulously coiffed jet-black head of hair. I'd met her only fifteen minutes earlier and already I was irritated. Her manner was patronizing; she seemed to speak only in clichés and backhanded compliments. But Celia did, quite literally, hold the key.

"I don't know what to expect," I replied cheerfully. "I'm not even sure they were completed paintings. Hannah refers to them as 'sketches' and 'studies' most of the time."

Celia let the three of us in to a space so dark that the only light came from the open doorway behind us. She flicked on a pocket flashlight and sliced the beam along the wall. Her beam illuminated a switch, which I pressed, and the fluorescent lighting flickered to life.

"It's mostly a great deal of claptrap," she said, leaning toward me in confidence. "Whatever Teddy and Barnaby didn't want."

"*And* yourself, Celia," said Barnaby. He stumbled over a hat rack. "Good heavens, I don't remember half of these things."

She produced a pair of plastic surgical gloves and took her time tugging them into place over her fingers. Not knowing where to start, I followed her through the maze of furniture and stacks of boxes. "No, sorry," she would mutter, whenever we arrived somewhere, before setting off in another direction.

"How long ago did you remove the paintings from the letters?" I asked. "Or rather, the letters from the paintings?"

"I suppose it was when we were going through Alice's estate."

Celia was stooped over a stack of wooden frames, parting them with her hands. "No. Someone else's paintings."

So she knew enough to recognize Hannah's work on sight. Or at least, what wasn't Hannah's work. "You have a good memory," I observed. Alice Munk had died in, when was it, 1988?

"Ha. Not so good that I know where they are!" She moved off to another stack of boards, this one lying horizontal on a chest of drawers.

The possibility of having to systematically sift through the contents of the lock-up was discouraging but not off-putting. I broke from Celia to rummage through an oversized box.

"Here," said Barnaby. "Here they are. I believe."

By the time I made it over to him, he was propping one up against a dismantled headboard and blowing away some of the dust. I peered at the bottom corners of the canvas. No signature I could see. The work was a dark composition of what looked to be orchids, hovering like tiny luminescent aliens in a shadowy field of ochres and sage greens. I took a step back. Looking at it felt invigorating, like a layer of ordinariness had just been scrubbed from me. "Yes, it's hers," I said.

Barnaby was already moving his way down the stack, propping each painting wherever there was a horizontal surface to be found. They were all stretched canvas on wooden frames and seemed to be completed paintings. A vendor selling coconuts. Fishermen. A boathouse with Malay women in sarongs, huddled together in secret conversation. The severed head of a tiger, sitting on a veranda.

"Wow," I said.

Barnaby was standing on the other side of the enormous desk where he'd found the stack of paintings, gazing down into one of them.

I said, "Is that...?"

"Clouds."

I came around the desk and we stood side by side, staring into her sky. A thundercloud was forming, or was it dissipating? Warm yellows and pinks spread in broad strokes, while blues and greys were accumulating in narrower, surer lines. A bottomless, shifting sky that left me suspended between hope and despair. All we had was time, and such little time we had. I wanted to tell Hannah that I couldn't make sense of it either. To let her know that, somehow, she'd understood me—and maybe that could be enough?

"It's almost...simple," I said. "You wouldn't expect it could do what is does to you. It's...but you have to give it time, and your full attention."

"Yes, fine art is not like a bus shelter advert," Barnaby said. "Probably why it tends to fare rather poorly in this day and age."

"Ha!" I snorted. I might have asked him what had got up his nose, but I knew it was Celia. She'd moved into our range, along with the citrus-sweet scent of her perfume, and was gazing witheringly at the paintings on display.

"I can see that you two dreamers would spend the rest of the night here. Without a care in the world!" She pinned Barnaby with a knowing look.

As Celia had predicted, there were blankets, empty boxes, and a dolly in the locker. She and Barnaby wrapped and loaded the works while I looked on helplessly. Our minicab arrived before we even reached the sidewalk.

"I'll return the dolly," Barnaby said dutifully. He caught my eye as he grabbed its handles. "You're right, all of her works are realistic."

We climbed into the middle bench of seats, leaving the shotgun spot for Barnaby, and for a few moments Celia chewed the corner of her burgundy lips. The cabbie was racing through his playlist, sending a sequence of jarring first chords through the stereo system.

"Celia, I forgot to ask you about *The Descent of Woman*. The book? Barnaby mentioned that some correspondence existed between the Peterboroughs and their publishers and the engravers. Hannah's art was used for at least one engraving in the book. As you probably know. So…if you happen to have anything that could shed light on why her artwork was chosen, that would be really helpful for me."

"Well," she said, without a glance in my direction, "it's obvious you're not from the tabloids."

I wasn't sure if that implied something about me or my outfit, but I was pleased she seemed prepared to trust me. "I read David Maikin's article. I'm so sorry he…he used you in that way." Not that his disingenuous muckraking exculpated the Peterboroughs, I replied to myself. I could nuance my position later, once I got my hands on their correspondence and research notes.

"Once bitten, twice shy," she muttered. "But all right. It's not like any more damage can be done, I suppose."

"Thank you."

"Don't Worry Be Happy" burst into life on the car stereo.

She touched a hand to her hair. "Oh, he's frightfully slow, isn't he?"

I ducked and looked back toward the storage building.

"They're at home," she said. "After *it* broke, I took personal control of any contentious documents. From Fulgham House, from the lock-up. Irrational, I realize, as the cat was already out of the bag. I even persuaded the university to give me the Peterborough materials from their archives."

I was incredulous. "How did you manage that?"

"The weight of moral authority," she said icily.

That night, I slept in Celia Munk's guest bedroom. Barnaby stayed on, too, assigned one of the couches in her lounge. She owned a red brick conversion whose showroom minimalism felt surprisingly soothing. The guestroom was decorated in a palette of greys and whites, accented with dashes of fuschia; there were strategically placed glassware, decanters, stoppered perfume bottles, and candy dishes; the surface of the armoire was covered by a shallow, tentacled bowl, something like a Chihuly sculpture or a miniature alien spacecraft.

Exhausted, I dropped my backpack, stripped off my jeans, and jumped in bed. I fell asleep looking at clouds.

In the morning, I nearly collided with Celia as she was coming out of the washroom.

"You're awake!" she said in a raspy voice.

"Yes! You, too."

She stood there looking bewildered, unguarded, un-coiffed.

I smiled. "Going for a run," I told her, inching by.

With the slightest of flinches, she turned and padded off in her silk pajamas.

All night I'd dreamt of paintings, and as I ran through Celia's imposing urban village, these dream sequences came to me like puzzle pieces for a jigsaw. I'd dreamt of Hannah painting in Rome's Coliseum, with tigers prowling the arena and a capacity crowd making a soccer-match-style din. She kept the tigers occupied by throwing mussels at them. The great cats hooked the tips of their claws sideways into the shells to crack them open, then speared each tiny knot of flesh and brought it to their whiskery lips. Party guests popping hors d'oeuvres from toothpicks. All the while Hannah was deliberately, meticulously stroking paint on canvas. I remembered the nape of her neck. Her long hair was up, several brushes poked into it. I remembered her feet planted wide apart, the way she would lean forward, absently, to pick another mussel from the pail and fling it. I had the distinct and ridiculous thought: *this is not the way Victorian women handle themselves in the movies.* "Mrs. Inglis!" I called. "I can help!" The supply of mussels was running low, the tigers closing in. Across the dusty stadium I sprinted, carrying a huge, tentacled glass bowl—somehow this bowl was meant to help—and laid the empty vessel at her feet. "Mrs. Inglis! I can help!"

I sprinted the last fifty meters to Celia's door. Then took a few minutes to stretch before letting myself in quietly, only to find Celia and Barnaby knocking around in the kitchen.

"You're up," I said, still breathing a little roughly as I came through.

Though un-coiffed, Celia looked herself again. "When you left, my dear, you set off the alarm."

"Oh, shit. Pardon my language. Did the police come?"

Barnaby laughed. "Yes, we've only finally got rid of them. Sent the officers away with some pastries."

A rather large plate of pastries was glistening beside the coffee maker.

"Of course not," said Celia. "I merely had to come down to the control panel and turn off the blaring ruckus." She nodded at Barnaby. "He was up by then, of course, but has no clue of the combination."

"By then? I was awake half the night," he grumbled.

Celia handed him a cup of coffee. "You told me you slept well!" She poured me one, too, asking what I took in it. Then filled me a glass of water from the filter on her refrigerator and told me she was adding a wedge of lemon.

"I did sleep well," Barnaby was saying over our conversation. "In the sense that your £5,000 sofa bed is comfortable. That's what people really mean when they ask if you've slept well. 'Is my bed comfortable? Is it worth the money I've spent to host a guest once a in blue moon?' Yes, your bed is comfortable."

"That one was closer to £10,000," she murmured, carrying the pastries to the table.

"I was awake"—and here he paused to see if I was paying

attention—"because I couldn't put our Hannah Inglis and her paintings out of my head."

"Neither can I," I said.

After breakfast we managed to lean all twenty-two of the paintings around Celia's lounge and match each to the letter that had accompanied it, thereby putting them in chronological order. Having done so, the three of us lapsed into silence, sunk into ourselves, like visitors at a gallery. I'd always considered it a bizarre-looking behavior: humans, drinking in works of art. There was something primitive about it, some sort of animal magnetism in the activity. Like sitting at a campfire or lying under the stars. Like standing before a waterfall, mesmerized by all that ever-changing, ever-remaining matter.

I said, "When the aliens come and they ask why should they spare our miserable, self-destructive little species…what could they ever have to learn from us? We'll have to show them some art. Our best works of art."

Where on earth had that come from? The words had seemed to speak themselves, and now it was too late to recover and make myself sound normal.

Barnaby addressed Celia. "Why didn't we notice them before? After Mum's funeral?"

Celia was examining one of the smaller paintings, of a vine arching over a pergola. She didn't reply.

"I suppose I had a lot on my mind," he mumbled. He saw me looking at him and said, "You've got my nomination, Nancy. To speak to the aliens for us."

I did blush a bit, then, also because Barnaby looked unabashedly happy. He had one of Hannah's letters in hand as he stood back from a painting of a lotus flower. A pale pink lotus and trail of lily pads floated on glassy water. The canvas shimmered with pinks and greens and somehow it was all laced together: the shadows on the water, the glow of the slanting sun, the tumble of sky above.

Hannah had made dozens of versions of the lotus flowers, practicing color and stroke patterns. She'd written to Godot to send one in which "color is used for its building power." The obscure phrase had stuck with me. I repeated the phrase to Barnaby, knowing it was lying somewhere on the pages in his hand. "She's building connections, do you think? What does the color build? Is it showing the interrelation of everything?"

He pinched his nose, making a sort of purring noise. "That would be very Buddhist of her. Did she have any exposure to Buddhism?"

"It would be very human of her," Celia interjected, "to be awed by nature. To feel God's presence in it."

I wasn't convinced that the interconnection, for Hannah, was quite so godly. Her subjects were so vividly *themselves*, alive in the moment and not a whit beyond it. "This one of the severed cow's leg," I said, "I just *love* that she painted this. The hoof looks like a polished fingernail. So delicate. And sad. But, like, funny. Do you remember that, the morning of their tiger attack?"

Barnaby came over and had another look. "It's rather like she painted the tiger at the same time she painted its prey, if that's possible. Not sure I feel more for the prey or the predator."

I chuckled. "Exactly."

At some point, Celia entered the room balancing a box of pizza. She picked her way around the rearranged furniture, dodging our notebooks and computer cords. The pizza looked incongruous in her arms. Peasant food. Really, she was being a great sport, allowing us to take over her house.

"Here we are," she announced. "They've brought a pack of fizzy drinks as well."

"Dinnertime already?" Barnaby and I said.

I tried to pay for my share of the takeout, pushing a ten-pound and a five-pound note toward Celia, but she waved me away. Nor did she eat with us. She returned only after we'd decimated the large Mediterranean Deluxe, this time carrying file boxes. I jumped up to help, and we lowered the boxes onto the table.

"Celia?" Barnaby said in surprise.

"Honestly, Nancy, I don't think you'll find much about Hannah in all that," she said to me. "But you're welcome to try."

It was, of course, the notes and letters surrounding *The Descent*. All the 'contentious documents' Celia had been hiding in her closet or under her bed.

"Thank you, this is wonderful," I told her. To Barnaby, I said,

"There may be something more in here about the parasol flower. Or something to give an indication of why Hannah's art ended up with the Peterboroughs."

He nodded cautiously.

"Have you ever tried to locate Hannah's descendants?" I asked them. I thought of the letters in which Hannah had characterized her husband's opposition to her art.

Barnaby and Celia looked at each other.

"What for?" she said. "If you don't find proof of ownership in those documents, that says nothing about who rightfully owns these works, Nancy."

Barnaby was looking around the room at our private, stunning exposition. "These paintings have been in our family for generations."

"What Barnaby means to say is that Eva and Charles Peterborough collected art from all over the world," said Celia. "They were patrons of the arts. *That* is certainly well-documented historically."

My heart was thrumming. The Munks had not even cared to look at the paintings in decades! "I'm not trying to cause any trouble," I said. "But you agreed with me, Barnaby, how strange this situation is. Hannah was mailing these paintings to Henri Godot. So how did they end up…" My hands floated upward at my sides. "One could argue these paintings belong to Godot and his inheritors. She was trying to send them to him."

And if they'd reached their destination, I wondered, what difference might that have made for Hannah?

"Perhaps one could say that," said Barnaby, his bass voice sounding even deeper than usual. "*Is* that what you're saying, Nancy?"

The Munks looked at me anxiously.

No, I wasn't saying that, I told them. "Are you saying you want to stop?" Kenneth Cavanaugh had asked me. I excused myself to visit Celia's peacock-themed powder room, where I scrubbed pizza grease from my hands with scented soap and water.

THIRTY-EIGHT

In the Ladies Association boardroom, Lucy Finch taps the gavel several times. "Thank you all for coming to our emergency meeting. I'm sure you know by now that Mrs. Peterborough and her family are recovering at the Residency from their terrible ordeal."

Ladies make sympathetic noises. Beatrice Watts makes the sign of the cross. Hannah closes her eyes to stop from rolling them. She *had* been alarmed, of course, on the night of the fire. She woke to the sounds of whinnying horses and doors banging open along the street. In her dressing gown, she'd tiptoed onto the veranda. Next door, at the Residency, lanterns were glowing through the windows.

"Hannah." It was Hazel, not three paces away, a night bonnet wrapped around her full face.

"Cripes, Hazel! You startled me!"

"I was coming to your door as you walked out. They're rising against us, Hannah. Do you remember, a few years ago, how they lit up the train depot?" Hazel didn't wait for her to recall. "This may be hardest for you to bear, of us all."

"For me to bear? I don't understand you, Hazel. What time is it?"

"The darkies have torched Idlewyld."

"What? What do you mean?"

Hazel was unable to offer any concrete information. Hannah finally gave up and sprinted across the lawn to the Residency in her bare feet.

As she approached, two cadets on horseback trotted past her. A third horse, a russet mare, danced and circled near the veranda.

Seeing her, Darshan stilled the horse with a gentle "woah."

"Idlewyld is…? What has happened, Sergeant?"

"Fire. I don't know much more than that."

"May I come with you? Ride out with you?"

His face was grim, his eyes shadowed. "Of course not, madam." He turned the horse as the door opened. James Finch stepped out, shouted something—a number, she recalled—and Darshan signaled with a wave.

"Darshan. Wait."

The horse whinnied as he tightened the reins.

"Do be careful," she said.

He nodded, kicked the mare's flanks, and cantered away.

When she later learned that it was the doctor's cabin alone that had been destroyed by fire, she felt an overwhelming relief. It was a guilt-laced pleasure, offset by a certain amount of sympathy for the Peterboroughs. But this, she thinks, this meeting is too much.

Lucy is droning on. "...growing stronger by the hour, poor child. They've all had quite a shock, but Dr. MacGillivery assures me they will make a complete recovery."

The association's secretary, at Lucy's request, begins reading out a long list of items starting with candelabras and ending with a soup tureen. An emergency fund, what rubbish! Do they not know how well-provisioned the Idlewyld mansion is? Lucy must be under the impression the cabin contained household provisions and family heirlooms. Eva had not bothered to set her straight.

"How is the colonel?" whispers Hazel, who is seated to her left.

"Oh. Recovering. From his illness, not from the announcement."

"Yes, well, I was rather in shock about that, too. After all George has done for the man." She nods towards Lucy. "To be passed over like that!"

The list having been finally itemized, Lucy Finch addresses the group. "I thought each one of us might volunteer for at least two items, with an aim to supplementing the Peterboroughs' family belongings within the month."

"And don't forget, Lucy, the church has an emergency fund for..." Beatrice's voice trails off, her brow knuckling.

She has remembered the family's atheism. Hannah wants to laugh. God, none of them even know Eva! She swallows and raises a hand, then speaks without being called on. "I'm just not—" Hannah clears her throat. "Ladies, I'm just wondering...thankfully the main house wasn't damaged at all, as I understand it. I don't wish to seem insensitive, but are we certain the Peterboroughs *need* any of these provisions?"

Lucy pounces. "This family is homeless, distraught, and in fear for their lives, Mrs. Inglis. Yesterday Mrs. Peterborough was perfectly grateful for the assistance I could offer her. One has to take care not to sink into a reverse prejudice, in which the very wealthy are discounted on the basis of their wealth. I imagine this might be especially challenging for a socialist such as yourself."

"I'm not a socialist, Lucy." Hannah frowns at them. "Nor are the Peterboroughs homeless! And I know it wasn't bed linens and crockery they kept in that cabin."

The ladies are staring at her, expecting a reasonable explanation. If not crockery, then what? Hannah shakes her head and apologizes. No, she's never gone in the cabin herself. In despair, she lapses into silence.

Lucy, hawk-eyed, is about to resume when Eva herself enters the room. The half-circles under her eyes look as if they've been scored with scissors. A navy dress sits awkwardly upon her tensed shoulders.

"Good morning, everyone. I'm sorry to be late. I must take my sleep when I can get it these days."

"How are you faring, Eva?" Lucy replies on behalf of the group.

"Fine, thank you. As best as can be expected." Her voice is raspy. She moves to a place at the table.

"Does the family need suet?" inquires Marilese Blumengard, a Dutch homesteader.

Eva ignores this. "Have there been any arrests?" she addresses Lucy.

"No," reports Lucy. "Not as yet."

"Terrible," says Hazel, uncorking a flood of sympathies from around the table.

"Oh, you poor, poor thing," says the treasurer.

"Makes you wonder if you're safe in your own bed."

"You're not safe in your own bed."

"With these darkie servants everywhere."

"And these darkie *police*!"

Hannah shifts in her chair, regretting once again that she has come.

"All of them, bone idle," says Hazel. "That Kling sergeant, they found him sleeping at his desk, didn't they?"

"Well, it was the middle of the night," Hannah can't help but point out. "It's a wonder he was even at the station!"

A hush falls on the room.

"Think twice about whom you choose to defend, Mrs. Inglis," says Lucy. "People will question whether to include you at this table."

Around the circle, heads are nodding almost imperceptibly; eyes are averted, hands folded. Hannah grips the sides of her chair. Underneath all the niceties the world has corners, is ever angled into sides. In the Perak Club next door, their husbands are no doubt talking about retribution rather than bed sheets and hairbrushes.

"Please." Eva's voice is bamboo splintering. "I came here today, because I have faith in the solidarity of the women of this town."

"Well said!" Lucy exclaims. "Didn't I assure you, Mrs. Peterborough, that it would be worth attending one of our meetings!"

"Ought we to pressure the administration?" someone suggests.

"The administration must ensure the police do their job."

"We must get an arrest," Eva says with conviction.

Admiration shines from Lucy's pores. "Yes, Mrs. Peterborough, an arrest is precisely what we need."

"It is? Why?" Hannah blurts out, beside herself with frustration. "The fire might have been a horrible accident."

"Yet it wasn't." Eva smiles sourly.

"You didn't get word from your friend and colleague on the police force?" Hazel says innocently.

One or two of the others titter.

Lucy gives Hazel a sharp glance before addressing Hannah. "The scope and severity of the burn suggests that an unusual quantity of flammable oil was present. More than would be contained in a lamp. Then, just yesterday, an empty kettle of kerosene was found in the forest behind the estate. Ladies, this is undoubtedly a case of arson."

At the close of the LAP meeting, Hannah slips away immediately, leaving the others to coo at Eva. She is marching up Cinnamon Street when the Peterboroughs' blacktop slows beside her and releases Eva from its belly.

"Well, that was a majestic pain in the hindquarters," are Eva's first words.

Hannah tilts her umbrella for a clearer view of the woman. "I was starting to wonder whether that was you in that meeting room, or a look-alike automaton. 'I have faith in the solidarity of the women of this town,'" she mimics. "You must have practiced that one a few times."

"I called on you, Hannah. Twice."

"I know."

"I wanted to apologize. I brought your portfolio and your supplies."

"I know. Thank you. I did send you a note."

"Your girl said you weren't taking callers." Eva waves at the syce and the carriage drives off. "May I walk with you?"

"Feel free," Hannah replies drily. They chug up a particularly steep portion of the switchback before she glances again at Eva's terrible face. "Look, I'm glad none of you were hurt. You must focus on that fact."

"I'd rather she'd torched the main house."

"Eva!"

She coughs spasmodically for a time, stooped over a handkerchief. "All that work."

"Was *everything* destroyed? Surely not your book. Didn't you keep your documents in the study?"

"No, the book is fine." Eva wipes the handkerchief under her nose. "It's everything of Charles'. All the clinical observations that are required to undergird the book's arguments. A pity that scientific treatises require evidence."

A pity indeed. But there is no point rehashing her objections. "You'd better get back to the Residency," says Hannah, striking out again.

Eva hastens to keep up. "I'm in no rush, believe me. Between Lucy's warbling and the brigadier's preening, I'm losing my last shreds of sanity." She enters into another coughing fit, though her eyes start twinkling. "The thing is, if we want their help, it's better to appear to need it. I was quite proud of myself for coming to that realization. I've been so stubbornly competent all these years."

"Ye-es," Hannah says. "Eva, what do you mean 'she?' You said you'd rather 'she' had torched the house."

"The girl who destroyed our studio. I know who it is."

"And you want her arrested." She recalls Eva's insistence at the meeting. "Who?"

"Charlotte's genduk. The girl Charles took on as an assistant. She did this to us."

Hannah thinks of the light-skinned girl with the round shy face. Standing in the shallows, collecting river rocks by Charlotte's side. "The one who came on our trek."

"She's clever, all right," says Eva. "Clever enough to know that razing the studio was the best way to attack us. She wanted revenge."

Hannah starts at the word. It seems far-fetched. Yet she's forgetting the obvious! The girl must have wanted revenge for what Charles had done to her. A shiver scuttles over her. "In that case, any one of those poor things had cause to—"

"I'm telling you," Eva snarls, "it was her."

Why *are* you telling me, Hannah wants to ask, when you have the audience of the serving Resident and his successor? And the Ladies Association wrapped around your little finger? She must know that Hannah won't be inclined to leap to her aid, after everything that's passed between them. They walk in silence for a time, turning onto Ridge Road, cresting its slow rise along the hillside.

"Will you speak to Sergeant Singh for me?" Eva says, on cue. "Tell him what I know, that the genduk has done this."

"Me?"

"Resident Finch is not inclined to *require* an arrest."

"The ladies have just agreed to 'pressure the administration,'" Hannah points out.

"I don't believe James would go so far as to overturn a police investigation. Not as his last act from the chair, as it were. And this ridiculous Effingdon-Watts, he's for arresting the entire village, so long as it makes him look efficient. One sniveling, puffy-faced girl won't look efficient. Please, tell your sergeant who he needs to interrogate."

As they approach the acacia, Hannah slows and looks up into the tree. No sign of Roderick. Where has he been lately?

"What is it?" asks Eva.

"Nothing."

The wind is picking up, making their umbrellas less than useful. Soon the familiar turquoise clapboard of Hannah's house comes into sight up the rise, and she has yet to give Eva an answer.

"I believe you are sincere, Eva. You seem to have quite thought this through. But what do you know, really? Do you have any proof? And if so," she shakes her head, "then you should tell him yourself. I have no special sway over the man. Nor should I."

Eva looks at her sideways, pursing her lips in disbelief. "It's *his* job to find the proof."

"I don't know, Eva. I feel…"

"Oh, forget it," she snaps. "I thought for once *you* might be willing to help *me*."

They walk on more swiftly than before, a lump growing in Hannah's throat. At the flagstone pathway that leads to her veranda she says, "I'll talk to him. I can promise you that much."

Eva nods and rubs her eyes, offering her thanks as Hannah turns away. She doesn't see it until she's almost swung her foot into it, and that is when she shrieks. A tiger is gaping at her from the welcome mat, its tatty head bodiless and forlorn. One ear is ripped nearly off. A grey-pink tongue lolls out one side of the mouth. It is the sound of the sad face that hurts, the sound of so many flies whirring and buzzing and burrowing.

"What are *you* doing here?" she asks it.

Hearing a thump, she finds a boy in a grey miner's jumpsuit, squatting in one corner of the veranda. Heat rises in her, anger that she does not wish to contain.

"I suppose you're waiting for payment, are you?"

He stands and bows.

"Stop this. Do not kill any more tigers. Do you understand me?"

He blinks. "Tuan say?"

"*I* say. It's over! Tell the others your hunt is over." Hands shaking, Hannah opens her purse and pulls out two Straits dollars. "That's all you'll get. Wait. Take this…head away."

His eyes are wide as he points at the severed head. "For keep the bounty, too? Take plenty fast, memsahib, plenty fast. You wait here." He bows again and sprints off, presumably to seek some help for the removal.

Hannah walks around to the back entrance of the house and enters through the scullery, nearly tripping headlong over a pile of laundry.

THIRTY-NINE

Inside, the house is silent. Hannah can almost imagine that the great cat has padded quietly back to the woods. She plucks a banana from the fruit bowl. Far quieter here than it must be at the Residency. Eva will be arriving to a very concerned Lucy Finch. *Gracious me, you've walked home? In this wet! In your condition!* Lucy will probably towel her off and prop her up in bed with a cup of warm cocoa.

Could it really be that Charlotte's babysitter, barely more than a child herself, managed to foil the entire operation? And where is the young Malay girl now, who was once Charlotte's playmate? And Charles' assistant: what experiences does that word conceal, she wonders, in order for "revenge" to tally? Where are all the other servants who were at Idlewyld? Perhaps they've been sent home. Just as likely, they are still there at the great house, keeping up with the cleaning and gardening. *Think twice about whom you choose to defend.*

"Mem? You okay?" Suria is peering at her through the bars of the staircase, stooped over on the landing.

Hannah hadn't noticed she'd wandered halfway up the stairs. "Yes," she replies. Despite everything, or maybe because of it, she feels expansive. That expansive, hopeful stirring that tells her she should be painting. She can't ignore it any longer.

Suria has plodded down the stairs and stands with her hands on her hips. "You want me make lunch?"

"No, no, this is fine." Hannah takes her last bite of the banana and folds the peel.

The housemaid holds up one palm for the refuse.

"Suria, do you know anything about this fire at Idlewyld?"

She shrugs, her palm still raised.

"Of course you do. Servants talk as much as anybody else. But we can't talk about it together, can we?"

Suria shakes her head.

Hannah turns over the peel. But the ayah doesn't leave. "What is it?"

"You look...strange, mem."

"Why, thank you, Suria. Trust you to be honest. I must admit, I feel a little off-kilter. In point of fact, though, it's this town that's off-kilter. But one can't say that and be believed. One can't say, 'It's not me, it's you.'"

She's stashed her paint box and portfolio in the room they set aside for a nursery. She will lock the door and paint. George must still be out, trying to manage this mess with the natives.

A commotion outside the front door sends Suria to look. "Miners!" she cries. "Mem!"

Two miners are jabbering at each other as they seize and lift the stiff-ened tiger head onto a stretcher. In no time, they hoist the stretcher by its handles and scamper away with their loot. Hannah watches it all through the translucent drapes of the sitting room window.

"Mem!" Suria shuffles over. "They take tuan's head."

"Yes," she agrees. "They do."

Dismissing Suria, Hannah walks to the colonel's office and tests the doorknob, letting herself in. Alone, she has only ever stood in the doorway. Now she shuts the door behind her. The desk draws to her to it, and she moves smoothly around to the chair and, with a stutter of hesitation, sits down in it. The surface is mostly uncluttered. Only a few piles of paper that have nothing to hide and a paperweight with a skim of dust upon it. The entire room smells faintly of his shoes and shoe polish. On the wall facing there is a print of a Titian's Venus. Titian's Venus, of all things! Plump and bare and unabashed. So passive. So much in control. What could the colonel understand about Titian's Venus?

She opens one desk drawer, then the others. Some sort of shipping files are stacked in the bottom one. Biscuits and a flask of gin in the middle. Pencils, a straight rule, a tin of dominoes in the shallow top drawer. She falls to her knees, groping for the catch for the slender secret drawer that pops open sideways. There, next to a billfold, is the photograph. Hannah takes it and pushes the drawer back onto its catch.

George has not set foot in the men's club since "the incident," as he mentally refers to it. There was "the incident," as well as "the be-trayal," although he is unsure quite which came before which or why it bothers him that he cannot settle on a satisfactory order. (There is no answer to the question of the chicken or the egg, is there?) The fact is both events were humiliating, both took place, and he lives on in disgrace and discomfort. All of the staff manning the club, such as the boy who is showing him upstairs now, appear unusually welcoming. Laughing up their sleeves, the bastards.

Slipping into the smoking room, George is surprised to find a crowd gathered. Edgar Swinburne, Minister Watt, and several other members who are not normally part of Finch's inner circle. Charles Peterborough sits in a striped wingback, looking as he tends to: distracted and somewhat pained. Effingdon-Watts is present, too. Indeed it is E.W. lecturing to them all, speaking softly and firmly, one hand gripping the mantelpiece.

"The Malays have a history of going amok. Killing sprees and such."

Finch grumbles a little at this, the sounds from his mouth not quite forming words. Others murmur to each other.

"This is not something any one of us likes to come face to face with, gentlemen. I have the benefit of fresh eyes," E.W. waxes on, "and I can see all too clearly that the community in Kuala Kangsa is suffering a loss of innocence. Like the colonial experience around the globe. I've seen it in Africa, in India, the Americas…and I tell you, they won't stop at one fire."

"Now, Arthur," Finch grumbles. He's caught sight of George. "We've usually relied on diplomacy. Colonel Inglis has made great inroads with the local sultan, for instance."

E.W. glares at George and seems prepared to object. Instead, he shares his own fresh-eyed impressions of Izrin, formed during a recent stroll through the lower town. George turns away, occupying himself with the familiar plaques and the group photographs mounted on the wall. Hunting, cricket, cart racing. When he came to Kuala Kangsa, it was little better than a swamp, and they'd busied themselves with making houses, making roads, making order out of chaos. It was, in retrospect, a genesis not unlike the biblical one. It certainly seems a miracle from where he is standing now. E.W. tells them how poorly the sultan comes off, followed by that pack of stray dogs.

George wanders away to the billiards room. It's a scant few minutes before Finch comes through to find him. "He's a wally," George says.

"Didn't anybody tell him about the dogs?" The sultan is bound by his religious tradition to offer charity to all homeless creatures, human and animal alike.

"Arthur's only just lost his wife, you know. To the African yellow fever."

George smacks his hand to his forehead. "Yes, I do remember his tale of woe."

A pet bird trills suddenly in its cage in the corner.

"Look. I'm sorry, old boy. Did you get my note?"

The letter was classic Finch, the better portion of it spent trying to convince himself that Kuala Kangsa would be in good hands after he left, a much smaller portion spent on sympathy for George. *Well, the province fucking won't be in good hands, not with E.W. at the helm.* Surprisingly, though, George doesn't harbor any hostility toward Finch. He'll miss him, the fat old bugger. In any case, even Finch couldn't have gone against the wishes of the Resident-General. The question is, only, what to do about the rest of his life? Perhaps nothing.

"What are we going to do about the arson?" George asks, setting the billiard cue back in its rack. Finch pushes his lips into a thoughtful pucker. "Baldy doesn't know what was in that cabin, does he?" says George.

"No. I would like the whole damn thing to go away."

"Well, you're still the Resident," George says, "for a few weeks yet. And I'm still your deputy." He can't resist adding, "If Baldy hadn't got involved, the whole damn thing would have gone away by now."

Finch shakes his head. "I don't know about that. She-Peterborough is pushing quite hard." Conscious of the various ears in the adjoining room, they agree to reconvene at the office later.

"Didn't think the place would be overrun like this," he mumbles.

"Have a smoke, old boy," Finch suggests. "Do you good." He puts an arm around George and George surrenders to it.

"Maybe I won't be far behind you."

"Eh?"

"I'm thinking of going home. Take Hannah home. Start over again."

FORTY

To begin, Hannah sits with the canvas on her lap and draws directly onto it in pencil. Working fast, almost in gestures. Then breaks from this to arrange her palette and test colors. It is a pleasant kind of empty in the nursery. Cracking open the window, she hears birdsong. She touches her brushes, selects one, two, three different sizes and draws one, dry of paint, along the main lines of the portrait. Reds and ochres. Richness. Impoverishment. The barest dirt that nonetheless sustains. The earth and its bounty, mined for pigments. And she is no longer "mem," and in truth she never has been. She is an insect on the wing or one crawling up the wall, some minor hand of the divine—a witness who feels all of the doing in her being. A witness to sing to them in shapes and colors.

The photograph itself, this mesmerizing arrest of time, is not the living reality. Yet the painted portrait is alive, or it can be so. Hannah imagines she is working backwards, then, from death to life. Until the blood is pumping under the woman's skin, until the thoughts are lurking behind the eyes, and the words come like wrens, twitching and alert but caught behind her teeth. Until the whole of her feeling life, bounding and fluttering beneath the ribs and breasts, is present. Her brushes bring all this to view by providing the right forms of concealment—it is paradoxical, of course—so that life can establish itself. Not only the living body, but one person's unique awareness of her days.

Coming to the open window, Hannah lifts her face to the sunlight and lets the anticipation build like a symphony of strings. Then begins again.

With certain close strokes, she feels as if she is opening the woman up. Others, suturing her shut. She makes one ear nothing more than a gash. The left eye becomes swollen-lidded, almost bruised. She turns the woman's shoulder slightly into the center, rounding her upper back. As her brush strokes the thighs she can feel the weight and resistance of the flesh. The breasts will hang, unconcealed. The collarbone is jagged. The broken mouth opens, perhaps to object. *There is more,* the woman says to her. *More than this.*

Between forays at the easel, she chews at her fingers and shifts her weight back and forth. Sometimes, a floorboard creaks. Time flows away.

FORTY-ONE

On the way home, George feels freer, younger, for having said it. He needn't worry any more about gaining the Residency. He needn't worry about having to work under this preposterous, bloodthirsty E.W. Perhaps he needn't work much at all, depending on what Finch and the Home Office could arrange for him. And then, God willing, they could finally start a family.

He enters the house with a bang of the screen door. Shrugs off his outerwear, props his umbrella in its stand. "Memsahib?" he asks Suria, who has ambled out to greet him.

The ayah points upward, an anxious look on her face.

He takes the stairs faster than he has in weeks. He'll bed her, then tell her his plan. It's enough to have the plan; dates and times and details can be sorted later. The plan is solution enough.

Hannah is not in their bedroom or bathroom. Nor the guest bedroom. The only other room, what would have been the nursery, is shut and locked. "Hannah?" he calls through the door. "Are you in there?" Floorboards creak. "Why have you locked yourself in there?"

Another long minute passes. At last the door swings open.

Cautiously, he steps inside. She has not bothered to conceal the tubes of paints and rags strewn over the bare floor. Brushes, a palette, lying on the top of the dresser. A canvas in progress is on an easel facing them. He can't quite parse what he is seeing as he walks toward it, trying to decipher the colored shapes and forms. Finally, he recognizes a face—a scarred, ugly, swollen face with a cleft palate—sitting upon a heap of limbs and breasts and body parts. The girl on the canvas stares back at him, daring him to believe.

"Disgusting," he says.

His wife is standing, observing him, a long brush between her fingers. Her sultry eyes lower to his chest. They are weapons—hostile, single-purposed things. Her chin is smudged with red-brown paint. Her feet and hands are bare. Strands of her unwashed hair have come unpinned and lie lank upon her neck.

238

"Disgusting," he repeats, pointedly this time.

What in God's name is she doing painting! He asks her this.

"I'm doing…what I must do," she stammers. She doesn't appear remorseful at all. Dazed, more like.

He then notices the postcard photograph propped in front of the canvas. She must have stolen it from his study! Seeing it transports him back to the doctor's cabin: the fermented scents, the tools and maps, the drawer of faces. Before that, this very house girl shoving him off like a boat from a dock. And earlier still, hurrying through the Peterboroughs' stable, finding his family's bullock, as expected. Seeing the police mount—unexpected. The chestnut mare with its white marking. The chestnut mare with its white marking.

"He was there that day," George realizes. "Sergeant Singh."

Hannah listens, her eyes luminous, her whole being luminous.

"And you spent so much time away… So much time."

She continues to study his face.

"You were painting *there*," he suggests. "You were trekking there. That very day I visited. With that Kling." He laughs; something odd has popped into his head. "You know, Finch once tried to tell me those darkies were debating metaphysical matters, out there on the high street. The truth is our police force has nothing better to do than stand about and scratch their balls. Or, or, or…ingratiate themselves with our women."

"Ingratiate themselves." She seems to have woken. "'Our women.' So you've figured everything out for yourself, then. Do I get to speak, George?"

"Why should you? You say whatever serves, then do as you please."
This jab seems to register.

He moves closer. It's like toeing an abyss. "Here is a question for you, Hannah. Have you and that sergeant been alone together?"

Her eyes fall to the photograph for a moment before she raises her head, drawing herself up almost regally. "Yes," she says. "I was painting at Idlewyld all summer. In the house, with Eva's permission. And on their property, out of doors." The reek of paint must be getting to him. He puts his sleeve to his nose. "In the forest, with Darshan Singh."

Darshan Singh. In a blink the two of them are fording a stream, pulling off each other's clothes, lying in each other's arms. George's own arms are numb at his sides. "Is that...well, is that...all you have to say for yourself?"

"No," she murmurs. "I called off your hunt."

George backs out of the room, his chest burning. When he reaches the stairwell, the fury hits him. He marches back to the nursery. "Get out!" he shouts into the room. "Get out of this house! Whore!"

FORTY-TWO

The two police officers, the sergeant and his deputy, are arguing again. Malu keeps splitting straw. Manang is splitting straw, too. They squat beside each other in the holding cells, saying nothing. Last night he gave her both of the scratchy blankets that the officer slipped between the bars. She thinks of Umi at home, wondering about what her daughter has done. "I'm sorry, Amah," she whispers.

"Stop," Manang commands.

"I'm so sorry. Manang, I—"

"Shhh. Say nothing."

She should have stayed inside that cabin and let the flames swallow her up. In the place after this life, the bad place, she and Amah could be together. Instead she scuttled away like a rat.

Manang's fingers are splitting a husk. "Cry if you like," he says. "Say nothing."

Crescents of dirt are under his fingernails. She thinks of all the hot summer days his hands worked the black earth as he built and tended their gardens, turning tiles, hauling stones, mixing the air into the soil by pitchfork and mounding it to plant shrubs and herbs. Honest, useful work. "You shouldn't be here," she says. "You did nothing wrong."

"I did nothing." There is anger twitching, just under his skin.

He knows. He knows. He knows. The heartbeat of this new life.

"And I tell you," Manang goes on, "don't speak like that again. Big ears in police stations. All of the time they listen. Even—" he glances at the bickering officers, "even when their big mouths are going."

"But, Manang, I don't care. Big ears, big mouths, I don't care anymore."

She flinches when she sees the disappointment on his face. Some kinds of shame will never fade, will they? Being close to a good man like Manang is only making her shame grow.

"Hear me, Malu. Say *nothing*. To nobody."

She looks at the Sikhs, trading angry words and angry silences. They seem to have other problems on their hands.

FORTY-THREE

"I'm going out," Hannah informs Suria, who has come to the bottom of the stairs. "To the police station."

"No, mem," Suria answers, hushing her voice. "Mem, where you go?"

"To the police station, I've just told you."

She's not afraid of the colonel overhearing this news. Somehow, strangely, she's no longer concerned for what he thinks at all. For the first time in a long time, she feels at peace or, at least, emptied of worry. Ironic that George commands her to leave when he's just complained she's been out too much. He commands her to leave as if this weren't her home. She runs her fingertips over the textured wallpapering. Perhaps it isn't. "I can stop by the market afterward if we need anything. Do we need anything?"

"Don't go." Suria glances toward the study, faltering. "Sahib, he…"

"Sahib, what?" Hannah strains to imagine what the old woman wants her to understand.

No doubt Suria's heard every nasty word she and the colonel have just exchanged. Is she afraid to be left alone with him?

She whispers, "He will ask me where you go."

"Say what you want to him, Suria." Hannah observes the housemaid ruefully. There is really no way to politely assure her she's not an adulteress. "I'm going to the police station about the arson."

It is raining steadily. And it feels so good to be touched by the sky, her legs and arms and mind in motion, that she takes a circuitous route. In the stilted homes, the flow of the river, the overhanging mangrove trees, there is such beauty. The women, wrapped in their brilliant headscarves, squint at her through the fog. Mr. Lim the barber is vigorously sweeping the front stoop of his shop. There is so much beauty. She wishes more earnestly than ever before that Monsieur Godot were there in Kuala Kangsa to see it all. What would he make of it? What would he make of *Nude House Girl?*

By the time Hannah reaches the police station, the rain has lessened to a patter. Two British officers—the ones named Oakeshott and

Dennison or Debenham, who are always paired—are on their way out of the building.

"Mrs. Inglis! Why, hello!" one of them stammers.

"Can we give you a lift home?" says the other. "You've been caught out without an umbrella it seems."

"Oh no, thank you, gentlemen. I have some business here." She smiles politely and moves past them before they can object.

She's never had occasion to visit the police station. It turns out to be small and grubby. In the foyer she counts four cockroaches in plain sight. Indeed, they outnumber the furniture: two chairs, one desk. Behind this desk stands a young pimple-faced officer. Remembering Darshan's stories, she says, "Congratulations are in order, I hear, on the birth of your son."

"Madam!" he says, beaming. "Why, yes, thank you. Thank you. He is doing so, so well. Very big already!" They smile at each other uncomfortably until he adds, "Do you come to report something?"

"No. Yes. Not exactly." She leans to look down the hallway and several drops of water fall from her hat and collar onto the desk. "Oh dear."

He springs into action, mopping up the splashes with his cuff then hurrying to a closet.

"Oh dear," she repeats, seeing him return with a white bed sheet.

He offers the armful of fabric to her so she is forced to remove her hat before pressing the cotton against her face and neck and shoulders as he waits.

"I've come to speak with Sergeant Singh," she tells him. "It's about the arson."

"Oh yes. Popular topic these days." He smiles generously at her as he takes the bed sheet back. Tapping the logbook, he says, "Please sign here. I will check if Sergeant is available."

Pen poised, Hannah scans the grid of names. Nothing resembling "Oakeshott" or "Dennison" is recognizable in the log.

"Here, madam." He is waving her toward him, down the hallway, still holding the ball of damp bed sheets under one arm.

As she approaches, a holding cell emerges on her left and through the bars she sees two Malays squatting together, tearing, husk by husk, the straw covering the dirt floor. Like animals in a pen, is her first thought. Her second, with a jolt, is that the female prisoner is Charlotte Peterborough's genduk.

"Mrs. Inglis!" Darshan exclaims as she appears in his doorway.

The young officer looks with curiosity from her to his sergeant, then pivots and flees.

Hannah closes the door behind her. "I'm sorry to intrude, Sergeant Singh. You must be busy."

The skin around his eyes is puffy. The cuffs of his sleeves, ruined by stains. Hannah holds herself back from commenting.

"Long day," he admits. He gestures at the chair facing his desk and watches her as she settles in, fondness growing in his eyes.

"First, please forgive me for being so rude to you about the parasol flower. I suppose I felt...betrayed, on some level."

"Mrs. Inglis, I—"

"What I regret, wholeheartedly, is that I ever doubted your good intentions, Sergeant."

"You were unwell."

"I'm truly sorry."

He nods, smoothing one hand over his beard, listening.

"And the truth is I wanted the parasol flower so badly to exist. Even though I'd never encountered one, it felt like...well, like something had been taken away from me."

A touch of gloom seems to come over the sergeant as he considers this. But he says, stalwartly at first, "It very well may exist, Mrs. Inglis. Don't forget that. Why else would there be a legend? I may have added a few details here and there, how *I* imagine the legend, but those details can't negate what's out there, somewhere. In fact, I'm sure my depiction is not half as wondrous as a real parasol flower. When I'm done with this infernal case I may finally have a chance to get back to the woods."

Quietly, she says, "I can think of other reasons why there would be a legend."

"Can you?"

"Well, yes. Why are there legends about anything? People like something extraordinary to talk about." He appears unconvinced by this alternative. "Parasol flower or no parasol flower," she tells him, "I have fond memories of our time together."

"This is sounding like our time together has come to an end." He leans back in his chair.

"I don't know." She looks down at her hands and notices they are shaking slightly. Her nails are rimmed with burnt sienna. She tells him the good news first. "I've been painting, Darshan. Something quite good, I think. I think it could be a contribution."

"A contribution! That is wonderful."

"Yes." She smiles at the space between them.

"Is it a botanical?"

"No. A portrait of a house girl. Not a traditional portrait. An abstract, I suppose you'd call it. Darshan, did the cabin burn down completely? The cabin at Idlewyld."

"Oh. Odd question." He laces his hands together behind his head. "Three walls and a few of the beams are holding up but—"

"And are they"—she points through the door behind her—"suspects? I'm assuming you are in charge of the investigation."

"I am. Although you are proving rather good at interrogation, Mrs. Inglis. I could use your help."

"Pardon me." She twists in her chair, looking down for a time at his desk. "The girl out there in the holding cell. But, of course," she remembers, "you know her from our waterfall trek. She's a suspect, is she? That's why you are keeping her?"

"Mrs. Inglis, I cannot speak with you about the investigation." He frowns, his eyes unfocused. Where the blue cloth of his turban meets his skin an uneven ring of sweat has formed and dried. "I am keeping the two of them at the request of the Resident. For questioning."

"Eva is convinced *this* girl set the fire."

"I thought we agreed that Madam Peterborough's judgments may not be the most reliable." He is choosing his words with care. "Why would this girl set the fire?"

Hannah meets his eyes. She thinks of the photograph of Roki, which would have proven her point neatly. Out of embarrassment, in part, and out of consideration for poor Roki, she'd decided against bringing it to show him. As evidence, it should have been destroyed along with the rest; she would have to explain how she'd got it. And if she were honest with herself, there is also the plain and rather ugly fact that she wants the photograph for herself. She could not risk him seizing it. She replies, "Eva believes that the girl wanted revenge."

"For...?"

If she thought for a moment that Charles Peterborough was continuing his "research." If she didn't feel so strongly that what's happened was apt and just in itself. *Coward*, she tells herself. *You're no better than George.*

"Revenge for what, Mrs. Inglis?"

"I don't know," she replies unhappily. "She felt mistreated, perhaps, by her employers."

Sergeant Singh hangs his head for a moment, arms planted against his desk. "Let's consider this. A servant wants revenge, and so she sets fire to an abandoned shed in the middle of an abandoned coffee orchard. Instead of setting fire to the main house? Or stealing something? She was their genduk, after all, Mrs. Inglis. She had access to everything in that mansion, including their only child."

"You're very good at this," she says without thinking. "But of course you are." She shifts again in her seat. "I warned Eva that it didn't make sense, but she begged me to speak to you on her behalf. And I felt, considering how much she has helped me over the past months, that I owed her at least that much."

He cracks his knuckles loudly. "I am fed up with this blasted investigation. Nothing making sense. Everybody sticking an oar in."

"I'm sorry."

"Not you, Mrs. Inglis. You are simply discharging a duty to a friend."

She senses he is just being kind, which makes her feel even more badly. She takes a breath and says, "There's another reason why I've come. I told you I've been painting."

"Yes," he beams, "a contribution."

"I was painting at home, you see. And the colonel found me out." She tips her head back a moment and shoots air toward the ceiling. "He was so...angry. He confronted me."

"*Confronted* you?"

No suspect, she thinks, would be able to withstand that look! "He didn't touch me. Though I'm surprised he didn't!" She laughs self-consciously. "He told me to get out of the house."

"Mrs. Inglis."

She looks up to find him rapt, leaning toward her. "The *problem*, really, is that I admitted to George…that I had been trekking this summer at Idlewyld, and painting. That I had been trekking with you."

"What?"

"He was just so condescending! So insulting! He had that look on his face. And was making accusations and…I didn't want to deny you, when you've been such a help, a *friend*, to me. At the LAP meeting they were all slandering you, Darshan, and I tried…well, I didn't try very hard. I felt sick inside. Rightly so. But with George, I didn't deny anything. I couldn't deny you. I simply couldn't."

The sergeant unleashes a long, guttural groan. "Trouble and more trouble."

Trouble for him, he means. Fumbling, she finds a handkerchief and gets her feet under her.

"Stay, Mrs. Inglis. Please. The fact is any of the Peterboroughs or their servants could have made this information known to him at any time. Or your servants. Or my men. Eh?" He waits until she looks up at him. There is no animosity in his eyes. Only fatigue. "I appreciate, Mrs. Inglis, that you did not deny our friendship."

"I never told you. I've heard from the Kew Gardens jury."

"And? Well?"

"They hated *Strangler Fig*. They called it 'displeasing to the eye' and 'childish.' Oh, and they said the composition was 'wildly imbalanced.'" She pats her eyes.

"Wildly," he says. "That is…kind of a laugh."

She giggles. "Yes, isn't it."

"I am only glad to hear you are painting again."

"You are?"

"Of course, Mrs. Inglis. I was wrong. You must let no one stop you. Not Madam Peterborough, or lack of Madam Peterborough. Not your husband, not your neighbors, not even your famous art teacher. And certainly not the jury of the Grand Society of Pompous Criticizers of Paintings."

"Goodness, Sergeant, I take your point!" She can't help but grin.

Just to think of her new painting in the nursery makes her feel a little triumphant. The labor she has put into it, and the further labor she will do. Her commitment to the work itself. She must try to show some of her paintings, somewhere, for who will ever see them at this rate? Would Monsieur Godot have any… No, she mustn't count on him. He's never going to write to her again, is he?

Darshan has found a fresh page of paper and is writing in his impeccable tiny script, glancing up at her occasionally. What a minefield the poor man is navigating! Of course he must get back to work. Can she help him with that? She must help him, for once. How was this all going to end? The distress of the poor Malay girls, George's hostility, everyone's hostility, even Monsieur Godot's disappearance. If it weren't for art, how could one bear any of it? *But you can bear it, Hannah. Because you will always have this work, which is your life's work.* It is a knowing that wells up into her out of nowhere. Surprised, she remarks, "Perhaps nothing is coming to an end, after all."

There is a hard double-knock and Deputy Onkarjeet opens the door. He sizes them up and says, "Sir, we are required to submit the report."

"We were discussing the case, Deputy." Sergeant Singh glares wearily at him. "Continue drafting the report. I will join you shortly to make corrections."

"Thank you so much for your time, Sergeant. I'd best be going," Hannah says loudly. Tying her bonnet on, after Onkarjeet has left the room, she whispers, "What's bothering the deputy?"

"Me."

"That was his look exactly! Sucking politely on a lemon."

"Never mind. He and I, we have been working much too closely this past week, that is all."

Darshan rises to see her out. For a moment, standing near him, she feels a tremor of foreboding pass through her.

He voices it first. "Will you be all right? At home?"

She nods, hardly knowing how to reply. *Will you?* she wants to ask him. Instead she says, "Do take care." And, "Thank you for understanding."

FORTY-FOUR

Hannah times her return: away long enough that the colonel will have cooled off considerably, not so long that her brushes are irreparable. In the public gardens, she delays herself, huddled from the drizzle under a sycamore, schooling her imagination in the colonel's pain and humiliation. She will need to speak with him and apologize fully and sincerely. Then try to reassure him—of what? That she is not a monster. He won't trust her again. How, then, could she ever give him what he wants? It's a riddle she cannot solve, so at last she resolves to ask George himself.

Darkness has fallen by the time she arrives home, and it is only once she's indoors that she realizes quite how wet and chilled she has become.

"Come, mem!" Suria appears at her elbow to take her coat.

"Good grief, you must have been hiding in the closet." Hannah's heart bumps belatedly from the surprise. Slipping off her overcoat, she rubs her arms. "What's the matter?"

The old woman says nothing. Throwing Hannah's coat over the banister, she pulls her by the hand, leading her through to the kitchen. The room is quite warm, the stove still hot from the supper preparations. Hannah sighs with relief, stepping up to it to be warmed. But Suria moves her aside to twist open the oven door. She jabs a finger at the glowing coals. Weightless ashes swirl in the in-rushing air.

"What? For pity's sake, what are you trying to show me, Suria?"

The old woman looks petrified by the cast-iron stove. "Tuan make us burn them. Anjuh and me. Your big paintings, mem. Tuan watch me do it. Ooh, such a look on his face, mem, I think he asks me to climb in after."

Hannah sinks to her knees at the oven door, squinting into the wave of heat. Nothing. She sees nothing at all. That can't be right. "What are you talking about, Suria? They were on stretchers, on frames. These were canvases. Some of them quite big canvases." She draws rectangles with her arms as if they are playing charades.

"Yes, yes! Anjuh break with the axe. Tuan, he gives me garden scissors."

"My paintings? You're saying he had you chop up and burn my paintings?" Tuan might as well have taken the garden shears to her lungs. It was breathtaking. And deliberate. For this would have taken some time to accomplish. If only she'd come straight home, instead of stewing over how to make amends with the colonel's precious feelings. She might have saved some of them!

"Where is the case?" she manages to ask. Monsieur Godot gave her the leather portfolio as a leaving present. *The real learning,* he'd said to her, *will be outside these walls.* "Suria, where is the actual case?"

"In," she says, nodding fearfully at the stove.

"And...and what about the new painting? It was on the easel in the—"

"Mm." Suria sucks her thumb. "He do that one himself, first."

Hannah looks around the room. The colonel could be spying on the two of them now, standing quietly against a wall, to witness her in agony. Had he torched all of that effort, all the undiscovered and undocumented specimens, all of her precious learning, and simply gone to sleep? "Where is he? Where is sahib now?" she demands.

Suria raises her eyes to the ceiling.

"And my copybook? The book!" It was one fresh horror after another.

Before the ayah can reply, Hannah bolts upstairs to see for herself. The nursery is bare except for a bundle of paint-smeared rags. On the third floor, in her writing garret, all of the crates have been shifted and pillaged. Her satchel has been pulled-open, plundered, her notebooks are missing. Her copybook? Gone, too.

Nor is there any sign of the colonel. Except, as she treads toward their bedroom, the soft clunk of a key being turned in the lock.

At some point, Hannah pours herself a brandy and sits at the dining room table.

"Mem."

"What? What now?" What is the woman still doing, hovering, awake? Why had she bothered waiting for her arrival in the first place? The paintings, everything, is gone and nothing could be done about it. Hannah lifts her head.

The lamp lights Suria's creased forehead and high cheekbones. "I very sorry for you, mem. Very sorry."

She nods, exhausted. "It's not your fault, Suria. I realize that."

"Maybe not. Still, I am telling you I am very sorry for you. For what happens to you."

"Thank you, Suria."

"I'm telling you, too," says the ayah, bending to Hannah's ear, "about the box of the paints and the brushes. Sahib want, but I save. In Anjuh and my room, I hide them under our mattress."

"What?" Why had the old woman chosen to save the paints but not the paintings? Or the copybook? Hannah would never be able to replace her paintings, unique as they were. Yet the brushes and the box, the paints, these things could have been purchased again!

Suria's shaky smile opens into a grin. As is the custom with the natives, her teeth have been filed to points, and they are stained red from chewing betel paste. A devilish effect. "I tell tuan I not know where. And I am *think* for you, memsahib." She taps her temple. "With paints and brushes, she can make more paintings."

Hannah squeezes the old woman's hands. It does have a certain logic. Besides, Suria has risked her job, and likely her skin, to disobey the colonel. "Well done, Suria. Thank you. Truly. I'll get them from you in the morning."

FORTY-FIVE

I worked my way through every single document the Munks had retained in relation to *The Descent of Woman*. (Barnaby returned home to his cat. Celia kept up a brisk daily routine of comings and goings that involved tai chi, shopping, advisory to various boards, and rose gardening.) The bulk of my reading was Eva's research notes: copious observations about the natives, particularly the various Malay customs and rituals concerning the relationships of family members, "courtship and mating," and fashion. The Peterboroughs' retinue of servants—no doubt an easy source of information—provided much of the fodder for her anecdotal observations. One girl named Malu, a biracial teenager, seemed to fascinate Eva. This hypervigilance was understandable, given the girl was apparently charged with Charlotte's care and amusement. Yet, knowing Eva—as I now felt I did—I understood her fascination (and the almost paranoid surveillance of her employee) to be scientific at its root, having to do with Malu's mixed parentage.

Whereas Eva's research notes featured the family's experience in Malaya, Charles's logbook consisted of entries for Indonesian and Australian subjects. Flipping back and forth from the published book to the logbook and research journals, I realized that *The Descent*'s key chapter, "Sexual Selection in the Human Races," did not cite any empirical evidence for the "Malay type" presented. Remarkably, the book's crowning arguments relied solely on the field studies Charles had performed elsewhere.

I was conscious, too, of the fact that David Maikin must have worked from at least some of these same documents. The entries in Charles' logbook were the most incriminating. Here, he had dated and documented his physical observations of hundreds of research subjects, first Indonesian and then Australian aboriginals, women between the ages of fourteen and seventy-four. It was a gruesome read, partly because of the vast number of entries, partly because of the stark, objectifying language. Yet, as Barnaby had reminded me in

Oxford, the findings collected from the research had been published in scientific journals before being abridged for a key chapter in *The Descent of Woman*. At the time, nobody had so much as flinched.

Neither had I, when I studied up on *The Descent* prior to meeting Barnaby. All that I remembered clearly was striving to understand the Peterboroughs' theory. Granted, in the book, the dehumanizing details of the "empirical evidence" had been mostly stripped away, and the language was formal, to be sure. Still, how could I have read quite so uncritically? Why? Perhaps, quite simply, because I agreed with the book's conclusion: biology did not support the (then prevailing) idea that the female sex is inferior to the male. I appreciated the book's conclusion, so it was all I wanted to see. By contrast, David Maikin had smelled a rat. He'd sifted through the scientific evidence for gender and racial equality, searching for something to outrage his readers.

For all that Maikin did uncover, he must not have found the photograph. Pressed seamlessly between the blank latter pages of a logbook, it was an image of a Malay woman. She was completely naked, of middle age, and posed in a sexually provocative position. The effect was disturbing, to choose an insufficient word. Part catalogued specimen, part pornographic muse, she glared dully at me through the camera lens.

I could see no markings on the back of the card. No indication as to who had taken the photograph or where. I guessed, because of this, that it had been developed by the photographer himself. Charles? Or had one of his colleagues sent it to him? Whoever she was, had she complied, to be posed wearing nothing more than bangles? I decided it made no sense to ask about her consent or complicity, given the context. Then I decided that it did make sense to ask. I shouldn't presume the woman to be some sort of slave.

Although she had a grim expression on her face, it was perhaps no more grim than the other Victorian-era women I'd seen in family photographs, standing behind their seated husbands. I thought I'd once read that this aloofness was owing to camera technology; the exposure time needed for the shot was so long that no one could maintain anything but a "flat" expression. But when I went looking, I couldn't find this supposed fact anywhere; I began to wonder if I'd made it up. Could a whole generation of people be rendered humorless because of a technology?

The Malay woman had a cleft palate. This—her broken mouth—haunted me the most. Had she been singled out because of this abnormality? And yet the image was of her sexuality, surely, not her pathology. Was that any better? But how could it be? The questions that proliferated in my mind around my discovery created bad feelings. I felt exposed in some way I could not quite fathom, or consider legitimate, and I felt ashamed by my inner protestations. Maybe because I was feeling dubious and defensive, whatever the reason, I kept the photograph aside when I boxed up the Peterborough documents. That is, I kept it aside, then slipped it into my own notebook. I took it with me when I left Celia's. I took it. And never told her I'd done so.

Of course, I never mentioned the photograph to Barnaby either. Barnaby had "reopened," as he put it, his original investigation into the parasol flower. Although he'd turned up nothing decades earlier, he felt that perhaps something new might have come to light since then. Wasn't the world smaller and less wild? And, at the very least, he reckoned he could make faster and further inroads since the invention of the internet.

When we caught up on Skype, I told him I'd found nothing about a parasol flower, or anything similar, in the Peterboroughs' research notes. Indeed, they had spent relatively little time on botany. The Parasol Flower illustration must have been a late addition to *The Descent*, perhaps included even after the manuscript had been penned and prepared for press.

For his part, Barnaby reported that none of the organizations he'd contacted in Asia, or the databases he'd searched, made any reference to an enormous whorl-shaped bloom. "It's rather a delicate business," he told me. "One doesn't want to come off looking like a nut."

"Yeah. The botanist I spoke with at Kew told me a flower like that wouldn't be biologically possible, or something similar. Not evolutionarily possible? I don't know, he seemed to consider me just really confused."

He grunted. "The trouble is that there isn't a plausible explanation for how such a plant could enact photosynthesis on that scale, if it really were under the jungle canopy as she depicts it. Besides this, the blossom violates a sort of naturalistic economy. Why would a species dedicate so much of its resources to support an enormous bloom when a smaller one would do?"

"I don't know." For some reason the question irritated me. "Maybe a smaller bloom wouldn't do. Why does the *Rafflesia* bother?"

"The *Rafflesia* is a parasite," he reminded me. "Technically speaking, that's not a flower head."

"Well, it could have been a smaller parasite, on this logic."

"I must admit it's disheartening." He ran his hands through his hair, sending it springing off in all directions. "I'd hoped to be able to find *some* sort of lead on it. Even an amateur snap. Hasn't the entire planet been photographed by Japanese tourists?"

"Maybe it's heartening, in a way," I countered. "The planet still has more remote and untouched acreage than we imagine."

He leaned toward his screen. "Mmph. At least you'll be seeing the painting of it shortly."

Celia had helped me to arrange a visit with her son, Thomas Munk, in Brighton.

"I'm looking forward to it," I said.

The truth was that I was looking *beyond* my meeting with Thomas and his two paintings, precisely because there didn't seem to be much of anything after. There were the few paintings on Charlotte's list, spread now amongst the Munks, and those that Hannah had enclosed in her letters to Godot. I was coming to the end of the road and I didn't like it. Surely Hannah Inglis had created more than a couple dozen "sketches," promising as they were, and the few paintings for the Peterboroughs.

As my conversation with Barnaby grew more meandering, I floated the topic. Surely Hannah had left more artwork? There was mewling, and I watched him reach off-screen. Setting Pluto on his lap, Barnaby began rubbing the cat's little chin vigorously. "She could have died young," he cooed to his baby. "Tropical fever. Heatstroke. People died young in those days."

"Meh."

"She could have become pregnant. Suppose she finally had children, and involved herself with home decorating and her husband's career. That's what women were supposed to do."

"Hannah never willingly stopped painting," I heard myself say with conviction.

"What?" He laughed. "What makes you say that?"

"I—" What had made me say that? Taking a moment, I tried to articulate my intuition. "She wrote about how important it was to her to make a contribution. She wrote about how she couldn't stop painting. She wrote in ways that…about painting, about life… I just can't believe she would have given up on it."

"She gave up on Godot," he remarked.

"Hardly. It was a miracle she kept writing to him for so long when he wasn't replying."

I thought of Hannah's letters to her teacher, in which she was increasingly critical of her husband and their British community. Increasingly disturbed. Lonely. Reckless. Privately, I'd debated whether she'd been forced out of society or had chosen to leave it. And I reckoned that, apart from the Peterboroughs, Hannah's drawings and paintings had probably never been appreciated by anybody. For all intents and purposes, she had died without "making a contribution." But the thought of her giving up painting? No, I couldn't abide that.

Onscreen, Barnaby Munk was blinking at me. *He's stopped arguing with me because I'm beyond reason.* I very clearly remember thinking that.

"Let's go then," he said.

"What?" Even for Barnaby, it was an abrupt goodbye.

"I've been looking for my next walking holiday," he said. "Let's go *there*." He waved at me with Pluto's paw. "Hello? Kuala Kangsa?" he said. "Malaysia!" My mouth opened and a sound slid out. "Well, I believe the place is still there," he said. "So let us go, Nancy. We must. We will see what the locals can tell us about parasol flowers. And Hannah Inglis."

"I'm supposed to see Tommy's paintings next week," I said, stupidly. "But…sure. Yes. After that." I nodded my bulbous Skype head sagely. My stomach was suddenly alive with butterflies.

"Good-o!" He grinned at me.

"I'm supposed to call him Thomas," I added. "'Tommy' was reserved for family."

"Quite. And he's rather fashion-conscious." Barnaby wrinkled his nose. "Might be worth spiffing yourself up a little, Nancy."

FORTY-SIX

I was secretly pleased that Daphne insisted on driving me to Brighton. I would get a break from public transportation. Bob had insisted, too. "I'm self-sufficient," he murmured behind his hand, "even though I don't let on."

Daphne drove slower than I might have liked, but we proceeded without rest stops and traffic was flowing. We arrived in Brighton half an hour before my one o'clock meeting with Thomas Munk, just as planned. Having spent some time gazing at the coastline from the car, we rolled into the little parking lot of his office.

I'd made it obvious, or so I thought, that I was meeting Thomas on my own. Daphne exited the car when I did, hurrying after me. "I'll step away after the introductions," she promised. "I need to know you'll be safe. This way," she whispered, for we were inside the building by now, "he knows that I know that he's alone with you."

Since I'd told the Plewetts I would be traveling to Malaysia with Barnaby Munk, they were more protective than ever. "He's seventy-one," I'd said to them, of Barnaby. "We're not having an affair!" Somehow, saying that had just made the situation seem weirder.

Outside Munk, Misener, & Wallenstein, I told Daphne, "I doubt that I'll be 'alone with him.' It's a busy office building."

Indeed, the reception was filled with couples and singletons, all checking their phones. The receptionist, encircled by a high desk veneered in faux birch wood, rang Thomas for me, who came out without much delay. As promised, Daphne introduced herself, begging off right after to sit down with a *Conde Nast* magazine. Tommy was slim, short-haired, and, as Barnaby had predicted, extremely well-tailored. His dark almond-shaped eyes were Celia's. I guessed that he'd inherited a great deal from his mother, because he looked nothing like his uncle Barnaby.

Walking me to the elevator, Thomas explained he was full partner, practically a managing partner. With a glance at my attire—I'd worn my one pantsuit—he remarked that at various times he'd put in his own fair share of pro bono at "rough spots" in the city. He pressed

257

the button for the penthouse. Yes, he'd always liked the south, he said; really, he couldn't get away from London fast enough.

His L-shaped office had a charming view of a verdant park with an old-fashioned bandstand, a view I forgot the moment I turned my back to it. For hanging on the wall opposite the large windows was *The Parasol Flower*.

I nearly toppled headfirst onto the boardroom table as I walked toward it.

"Impressive, isn't it?" I heard him say.

Recovering myself as best as possible, I answered, "Very."

"So I understand you're something of an expert? When it comes to pioneering women artists?"

I didn't reply. I wanted to not talk to this man. To not talk at all. I needed to be alone with the painting, and I was soon seized with a horrible feeling of frustration that I would never be alone with it. I would never be able to return to it, even. To sip it in slowly. To look up from my armchair, from my table, from my lover, to find something new and peculiar in each viewing. Because I was not Thomas Munk, this man who was bothering me while I tried to drink of this flower, just sip a little of its shifting palette of oranges, pinks, and yellows. They were all the more surprising to me, having held on so long to a black and white etching, a pale simulacrum. Yet it was the richness of the texture of the work that struck me first and foremost. The sumptuousness of the glossy leaves and razor-sharp spikes of palm. Filamentous tendrils curling over themselves. The blossom's paper-thin petals, almost transparent at their edges and shimmering slightly. I had to pull myself back before I was drawn too far into the center of the whorl, of that whole incredible world—a place, a moment, an abundantly lush moment, that could not possibly have been so intense. Could it?

"I'm sorry," I mumbled. "I've not seen it before."

"Of course."

Silence for a while.

"I understand you saw the etching of it in *The Descent*, is that right?" he asked.

I nodded. "White does a…magnificent job, but…of course it's not the same." I judged that I'd better bring myself to talk properly to my host. I closed my eyes and turned to smile at Thomas Munk. "How did you happen to inherit this particular painting?"

"Oh, well, I wanted it. I asked Mummy for it, I suppose. I was on hand when she and my father were sorting through Nan's estate."

You wanted it, and so you took it. If only life were so simple. Without realizing it, I'd turned again toward the painting, again felt its spiralling contours reaching into me and pulling me closer. "Nobody else wanted it?"

"No, I don't think so. I don't think my grandmother much cared about collecting, from what I could tell. Old Barnaby took the one of the Sikh man. A few went to the Trust..."

I forced myself to turn away from the painting in a renewed effort to get my wits about me. I only had so much time with Thomas Munk; I ought to be using it effectively.

"I enjoy jungle scapes," he said rather shyly. "You know, palms in the garden, tropical motifs. I don't know, I always have."

"And you took one other Inglis, right? *Nude House Girl.*"

It wasn't my imagination that the man flinched when I spoke the name of the work. Really, I thought, men could be such children.

"That one I have at home." He fiddled with his lapels. "Oh dear. I thought you were only interested in seeing the flower painting."

"Oh, I—I'm very glad to have seen *The Parasol Flower.*" My mind raced. How had I possibly given that impression? Our correspondence quite clearly referred to both works; I was meant to be seeing both works. Now he was backing out? I decided to fib as necessary. "It's absolutely no trouble for me to make a second stop, Mr. Munk. We're staying the night in Brighton. Such a nice city to visit, too."

He and I batted questions of time and convenience back and forth and ultimately agreed that we would stop by his house early the next morning before he left for work. I spent a few more minutes savoring *The Parasol Flower* and recording some notes and images—Tommy even helped me remove the painting from the wall to see if there were any markings on the back of the frame or canvas—before steeling myself to leave. It was a good thing I had Daphne waiting for me in the lobby.

His home was in Hove, a ten-minute drive from his office and about the same distance from the bed and breakfast we'd found, though it took us thirty minutes to locate it and find a parking spot. Daphne and I had given ourselves extra time. Nonetheless, we arrived ten minutes late and flustered.

"Thank you again for allowing us to see *Nude House Girl*," I said to him, having apologized at least twice for our tardiness.

"We're only fashionably late!" Daphne had been hissing as we came up the steps.

"It isn't a dinner party!" I'd been hissing back. "He's a busy man."

"Not a problem," Tommy replied, pulling out his phone to check the screen. "Well. I'll show you up to it."

The bright, semi-detached home had a tidy playroom in place of a dining area. He led us upstairs as Daphne and I took turns complimenting him on the stone flooring, the natural light, the sturdy banister. The upper hallway featured a gallery of white-framed family photos. A woman with long wavy hair and large dark eyes, smiling professionally into the camera. Tommy and the woman alternately romping with a poppet of a child in various ages and stages. A Scottie dog made frequent appearances.

"And it's so nice and quiet, this neighborhood," Daphne said, giving me a look.

As we walked past an upstairs bathroom, I glimpsed an alligator toothbrush in a holder. Where had he mounted this painting? I was beginning to wonder.

"It's an unusual work," Tommy said over his shoulder, as we entered the master bedroom. Cardboard boxes lined one side of the room, most of them full and taped. An enormous mirror above the bed's headboard gave me my first view of *Nude House Girl*. The painting itself was hanging at the opposite end of the room, in an alcove that led onward to a balcony.

"Oh, are you moving house?" I heard Daphne say behind me. "That's such an ordeal, isn't it, packing everything up."

Thomas Munk didn't respond. He'd arrived at the painting and was clearly more interesting in explaining that. The work, to my surprise, was double-sided. That is to say, two paintings had been created on one loosely rectangular strip of canvas. It was mounted, quite ingeniously, to stretch between a floating frame, sandwiched by glass so that one could view both sides of the canvas. And, in order to facilitate this dual viewing, Thomas, or someone in the family, had suspended *Nude House Girl* from the ceiling. I walked around the hanging artwork as he spoke, marveling first at this engineering of perspectives. The mirror over the bed, as well as a second upright mirror, positioned against one angled wall of the alcove, meant that almost wherever you walked in the room, her large dark eyes were watching.

The paintings themselves might have been called portraits, though they were non- representational in style. They were, I thought, vaguely cubist-looking, with many angles and curves and sharp corners. The color work was muted, in a palette of ochres, dark purples, and the occasional dart of red or spidery fringe of black. Although there were differences between the two portraits, they seemed, in my opinion, to be versions of the same subject. She was naked, and the naked parts of her body did not fit together. Her face looked as if bruised, her mouth, broken. A cleft palate? Fireworks were exploding in my brain.

On the upper torso, one nipple and one breast were clearly visible, the rest of her chest being skeins of color. As if she had twisted out of her skin to turn toward the painter. On both versions, the woman's legs were small and crossed and crowded into the bottom of the page, like a child's drawing when she has suddenly run out of space. Between the legs, in both works, and which you have might have first taken for background, sat an upturned black-brown oval surrounding a slash of clitoris. Once I understood this feature as the woman's genitals, the curved legs transformed into fleshy mounds of mons veneris. And the woman's eyes became portals of defiance. You will not own me. I searched but did not see a signature. Had I not known the provenance, I might have wondered if they'd been accomplished by the artist who had painted *Murdo* and *Jane* and *The Parasol Flower*. I said this to Thomas, who readily agreed. He told me he preferred *Nude House Girl*, though it was obviously unfinished and "too raw for most people to enjoy it," as he put it.

"There is something very tender about them," he said.

"And fierce." I glanced at Daphne, who had a politely disturbed expression on her face. I asked, "Did you always have the canvas framed like this? It's ingenious."

"No. Until…fairly recently, as a matter of fact, I didn't have the painting up at all. Gemma always thought it hideous."

"Funny, isn't it, how different peoples' tastes can be," Daphne commented.

There was a long silence.

"So…um…why did the artist paint on both sides?" asked Daphne.

Thomas Munk appeared to be deferring to me. I replied, "It's not uncommon, actually. Lots of artists have done it. Or even painted right over other paintings. Van Gogh, for instance. Usually it's to make use of the canvas. For instance, if you've run out and don't have more handy. Or can't afford more."

"Oh," said Daphne. "So she must have been shorthanded."

"Presumably. An artist typically wouldn't prefer to paint on the back of the canvas. It's rougher and doesn't take the paint as easily, and it won't hold up as well over time."

"Oh," Daphne said again, keeping her expression neutral. I smiled to myself. She was trying to imagine being quite so desperate as to *need* to paint *that*.

I considered the situation in which Hannah Inglis had come to the end of her stock of canvas. By the dates on her letters, I knew that *Nude House Girl* was not her last work. Whatever the problem, she'd surmounted it and managed to obtain more canvas.

Tommy's phone buzzed, and he left us alone in his bedroom to complete our viewing of the two nude house girls. Daphne nosed around the room while I tried to swim through the layers of consciousness surrounding the art before me; I shifted my focus from the artist to her muse, who might well have been the same woman who'd posed for the photograph I'd stolen. Who was she, this one looking back at me with quiet defiance? And her twin—slightly more elongated, slightly more melancholic in aura. How were we all related? I agreed with Tommy, there was something very tender in the portraits.

He reentered the room, apologizing. So-and-So had called, and Tommy needed to leave for the office.

"Of course!" Daphne exclaimed. She pulled me away and we followed him downstairs.

He chatted to us as we put our shoes back on—now that we were leaving, he was very chatty—asking me about my investigation and where it was leading me. Word had gotten to him that I was heading to Malaysia with his uncle. I told him I was excited to see what we could find in and around Kuala Kangsa. There were still so many unanswered questions.

"If I have any follow-up questions, may I contact you?" I asked him.

"Of course," he said unenthusiastically. He threw on his coat.

"Yes, actually, there are a number of things I'm still trying to piece together. How your great-grandmother wound up with these two paintings, for instance."

He looked startled. "Didn't she purchase them?" he asked, ushering us on to the porch. We descended and waited while he set the alarm then locked up carefully.

"How the other half live," Daphne mouthed to me.

"Follow the money," Thomas said, coming down the stairs after us. "I would think the art executor has a record of payments. Perhaps the family accountant may even have a ledger from that era or some records he can share."

Yes, follow the money! And who were these people, I wanted to ask him. The art executor. The family accountant. "That's a great idea," I said. "Thank you!"

He pointed toward his garage to signal his path. Then he leaned in to shake Daphne's hand, my hand. I expected him to bolt for his car. Instead he sucked his bottom lip for a moment, squinting in the morning sun. "This is a bit awkward. If you wouldn't mind doing me a favor?"

We agreed readily and he said, "Don't mention anything to my mother about Gemma and Blake. You know, the fact that they've moved out."

"Right," I said with authority. "Of course not."

FORTY-SEVEN

Malu is moved to the interrogation room when two other men, both servants at Idlewyld, are brought to the station. She hears their feet moving in the dirt and straw. She puts her face to the crack of the door. Somebody has allowed the men betel paste and a tin spittoon, though they've done most of their spitting on the back wall of the cell, now streaked blood red.

All these months she has been so witless and young, keeping herself away from Amah, playing at being brave. Now she's stuck and can't go anywhere. What will happen to her? The lash? There is a new prison, she has heard say, in Kuala Lumpur. How many more days will she be waiting to know? She decides to ask the sergeant. When his footsteps pass in the corridor, she bangs on the door.

"Not up to me," he tells her. He closes the door and sits on the stool in the room. It looks silly because his legs are long and the stool is low. He adjusts himself, pulling a book from his back pocket and putting it instead in a front pocket to be more comfortable.

"Your book," she says, keeping her back to the wall, "is it the book of the rules? For punishment?"

He tells her it is a book of notes. Notes of incredible things that he has discovered in the forest.

"Incredible things," she says. "Like waterfalls?"

He smiles at her. "Exactly. Like waterfalls."

"What does it feel like to read?" she asks. She can read some words, but reading whole pages of them, she is sure that brings a different feeling. "Good?"

Sergeant Singh nods slowly. "Good, yes. Sometimes sad or frightening. Many different things at once." He looks at her a long while. "Malu, I think I understand what you were doing for Dr. Peterborough. In the cabin."

At that, she makes her eyes dead to him. Her bottom lip does not behave itself as well.

"I'm not going to ask you about it," he says. "What good will that do now, eh?"

"My mother is very sick." After she says this, she realizes how out of place it sounds. To her, Umi is the center of day and night. To other people, Umi has nothing to do with anything.

"I know," he says, surprising her again. "Your friend has been telling me a few things." The sergeant turns toward the holding cell.

Manang? Manang! After all his warnings for her to keep quiet in front of the police!

The sergeant says, "They want to send you to an orphanage in Kuala Lumpur." His gaze floats away. "In place of a punishment. You will be clothed and fed there, schooled even. And I suppose it may only be for a year or two, or three. Until you are grown."

In *place* of a punishment? Malu searches the room for something, anything to grab onto, but this floor is wood planking, not the straw and dirt of the cell. There is only her pallet bed and a chamber pot. She leaps on the bed, bashing her fists into her mattress. Then, grabbing the pot, she flings it across the room, and begins tearing at the bedsheet they've given her. Beating against the man's big arms as they come to restrain her. She would tear at his deep voice, too, if she could, and rip it to shreds.

One day, the soldiers come in and take Manang and the two others. They chain each man's wrists behind his back. Malu begins banging on the door of her locked room.

After the men are gone out of the station, the sergeant unlocks her door and looks in at her. "What do you want?" he says in Malay. "Stop banging."

"I made the fire at the doctor's cabin. Me. I did it." Sergeant Singh does not blink. "Manang didn't do it. None of those men did it. *I* did that fire, I promise you." Still, he says nothing and does not move. "Tell the soldiers to stop! Stop them from…where they are being taken, sir? Make them free Manang! I lit three matches. I poured the kerosene. I—I knocked over the jar with the long scissors."

He coughs and shakes his head, letting the door swing fully open. "I cannot, Malu. Even if what you say is true."

"It *is* true."

He puts his hands on his hips, looking inward. "They have confessed. And the administration…wants what it wants."

"What? No! I am the one, I swear it!"

The administration, who is that? The two English officers with waxed mustaches? They had come once before and argued with Sergeant Singh. This last time, the sergeant barely said a word, from what she could make out. And after the visitors left, he paced the hallway not blinking and not seeing. Just like he was doing now.

When Sergeant Singh leaves she comes to the doorway. He has left the door to her room wide open. Malu stops at the threshold. In his office across the hall, he is bending over his desk. Glancing at her, he takes a pistol from a drawer, tucks it under his belt, and walks past her out of the station.

"Where are you going?" she asks.

Seconds pass. Malu inches into the entry room. No one. Her eyes lock on the empty entranceway. Inching forward, she darts out of the police station, tearing down the street as fast as her wobbling legs can take her.

FORTY-EIGHT

When Hannah awakens, there are a dozen tree caterpillars treading her blanket. Instinctively, she kicks her legs, causing the insects to bounce into the air and rain down on her. "Ugh!" Scrambling to her feet, she picks off their fuzzy, squirming bodies. Roddy, her companion of late, jumps into the fray, pinching the fallen bugs one by one and popping them in his mouth. It would be handy to enjoy the taste of insects. In the past two days, she's eaten little more than fruit.

She hasn't slept much, either, in the two nights since leaving Ridge Road. Trying to catch up on it during the day doesn't seem to be working. Her head is full of thoughts that won't obey any sort of order, like these shrimping boats flitting back and forth across the river. What of that pitch-black steamship, immense and sinister by comparison, wedged against the dock? She feels sure the ship is a sign of something...

Hannah crouches and feels inside the satchel she has been using as a pillow, touching each item. Anjuh and Suria salvaged a roll of canvas and her complete paint box. She has also two sponges, a bar of soap, several rags, and her palette knife. The photograph of Slow Roki, which survived unscathed in the pocket of the bag, and is now only a little worse for wear around the edges.

If she could begin the painting again soon enough, she could reproduce it. She'd put her faith in that idea. And as she explained to Suria, "Faith is more important than breakfast."

"No, mem," said Suria. "At breakfast time, breakfast is more important."

To be agreeable, Hannah allowed Suria to slip a boiled egg and two packets of coconut biscuits into her bag before she left the house. "*Don't* let anyone follow me," she insisted, taking the housemaid by the shoulders. "No one. I need peace. I need to be sure that I will not be interrupted."

"Outside?" Suria sounded incredulous. "Where you go, mem? How long you be gone?"

Hannah didn't try to explain. Leaving had less to do with being physically interrupted and more to do with a choice, in herself, to make art. And if she no longer had the portfolio Monsieur Godot had given her, she had his words. *The real learning will be outside these walls.* She had prayed on his statement. What was she supposed to learn from the destruction of her work? All of those paintings, had they not been the learning?

With Suria trailing her to the edge of their yard, Hannah headed further along Ridge Road, higher into the mountains, eventually breaking from the road. She intended to stay in the woods all day if need be, to repaint the portrait of Roki. At first, the shady green of the forest helped her to breathe more deeply and shake some of the tension from her shoulders. The silence, broken only by the softened crunch of her footsteps, took her in. She trod on tiny plants, breaking their spines. Slender branches snapped as she pushed her way through the denser areas. If she had been swinging a machete, as Darshan used to do for her, the forest would accept that cutting and scarring, too. Was she truly welcome there? Or was the jungle so vast and pliable, unspeaking and acquiescent by nature, that it only seemed so?

Where the first rise leveled off and the vegetation thinned a little, she stopped and unfolded her three-legged stool. Though her mind kept moving onward, pausing at each person it encountered to ask, *What am I supposed to learn? What am I failing to see?* Her mother, bearing a steaming bowl of soup, a sympathetic and inquiring expression on her face. Jane Hemming from the academy, blowing smoke to the sky and laughing, telling her that Paris was full of surprises. Suria, bowing her head and opening the oven door to reveal glowing embers. None of these people had an answer for her. Neither did Roki, when Hannah fished her out of the pocket and studied her.

With a pin, she fastened the photo card to a glossy leafy so it was available for easy viewing as she painted. As she plunged again toward the satchel, she checked herself. Leaves were moving near her feet. A wide triangular head rose, pulling back into an *S*.

Hannah knocked her stool backwards, stumbling away. A second later, her body was exploding inside—all breath and blood and sensation. A pit viper! One of the deadliest snakes in the country. Venom that killed. Unless you could cut it out faster than it spread.

She remembered Darshan describing victims who had "bled from all orifices"—eyes, mouth, ears, nostrils.

But surely her imagination was getting the best of her? Mightn't it have been an ordinary rat snake? She stood frozen in place, scanning the leafy forest floor around her feet. She felt a fool. A fool if it wasn't a pit viper, a fool if it was, and she wound up dead so haphazardly, so quickly and purposelessly, like an animal. Where no one would ever find her. Yet she was not dead. Or even injured.

Hannah tiptoed back and unpinned the photograph. Hastily she grabbed her gear and snuck back down the rise. Thoughts tumbled through her unheeded as she continued her descent, following the light and the forest markers she'd noted on the way in, not slowing until she'd broken into the clearing by the road. There she came to a stop on the shoulder to suck back water from her canteen. *Coward! Who can't manage a few hours in the woods on her own? Who can't manage a night in her own home?* Walking back down Ridge Road during waking hours, now, she was conscious of the wives' eyes upon her and their mouths snickering behind gauze curtains.

She wanted to tell Eva that at least she'd discharged her debt. She'd asked the police to interrogate a troubled young servant. Good fortune, she thought bitterly, that they'd already begun. Was Eva looking out at her now, from her new vantage point at the Residency? Watching a frightened, sweaty woman, lugging the remnants of her life upon her back. Hannah reminded herself that she was supposed to paint. That was all she had to accomplish. There was no point trying to string words together, no point trying to fight. She must paint Roki's portrait before it was too late. It had been so good, so perfect. She must recreate *Nude House Girl* and show it to them. Show them what they'd done.

In the public gardens, it did not go well. Here, on the quiet hill overlooking Kuala Kangsa's harbor, it is not going well, either. She tries, and there is something, some glimmer of life, but it is not enough. And down below, the shrimping crews flit back and forth, coming and going and coming and going, so industrious. There is a never-ending supply of shrimp to be taken. She tries, and she has no easel, and she has to make do without a gesso. Not that these excuses matter. No time for excuses.

"Let's go," she tells the gibbon. "Let's go!" Hannah hoists her satchel onto her back, picks up her stool, and heads downhill, Roddy tripping on her heels. Ahead, the harbor slowly sinks into the peaked roofs lining the streets. River water is making everything swim before her eyes.

There is nothing romantic or mysterious about it at all. The lesson is this: she should stop painting. As one might stop eating a food that disagrees with one's bowels.

Monsieur Godot had supported her for a time because she was once his student. He'd felt honor bound to teach her; after she'd left, he'd gone on shining on her a little longer. Part of her had even imagined his silence as a new way of caring. He was encouraging her to fend on her own or to become accustomed to her instincts. He was guiding her to become her own arbiter, to resolve her own technical dilemmas about what worked and what didn't. He was confident she was strong enough to answer her own questions and make original art. Really, that was all in her imagination.

"Special bird for nice lady," sings the clerk at the menagerie. "Special bird for nice lady."

The songbirds hop and twist in their cages, preening. So tiny! Some are feathered in flamboyant pinks and yellows, others in neutral browns and taupe. They cock their little heads as she moves down the row; they seem to tick like clocks.

"I love you," she tells them.

"Yes! So special!" the clerk exclaims. Embarrassingly, the woman has heard her.

At the end of the row is a little owl whose eyes are tightly closed. He clings, upright, to a bough that is propped in the cage. A barred eagle-owl, an unmistakable jungle bird. This one looks to be a juvenile. Had it fallen out of its nest? On the other side of the table, the clerk is following Hannah along the row. "So special!" she says again.

Surely nobody wants an owl as a pet. Without song, with a need to kill. Poor thing. Hannah tugs her hat down and turns toward the flower seller.

"Moon orchid, memsahib? Angel's-trumpet?"

It's not the prostitute who is usually at the booth. Today it is a man she does not recognize, likewise petite and dark, with large ears and a firm voice.

"Have you ever sold a parasol flower?" she asks him.

He cups a hand behind one of his ears.

"A parasol flower. Big," she says, holding her hands out wide, then slicing a circle in the air. Her satchel shifts on her shoulders, knocking her sideways a little.

His forehead ripples delicately. "Ah! Stink flower."

"No, no. Never mind."

He pulls a stem of moon orchid from one of the buckets and bows to her, offering it. "No cost, madam."

"No, thank you," she says curtly, backing away.

"Help you, mem?" says the vegetable grocer, for she has come to a stop in front of him. Between the two of them are little heaps of zucchini and green beans. A bucket of rambutans. "Shoo!" He lunges for his duster and waves it menacingly at Roderick, who sits calmly at her feet.

Hannah searches her purse and finds nothing.

The grocer is squinting at her. He looks kind, she thinks. Concerned. Somehow old and young at the same time. He holds up a pear. "Pay later," he says.

"Oh. No! That's not what I meant. I—no, thank you."

If she goes home, she would be fed. Truthfully, her stomach is beyond hunger, now. Food is important for steadying her hands. The tremors will make it more difficult to paint. But she cannot paint if she goes back, only if she goes forward.

And is she already forgetting? The lesson is this: she should stop painting.

No. She *won't* bother the sergeant. He is so very busy. She has burdened him enough. She can find him After. "What do I do now?" she might have asked him. "It is done," he might have answered. "Do you not see its light, Hannah? Fierce and white." Like the stars overhead. She searches the stars, trying to make out what is coming for her. Something is coming that she cannot quite see, something to divide the "After" from the "Before."

Is this the true problem, that her head is likely to explode? Her neck hurts, her teeth hurt. Her head is going to… She taps at her chest in disbelief. There is a dog trotting along with a rat between its teeth. She is the rat between the dog's teeth. Her teeth hurt, her bones crunch. These pruney, useless hands that cannot paint a true painting. A "contribution."

"What do I do now?" she asks Roddy, but Roddy is gone.

Covering her face, unseeing, Hannah staggers ahead for a time before she stumbles and lands on her hands and knees. She struggles to breathe, hating herself. Hating herself for being unwilling, even now, to ask the colonel for mercy. *You must keep going,* Darshan advised her. *You must let nothing stop you.* "But why?" She laughs at herself. "If I'm just…not…going anywhere."

She sits down where she has fallen. And, because the sky has started spinning, closes her eyes. Like a parade of ghosts, they come to see her off—each misshapen, imperfect attempt at true art. When she arrives at the last page of her portfolio, she wrings her hands and prays for the strength to see life. To truly see it. *Because there are plenty of people who can paint anything, he told them. Technically competent, even technically perfect, but lacking the seeing power, they paint nothing worthwhile.* Nothing. "Let me have the seeing power." Squeezing her eyes tight. "Please, God, tell me it's worthwhile."

A sudden crack of thunder.

Her eyes open. "Very funny."

The drumming of rain, unhurried and almost random at first, then quickening, like applause. In no time, she is wet through. With a surge of alertness, she memorizes the shape of the sprawling honeysuckle bush in front of her, and, behind that, the outlines of a pretty clapboard home. There is no point trying to move. The old tenderness in her ankle throbs hotly. Cool rain is good. This cool rain and this quiet street…somewhere near the Perak Club? It's not so bad a place.

Sit for a while. Try to rest.

FORTY-NINE

The next thing Hannah remembers is the smell of lavender. Steam rises from the bath they have drawn for her. A house girl waits in an alcove, a human towel rack. Choose a bar of soap. Step in.

After, she stands in front of a mirror staring at someone pink she doesn't recognize.

"Hannah? Are you listening to me? George is very worried about you," Lucy is saying so earnestly. "*I'm* very worried about you."

She looks down to see that she is clothed, thank goodness. In a robe and a set of nightclothes that couldn't be Lucy's, for when she holds her arms up, the cuffs lie perfectly at her wrists. They are in a dining room. Not the main one of the house, she thinks. A plate of cured meats and cheeses sits in front of her, along with a cup of broth.

"What are you doing?" says Lucy.

"Whose clothes are these?"

"Oh, I don't know," she answers snippily. "I took them from the provisions assembled for the Peterboroughs."

Hannah laughs—for too long, by the look on Lucy's face. It's the first true laugh she's had in… Yes, she remembers she has already demanded to see her satchel. She checked through it. Had anything been taken? Her clothes, they told her, were being washed.

Lucy is going over the story of Hannah's "capture." Makes her sound like a rabid dog. It seems the colonel sent Anjuh out to look for her at some point. Later, Anjuh enlisted two friends from the lower town. It's incredible, she thinks, how much better one can feel from a bath and three bites of cured pork. Except she's so tired. As if her very soul were weary.

"Why was I brought *here*?" she interrupts Lucy.

"Because you screamed at your houseboy that you wouldn't go home." Lucy is using the slowed-down speech she reserves for servants and clerks. "Hannah, you were kicking and shouting so loud you woke the Tallymans. You struck their servant in the face."

She feels her cheeks pinkening. Can she make out three men

approaching in the gloom? A feeling of being cornered. "Poor Anjuh," she says.

"Poor Anjuh! Hannah, you've had some sort of breakdown! You've been behaving…"

Hannah reaches for the cup of broth and sips at it until she's certain Lucy has shut up for good and is ready to listen. "George burned my belongings, Lucy."

She looks confused. "Your belongings?"

"All of my paintings, my portfolio, my notebooks."

"Ah."

She pushes her chair back from the table. "I'm just going to check on them."

"Wait, Hannah! Stay here. We're talking, you're eating. No one's done anything with—"

"My satchel. That's what I need."

Lucy's eyes narrow. "Why did George burn your paintings?"

"Because he's a hateful, mean-spirited man!"

She inspects her fingertips. "Because he'd told you not to paint, isn't that why?"

Hannah folds her fingers over her cuffs and extends her arms wide and high. A barred eagle-owl, soaring. "Why can't I wear my own clothes?"

Lucy ignores this and says, "In your satchel, I found…an unfinished painting, I suppose it is. It appears to be of a naked woman."

"Yes." She lets her arms fall.

"Yes? Doesn't this strike you as problematic?"

Her head feels thick and her thoughts are taking too long in coming. "Are you familiar with the history of art?"

"Of course," mutters Lucy.

"The naked female form…is a classic subject."

Hannah clutches her torso, all at once remembering the photograph of Roki. She'd planned to stuff it into her corset but the men were coming at her too fast, pulling at her, circling her in that bouncing cart, wherever it was taking her. Here, to the Residency. Was the photograph still in the pocket of her satchel?

"When I arrived, what happened…?" She can't recall undressing. "Who helped me out of my clothes? Where is my satchel?"

"One of my girls. I've told you, we left everything of yours in the yellow bedroom. Hannah, are you all right?"

"I was working backwards, from death to life," she tells Lucy, remembering, feeling as if she's swum into a pocket of clarity. "All of the secret places need to pulse with life, in a portrait. You see it's not about exposing her *body*. Our bodies. Who owns them, Lucy? But. George *destroyed* the original." This last she can't help but speak viciously.

"He probably found it disturbing."

"We come here and we bully them into doing what we wish, and we don't even admit we are bullying. We call it governing or employing or scientific research."

Lucy is stunned for a moment. Then says, "Hannah, I'm afraid you simply don't know what you're saying anymore."

"I want my painting back. And my clothes. And all of my property you've pawed through!" She rises from the table, pushing the plate of meats away. It strikes the mug of broth, overturning it, and oily brown liquid sploshes across the table, dribbling into Lucy's lap.

Lucy says quietly, "I'm going to recommend that you see a medical doctor."

"What?"

"If George wants an *opinion*." Lucy takes a napkin and begins dabbing it on her crotch and thighs. "If he can't manage to…"

"What do you mean? God! Is this why you're here with me, asking questions? To observe me for an 'opinion'? I thought you were being *friendly*, Lucy, in your own…pretentious way."

Across the table, her host looks genuinely miserable. Lucy's reaction, the way in which she wilted so quickly and completely, will haunt Hannah in the hours to come, as she regains some clarity of mind and purpose. And when the subject is broached again, she decides to cooperate for a medical examination. Perhaps there *is* something wrong with her if she's flinging punches and toppling soup.

The gardens at the Residency have an old and impressive traveler's palm, one of the original specimens, most likely. It is planted toward the middle rear of the grounds, surrounded by bright, jagged stands of *Codiaeum* and *Cordyline*. Past Residents have interspersed subtler, less conventional tropicals here and there, including blue pea and a climbing vine called a porcelain plant. A plot for vegetables is tucked in behind two white Romanesque statues, and one section, along the eastern flank of the garden, appears to be dedicated to samples of tropical trees. There, a rubber sapling stands alongside eleven different species of palms, all of them extensively labeled. On the night of the gymkhana festival, the last time Hannah wandered through the grounds, it was too dark to read the tags.

She is tipped slightly over, doing just that, when Brigadier Effing-don-Watts comes toward her through a stand of bamboo. They exchange greetings, if a little warily. He seems on edge, in a bouncy sort of way, and she expects him to move on. Instead, he invites her to comment on the bamboo.

"It's quite striking," she says. "I do love the great thick stems. Also the swishing sound when the wind is moving through a grove."

There are, he tells her, over eight hundred uses for the bamboo plant. Bamboo, in his estimation, is the future. He grins at her under his safari hat.

"How are you finding Kuala Kangsa?" she asks in return.

"Still getting a measure of it. To be honest, Mrs. Inglis, I've come into rather a mess here. No offense to your husband!"

"Oh, none taken," she says lightly. Knowing how George detests the man, she feels like she might burst into laughter at E.W.'s eager, sunburnt face.

Perhaps she looked coy, suppressing this humor, for the man's eyes begin to crinkle warmly as his gaze travels down the front of her dress. "Tell me, Mrs. Inglis, what sort of entertainment is there in Kuala Kangsa?"

"Entertainment?" The idea of fashionable leisure activities in Kuala Kangsa makes her smile harder.

E.W. smiles back, somewhat tenderly. What have they told him about her? That she's an invalid to be pitied? Perhaps his compassion is making him over-emotional. She remembers the man's dead wife and feels a stroke of sympathy herself. She must stop teasing the fellow.

"I suppose there's the gymkhana festival," she says. "The way we celebrate it here I've always found entertaining. There are the horses and their show, of course—poor creatures. Music. Plenty of music. The Ladies Association sells home baking to the few who prefer treacle tarts to shaved ice. And the Chinese miners come over from Ipoh to run several of the games for the children. Frog races, boat races, bobbing for pears. All the women come wearing their brightest keftis and scarves, which doesn't stop them from bobbing for pears. Oh, the Sikhs host an exciting tent-pegging competition with competitors from Kelangor and Ipoh. There is our elephant, Elmira, who will take you up on her back. She walks along at the bottom of the slope. The cadets pitch a handsome tent right in the middle of the green and will stand in their plumed hats all morning, waiting proudly for you to enter. Inside, a full course lunch is served on silver platters. And no doubt you'll see Sultan Izrin and his family touring the meadow in their finery, with a pack of skinny kids tiptoeing after them, hoping for a stray penny. It will pour, absolutely pour, from four o'clock to a quarter past. So that everyone will run, helter-skelter, screaming and dancing and giggling and pulling each other here and there. Peacocks vibrating and crying like fallen angels. Ladies, shoveling treacle tarts in their mouths before they go soggy. And then the rain will stop as abruptly as it started, and the entire village will laugh at itself for forgetting just how wet rain can be. Between you and me, Brigadier, the most fun is simply to wander with a kebab in one hand and a pair of binoculars in the other. Sightseeing."

He nods politely after she has finished all of this and says something stiff and witless about her charity toward the natives. He must have given her the wrong impression, he says, using the word "entertainment." "In point of fact, I'm less interested in play, Mrs. Inglis, than in having this village start working."

She nods, tells him she should be heading back inside, and they part ways. Later, she spots him rapping on the trunk of the traveler's palm as if he were testing it for its timber yield. Whatever else the colonel is, he's not such an idiot as this man. George decided long before he ever met her to accept Malaya on its own terms.

Yet he won't let her live as she must live, will he? And how must she live? Weaving her way to the westernmost point of the gardens, she hides behind a fruiting tree—a *Dillenia*, she sees on the label—and looks toward their house. She can see nothing animate, only the bulky blue shapes of the building, with the little barn sitting some distance away. Without Cleopatra to graze it, the stretch of meadow between here and there has sprung up rather recklessly.

Conveniently, but somehow unexpectedly, Charles Peterborough is the physician to assess Hannah. The colonel is prepared to welcome her home, Lucy notes brightly, after she has been assessed by a professional.

"And that's Charles?"

"Oh, he's unassuming, I know. We think of him as a shortsighted, rather awkward conversationalist. Pathologically shy," Lucy whispers behind her hand. "Actually, he's a prominent specialist in women's health. He's not been practicing here as a medical doctor, in favor of focusing on his research."

Charles is installed in one of the wings on the third floor, quite apart from Eva's rooms, Hannah remarks, as she climbs the winding flights of the rear stairwell. The air on the upper level is noticeably thicker. In summer, it must be positively unlivable. Though, of course, in summer, Charles had been at Idlewyld.

"You must be pleased by the sentencing," she says, after they greet each other and he is fussing with his pen.

The news of the day is that three of his former servants have confessed to plotting and committing willful destruction of property by fire. Each will serve three years of hard labor. The new prison in Kuala Lumpur, says *The Malay Mail*, will provide "suitable accommodation." Most of the article concerns the prison facility's construction and modern features.

"Not particularly," he replies and does not elaborate.

She wonders if he shares Eva's opinion that the genduk is the true culprit. Charles looks anything but outraged. Saddened, perhaps. His research, she reminds herself, has been destroyed.

Before he begins his formal questioning, she ventures, "I don't suppose you know, Doctor, but my husband incinerated my artwork. He ordered our servants to cut my paintings to pieces and feed them into the stove. Each and every painting that I have done here, sir. Many of them were botanical specimens discovered at Idlewyld."

He listens to this keenly, once or twice pushing his spectacles up his nose.

"I thought I might be able to recreate one of the works that…that I considered especially promising. I tried." She struggles to keep her throat from locking up. "I couldn't do it."

Charles nods slowly. "Yes, I understand that when your husband learned of your deception, he lost his temper." She nods. "And so you left your house. Were you afraid of him?"

She remembers the feelings of release and relief that came after she told the colonel of her summer spent trekking and painting. "No, Doctor. Just the opposite. I wasn't afraid of George. I left because I wanted to recreate one of the works."

"Why did you not return? Apologize? Try to patch it up with him?"

All she can think about now is the original portrait of the hare-lipped house girl, waiting on the easel in the nursery. What she had planned to add to it—the shadows to be deepened on the neck and the fine work still needed for the eyeballs, and how she intended to heighten the intensity of the purples in the small of the back and repeat them in the left nipple and the upper quadrant of the background. She says, "I don't know."

He asks her several questions about how she is feeling, physically, emotionally. Then about how she was feeling, physically, emotionally, during the duration of "the episode." This is how he seems to be referring to the time she spent on her own in the village. She answers as truthfully as possible.

"I think," he says, "that at the very least you feel life too deeply, Mrs. Inglis. Would you agree that you are oversensitive? Do you care about things that others don't?"

"Perhaps," she assents.

"And that the artwork you create is contributing to this imbalance," he continues, "this excess of sensitivity?"

"Yes. I can see that it does." She asks, "Have you seen the paintings I arrived with, Doctor? They were removed from my satchel."

He takes a moment to consider this. "Yes, as a matter of fact. Mrs. Finch thought it might give me some insight into your state of mind." He tells her it is not unusual for artists to succumb to monomania and even certain states of hysteria. These conditions are aggravated by poor eating, poor socialization, and poor hygiene.

Hannah is close to tears, absorbing what he is telling her. She expected to dispute him, to dislike him. "You think I am an artist?" She seizes her knees, knowing that this question and the hope that stirs it will only reaffirm her obsession. Before he can answer, she says, "You do. You've said as much."

Charles Peterborough advises her to stop painting. She must focus on taking care of her own needs properly—washing regularly, brushing her hair and teeth, wearing clean clothing, paring her fingernails and toenails—and that her husband should arrange for her treatment as a day-patient at a new psychiatric clinic in London. Charles Peterborough, it would seem, knew before Hannah did herself that the colonel had plans to relocate them.

He also prescribes ether on the occasions she is feeling particularly anxious to paint. Also, to overcome any qualms about social interactions. She is to build friendships with "decent people" and avoid being alone. Eat more meat. Eat more frequently. Take up a restful hobby such as gardening. And, once she is given a clear report from her psychiatrist, she (and her husband) could greatly benefit from having a child.

FIFTY

Eva Peterborough is the last person George expects to see heading for his house. Not when her pet friend is already there with her at the Residency. He opens the front door himself, just as she's about to knock.

"Ah. May I have a word please, Colonel?"

She and Charles are such a match, he thinks, and not for the first time. Unattractive, demanding. "Of course," he replies, ushering her inside. "Would you like me to have some tea pre—"

"Don't bother."

It is a rare opportunity to use the conservatory with a visitor. They settle into place overlooking the back lawn. That particular morning has been clear and cool, almost bearable. The bougainvillea is ever-blooming.

"Aren't you going to ask me how your wife is doing?"

"I believe she's in good hands. In fact, I'm told that she's been seen today by your husband, Mrs. Peterborough. Should I be worried?"

She pins her green cat's eyes on his. "I'm referring to her state of mind, Colonel. Which you ruptured by burning her art and casting her out of her own home."

George takes a moment to breathe. He must keep his cool with this quick-witted witch. "Perhaps," he says, "you would be kind enough to tell me how *you* were supporting Hannah's mental hygiene by encouraging her to have adulterous relations in the forest, like some animal? And then to deceive and disobey her husband. You forget, Mrs. Peterborough, that I know exactly what kind of depravity you and your husband engage in in the name of research."

"Yes, of course you do. You came into our home uninvited and snooped through what wasn't yours. Then you stole from us."

"Stole? What, the photograph?"

"Trespassing, theft," Eva cites. "And then, in breach of a promise to your supervisor, you broke confidence by telling Hannah all about it."

"Come now, talking to one's wife is no breach of confidence.

Besides, this isn't state espionage we are talking about; this was your husband's grubby little operation to look up girls' sarongs."

Zinger! He's longed to tell the woman exactly how he feels about her, the preposterous bitch, and if ever there were an occasion, this is it. Hasn't she just barged into his house and blamed *him* for his wife's undoing?

"It's outrageous," George goes on, "that you should accuse me of harming Hannah. God knows why, but she put some sort of store in your opinions. Now look at her." Rising to stand, he says, "I think you've got some sort of unnatural hold over her!"

"What?" she laughs, blushing, incriminating herself.

"And I've had quite enough of it, Mrs. Peterborough. You may think you can do as you please with her, but Hannah is my *wife*. And you are…you are nothing to us. You are pitiful. I'll ask you to leave our house. Now."

Eva rises to her feet but moves no further. "I apologize," she says, sounding nothing of the sort. "Coming here, my intention wasn't to hurl accusations, Colonel." Looking down, she begins picking at the tips of her gloves.

"Well, I…don't…" He is gruff and remains standing, hoping to expedite whatever conversation is left. "Fine. I accept your apology."

"However, I know that you are planning on taking Hannah to London."

"As I said, Hannah is my wife!"

"I mean, the two of you are moving back to London. I realize that this has all been arranged with Lucy and with Charles, and what will no doubt be a convenient diagnosis. The coaching that is going on over there—" She rolls her eyes upward. "Even your rival, E.W., is making himself useful by singing the praises of modern health care and urban appliances for 'the gentler sex.' James, to his credit, is the only one keeping out of their game."

The clever shrew must have her big nose in everybody's business. She's making it sound like he went to the Residency with a plan and had them sign to it. He hadn't. Quite simply, he'd looked down at his unconscious wife—the ether had kicked in, said Lucy—and vowed to save her soul. They'd showed him the state of her clothing, ruined by mud and monkey shit. Those grotesque, perverted half-paintings on the rolled strip of canvas. He'd regretted, honestly regretted, having ever told Hannah to leave, and he vowed to do better by her.

"And what are *you* telling her, Mrs. Peterborough?"

To his surprise, when the lady responds she sounds genuinely humbled. She tells him she has not been saying much at all. Instead, she's been listening to Hannah and observing her as she recovers. Hannah has spoken a good deal about Monsieur Godot and of other artists who inspired her. Of her faith. Of letting go.

"Letting go?" he says, querying this phrase. Perhaps Hannah is, with God's help, willing to stop this nonsense. It occurs to him Mrs. Peterborough could be a helpful source of information, if only he could manage his own irritation with her. "Please," he says, gesturing for them to resume their seats. "Do you know," he asks, once they are seated, "has Hannah…expressed a desire to paint since she was brought to the Residency?"

Eva appears to think carefully about this. At last, she says, "I will be perfectly honest with you, Colonel Inglis. Yes. She has."

"So then this 'letting go'…what does this letting go amount to, Mrs. Peterborough?" When they left Europe, he imagined that without her precious academy, Hannah might tire of painting. But there was this Henri Godot, lingering, fueling the fire. George had even wondered if Godot had been the true purpose and value behind the art. But Hannah had kept on painting, without Godot and his enthusiastic letters. Without a studio. And if Mrs. Peterborough was right, Hannah may keep on painting even without Sergeant Singh. Exasperated, he says, "It amounts to nothing, that's what. It's another lie."

"Hannah is not in a sexual relationship with Sergeant Singh. She never was. She's not cuckolded you, Colonel. The only deceit she's ever engaged in was so that she may pursue her talent."

"Why are you speaking to me as if I'm an imbecile?"

She runs her tongue over her lips and says, amiably, "I find that with men, mostly, it can be necessary."

"Excuse me?" These two women have been sharing secrets for months, just as women do, and now it appears Mrs. Peterborough has come to plead some sort of case for her friend? "Has Hannah sent you?" he demands. "Why are you here? What do you want?"

"To warn you, Colonel Inglis. I will ruin you."

"What?" He is caught off guard by this blunt and vicious message.

"If you do not let Hannah live—let her live and paint as she must, respect her, care for her—I will ruin you. For example, my connections will ensure you do not receive a transfer or a pension, but rather an administrative discharge. 'Unsuitability due to causes within the officer's control' is one option. Not as concise as, 'dismissed with disgrace.' Either one would make the rest of your life, socially speaking, full of shame and quite uncomfortable. Financially speaking, well…" She shrugs.

George grips the arm of his chair as he takes this in. Her connections—is that Swettenham? What had James mentioned? Had *she* already arranged to have the Residency handed to E.W.? He shakes his head, unable to accept what she is telling him, yet unwilling to ask her for some sort of proof.

"I'm not speaking merely of Perak, or even Southeast Asia, Colonel Inglis. I can and I will ruin you in London, or its suburbs, or in some country town. If it comes to that."

He stares. Incredibly, the woman is as cool as a cucumber. The only possible sign of upset is the flaring of her large nostrils. Finally, she asks in a pitying voice, "Are you understanding me, George?" and for a moment he is back at his mother's knee, flummoxed by what he's done wrong.

"I—I assure you," he answers, sticking his chin out and clearing his throat, "I am not proud of how things have unfolded, Mrs. Peterborough. And I appreciate your concern for Hannah. I must tell you: I love my wife. I love my wife very deeply. I can assure you, I will do my utmost to care for her."

Eva Peterborough looks him over, perhaps considering whether to say anything further, then makes her excuses to leave.

FIFTY-ONE

A week or so after I'd seen Thomas Munk's *Nude House Girl*, he emailed me. I was packing for Malaysia at the time and when I saw the subject line on my phone, I tossed my wicking travel socks aside and lay down on the bed.

To: nancyroach21@gmail.com
From: tmunk@mmw.co.uk
Subject: ledger of art expenditures

Dear Nancy,

It was very nice to meet you the other day. Your obvious appreciation for my paintings quite moved me. As I happened to have some time on my hands yesterday, I took the liberty of contacting Miranda Buckley at Fulgham House. Miranda has access to the many archival ledgers that comprised the financial accounts of the estate while it was owned by the Pellingham-Peterborough family. Attached is a scanned copy of several pages of the ledger for Art Acquisitions and Expenditures, roughly 1885 through 1914. I've had a quick look myself, and noted that there appear to be multiple expenses related to Hannah Inglis. See what you think!

Warm regards,
Tommy

I charged out of the bedroom to find my laptop, in the lounge, and opened the email message there, clicking immediately on the attached PDF. The old ledger pages were better described as browned than yellowed, over which lay the black grid of the chart and a steeply slanting inky script.

Daphne was saying something, coming up behind me to peer at the screen. I focused on the line entries, scanning down the rows. Who had kept the books? I wondered. Surely not Charles or Eva. Their family's status warranted a professional accountant. Eventually I came to an entry whose description read: *Comm. for ptg H. Inglis.* The entry was dated 1896 and associated with £200. Not a bad sum for the era, I was pretty sure. Comm., I surmised, referred to "commission." At least, I could think of no other possible meaning. Here, it seemed, was empirical evidence that Eva and Charles Peterborough had purchased Hannah's art.

"Jackpot!" I said, causing Daphne to gasp. She set a cup of tea down next to me.

"Thank you," I said. "How much do you think £200 was worth in 1896?"

"I'll Google it!" She beetled off to the kitchen, where their old PC was tucked in a corner.

I continued scanning down the ledger, conscious of Tommy's forewarning of "multiple expenses related to Hannah." Sure enough, after a stretch of a year or so, I saw a similar descriptive note, *Comm. ptg H. Inglis*, this time associated with £25. Then another with the same phrasing, another £25. None of the entries, I remarked upon, referred to numbers or the names of paintings. What exactly was being commissioned? On such a regular basis? The entries for H. Inglis came once every two months for a period of…thirteen years. Thirteen *years*!

This pattern was fairly easy to see during the Peterboroughs' relatively nomadic travels through Australia and Indonesia (because there were often only two or three other line items), and more difficult to spot once the family had returned to the home in England and was selling and purchasing many other works of art.

"Adjusting for inflation," Daphne called out, "£24,173."

"Oh my God. That can't be for a painting," I mumbled to myself. What was it for? I took a gulp of tea and sat frowning at the screen. What was it *for*? In Malaya, where the British pound must have gone far further than it did in London, Hannah could have bought a home with that amount. Or traveled. I skimmed down to the next H. Inglis entry I'd highlighted. "Or lived for fifteen months without needing a penny."

Daphne had come back into the room. I told her at last what I was looking at. "Ooh," she said, "imagine giving that amount of money away! So posh, weren't they? And you say they kept giving her money, did they, for thirteen years?"

"It's not exactly charity," I corrected her gently. "The payments were in return for Hannah's artwork."

But I'd done a quick tally of the ledger entries. Depending on the price per work, ostensibly the Peterboroughs had commissioned Hannah for something like seventy-eight paintings. At minimum. "Well, the Munks certainly don't have seventy-eight paintings by Hannah Inglis," I said.

"Perhaps they were resold?" suggested Daphne.

"If the Peterboroughs sold any, it must have been after 1914. I don't see anything on the black side of this ledger relating to Inglis paintings."

I had already planned to revisit Fulgham House before leaving for Malaysia. It was so close, after all, and I wanted to compare *Murdo* and *Jane* to Tommy's paintings. I wanted to see the engraving once more. And perhaps, I thought now, there was a way to speak to Miranda Buckley about this ledger.

By the time I arrived at Fulgham House the following day, I'd developed a strong hunch: Eva Peterborough had been supporting Hannah financially. What I still didn't comprehend was why. Had Maikin's speculation been right—the two were lovers? Sheer generosity was another option. As was, on the other end of the spectrum, some sort of blackmail. There remained, of course, the more straightforward possibility that Hannah was creating paintings for the Peterboroughs on a regular basis, thus earning the income. The family did end up with a handful of Inglis paintings, though certainly not thirteen years' worth of output. And we couldn't count the cache of paintings intended for Monsieur Godot. I was hoping that Miranda Buckley would be able to shed some light on the matter.

Miranda's small windowless office at the estate might originally have been a closet. It was odd, I confessed to her, to imagine Eva and Charles Peterborough actually living at Fulgham House. Taking their hats and coats off, having them stashed away as they brushed down their elegant outfits. Miranda cocked her head at me. "How can I help, Miss Roach?"

"Did the Peterboroughs own, let's say, one hundred Hannah Inglis paintings at any point in time?"

"Oh, I don't think so!" she exclaimed. "They had rather a large collection of art, generally, but…"

"And the ledger," I said, "Tommy sent me a digital copy, as I think you know." I paused until I saw the recognition on her face.

"Yes, I scanned it for him."

"That ledger shows *all* of the paintings the family sold at auction, or sold to a gallery, and the price received?"

She nodded. "Unless they were given away, I suppose."

"And so what I'm seeing there is correct? The family didn't *sell* any works by Hannah Inglis?"

She screwed up her face. "I'd have to take another look at the ledger after 1910 to be…"

"1914," I said, "is how far the PDF goes."

"Okay," she agreed.

"Perhaps I could see the rest of the ledger? Save you bothering."

"I can't remember if *any* Inglis paintings were sold, but I can safely say that it wasn't hundreds of paintings. I would have remembered that."

I winced at Miranda Buckley, a wince full of longing and gritty determination. It was an expression I'd perfected on the librarians at Richelieu. Five minutes later I was sitting on the floor of her office with the ledger on my lap, delicately flipping pages. Sure enough, there were no entries showing sales of any H. Inglis paintings, right up until the sale of the estate to the National Trust.

During my review, Miranda came and went from her desk, practically stepping over me. Apparently "the system had gone down." She'd been on the phone all afternoon with a software company called The Edge. Since the software was only installed on the check-in ticket machines in the lobby, and the only line Miranda could allow to be tied up was in her closet-office, the situation meant for a lot of "backing" and "forthing."

"*You'll* be over the edge soon," I punned to her, feeling that we'd developed a good rapport by then.

"God, I wish I was still in graduate school," she replied. "I thought that was a special kind of torture."

"Oh, it is," I said. "Don't worry, we're both circling hell."

The thought of clicking open the pink file I'd labeled NEW DISS!

made me want to vomit. Kenneth was all over my notes, my research, my lists and outlines. His name was literally all over the annotated bibliography I'd developed. Kenneth had passed my dissertation prospectus, but told me my ideas needed to be "redirected." It was understood that my pass was conditional and exceptional—at least, that's how I understood it. And that redirection would be in the direction of his theory. "New diss," I murmured. "Nudist. Ha!"

"Sorry?" said Miranda.

"Nothing. Just talking to myself."

Soon I was scribbling furiously, taking down all the names that, I was beginning to realize, referred to art galleries. Were these places the Peterboroughs had sent Hannah's paintings? Beginning in 1922, there were names that showed up repeatedly on the ledger in association with income rather than debt. Baird-Carter, Tooth, Goupil, Lefevre. Had I in fact been a graduate student of art history, I probably would have recognized them definitively.

"Miranda," I said, "I think they might have been placing her paintings in galleries." I listed the motley collection of surnames. "I think people must have bought her work!"

I looked up to see her with the phone to her ear, nodding and listening to some techie on the other end of the line. She set the phone down. "Thank Christ. The system's up."

"Aw, that's wonderful," I told her. I scrambled to my feet, eager to repeat my own good news.

FIFTY-TWO

When Malu arrives home to the tippy hut, Uncle Nito shoves her back out the door. So hard she almost falls from the ladder.

"You are arrested by the police, girl, you bring deep shame on this family, and you expect a welcome from us?" Nattie follows her outside, hand raised to strike. "So hard on her," she adds with venom, jabbing her thumb behind her, "my sister who loves you."

"But I wasn't convicted," Malu says, desperate, frantic to see Umi. "Why do you think they released me?"

Nito looks out at her from the window, stone-faced. Nattie curls her lips and spits. "Get! Too much shame. Go away. Go! Go! Go!"

"Auntie Nattie, I need to see Amah," she begs. "Please. Then I'll go. And I won't come back."

Her mother, propped up on her bedroll as usual, seems much worsened. Her eyes lie deep in their sockets and her mouth twitches soundlessly. "Amah," Malu cries, running over to her and holding her close. She is as light and hard as bone; her cold hands move by themselves and won't stop to be squeezed, won't stroke Malu's in return. Malu weeps into this bundle of rags. Incurable.

"I did do the fire," she whispers in her mother's ear. "I did it, Amah." The words have no effect.

Scrambling to her feet, Malu is unable to contain the rage that roars through her. She staggers toward Nito and Nattie; he puts an arm up to shield himself and his wife. Malu backs away, her eyes filling. She snatches the money tin and empties it into her spreading hands and fingers. Then, thinking better of it, throws the coins to floor and runs.

Down by the river, she hides in the tall grasses, doubled over in pain. The only relief is to imagine walking out through the rushes and sinking into the cool water. Lord guide me, she prays, over and over.

Until she sees Sergeant Singh walking along one of the pathways through the grassland. Heading for home? Malu stays put to begin with, unconvinced that he won't drag her back to the police station.

But then it occurs to her, *he* is Allah's answer to her prayers. She must talk to him. Ask him if she can still go to the orphanage. She would at least be fed there. Maybe she will be able to find work in Kuala Lumpur? In this town, nothing good will ever come of her.

Just as she rises to show herself to him, she spies the two English officers coming from a nearby building. The same mustache men who came to the police station, she decides. Though they are not wearing their uniforms. They walk together, swiftly, so focused on Sergeant Singh that Malu is able to keep up without anyone noticing.

Where one street meets another, the sergeant turns, looks far enough around to discover the officers rushing him, now, each one pulling at an arm and wrestling it behind his back. The sergeant is bigger and stronger than either of the men on their own, she can tell. And if she came to help him? No sooner does the thought cross her mind than one of the longos puts a knife to Sergeant Singh's throat. He stills.

Malu presses her eyes closed. She will never forget the sound that starts her running.

FIFTY-THREE

Hannah knocks at the front door of her house. She and Lucy wait on the step until Suria receives them and ushers them inside. "Oh, mem," Suria cries, squeezing Hannah by the hands, ignoring Lucy's icy stare. "Good now, mem?"

"Yes, thank you, Suria." She *is* good. Though her ankle still requires her to limp a little. Being considered an invalid of sorts, a damaged person, has turned the ladies' hostility to pity, or at least, pity has been the only appropriate social response. Pity sent from a distance. Which has suited Hannah fine. Mostly, she's had space and time to herself.

She humps in after Lucy, who has noticed the colonel in the front parlor. What is he doing there, just sitting by himself? Waiting for them, she supposes.

"Hannah's been seen by Dr. Peterborough," Lucy reports, making the words seem cozy. As if she's said, "Hannah's been given a mug of warm cocoa."

George is frowning at a patch of air near their heads.

"Hello, George," Hannah says.

"Hello," he mumbles, eyes shifting.

Lucy delivers him the written report from the doctor. Two pages, folded into quarters. Hannah has not read it. The colonel immediately unfolds the paper, fishing his spectacles from a pocket, and they watch him reading. After a moment or two, Lucy pats Hannah's back. "Well, I'll leave you now, dear. Do take care." They embrace lightly. "I'm just next door," Lucy reminds her. She gives a last glance at George, who hasn't looked up from the page. "I'll see myself out."

When the colonel is finished reading, he removes his spectacles and comes over to where Hannah remains standing. She clutches the straps of her satchel. She's kept it on her back.

"How are you?" he asks. "You look well."

"I'd like to read the doctor's report, please."

"Of course," he mumbles, fetching it and handing it over.

Hannah takes the pages with her upstairs to the guest bedroom.

At breakfast the next morning, the colonel enters the dining room with the biggin and two mugs and pours them each a cup. Hannah has been leafing through a catalogue and has a cup of coffee already. When Suria brings in the tinned milk, George adds a dash to his coffee, catching her eye.

"Perhaps an old dog can change its spots," he says.

"It's a leopard," she replies, "that doesn't change its spots. An old dog can't change its tricks."

George chuckles happily. "What are you going to do today?"

She shrugs. The last thing she wants to do is chat with him. To have to talk blandly to the colonel is to risk being consumed again. She is already much at risk, walking in the old places, drinking from the old mugs, as if nothing has changed. Just above her sternum, where her heart should be, is a muscular knot of enmity and frustration and bitterness. She imagines it churning, in place, like a little engine. The anxiety is about how she will manage with this new installation, this new technology. If she were strong enough to pry open her own rib cage she might rip the whole thing out and fling it at him.

Instead they drink coffee in silence, eating two fried eggs each. She can tell he is pleased with her appetite. He feels compelled, it seems, to tell her about how terribly he's gotten on in her absence. Then describes, once again, the entire horrendous scene at Finch's retirement party: George's nauseated boredom, the dressing down by Swettenham, the surprise of James' announcement, his stomach coming up and onto his shoes as all of the guests looked on. Perhaps, she thinks, the colonel means for them to go on by recommencing their life from that night forward. And she would tell him about her feverish aches and her walk to the lower town. Of wading through the ditch to knock on Darshan's door, drinking his Indian tea, and instead of falling asleep on his chesterfield, interrogating the poor man about an imaginary flower.

On the second night after her return, the colonel pads to the guest bedroom in the evening. She is reading a cookbook in bed, and this, too, he seems pleased to discover. He asks if she will consent to return to the marital bed. "The marital bed." She wants to laugh at this ancient formulation and his formal, nervous choice of phrases. His face looks ruddier than ever.

He adds hastily, "I won't…touch you. You have my word."

On the third night, she does return to their bedroom. It is an effort of forgetting. As promised, the colonel does not touch her. In the sleepy haze of the early morning, though, he forgets himself and nestles into her like a boy with his teddy. She does not move away. Later, when she is stirring, he wakes and whispers an apology for being a jealous fool, for overreacting, for calling her a horrible name. It is a secret, sleep-drunk apology, delivered in fragments. He does not seem to care about a reply, and she gives none.

Later, when he comes downstairs for breakfast, it is as if this confession never happened. Except for something lingering in the colonel's air—humility, perhaps? Good sportsmanship?

She is wondering at all this, when he says, "I've booked us berths on the November steamer to London."

"Why?"

"You need to get well, don't you? You cannot be well in a place like this." He glowers at a spider that has frozen in its tracks on the ceiling. The spider sets off again. "You read the doctor's letter."

They look at each other across the table. *You no more think me mad, than I think you mad,* her eyes tell him.

The colonel's announcement is not unexpected, given the doctor's prescription. Given what passed for conversation at the Residency, as she convalesced. Her own reflections on the incompatible positioning of the colonel and the brigadier have led her in the same direction.

She says, "I can understand why you don't want to work for E.W."

He taps his teeth. "Nnnh, quite."

"But what about—"

"As I've said, there's your condition to think about."

"I don't have a 'condition' worth thinking about, George. What Charles has written it's…it's not what happened, is it? I'm fine."

London? They'd tried to sell her on the wrong things, of course, for what did she care about frocks or George's family? The promise of London is its position in the tides of art flowing to and from Europe. The Thames had come to seem to her, in daydreams, like it was made of paint rather than water. From London, Monsieur Godot or Madame l'Espagne would be close enough to visit; they might offer suggestions or put her name forward to collectors and galleries. And there must be others she'd not met yet, people who cared just as genuinely about what could be done with art, with life.

But she had nothing to show those people.

London, without making art? With the colonel pattering around their house, placing his perfectly reasonable demands upon her? No, with each exhalation. No, said the soft chime of her pulse. Not that. The clanging of a warning grows louder inside her each time she tries to imagine that London.

"I can't go," she says.

He flounders, apparently unsure what strategy to pursue. Insist that she leave? Agree to stay on? "When can you go? How much time do you need?" The colonel's freckled forearms push against the table, his eyes are down. When she doesn't answer, he adds, "You are still feeling fragile?"

"No."

"So you simply discount everything Dr. Peterborough has recommended?" His color is rising; he twists in his chair, throwing one leg over the other. "I mean, hell, let's just say it doesn't matter what Peterborough recommends, does it? Let's just say that. We need to go home. We need this, Hannah."

"My art," she says, faltering.

"It's gone." He crosses his arms. As if this is all he can say about it.

"My paintings are gone, yes. My art is not the same as my paintings."

This is the lesson of their destruction, and it was Darshan who helped her to see it. *You must not stop.* It's not about what she creates, but that she is creating. And didn't Suria save her paints and brushes for that very purpose? Suria understood before Hannah herself could appreciate it. She needn't, and couldn't, recreate any single moment, any one subject or vantage point. Yet if she lets go, there will be more. Always. The world is full of future paintings.

"What are you on about?" he demands.

Before she can consider how to reply, the front door bursts open. Lucy Finch is standing in front of them, panting and apologetic. "I've only just heard! Oh my, had you heard, George?" She seems to seize up, looking from one of them to the other, unsure whom to address, or how.

The colonel's face is white.

"What's wrong?" Hannah prompts her.

"Sergeant Singh."

"What?"

"He's been killed. He's been killed! He's been killed." Lucy clamps a hand over her mouth.

"I don't understand," Hannah says.

"God help us," Lucy says softly. "Murdered in the street."

Hannah lies in bed with her satchel. After a few nights, she dares to put the bag on the floor between the bed and the wall. (She has dragged the bed from the center of the room toward the far wall.) Not once, however, does the colonel seek to step inside her room. He appears to be quite productive, whether at the Residency or at the government office, helping Finch to hand the reins over to Effing-don-Watts. She hears his voice, his footsteps, his wardrobe doors opening and closing.

During the days, when he is safely out, she packs their belongings and cleans. Scrubbing floors and wiping walls and laundering all the drapes. Making it nice for the next family. Periodically, she walks out to the stable or sits on the veranda. But the cleaning is the most satisfying. The only time she and the colonel attempt to be in the same room together is for supper on the Friday he officially leaves his position. It is a special occasion that he has organized in advance. All day, Suria thumps in and out of the dining room and upstairs to Hannah, asking again and again about how to prepare Yorkshire puddings.

Hannah comes into the dining room as the colonel is opening a bottle of Whyte & MacKay. A glass waits empty on the sideboard. "Going away present, from the lads," he says sheepishly. "Nice of them, isn't it?"

"By the smell of you, I would have thought you'd already drank it."

"Women," he retorts. "Little police officers, all of you."

Looking at his face Hannah feels suddenly queasy. Gripping the back of her dining chair, she leans over to tug her serviette from under her knife and drops it on her empty plate. "I'm not hungry."

"You'll sit down and you'll eat with me tonight."

She glares at him, which he seems to expect and even enjoy. The colonel points at her chair, taking his own seat. He begins carving the roast chicken, piling slabs of the meat onto his plate, then exchanges his plate for hers. Leaning forward over the table, he scoops a fat dollop of potatoes and two of the puck-shaped Yorkshire puddings onto the plate in front of her. Suria stands frozen by the sideboard, holding a boat of gravy. George walks over and grabs it from her, then pours it over everything.

"You'll sit and you'll eat," he says again, jerking her chair out from the table. For she is still standing. "Pour memsahib a glass of port," he tells Suria.

Hannah looks over at the ayah, who has already turned for the bottle. She closes her eyes and lowers herself into the chair.

"All of it," he says.

The steamship to London is due to depart on November 10. For every supper prior, Hannah supplies Suria with an excuse for her absence. On several occasions, she is "out at a neighbor's." Fridays: attending the evening church service. Illness—which is in any case not far from the truth—covers several days at a stretch. There are also "women's troubles" and the fact that she is asleep, sound asleep. Eva and Lucy, who call on Hannah during this period, receive one of the same excuses.

When Hannah runs out of excuses, she leaves Suria to come up with her own account of mem's reclusive behavior. The colonel accepts it all, apparently, until the day that he doesn't.

There is a note in his voice so unnatural that it draws Hannah from the guestroom to the top of the stairs.

"Don't know, sahib."

"You do know."

"Mem not hungry. She say, you eat, please."

"*I* am asking her to eat with me. And who am I?"

"Sahib, sir. Tuan, sir."

"Who am I to *her*? Eh? What do you reckon?"

She hears Suria stumbling over a response. Then the unmistakable squelch of bone against bone, flesh against flesh. A heavy footfall. A loud grunt.

Hannah strains to hear what else may be happening below, though she cannot budge, as if the whole thing has unfolded within a bad dream and she is actually asleep.

That evening she goes to find Suria in her quarters with Anjuh. The ayah's jaw has some stiffness and bruising that will probably worsen before mending. Unfortunately, two of the fingers of her left hand are in worse shape. Anjuh unwraps the bandage gently for Hannah to see. They look badly sprained. The little one, perhaps broken.

"How did this happen?" she asks. Suria shakes her head. "Tuan has done this to you," says Hannah. He must have twisted them, hard, perhaps even stomped on her hand. Had she fallen from the initial blow? Hannah tries to remember the sequence of sounds. A coward, she was nothing but a coward, hiding out of sight and leaving Suria to face the colonel's rage.

"I'm so sorry, Suria. So very sorry." Hannah looks at the couple. "You won't have to put up with us much longer."

Suria says nothing, still shaking her head, as if she refuses to believe anything. Anjuh hovers anxiously beside her, holding the unspooled bandage in one hand and a bowl of noodles under the other arm. It must be excruciating for him to see his wife in this state.

"Do you have a doctor in town?" she asks. "Someone who can help you heal? I think you should be using a splint, Suria. You know, so the fingers can heal as straight as possible." She tries to demonstrate on her own hand.

They look at each other and mumble a few words in Malay. Perhaps they don't understand.

Hannah says, "I want you to go home. Back to the lower town. There's no point in you hanging on here for the last week or two, not when he's being…so unkind. Anjuh, please, help her get to a doctor. Medicine. Don't worry, I will make sure that you're paid for the last weeks of your service."

Anjuh and Suria look at each other again, exchanging a few more words in Malay. "No, mem," Anjuh tells her. "We not make you alone."

Wiping the tears away, more come in their place. And now she is embarrassing these poor people! "I'm so sorry," Hannah repeats. "I'm sorry for everything that has happened. Sorry for what we have made you do."

"Hush, mem." Anjuh puts the bowl of noodles down and takes her by the arm.

Suria joins in, moving around the table to ladle a new bowl of soup. "Please, eat."

She accepts a place at their table. Anjuh rewraps Suria's hand with the old bandage and pulls a crate up for an extra chair. Then they all begin slurping broth and spooling noodles onto their spoons. The table is so small their heads almost touch when they lean over the bowls.

"Noodles is good for sadness," Suria remarks.

She will need a lot of noodles, then. A river full. As Hannah eats, her insides warming, she considers her next steps. Just like Suria and Anjuh, she cannot stay on Ridge Road.

FIFTY-FOUR

One of Lucy's house girls opens the door.

"Good morning. Is Mrs. Peterborough available?" Hannah asks. It is nine o'clock in the morning. She would be surprised if Eva weren't in. Available is another matter.

The maid ushers her inside with a bow. Has she been one of the doctor's research subjects too? The girl returns before long and leads Hannah through to the back parlor. Eva is sitting in one of the armchairs with a pot of coffee and a newspaper on the table beside her. Seeing Hannah, she rises. "Hannah darling, how are you?"

"Oh…surviving, I suppose."

"Good."

"I'm sorry I couldn't receive you the other day."

"Or the one after that."

"No, well, I've been…" Broken is a word that comes to mind. Wallowing is another. "Eva, tell me what happened."

"What do you mean?"

"How he was killed. Why he was killed. Tell me everything you know."

Eva sits down, gesturing for Hannah to do the same and shooing away the remaining servant. "Hannah, I don't really know."

"I came to you, Eva, because I knew *you* would tell me the truth."

"Sit down, then."

Reluctantly, Hannah removes her satchel and takes a seat in the nearest armchair.

Eva glances at the satchel. "He was found with his throat slit. In one of the alleys in the lower town, quite near the river. It seems that no one saw or heard anything, or at least nobody has come forward. His body was found by some shrimpers heading toward the wharf. Apparently, they had some trouble finding an officer to report their discovery. Every available man was assisting with the transfer of the convicts."

She swallows with difficulty. So Darshan would have lain alone in the street. Died alone.

"My speculation," continues Eva, tapping her chin with her fore-finger, "is that those shrimpers were the ones who released the wretched genduk. They must have arrived at the station, found no officers about...and perhaps the girl pleaded with them. Promised them sexual favors. Or they simply took the opportunity to free one of their own."

"She was locked in, wasn't she?"

Eva shrugs. "Were there keys nearby? It wasn't the most secure of situations."

"I should have gone to his funeral," Hannah murmurs. She had felt too guilty and too anguished to show her face.

"What, his Sikh funeral? Hannah, my goodness, that would have sealed your fate, socially. What with your breakdown...and then the rumors that were already—"

"Right," snaps Hannah, "because now you're at the epicenter of Who's Who and What's What."

"Not for long, thankfully. I've convinced Charles to leave for Australia. That's why I called on you earlier this week. To say goodbye." Her expression softens. "To offer you my condolences, as well."

Hannah sniffs. Somehow, losing Eva is a blow. As much as she's come to dislike the woman, she likes her just as much. "What are you going to do in Australia? How soon are you leaving?"

"Tour, collect, write, conduct field research. What we do wherever we go." Eva reaches for her hand in an uncharacteristic show of warmth. "Don't look so devastated, Hannah. You're leaving, too, aren't you?" She looks down. "And despite, as you put it, being at the epicenter of Who's Who, I don't fancy living at Idlewyld if you won't be visiting."

Lucy enters the room with a discreet cough. "Hannah!" she chirps.

"Hello, Lucy."

Lucy registers the presence of the beat-up satchel at Hannah's feet with widening eyes and proceeds to interrogate her. *How are you feeling? How are you sleeping? Eating? Are you coping, poor dear, with your diagnosis?* Hannah is surprised there are no questions about her bowel functions.

At some point during the exchange, Eva excuses herself. "Come out to Idlewyld before we leave, darling. Please. I have something to give you."

Hannah stands for many minutes, possibly, looking at Darshan's bungalow from the street. She can't manage to move any closer; neither can she force herself to turn and leave. What of his laugh, that great boom of a laugh—hadn't she heard it, just now, around the corner?

"Madam," a voice says.

"Yes." Hannah wakes to find herself facing a Sikh woman, younger than herself, holding a child against her hip.

"What do you want with this house?" the woman asks. "Why are you standing here looking?"

Confused, Hannah says, "Do you live here now?"

"No." The woman shakes her head. She has jet black hair and black eyes that do not look friendly. "More important: *you* do not live here."

"Of course not," Hannah says, thinking at the same time that she wouldn't have minded living there, in the lower town. She likes the noises, the close quarters, the salty breeze from the water.

The child reaches out to her, a chubby hand, with pink fingers extended in a spiral. The motion shifts his weight, pulling him out of his mother's grip. She draws her son firmly back into her arms.

"This might sound strange," Hannah tells her, "but I am…I was a friend of Sergeant Singh's. And I wondered…" She fumbles for a moment with her handkerchief against her nose. *I wondered if I could tell you how much I miss him.* "I wondered if I might be able to have his notebook? Where he wrote about the forest species he was documenting? If nobody else has use of it. If…I don't know where it might be, you see, he usually carried it with him, but…and I don't suppose you would know, either."

The woman regards her silently. Her eyes have grown a little kinder.

"I suppose not," Hannah continues. "Only, I thought he may have left it at home. Or it, it may have been put in his house when they, when they…" She cannot bring herself to talk about the task, though someone must have had it, of removing Darshan's bloodied uniform. Emptying its pockets. Bathing his body clean. Preparing him for the funeral rites. What are Sikh funeral rites? He never spoke much of his faith, and, absurdly, she had not asked him about himself. Who did these things for him? she wants to ask the woman. What and whom did he love? He had never mentioned a wife, never a family. "He's remarkably content," says Hannah, of the child, "just sitting in your arms."

"Still sleepy," she answers. The woman turns and walks in the direction of the bungalow. "Wait here."

Hannah follows her toward the side door, where the woman enters without knocking. Who is she, this young stern thing? Hannah doesn't recognize her, and yet there are few Sikh women in the village. As she stands, waiting, she considers the matter. Could it be that she is a relation of Darshan's, come from India? There is no reason to suppose this except for his death, and the fact the two share a faith.

Shortly the woman emerges from the side door, her son still clinging to her like a koala. She holds out Darshan's square notebook with its leather tie. "This one?" she says. "Because there are ten more just like it."

At Idlewyld, the two women embrace warmly. It has begun to sink in, how much they will miss each other's company. That they may well never see each other again. Eva asks Hannah to come upstairs. The pleasant, lilting sound of syllables grows louder as they walk down the corridor.

"Let's stop in on Charlotte," Hannah suggests.

In the nursery, Charlotte Peterborough is reading aloud to a new servant, a temporary genduk. This Malay is grey-haired and stout. Her betel-stained mouth parts as she listens. The girl's cheeks are bright red in the heat of the stuffy room.

"Say goodbye to Mrs. Inglis," Eva directs her daughter.

Charlotte does so, and lets Hannah embrace her briefly.

"Be a good girl, then," Hannah says, for no particular reason. She wonders how much Charlotte talks to her mother and father. What does she know about their lives? "Are you still collecting butterflies?" she asks her.

"It's out of season," Charlotte replies, taking her seat again at the table.

"Ah. So I suppose not."

"Come," Eva says, "I have something for you, Hannah."

Further down the corridor, they enter her study. The room has been emptied except for the long mahogany desk. Eva moves around to unlock and then tug open a drawer. She removes an envelope, turning it over in her fingers, gathering her thoughts.

"I've treated you poorly, Hannah. And I'm very sorry that I can't change that, I know. Whatever justifications I may have had, I…I was simply struggling. This may sound awfully silly to you. But it seemed to me that, when you chose Sergeant Singh, you chose *against* me."

"What you do mean?" she objects. "I spent far more time here with you. I didn't choose him, Eva."

"Yes, you did," she insists kindly. "Here." She holds out the envelope. "Your commission."

Hannah peeks inside. "This isn't meant to be payment, is it? Eva, I didn't accomplish anything on your behalf. I never made you a painting!"

"You made plenty, but then your bastard of a husband burned them all to ashes."

Hannah draws out a bundle of British banknotes. Hundreds of hundred-pound notes. "I can't accept this."

"Of course you can."

"I wanted to paint you something special." A parasol flower, she cannot bring herself to add.

"Then say you *will* paint me something special. Because I'm not taking any of it back!" With her fingernail, Eva traces the grain in the wood of the desktop between them. She pushes at a char mark, a black wound in the wood. "Don't waste your talent, Hannah. Take the money and spend it on paint supplies. Then send me something. But we'll correspond, won't we?"

"Paint supplies! There must be at least—"

"You're right, that's far too much to spend on paint alone. Set yourself up with what you need. Keep going."

Hannah feels a rush of gratitude. "Thank you. Very much."

"Not at all," she says coolly.

"Eva, I just want to say…I'm so glad to have known you. For what you've helped me see. So much. And I wish—I wish you happiness, wherever you go."

Her mouth turns up. "If my theory is a good one, then I should be able to verify it from any location. After all, Mr. Darwin spent thirteen years peering at barnacles before he dared to present the idea of sexual selection. Charles and I can make up the fieldwork elsewhere. And when we do, I expect we'll see all of this here in Kuala Kangsa as nothing more than a setback."

Hannah flinches inwardly. Of course the fieldwork would continue; it is the reason the Peterboroughs came in the first place, and the reason they have to move on. Holding a packet of Eva's money, she's hardly in a position to object.

"I know you don't approve," says Eva, reading her face. "I appreciate your concern. I'll take it into consideration," she says, a little awkwardly. "He certainly won't be doing any more photography."

Someone is calling for memsahib, coming along the corridor. A head appears in the doorway; a houseboy asks a question about packing the kitchen crockery. He leaves with an answer but the women agree, Eva must get on with things.

"I'll take a little walk out back, if you don't mind," says Hannah. "Before I head home."

"A little walk." Eva laughs. "I know you. Three hours later, she'll have hiked to the highlands!"

FIFTY-FIVE

After an interminably long flight and a drive that gave new meaning to the word "pothole," Barnaby and I were recuperating in our guest-house when fireworks began shooting off. Separately, we stumbled into the hallway and out onto the enormous covered steps of the Sayong Resort.

"What for?" he moaned to me.

Our view of the impressive display was partly obscured by a cluster of high-rises closer to the city center.

"National holiday?" I guessed.

The desk clerk, who must have seen us exit, coughed discreetly behind us. He was dark-haired and light-skinned, with round gold-framed glasses and a sensitive aura about him. I wondered if perhaps he were a student at the local university. His name, he later told me, was Danish. "Very good guess," said the man. "But Independence Day is not until next week."

The bang-banging of the fireworks continued. I rubbed my eyes.

"What are they for, then?" snapped Barnaby, clearly cross that we were being put through a guessing game on top of everything else.

Danish beamed. "A football celebration. We've just walloped Thailand. You are fortunate to be here on this special day."

"Yes," said Barnaby, slouching back to the entryway, "fortunate."

I stayed out on the breezy step with Danish after Barnaby had gone, apologizing for his crankiness and offering my congratulations on the match.

"Yes, it is nice," he said. He smiled for a long moment, and added, "And nice to be traveling with your grandfather."

I laughed and explained that we weren't related, just friends. "Sort of," I added. "We're...uh...doing field research, I guess you could say."

The fireworks boomed on. The Sayong Resort itself was deserted, and I saw clearly now that poor Danish was stuck at work that night instead of celebrating the soccer victory with his friends. In the back room he'd probably had his television set on, but the resort wasn't the kind of place to deck itself out for a sporting event. Barnaby had insisted we go upscale, at least while we were visiting the Royal City of Kuala Kangsa, as all the guidebooks had proclaimed it. The party was clearly elsewhere.

"Did you grow up here?" I asked him.

"In Kuala Kangsa? Yes."

"So you know where everything is."

He nodded happily.

In her letters, Hannah had mentioned the Residency, the public gardens, the marketplace, the fishing wharf, the mosque, Ridge Road, the Perak Club, the police station, and the postal office on the high street. The outpost of Kuala Kangsa had grown into a city. Finding these landmarks was like peeling back the layers of an onion. Danish advised us on where to peel.

And so I walked where Hannah may have walked, through shady neighborhoods, and a bustling marketplace, along a road on a ridge with a view of the Perak River, though this road had sidewalks and palatial homes. In the public gardens, Barnaby and I sat with plastic cups of bubble tea, gawping at the ballooning clouds. We strolled the grounds, sniffing roses and marveling at how finely clipped the lawn was.

The police station had been relocated twice, it seemed, toward the periphery of the city, and we did not bother to seek it out. On the high street, we entered a few of the tourist shops. I put postcards in the mail for my parents and Daphne and Bob, even one for Chris and Zoe, using the same postal service Hannah had used over a hundred years earlier. And the same clerk, by the looks of him. How strange that her letters had somehow found their way to me. I'd touched them, read them, entered into her concerns, her hopes, her imaginings. I'd met her in her art, too, and in a weird way found myself there. Hannah Inglis would never know me, of course. Or know how she'd changed my life. Reflecting on the whole experience, as one tends to when traveling—and journaling, as I had started to do—it was beginning to blow my mind.

"I think this is it," Barnaby said. "Our stop."

We trundled to the front of the bus, not seeing how else we were supposed to make our stop known to the driver. The driver slowed as we talked at him and pointed to the sign for the cemetery. Danish had told me that in the immediate area, there were in fact seven cemeteries:

a small one in the center of town for the founding British officers and cadets of the region (with the latest burial being 1822), three others that had Christian Chinese bodies, two for the Muslim faith (a sprawling one for the Malay Muslim population and a much smaller one for those Muslims who had come from India), and finally the Western Highland English cemetery. This seemed our best bet. The Western Highland contained people of all faiths, including Catholics, Protestants, and even one or two Jewish graves. We discovered that although it was called an English cemetery, Germans, Dutch, French, and other nationalities were represented, too. Even someone from Argentina.

Bounded by apartment blocks and shaded by fine-leafed locust trees, the cemetery was larger than it had appeared from the road. Barnaby and I spent a good thirty minutes wandering in opposite directions before we caught up with each other in an area dominated by large, raised crypts. He read out the message on the end of one facing us: "Both parents expired on the morning of April 2, 1869, and their son on the previous afternoon, from jungle fever. Golly!"

"I know," I said. "There were some 'jungle fevers' over there."

"See any Inglises?"

"Not yet." Unfortunately, many of the stones of that era were almost entirely eroded. And it was of course possible George and Hannah had left the country, let alone the area. We strolled past Woolriches and Kavanblatzes, other Georges, and other Hannahs. One Amelia Burns, who had died at only four years old. It was a rough life, I thought.

"Perhaps Hannah couldn't afford a headstone," I remarked. Though I did not like to think of her penniless.

"She might have died in the jungle," Barnaby suggested. "She might have slipped and fallen into a cave or drowned in a rushing river. That's rather more exciting."

"Or been eaten by a tiger," I said, grimacing.

We kept walking. In one corner of the cemetery, bounded by a stone wall, was a small burial ground dedicated to the Sikh community. We picked our way over.

"I suppose they've been assimilated too," Barnaby said as we ducked under an archway.

Inside was a grouping of monuments for the fallen Sikh policemen of the region of Perak and a historical plaque set into a large plinth. I read the plaque with interest. It spoke of how the Sikhs had been brought by the British to Malaya as convicts. In Penang and Perak, these men had performed the dangerous and difficult labor of clearing the dense forest, draining the swamplands, and building the railroad that connected Taiping, a port, to Kuala Kangsa and the mining town of Ipoh. Essentially, after the railroad had been constructed they were released from service. Most of the men who'd survived went on to form the regional police force for the growing colony.

So he'd been a convict, her sergeant. What crime had he committed? I wondered. Had Hannah known about it? I looked up and inhaled the scent of the pine boughs above me. Going from criminal to police officer had probably been a natural transition.

"I've found a 'D. Singh,'" said Barnaby, who was stooped in front of one wall of the monument. The wall was lined with columns of engraved names. The Sikhs cremated their dead; there were no headstones to be found.

"Really?"

"Oh. Here's another," he said.

Together we counted five D. Singhs on the list.

We returned at the end of the day to our Sayong Resort with sore feet and bellies full of *ikan bakar*. In my head I was struggling to make peace with the idea that we might find no traces of Hannah Inglis in this place. Malaysia had moved on, and rightly so. I reaffirmed my vow to absorb and enjoy as much of the trip as possible, whatever happened. I was lucky to have traveled so far.

"It's ironic," I said to Barnaby.

We were in my room, each of us with a cup of tea.

"What's ironic?" He didn't look up. He was reviewing his topographic map yet again.

"Somehow I had the idea that coming *here* was going to bring me closer to the truth about who Hannah was. Closer. Like I could be an eyewitness or something. Find an exotic, alien reality."

"But she lived here well over a hundred years ago."

"It's not just the timing. The point is there's no way of getting outside of anyone's story. The story is all we've got."

He looked up, blank. "You've lost me."

"Forget it. I'm such an idiot. With Hannah, I've been going against every premise in the discourse."

I looked at him for a moment, head bent again to peer at his map, and decided I would try to explain it after all. Maybe less for Barnaby's sake than my own. I said, "Foucault identified it. People make recourse to something like 'nature' or the 'essential' to put an end to questions and to ground their authority. Take racial identity, for example. It's totally fictional. What makes somebody 'white' or 'black' or 'red' depends on whatever social conventions are in play wherever you're referring to somebody as 'white' or 'black' or 'red.'

"Same with gender. And so the line of reasoning that says to define what it means to be a woman, we have to double down and look at the 'biology alone'—that's deceptive. There is no 'biology alone.' That way of approaching things is just begging the question. Just privileging certain traits, calling *them* what's 'natural,' and saying *they're* the things that constitute identity. The whole thing is a rhetorical move. I'm falling for the same kind of logic, Barnaby. Why should Hannah's bones be any more *Hannah* than her letters or her paintings? Really, why should coming here bring me any closer to knowing her?"

I hadn't spoken in this way in a long time. It felt strange, like putting on an old pair of gloves.

Barnaby poked his head up again. "I'm glad I went into science."

I grunted, a little disappointed he wasn't going to engage me on the topic. Turning to the miniature dual-purpose tea/coffee maker, I set about replacing the round teabag in the filter holder to make more tea. Red Rose. No, probably not from a local plantation. I removed the wet bag, flung it in the garbage, tore open another. When I poured the new water into the machine, most of it dribbled down the front of the carafe and onto the carpet.

"Why can't they design a spout that doesn't spill? Is that really too much to ask?" And having replaced the round teabag, I couldn't get the miniature filter basket to slide back in place. I fiddled with the angle, ramming the little plastic cup back and forth, liquid sloshing.

"Here, here," said Barnaby softly, reaching to still my hand. "Fetch your cup."

I watched him slide the basket neatly into place as I handed him my paper cup. Hot brown liquid soon started dripping into it.

"You're disappointed," he said, "that we haven't found anything definitive."

"Sort of," I admitted.

There was a knock at the door. Danish was standing in the hallway, his hands pressed together as if in prayer. "Hi! Just thought of something," he said. "Have you tried the local library?"

Yes, I truly was an idiot.

FIFTY-SIX

Hannah finds the colonel is at the desk in his office, surrounded by bare walls and crates. He is skimming over what appears to be a shipping log. "I'm not coming," she tells him.

"What?"

"You heard me. I'm not coming to England with you."

"That's…" He presses his palms into the desk, looking intently at her before rising to his feet. "I won't pay for you to stay here, Hannah. I warn you."

"Of course not. I wouldn't expect that."

They eye each other, exhibits of themselves. It is late in the morning. The air is fresh and dry enough to feel through her pores that the rainy season is coming to an end. Her satchel waits by the front door.

"What's the matter with you?" he blurts out. "What will you do, Hannah? You're simply not well. You must be…you must be bewitched," he accuses her bizarrely.

"I will be fine," she says. She feels calm, quite calm, in fact.

"Good god, you're incredible! You know you won't earn anything. How could you earn anything? You'll be put on the streets. You'll destroy your reputation, our reputation. And your health. I hope you don't think I'm having that on my conscience. I'll let it be known that you—"

"Be quiet please, George. You can let whatever you want to be known be known. I don't care. What will you do, have my throat slit as well?"

The mask drops over his face. "You think *I* am responsible for—? I assure you, I am not."

Looking at him, she doesn't feel assured. She's had plenty of time to think everything through. Hannah says, "It's what you do, George. Or rather, who you are. You would have killed every last tiger in the bush. And for what purpose? Cleo was long gone."

The colonel appears transfixed, caught within his clothes. Hannah doesn't wait any longer.

Later, the colonel finds her in the public gardens. Who knows how long he would have been looking, to come across her here. He's likely never set foot in the gardens. She sees him walking up the gravel path and fights the impulse to gather up her tubes of paint and her palette and clutch everything to her.

She is painting the south gate itself: the honey-colored stone wall where it curls into an arch over the delicate wrought-iron door. A glimpse of the wild greens beyond. As he approaches, Hannah lifts her brush and slides it behind her ear.

The colonel looks for a long time at the unfinished painting propped on her lap. He appears to have been crying. His face is somber as he hands her a fold of bills.

"For the first while," he says. "To tide you over." He clears his throat. "I redeemed your ticket."

Hannah takes the money, knowing at once there is more there than the price of a steamship's passage. A terrifying abyss seems to fall open beneath her. The depth of the Pacific Ocean itself.

"Thank you," she tells him.

He half-shrugs, nods. Then he cups her shoulder a little roughly. "Take care of yourself, Hannah."

"You as well, George."

Later still, she hears the great horn sounding and resounding on the steamer as it exits the harbor. The silence that comes after is profound.

George, James, Lucy, so many others who've come and gone, inevitably, sliding along toward their destinies. Eva and her family have already left for a place called Darwin, fittingly. And yet it feels as if she is the one who has pushed out to sea, the familiar features of the coastline diminishing and blurring before her eyes.

Hannah picks at her fingernails, digging out the dried paint. A good wash is what she needs. She packs up her paints and belongings and is halfway up Cinnamon Hill before she remembers that her suitcases are in the opposite direction, at her new house. Amalaka Singh, it turns out, is landlady to half the townspeople in the lower village. Young as she is she knows her business, and most of the village's business as well. "Anybody give you trouble," she told Hannah, and her elder brother and father would "apply the muscle." The sort of trouble, Hannah imagines, that women who live alone are expected to encounter.

Amalaka had conducted the transaction. She'd brought Hannah into the sitting room of her family's home, the men looking on. "Three bungalows are available at this time."

"I don't want his," Hannah said immediately, her voice choking on itself. "I couldn't. I'm sorry."

She took a deep breath and pressed the soles of her feet into the thatch flooring. There were pictures of the Sikh gurus on Amalaka's wall as well. Everything else felt quite different: the light in the room, its vaguely sweet smell, like clover. Hannah could hear the child gabbling at somebody in an adjacent room.

Amalaka's brother said something in Punjabi, she supposed, and the three of them had a brief discussion.

"How long?" Amalaka asked her.

Hannah shook her head. "I don't know. Indefinitely."

Again, they spoke. Stealing glances, Hannah interpreted the father as reticent, the brother and sister more sanguine. All three must have considered her move unusual. If they had any qualms about her friendship with Sergeant Singh, they voiced no objections to her. Part of her ached for them to complain. They should castigate her for ruining his life. Rake her over the coals. Demand to know: how was anything ever going to be put right?

The family seemed to reach a resolution. Amalaka said to her, "So of the remaining two bungalows, one is fresher and one is older. Unfortunately, the fresher one is next door to the missionary family."

"Oh," said Hannah, "you mean Mr. and Mrs. Watts?"

"Yes," the three of them said at once.

The Watts children, apart from Jane, were known to be a rambunctious crew, it was true, and Mr. Watts came by his fire-and-brimstone reputation honestly. Yet Beatrice, for all her faults, was a kind woman. Without Lucy and the LAP members to goad her on, she might even take on some original qualities. "I know the Watts," Hannah said.

"Yes, and do they not know *you*?" Amalaka replied, translating for her father.

In an instant, Hannah realized how wrong she'd got it. The question was not whether she could put up with the Watts, but whether they could put up with her. Would their god-fearing family be content with a sinner, a rebellious and broken woman, in their midst?

Hannah said, her chest tightening, "By all means, I am content with the older bungalow. I don't want to cause trouble."

She heads there now, to the smaller, older bungalow situated at the end of one of the lanes running toward the river. It is less desirable because of its proximity to the stilted homes clustered along the river. The poorest of the village live in the stilted huts, whether Malay, Chinese, Indian, or people from the hill tribe who ventured out of the forest. The stilted community throws its kitchen choppings out its windows, and they urinate and defecate out them, too. Depending on which way the breeze is blowing, especially at low tide, the smell can be intense. Because of the kitchen choppings, there are dogs that make their homes in the tall grasses. They pace and whine and occasionally choke themselves on fish bones. Noisy carrion crows visit, too.

At the moment, Hannah sees only the boys as she turns down her lane. Two skinny black-haired things, kicking a ball back and forth. She avoids them, glancing over once or twice to see what they will do about her and smiling pleasantly at them. The taller one stops the ball under his foot and stares openly. Hannah moves ahead to the squashed-looking little home and its shuttered front door. Surely the Singhs would be fine if she installed a mesh one.

Tomorrow, perhaps, she could find Suria and Anjuh to say hello. Though perhaps not. They might feel…and she might feel…unsure of what to say, under the circumstances. Something strikes her hard in the rump, making her stumble forward. It is the ball, of course. Hannah pauses, brushes the dust from her backside, then turns to face the boys. The taller one is covering his laughing mouth. The smaller one looks terrified. She grips the straps of her satchel, feeling foolish. The ball, dirty and cracked, has not rolled far. Hannah walks over to it, lines up, and swings her boot, sending it high and, to her surprise, quite far up the lane.

"That felt lovely," she tells them. "I can see why you enjoy it."

But the pair of them are already off and running, either to flee her or to fetch the ball. It doesn't really matter. No doubt they'll be back.

Inside, she stands for a minute, wrestling with the unreality of the situation before wrestling a towel from her tangle of belongings. Clutching the towel, she surveys the drab lounge, the tiny cooking area in an alcove out back, the shadowy bedroom where there is a fist-sized hole in the uneven floorboards. It is perfect. It is a space that is all her own. Though there is nothing in the house, she soon sees, resembling a bathtub. Or water. She laughs. Up the street, she passed a well where people must draw their water for cooking and cleaning. She will have to buy a basin, or a jug, something for carrying water. My god, she is so ill-prepared. Who or what, really, does she need to be prepared for?

Hannah tugs open the one shuttered window on the back wall of the lounge. It looks out toward the Perak river, broad enough in this area to resemble a lake, shining in the late-day sun. A boggy shoreline of stilted huts clutters the foreground of the prospect. One of the huts looks tippy, precariously so, as if at any moment it might crash into the sparkling blue.

"Goodness," she says, "now that one's going to wring my nerves out."

Shutting the window, she fishes her bathing costume from her suit-case. A little further upstream it may be quite pleasant as a point of entry.

In fact, it is just as she imagines it, a wedge of shallows where the river meanders eastward. Where, during the day, it turns out, the women of the lower town come while their men are out fishing. Hannah wades into the blue, a dark phthalo blue with streaks of Veronese green, and washes herself clean.

FIFTY-SEVEN

I went alone to the library, leaving Barnaby to his topographical map and an episode of *Strictly Come Dancing* that he'd managed to find on the satellite TV programming. (What was it with the over-60s and that television program?) At the largest branch of the municipal library, there were a few Malaysian patrons leafing through the local news-paper and using the computer terminals for internet access.

I searched the government records area and was pleased to locate the 1892 and 1902 censuses. The first of these showed one Lieut. Colonel James Finch, Resident, to be living at the Residency, Kuala Kangsa. Wife: Mrs. Lucille Finch. The other inhabitants of the ad-dresses along Ridge Road did include Colonel George Inglis (age forty-three) and his wife, Hannah (age twenty-seven). I wrote down all of the other names, too: Mr. Edgar and Mrs. Hazel Swinburne, Mrs. Myrtle Cudmore, etcetera. I skimmed the list of names in the other kampongs, but did not see the Peterboroughs on record. In the 1902 census, there was a new Resident, one Arthur Effingdon-Watts, listed as 'widower,' and no Colonel George or Hannah Inglis living at #26 Ridge Road or anywhere else in town. They'd left, it seemed.

Invigorated, I went on to look up local history books by local au-thors. The database suggested a particularly promising volume, *Our Colonial Past: the British families who took Malaya as their home 1867-1907*, by one Amalaka Singh. Disappointingly, the book was not on the shelf. The librarian told me their records showed the book as missing.

"Missing?" I said.

"Yes. Could be lost by somebody, could be stolen."

"So, not just on loan. *Gone.*"

"Yes," she said with a little pout. She had a pretty face, framed by a glossy black bob. "Sorry for this," she added.

To be helpful, the girl printed out the book's bibliographic infor-mation while I waited at the check-out counter, book-less, craving something more, and looking blankly into the reading room at the microfiche reader. "Is that a…? What is that?" I asked her, pointing.

"The reading room?"

"That machine."

"Oh, the microfiche!" she exclaimed, looking a little fearful.

The Malay Mail, founded in 1890, had been run from Kuala Lumpur but took contributions from across the peninsula. Miraculously, it seemed to me, Hannah's Kuala Kangsa had had press coverage. While the librarian powered up the old machine, I scooped cassettes from the drawer. I found nothing of much interest until the May 1902 edition, *Perak Supplement*. The article, titled "We Saved the Best for Last," referred to the region's final gymkhana festival ever to be held. Queen Victoria had died over a year before, in January 1901, and it was somewhat awkward, the reporter implied, to continue celebrating her birthday. The article was comprised mostly of elaborately captioned photographs. One of them was a group photo of a weather-beaten assortment of people, some of whom were children holding up frogs or homemade boats. An Englishwoman wearing a sun bonnet and a joyful smile stood in the second row, looking over at the children. The caption read, "Off to the races!" The names of the participants were listed, along with "race convener" Mrs. Hannah Inglis, center back. Hannah, the woman wearing the sunbonnet.

The very same, yet so very different, woman from the anatomy class photograph. I sat at the microfiche reader feeling Hannah's enthusiasm, wanting to put my own boat in her race. In that near-empty and slightly musty-smelling library, I sat loving a person I'd never met, someone who had never and would never know me.

The photograph proved she was here, in Kuala Kangsa, in the spring of 1902. Before the census record had been taken? Had she moved away after that, or somehow escaped being counted? I checked the time chart I'd made. It had been five years since Hannah stopped writing to Godot. Five years since she'd written about the diagnosis and treatment advocated by Charles Peterborough, namely, that she return to England and give up painting. It would be another six years until the publication of *The Descent*, in 1908, with its etching of the parasol flower. And, for eight more years after this photograph was taken, Eva Peterborough's accountant would be recording his little notes, *Comm. for ptg. H. Inglis*, before those mysteriously vanished too. What exactly to make of all of this, I didn't know.

Hannah looked happy, though. "I'm glad," I told her quietly. "I'm so glad you were happy."

FIFTY-EIGHT

Danish agreed to drive us to the Cameron Highlands.

"You understand that we want something *off* the beaten path," Barnaby reminded him. We loaded our rucksacks into the trunk of our rental car. It was six o'clock in the morning; we'd asked for an early start.

"I understand, sir," Danish replied patiently.

We had explained everything to him one evening in the resort's Meeting Room B, reviewing the topographical maps Barnaby had brought with him. Danish had mentioned he was quite familiar with the highland hiking trails. His family had often taken him for outings there as a child.

As spry as Barnaby was for his age, and as much technical gear as he'd brought for us both, I was still a little nervous about going "off the beaten path." Inviting Danish to come along had been my idea, one that I probably should have discussed with Barnaby in advance. He'd been cool with me since Meeting Room B. Offended, possibly. Maybe he thought Danish would cramp his style.

We had described to Danish the flower we were most interested in finding, without actually calling it a parasol flower. Unassuming foliage, growing on the forest floor, enormous flower head, only rarely in bloom.

"The Rafflesia plant?" he said.

"No!" Barnaby and I screeched at the same time.

I showed the poor man the photograph of *The Parasol Flower* painting on my phone.

Danish glanced at it and said in a low voice, "No, never heard of it."

"Take note of the details," Barnaby commanded.

Danish had looked again, delicately taking hold of the phone and even zooming in on the image.

Now we were heading up, up, up, for an outing that, I reflected from the backseat, had several hazards. The weather was iffy; it was unseasonably cold, and rain was forecasted for that afternoon. Barnaby was already irritable. And then there was fact that, however much we'd downplayed it, we'd come halfway around the world in search of a flower that no one who lived here had ever seen. Today was the day we would very likely prove we were fools.

On the other hand, the countryside was breathtaking. Across every horizon, heavily-forested mountain peaks rose toward the glowing sun. Verdant tea plantations covered the undulating hills between. So early in the morning, the highlands felt like ours alone. Occasionally a pickup truck or compact car zoomed by us in the opposite direction; each time, Danish swerved and slowed, and I clutched the door handle a little more tightly. When we went around a sharp corner, he beeped the horn of the Toyota.

We were heading to trek a peak called Gunung Berembun. Using the trail system, it was a four- or five-hour loop. Since we wanted to spend some time bushwhacking, we were factoring in an extra two hours.

Danish veered to the right at an intersection with a stack of signposts. Some of them had been spray painted over with black lettering I couldn't make sense of. "That way is Gunung Jasar," he told us. "There are two *orang asli* villages and some very nice viewing points."

"What happened there?" I asked. Craning to look behind me, I could see something wasn't right. The road onward look widened and rutted.

"Protests," Danish said. "Developers bulldozed part of the mountain."

"Oh no!"

"I thought it was a nature reserve," said Barnaby, who had of course done his research.

"It is. Nature reserve means state-owned land. State decided on condominium developments and strawberry farms."

"Huh?" I said. It sounded like an odd combination to me.

"For tourists. The Cameron Highlands is becoming a very popular tourist destination for Malaysians and Thai."

Once popular only for the English, I appended mentally. I looked at Danish to see if I could judge what he thought about this change. He seemed to be simply concentrating on the way forward.

We parked the car where the road ended. Several small tour buses were lined up in what passed for a parking lot. Barnaby threw menacing looks at the empty buses as he rearranged his gear, pulling his binoculars out of one pocket and stuffing them into another.

I caught his eye. "Don't worry. I think we've got to at least *start* on the beaten path."

Danish said, "You'll see, it gets very quiet, sir. Especially the distance we're going to go."

He was right. At first the trail was slim but obvious, swerving endlessly, it seemed, through an enclosed forest of ferns. We crossed several boggy patches and rivulets. Later, the vegetation opened up to reveal the tops of the trees towering over us. Epiphytes and lianas dangled almost to within reach. I thought of Hannah in a place like this, lugging her paints and her three-legged stool. There was not much color here that I could distinguish, just green on green on green.

I slowed, deliberately taking a pause, and noticed a huge black worm slithering along the path beside me. The thing was big enough that when I listened closely I could hear it making a noise as it disturbed the forest floor debris. "What is *that*?" I asked. But the others were too far ahead to hear me.

I bounded to catch up and learned that my companion had likely been a millipede. "The size of a bracelet!" I marveled. "Not that I'd want it to touch me."

On our first leg to Robinson Waterfall, we spotted not only the millipede, but an orchid and a brightly colored bird called a black and yellow broadbill. The waterfall was breathtaking, or rather, would have been breathtaking. It was near a road and attracted a good deal of attention. A bridge had even been built at the base of the falls to allow people to view the falling water at an optimum angle. However, the bridge obscured all other angles. Onlookers here, Danish told us, were usually heading to and from Tanah Rata, the city that was now home base for the highlands. We took a few photographs but didn't linger.

He led us onward until our path joined with another, a signposted trail that looked overgrown and in poor repair. I could feel Barnaby's spirits rising. As we walked on, I scanned the uneven jungle floor for unusual flora. In most places, it was next to impossible to see further than a few steps in front of us, given the density of the undergrowth and the rocky hillocks that formed the terrain. A pack of tourists on a guided hike passed us by and we exchanged hellos. One of them informed us of an interesting mushroom up ahead. For all the use the trail was getting, it certainly wasn't being maintained. Raised roots frequently obscured our path, as did fallen trees. I checked my phone and discovered to my surprise that there was still cell reception. Ever since the path had forked, back by the waterfall, the trail had been steadily rising.

Barnaby clipped along in front of me, impressing me by showing no signs of fatigue. Once in a while, he directed my attention to bird-song, or a plant, or a patch of groundcover, usually by coming to a full stop and holding up his index finger to catch my attention. He was the one who spotted the sloth, high in a tree. We gathered around below the creature, staring at its hairy, motionless body. After the excitement of the sloth, we decided to eat lunch at the next decent resting place.

As my legs cycled onward, so did my thoughts, revolving around the mystery of Hannah's letters to Godot. Did she know that the Peterboroughs had wound up with the art and the letters she was addressing to her mentor? No, I thought not. At least, not at the time. For as much as Hannah must have lost hope in receiving a reply from Godot, the paintings were still arriving in France. Or were they? What if the letters and the paintings had never been shipped? That would certainly account for why Godot, who had corresponded with Hannah up until 1896, (in the exchange that was documented in Coles), abruptly stopped writing to her. What if everything had remained in Kuala Kangsa? After all, the Peterboroughs were located in Kuala Kangsa at the time. Might they have somehow intercepted Hannah's art before it ever left town? But how? And why?

"I've been thinking about the letters," I said to Barnaby as we were packing up lunch. I shared my newest thoughts on the puzzle.

"Let's focus on the how," he advised. "*Why* the Peterboroughs should have taken them seems impossible to know."

"It's all speculation. But okay. Let's focus on how it could have happened. And let's just say it was Eva, not Charles, who was directly involved. We know she was the one who was friends with Hannah. It was Eva who cared about Hannah's paintings, in my opinion."

"Good. Now, if Eva *intercepted* the art and letters... Let's think.

If the letters started at point A, with Hannah, and then they didn't make it to point G, Godot, we must ask: where else are they along the way?"

"Ha! It's like when you misplace your favorite pen and you have to backtrack to think of all the places you've been using it."

Barnaby laughed. "Ah yes, my young nerd."

We had set out again by this point, but Danish, I noticed, had purposefully slowed his pace. He was glancing back at us frequently; no doubt he thought the two of us a curiosity.

I considered the steps involved in posting a letter. "The only other people involved are postal workers, right? The clerk who accepted her parcels. Maybe somebody else who sorted them in the back room into the 'Europe' or 'France' pile or whatever. Then, after that, the person who delivered them from the post office to the steamship."

"But we'd said they never made it to Europe," he reminded us, "so they never made it onto the steamship."

"True. Unless the steamship sank."

"All of the steamships?"

"Point made."

"I think we say the clerk at the post office must have *accepted* her parcels. Because Hannah seems to have believed they were posted. She kept writing."

"Yes," I agreed, "and she even writes *about* posting them. So she definitely handed them over to the clerk."

We were silent for a long minute or two, each of us roaming through the back room of Kuala Kangsa's post office. Where it must have gone awry. Hannah's parcels must have been stopped there, at least temporarily. I said, "So it's either the clerk or one of the workers in the back room—a manager in the back office?—who failed to move her mail onward to its destination."

Barnaby had been imagining the physical dimensions of the situation. "It must have been quite the pile of mail to *not* send," he pointed out. "Think of what we loaded into the minicab."

We thought about that for a minute.

"Maybe," I offered, "whoever was stopping them from reaching Godot was doling them out to someone else? Eva?"

"Eva watched her friend pining for a response from her teacher all those months, knowing that she herself was the cause of that agony? I can't imagine her being quite so cruel."

She was cruel enough to the natives, I thought to myself. But the fact was I agreed with him; Eva wouldn't have let Hannah or her art suffer for what seemed like no good reason. Our path leveled off, and we emerged from the forest into a sort of rocky clearing. Bracketed between slabs of sedimentary rock, transparent green-blue water coursed across the clearing. Two planks of lumber had been hauled into place as a simple bridge.

Danish knelt and put his hand in the water. We followed suit. It was silky smooth and tepid. The current tugged at my hand. With no more than a word to each other, we abandoned the trail and began moving along the shoreline, stepping on the creased and divotted stones, the crowns of giant rock molars. I headed past a stretch of jostling rapids to a place where the river leveled and broadened into a little lagoon. Out of the gloom of the forest, now, the sun felt baking warm on my face and the backs of my legs. Barnaby was nearby with Danish, pointing at a butterfly that had just landed. We would be here a while. I tugged off my hiking boots, stripped my feet free of their socks, and swung my legs into the gentle flow of the river.

Closing my eyes, I returned to Kuala Kangsa's post office of 1896. Random snippets of Barnaby and Danish's conversation floated past me: technicalities about moth migration, something about bowler hats, somebody (a mountaineer?) who'd died from an infected blister. I thought of the effort Barnaby and I had made in Hampstead, unloading boxes of paintings from the minicab and walking them into Celia's home. Ten months of "failure" to send on the parcels to Godot had to have been deliberate. Someone must have asked for Hannah's mail to Godot to be held aside. Someone who had paid for this service, most probably. Someone who wanted to thwart Hannah.

I nearly kicked myself off the lip of rock and into the eddying water. *George* was the one responsible. In conjunction with the manager of the post office, or whomever could have promised him to keep his wife's art stashed in a closet or under a desk. It was George who had wanted Hannah to grow frustrated, isolated, discouraged. To give up painting. My hands stirred excitedly in the pristine water. Perhaps he'd even thought that eliminating Godot from her life would be a way of reinforcing their relationship, or her dependency.

Clambering to my feet, I shook each wet leg. George himself wouldn't have wanted to keep the paintings or the letters. He couldn't have kept them, could he? Hannah would likely have found out. Whereas Eva, who had supported her friend's painting, might have at least appreciated the studies. So George gave them to Eva? Eva must have found out, somehow, that they were sitting there. And took them.

"And didn't tell Hannah," I said.

Eva Peterborough had read her friend's letters. They were personal, intimate, addressed to somebody else. I had read them, too, of course. Neither of us had been entitled to invade Hannah's privacy. I could understand, then, if Eva Peterborough had kept quiet about what she'd done. Just what I would do, I wasn't sure. My current theory— an idea I'd come to in my travel journal—was that Hannah had kept writing letters to Godot all those months, without any reply, because she needed to believe in him. Or rather, to have his faith in what she was doing. If this made any sense, then perhaps she'd *stopped* writing letters to Godot when she no longer needed him. Had she started believing in herself? Or had she stopped painting?

"You're talking to yourself again," said Barnaby.

"Yes, and it's working," I replied. I didn't bother trying to explain.

He put his binoculars to his face and swiveled in the direction of a bird call. Danish, I saw, was waiting nearby, his backpack propped at his feet.

"Are we heading out, then?" I reached for my socks and right-sided them. "On or off the path?"

"Off the path," said Danish. "We'll head toward the summit by following this little river upstream. A good way to bushwhack. Less undergrowth."

As we climbed higher on the mountain, the river diminished, and the conifers multiplied. Afternoon sunshine leaked through the trees, revealing a tangle of ferns, vines, and palms rising from the earth, but no parasol flowers. We met several ancient and enormous trees, one whose trunk was buttressed by roots too tall to step over. Almost all but the smallest saplings, it occurred to me, would have been here when Hannah was trekking and painting in the region.

Even the mossy logs were so thick they probably took a century to decay.

Danish found us a pitcher plant. *Nepenthes alba*, Barnaby clarified. The tubular flower head, with its curled lip and bulbous shape, appeared to me like an animal organ. An esophagus or some part of the colon, perhaps, or even an inverted birth canal. This one was striated lipstick red and kelly green. Hannah had been struck by the pitcher plant's alien appearance when she'd first started trekking. Coles published a letter in which she described the plant's tubular body as "a gizzard masquerading as a bulb of blown glass." She'd painted several different *Nepenthes* variants that she'd sent to Godot for comment.

In a way that I hadn't appreciated on paper, hiking at altitude was dispiriting. I felt that I was down to one lung. For all our bushwhacking efforts, we'd uncovered nothing more exotic than the *Nepenthes alba*, and we now had very wet feet. Like me, I was sure, Barnaby had started looking a little worse for wear. His hair was slick with sweat and his stride lopsided. Only Danish seemed carefree. The view from the top of the Gunung Berembun allowed us a unique vantage on the other peaks in the highlands. It was stunning, we told each other. It didn't feel like much of a prize.

As we came around to the west side of the summit, we encountered twenty or so spandex-clad tourists, posing for a group photo using an enormous lofted selfie stick. Danish waved happily at them and began chatting to them in Mandarin.

"I'll tend to my blister," Barnaby informed me, flinging off his pack and rooting in pockets.

"Shall we rest for a while?" I suggested. I wanted to head back down on the main trail, whatever the other two thought. The idea that we would turn a corner and blunder upon a flower as special and unusual as the parasol flower seemed a ridiculous fantasy. "I suppose you've seen some amazing sights in your travels," I said to Barnaby.

He nodded as he squinted at his bloodied heel.

It emerged that Barnaby and Danish were just as happy as I was to descend along a quicker and easier route. We followed in the wake of the spandexed tourists, giving them a long head start.

I asked Danish if there were still tigers in Malaysian jungles.

"Not very many," he said. "It's extremely rare to see one."

"What about birds of paradise?"

He told me about a National Geographic crew who had come to the area two years prior to try to film the birds in the wild. The crew had camped out overnight in a tent they'd camouflaged with boughs of foliage in order to fool the birds. The crew masked their human scent by painting their limbs and torsos with mud every few hours. Apparently, they ate nothing but odorless granola-bar-like meal replacements. After *sixteen days* of such vigilance the photographers were rewarded when they spotted a male bird of paradise tottering along a nearby log, dancing to impress his mate.

"What hard work for a few minutes of footage," commented Barnaby.

"You should see the video," said Danish. "These guys are so cute! So weird and so cute! Somebody put all the dancing bird videos together, you know. Added the music: Michael Jackson, Ace of Bass... and it went viral. Prime minister was very excited about that."

"The prime minister?" I said.

"Good for tourism. They say 1.2 million tourist dollars over the next five years for ecotourism. Direct from the dancing bird video."

"Wow."

"Why do I feel like a walking punch line?" Barnaby muttered.

"Oh, Barnaby," I said, "we haven't come because of some silly bird-dancing video."

By early evening we'd returned to the Sayong Resort safe, over-hungry, and over-tired. I lay on the bed for a while looking at my photographs in the viewer. The sloth had been endearing. The waterfalls, picturesque. Now that I'd showered and had four walls around me, I felt a growing sense of accomplishment: we'd trekked a jungle summit at altitude. But my mood ran deeper than self-satisfaction. All of my anxieties and expectations had been scrubbed away by the forest, with its astonishing and peculiar abundance. By nature's way of being any which way, without having to do anything. I closed my eyes for only a moment before sleep overtook me.

Late that night, hunger seized us and we hobbled to a nearby Korean barbecue to eat. The possibility remained of trekking in other areas of the region, notably the Belem Forest Reserve, a nature preserve that crossed the Thai border. It was one of the largest untouched reserves on the planet, and was said to still support large animals like tapirs, rhinoceroses, and elephants.

"It did look amazing in the pictures," I said.

"Which ones were those?" quipped Barnaby. "From the Belum Rainforest Resort?"

Strange as it sounds, it was just like that, that we gave up the search for a parasol flower, without naming what we were doing. Other people, I consoled myself, may be inspired to go further. We ate for a long while in silence. Easy for Barnaby to have scruples, I thought. He'd spent a lifetime venturing through virgin wilds; he'd collected plenty of memories. And in his case, he'd built a career on it. I suppose I felt a little regretful.

"I think, based on the *Malay Mail* photograph, that Hannah stayed in Malaya," I announced. "Maybe she lived in the lower town for a time. Maybe she moved out of Perak to another area of the peninsula. I almost wonder if she went to live in the forest that she loved so much."

Barnaby laughed at me. "What, with her Sergeant Singh? The two of them, living off the land. You romantic, you!"

I looked away, a little embarrassed, a touch indignant. There were aborigines in the peninsula who lived off the land, plenty of them, and their villages existed to this day. They weren't a figment of anyone's "romantic" imagination. I wanted Hannah and Darshan to have made an escape; I was too much of a realist to believe that they had.

He yawned and rubbed his eyes. "Nancy, I meant no disrespect," he said. "Come, now."

"Oh, none taken," I assured him. "I was just...thinking of something."

"Or someone?" His eyes twinkled.

"Yes, someone," I admitted. An image of Kenneth had popped into my head, leaning back in his chair at the head of our class seminar table, on a day that I'd arrived conspicuously late. It was the morning after the first full night we'd spent together, and we'd made a point to arrive on campus separately. I had dallied and considered skipping the class entirely, feeling like my face was emblazoned with his fingerprints, his kisses, his cum. When I showed up, heart thumping in my chest, and quickly slid into my seat, I saw that Kenneth was perfectly at ease. In fact, he was entirely self-assured, proud, even cocky. And that, back then, had made me want him all the more. "Someone that I'm glad is gone," I told Barnaby.

"Ah," he said. He looked at me fondly for a time, then hooked his thumb toward the buffet. "I'm going back for seconds."

My life seemed to be a collection of items and endeavors and people that I had left behind as I moved on, gave up, moved away. Zoe and Chris, for instance: were we really going to keep in touch? This was what people did, wasn't it? Make traces that amounted to nothing. In Hannah's case, her letters undelivered, her art undocumented. Her spirit seemed to be scattered around the globe. Although there was nothing unusual about that, and she herself would not have hoped for anything better than to do what she loved, I realized I was in a position to make something of her contributions. I was alive.

The names of the galleries I'd transcribed from the ledger—most of them were no longer in existence, probably, but they were a place to start. There were other people who may have bought Hannah's art and enjoyed it. Or people who'd inherited it, knowing nothing about her. There were the works themselves to find and appraise, perhaps other letters, the descendants of Hannah's colleagues at the academy, Godot's inheritors; there were communities to infiltrate, a public to inform, so much sharing to be done. Or, more strategically put, a brand to create.

Hannah hadn't painted *The Parasol Flower* while the Peterboroughs were in Malaysia. I felt sure she would have mentioned it to Godot. So the question was whether she'd painted *The Parasol Flower* in the jungle, where she'd found it, or from some place in England, for instance. At the asylum Charles had recommended? Or, with the help of some ether, holed away in one of the back rooms of the colonel's country estate?

Barnaby returned with a pile of meat slathered in orange sauce. "You're contemplative this evening, Nance." He took a few slippery bites before wiping his mouth. "I really should renovate my bathroom when I get back. It's begging for an update."

I said, "I'm exhausted. I miss my family."

"Indeed. I'm a fried egg."

A server, passing by with a jug of water, did a double take.

"What?" I said.

"Something my mum used to say. Spent, is all I meant."

We chuckled. Moms and their sayings.

"To all the parasol flowers out there, wherever you may be hiding," he said, and we tapped drinks.

"Barnaby, do you think your family would cooperate if I were to write about Hannah? About finding her art?"

"Hmmm. Perhaps if we vetted your final draft," he said.

FIFTY-NINE

On a summer day in 1907, when the cicadas are crying and the British residents are hiding inside from sunstroke, Hannah packs her satchel with a wineskin of water and takes the remaining mangosteens from the fruit bowl. She tucks in a lump of rosemary bread, Suria's old recipe, and plods to the upper town. Her pace is not quite what it used to be, her hips have begun to ache in their sockets, yet her endurance is better than ever.

Where she and the colonel once lived there is a second new family, she has heard tell. A young lady from Brighton and her colonel. The couple has an infant, by the sounds of it. Hannah crosses the stiff grass at the side of the property, marveling at herself for coming so close and striding right under the shuttered window at the side, which is the window of the master bedroom.

When mosquitoes land on her neck she ignores them and keeps walking. If she had to swat at every insect that bothered her, she'd never make it anywhere. There is a tea that takes the itch away and she's had her two cups that morning. Crossing the lawn in the back garden, she walks on past the stable, with its ever-festive fringe of bougainvillea, and on into the jungle.

Here, it is much more difficult to walk without tripping over a root or vine or nettle, practiced as she is. Hannah has never visited these closest woods. The sergeant slashed no footpaths here. She picks up her skirts and perseveres, struggling along for a hundred yards or so until allowing herself a drink of water. The deep quiet is broken by the sound of her swallowing and by the occasional trilling bird. She surveys the terrain. The woods are always different from slope to slope, bend to bend, hour to hour. Here, in this moment, life is close and dark and dripping with moisture. Teak trees predominate: a layer of marvelous ferns. Already she has noticed several unfamiliar mushrooms sprouting from the detritus, but she can never be bothered to document anything, not like the sergeant did. There may be liparis orchids, perhaps, some kind of shade flower. If she doesn't come across any flowers she'll pick an interesting patch of foliage and sit down to that. She's already remarked on an ancient camphor tree, its mottled bark a kaleidoscope of warm greens and pinks and browns.

Looking back now toward that enormous tree, she glimpses something floating, it seems, above a bed of fledgling nipa fronds. Hannah backtracks, picking her way toward the flash of color. The object is both farther away and larger than it first appears. And what an incredible tint—the effect is a sort of glow. *As when you close your eyes against the sun and the light seeps in.* She stumbles, coming down on one knee, grunting her surprise. "Heedless woman," she chastises herself even as she quickens her pace, pulling herself forward with saplings. Her boots plant into the spongy black earth and moss. She dodges rocks.

It is just as he's promised, as big as a ladies' parasol. She inhales the mild fragrance, which reminds her of cardamom, in fact, not vanilla and citrus. But it is the exquisite color of the blossom that captivates her. She'll spend days just trying to get the color. Hannah's hands shake as she reaches for the long stalk, as smooth and vivid green as a young bamboo.

"My god," she murmurs. Then shouts, "I've found it! Darshan, I've found it!"

A wave of grief surges inside her, leaving her with such a depth of longing that she stands bewildered for several minutes. She has not thought of him as often, lately. His name, she's not spoken for years.

The petals are as thick as a tabletop. They curl together, locking perfectly around a central hole—a dark, seemingly bottomless cup that is growing, she realizes, from the inverse of the stem. Around this cup, the petals form a basin streaked violet by some pigment of nature. Ultramarine blue and Alizarin crimson? The underside of the bloom is a sturdy, spiralling network of veins that appear prickly or perhaps hairy. She is not inclined to touch. The edges of the petals ripple a little where the flesh thins. She laughs. Quite like the frill of a parasol.

As she is clearing a place for her stool and readying herself to sketch, a deep-throated rumble resounds to the west of her. Searching the shadowy tiers of green, she can see no movement. Slowly Hannah reaches for her satchel, feels for the paring knife strapped inside. From peeling a mangosteen to fighting a tiger—absurd. Nevertheless, she plucks out the blade and fits it carefully under her bootlaces on the outside of her ankle. Lately, she has considered buying a rifle to take with her. They have come down in price, though weight is a serious consideration. Machetes are handy for clearing, of course, but she prefers to manage without clearing and travel lighter.

No animal will come to her that day.

Hannah begins at the vortex of the colossal, alien beauty. A parasol flower. A rarity. And she has a brush in her grasp.

Acknowledgments

This book took a very long time to make, and was reborn in many different drafts. The idea for it came to me during my dissertation research, in particular, my reading of a postcolonial critique by Laura Ann Stoler called *Race and the Education of Desire: Foucault's History of Sexuality and the Colonial Order of Things.* The racial science hiding at the core of this novel is historically accurate and makes up part of Stoler's analysis of Southeast Asia. Several other books proved helpful to me for their representations of British colonial experiences in Malaysia: J. G. Butler's *The British in Malaya, 1880 – 1941,* Pat Barr's *Taming the Jungle: the men who made British Malaya,* and *Perak and the Malays* by Robert McNair. The Victorian journals of traveler Emily Innes, published as *The Chersonese with the Gilding Off* provided valuable observations about everyday life at the time. The well-known artist and teacher Robert Henri (1865 - 1929), whose lectures are collected in the delicious volume *The Art Spirit,* provided me nourishing food for thought about my own artistic journey as well a basis for the character Monsieur Godot. Finally, I took strength from the intrepid Marianne North, who trekked through rugged nineteenth-century jungles to paint botanical scenes and specimens. The book *A Vision of Eden,* published by Kew Gardens, is an excellent resource about her life and art.

My deepest gratitude to friends and colleagues who have provided help and support for this project, often well before it was clear it would ever have a place in the world. Thank you to Barbara Winter, Sheila Gale, Jennifer Mook-Sang, Donna Kirk, and Sherry Isaac for your supportive feedback on drafts, early and late. To Sherry Coman, a wonderful and wise writing coach: your questions, suggestions, and provocations have allowed this novel to truly come into its own. I am grateful to visionary Jaynie Royal for bringing me into the family of authors at her small but mighty publishing house, Regal House Publishing. I am equally lucky to have developed such a congenial literary collaboration with my editor there, Pamela Van Dyk.

My brother Christopher Skeaff has been an invaluable source of writerly as well as moral support from beginning to end, in good times and bad. I hope you know how special you are to me. Lastly, for reminding me on a daily basis how wonderful this life can be: thank you, my darling children, Maya and Zakir.